MEGAGOGO™

VOLUME 001

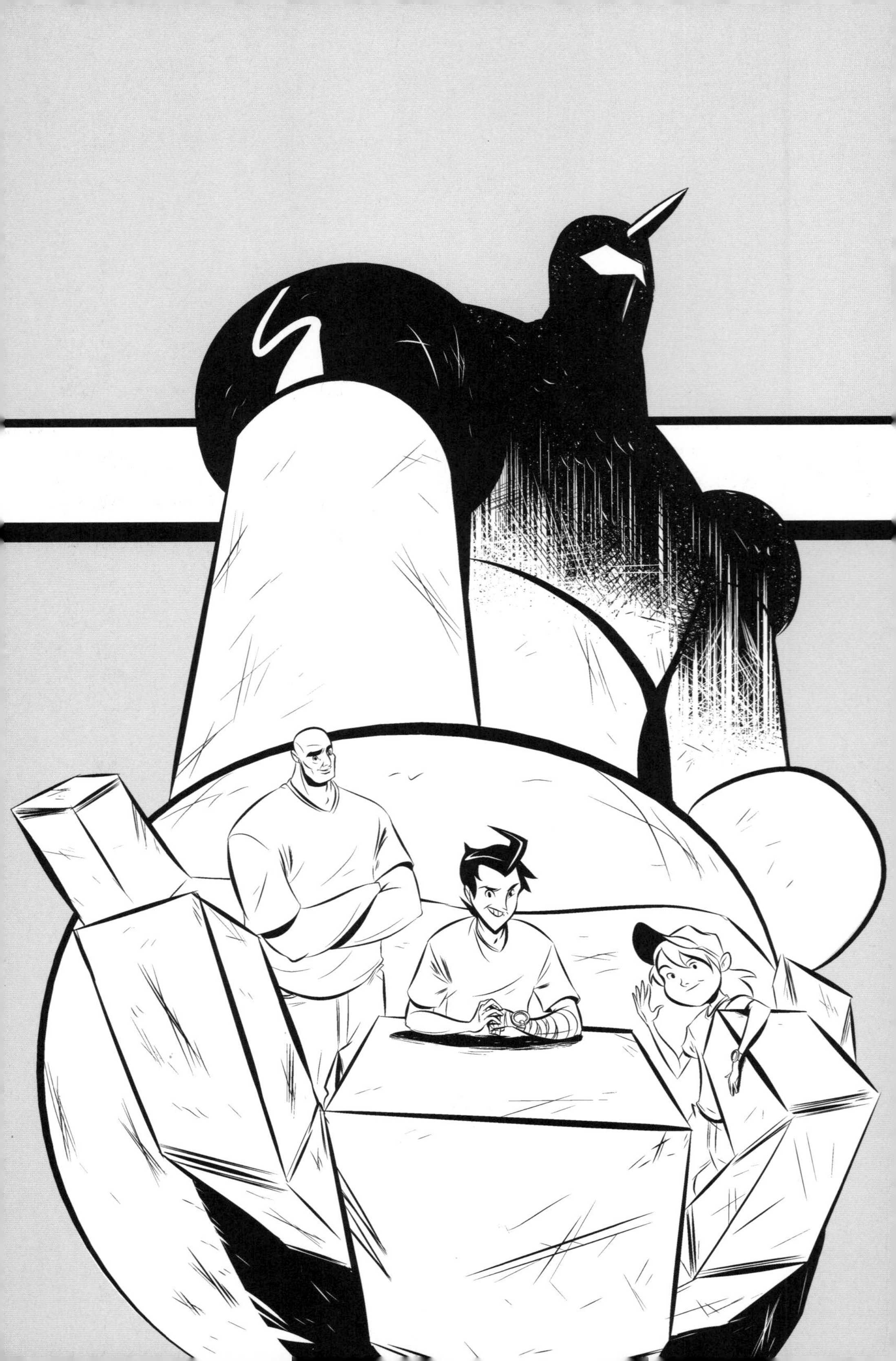

MEGAGOGO™

VOLUME 001

WRITTEN AND ILLUSTRATED
— BY —
WOOK JIN CLARK

EDITED
— BY —
JILL BEATON

DESIGNED
— BY —
KEITH WOOD

AN ONI PRESS PUBLICATION

ONI PRESS, INC.

JOE NOZEMACK PUBLISHER

JAMES LUCAS JONES EDITOR IN CHIEF

KEITH A. WOOD ART DIRECTOR

JOHN SCHORK DIRECTOR OF PUBLICITY

CHEYENNE ALLOTT DIRECTOR OF SALES

JILL BEATON EDITOR

CHARLIE CHU EDITOR

JASON STOREY GRAPHIC DESIGNER

TROY LOOK DIGITAL PREPRESS LEAD

ROBIN HERRERA ADMINISTRATIVE ASSISTANT

ONI PRESS, INC.
1305 SE MARTIN LUTHER KING JR. BLVD.
SUITE A
PORTLAND, OR 97214
USA

onipress.com | twitter.com/onipress
facebook.com/onipress | onipress.tumblr.com

wookjinclark.com | @wookjinclark

First Edition: February 2014

ISBN 978-1-62010-117-9
eISBN 978-1-62010-128-5

Library of Congress Control Number: 2013949081

10 9 8 4 7 6 5 4 3 2 1

Printed in China.

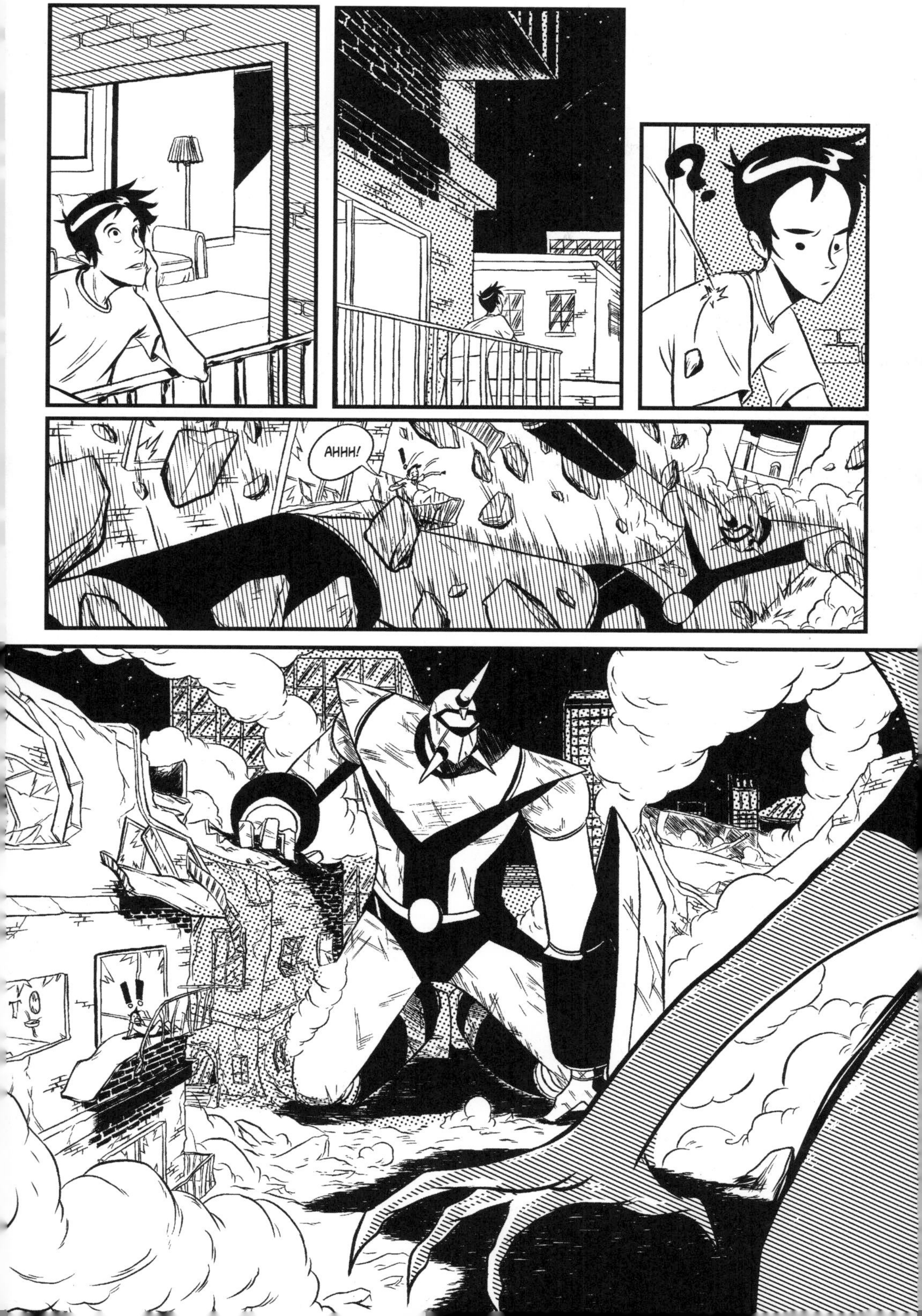
?
AHHH!
!
!!

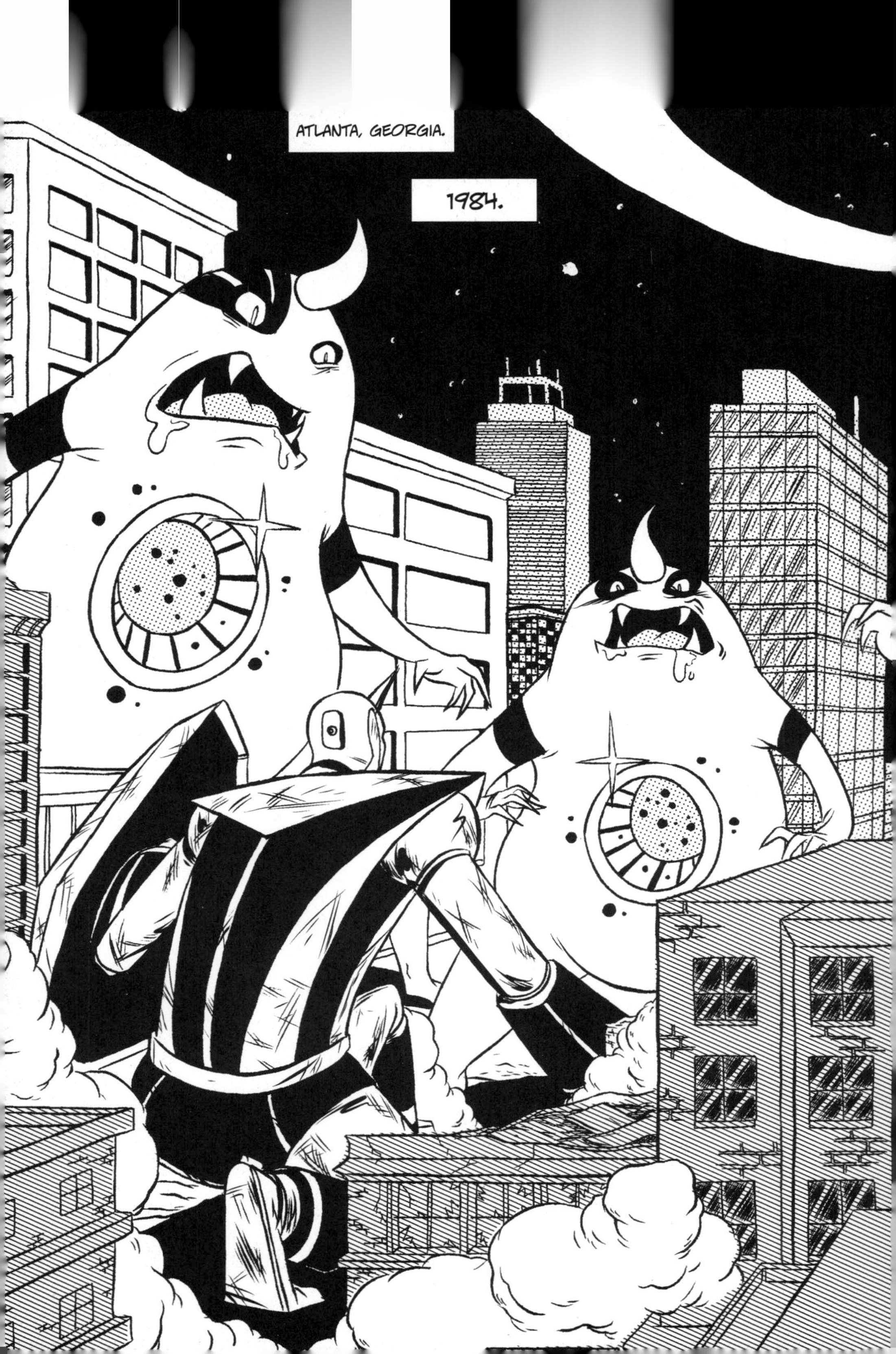
ATLANTA, GEORGIA.
1984.

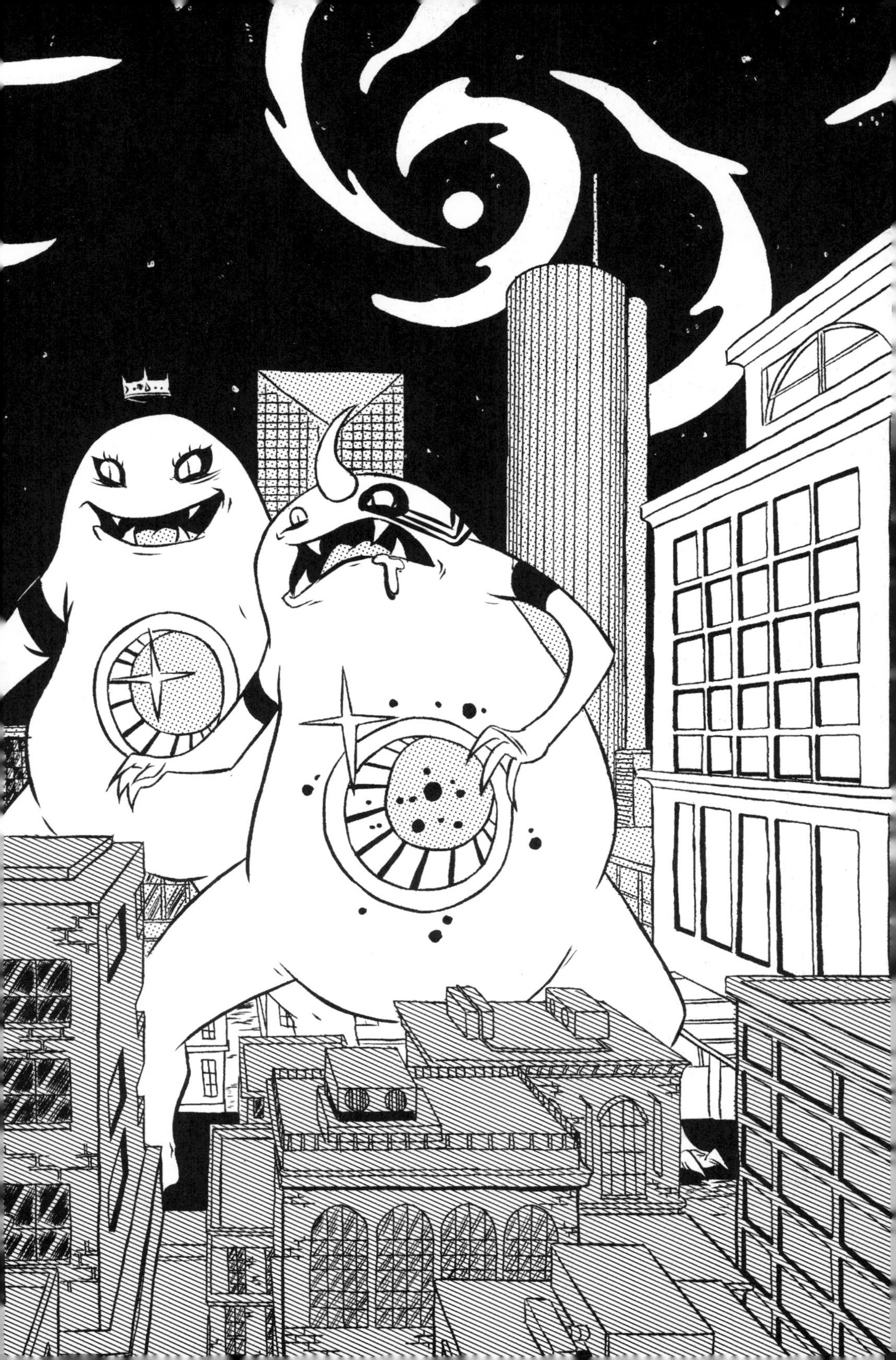

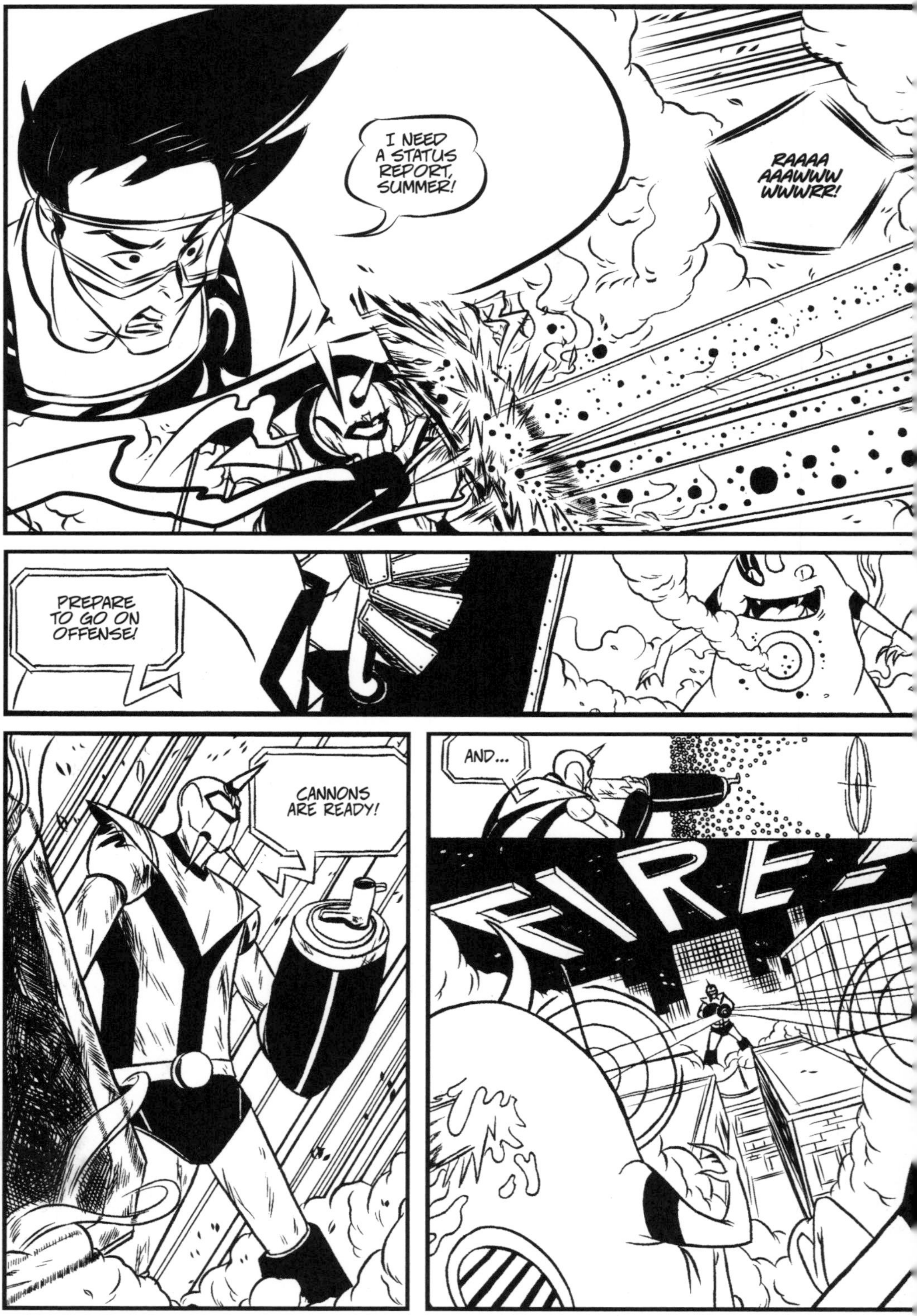
I NEED A STATUS REPORT, SUMMER!
RAAAA AAAWWW WWWRR!
PREPARE TO GO ON OFFENSE!
CANNONS ARE READY!
AND...
FIRE!

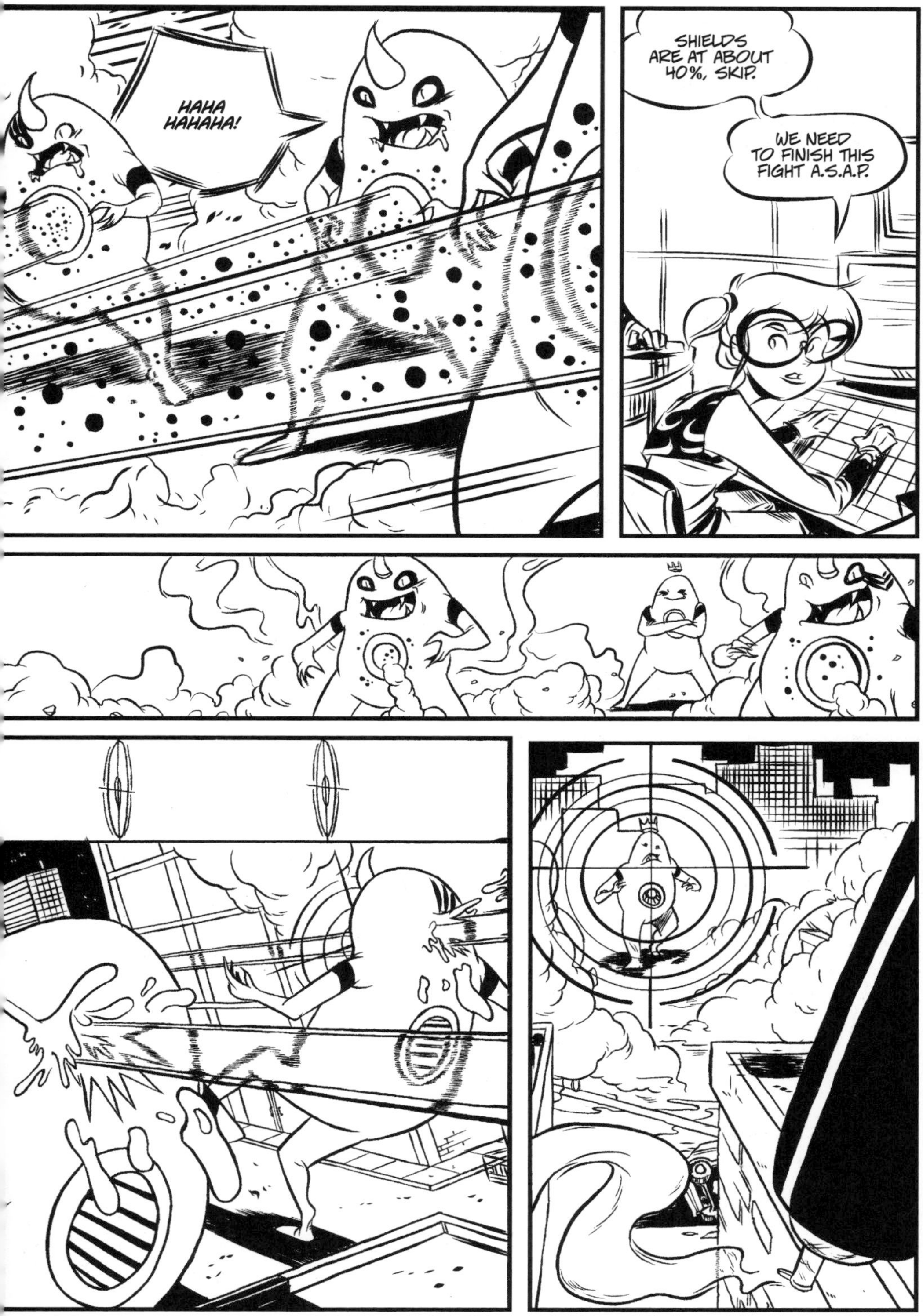
HAHA HAHAHA!
SHIELDS ARE AT ABOUT 40%, SKIP.
WE NEED TO FINISH THIS FIGHT A.S.A.P.

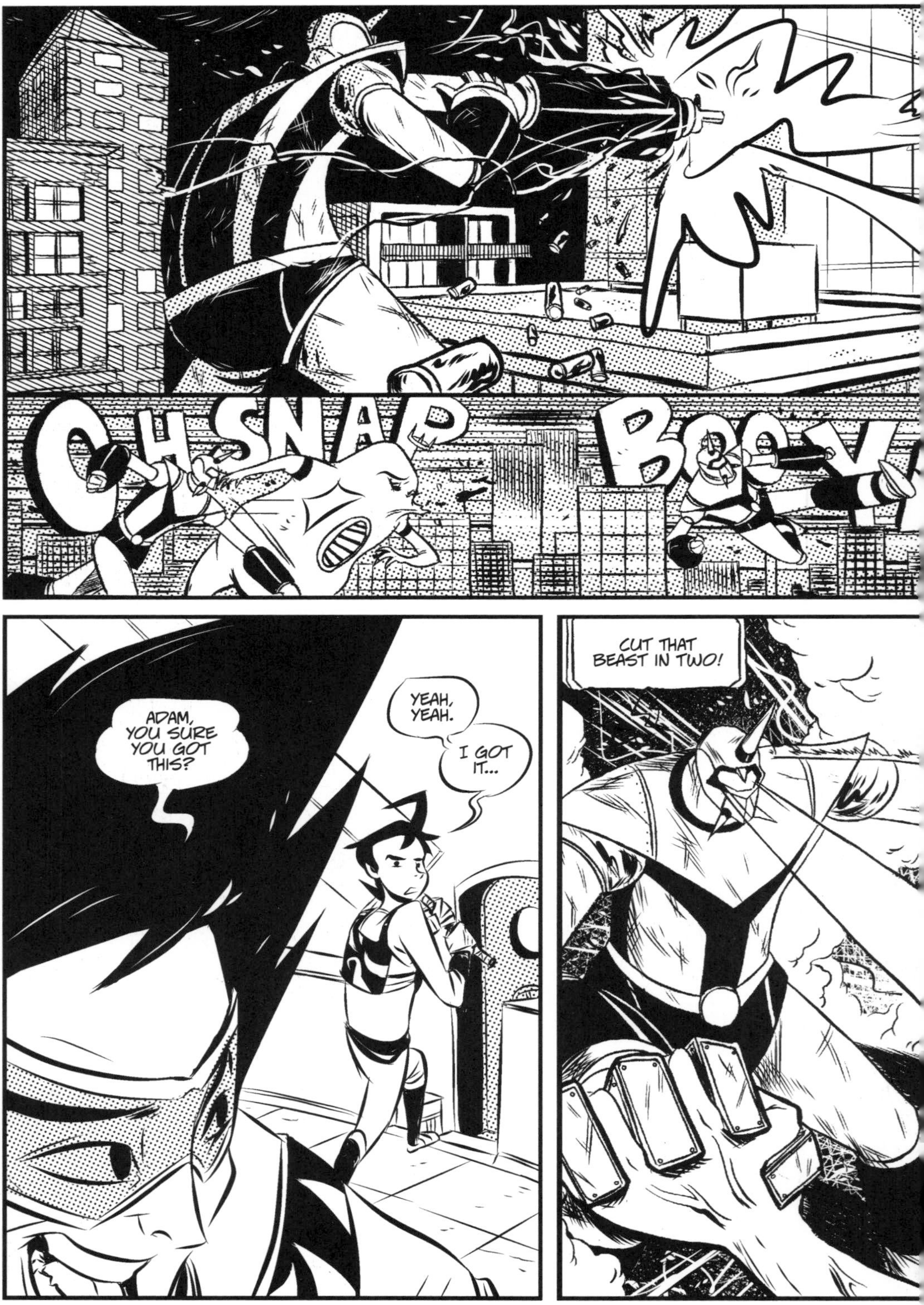
CHSNAP
BOOV
ADAM, YOU SURE YOU GOT THIS?
YEAH, YEAH.
I GOT IT...
CUT THAT BEAST IN TWO!

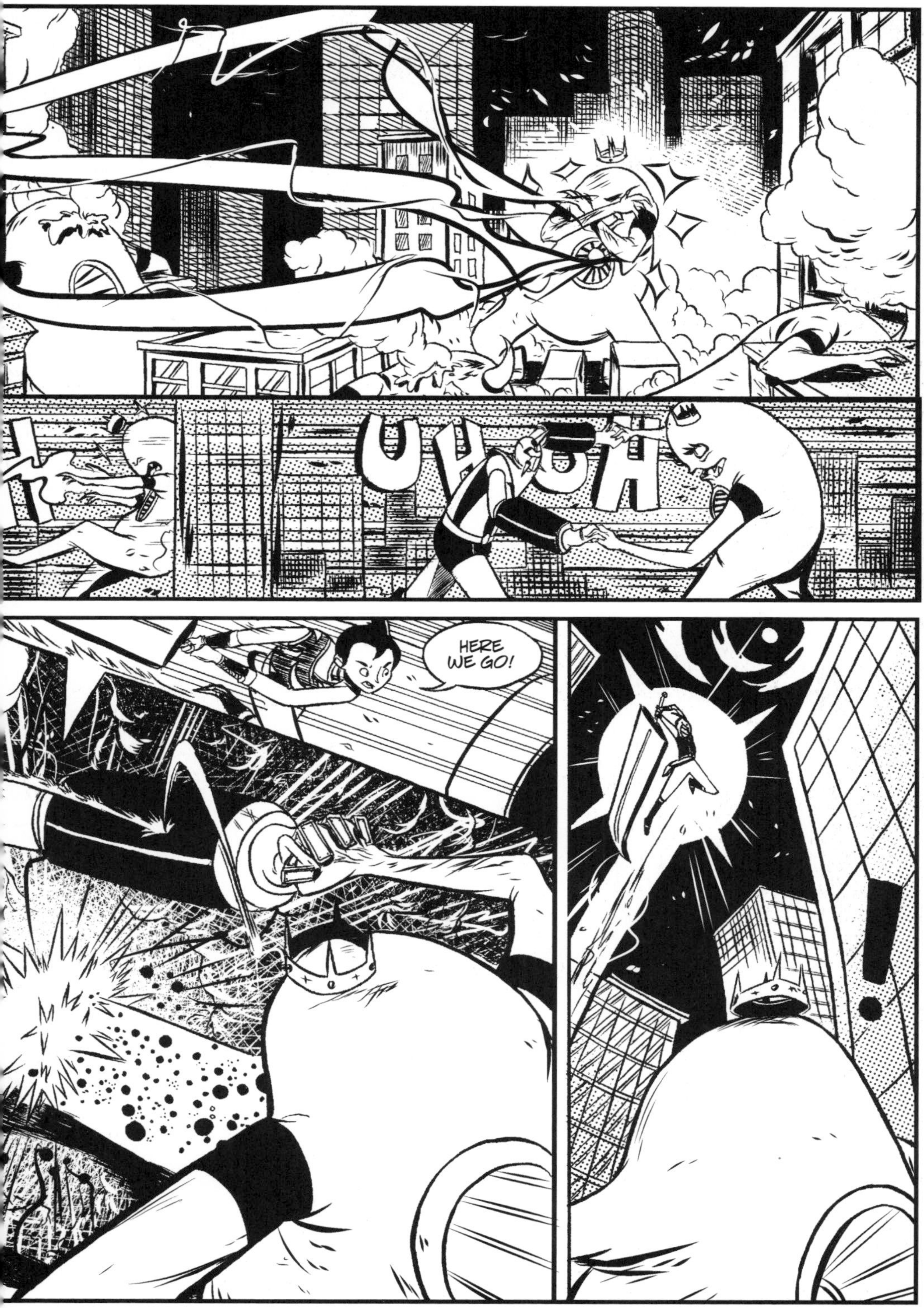
HERE WE GO!

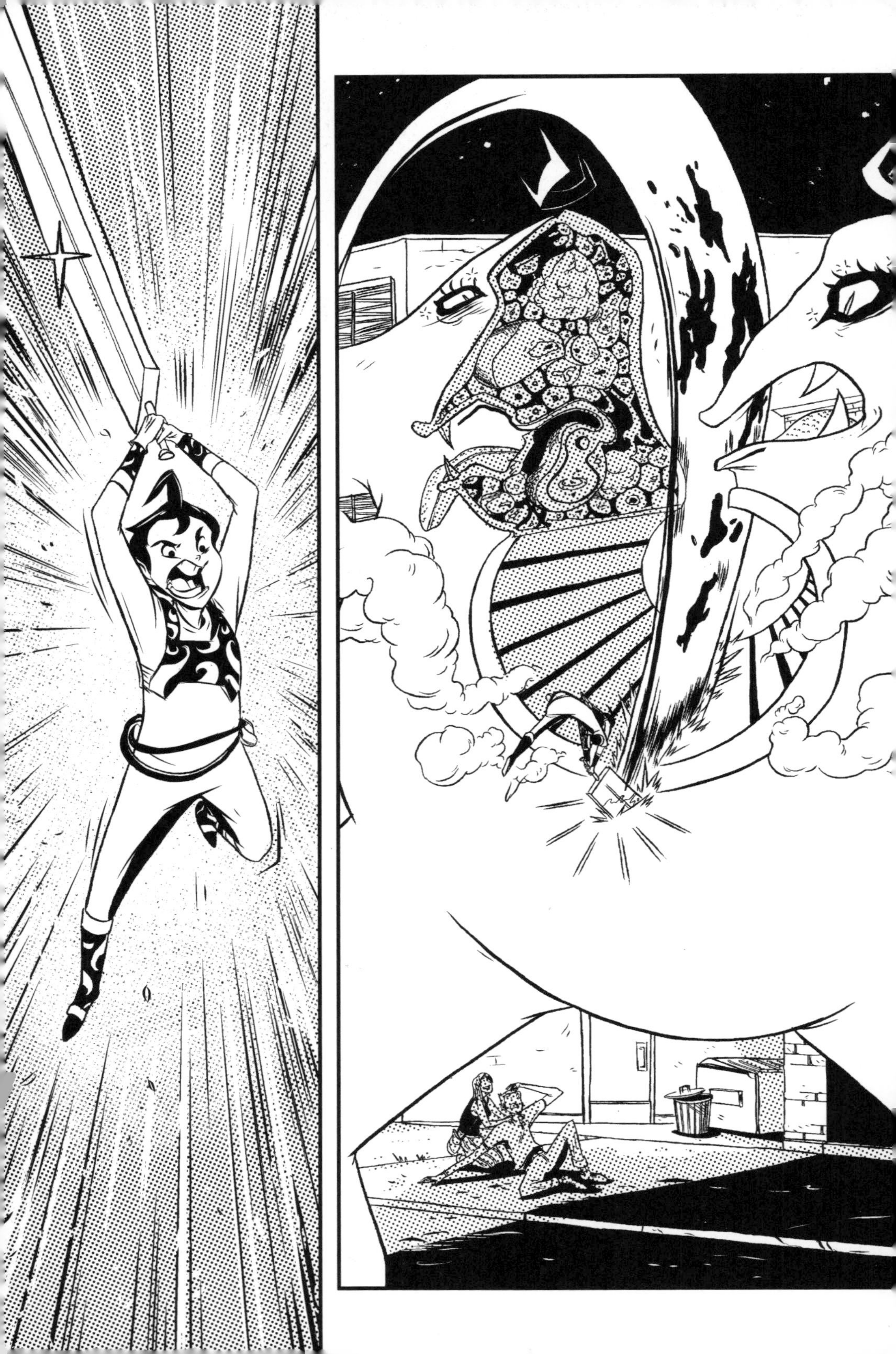

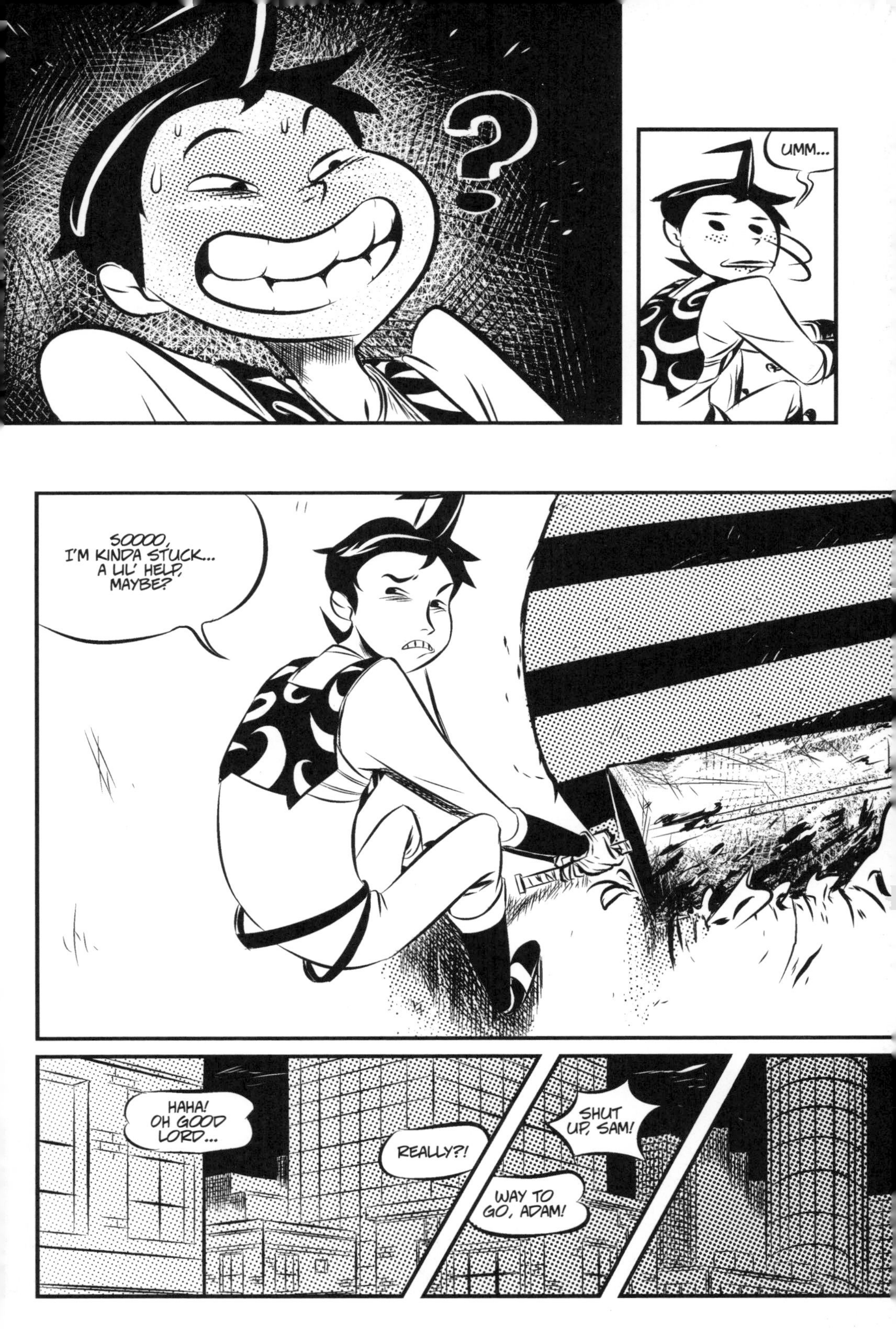
?
UMM...
SOOOO, I'M KINDA STUCK... A LIL' HELP, MAYBE?
HAHA! OH GOOD LORD...
REALLY?!
WAY TO GO, ADAM!
SHUT UP, SAM!

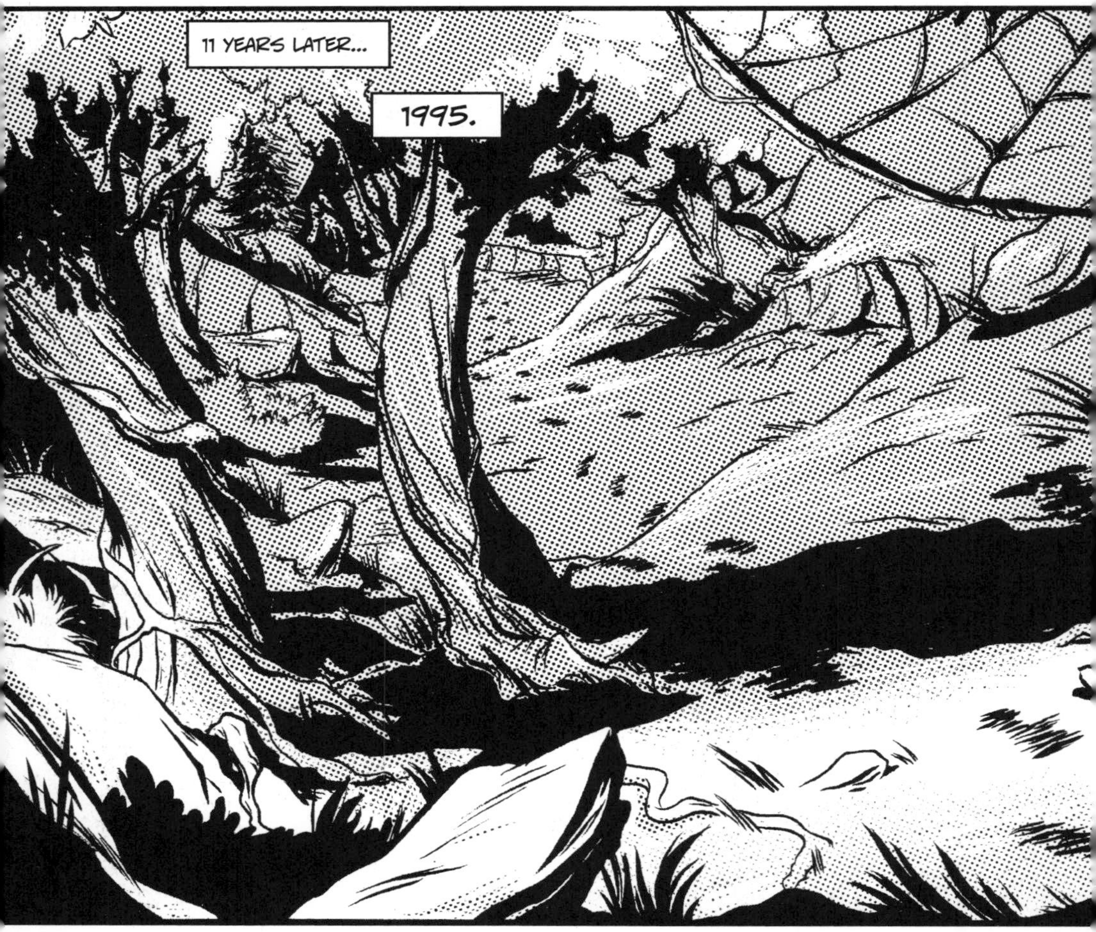
11 YEARS LATER...
1995.

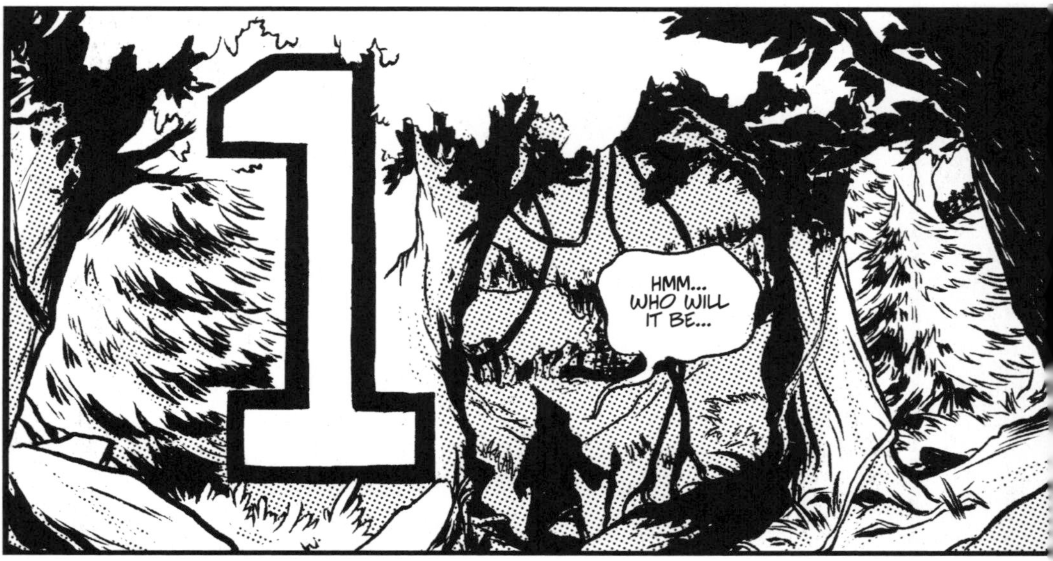
1
HMM... WHO WILL IT BE...

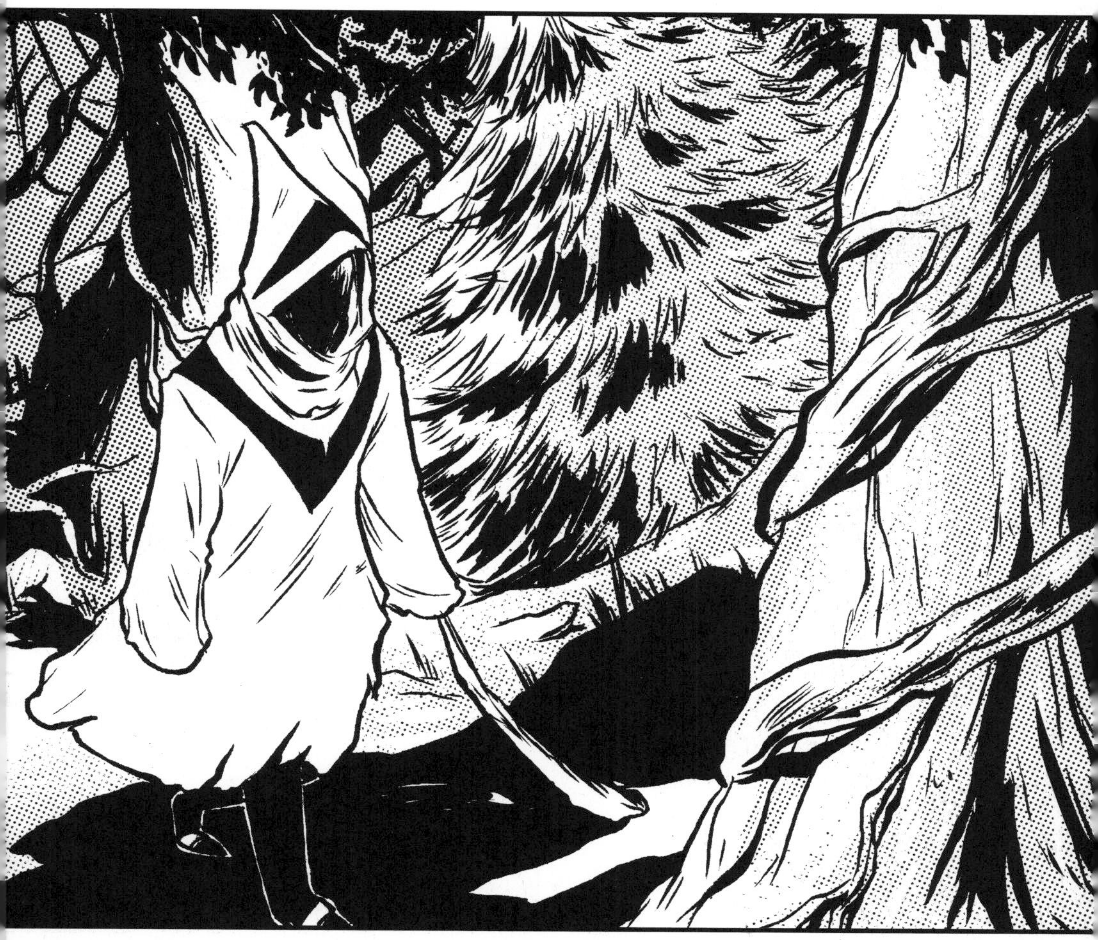

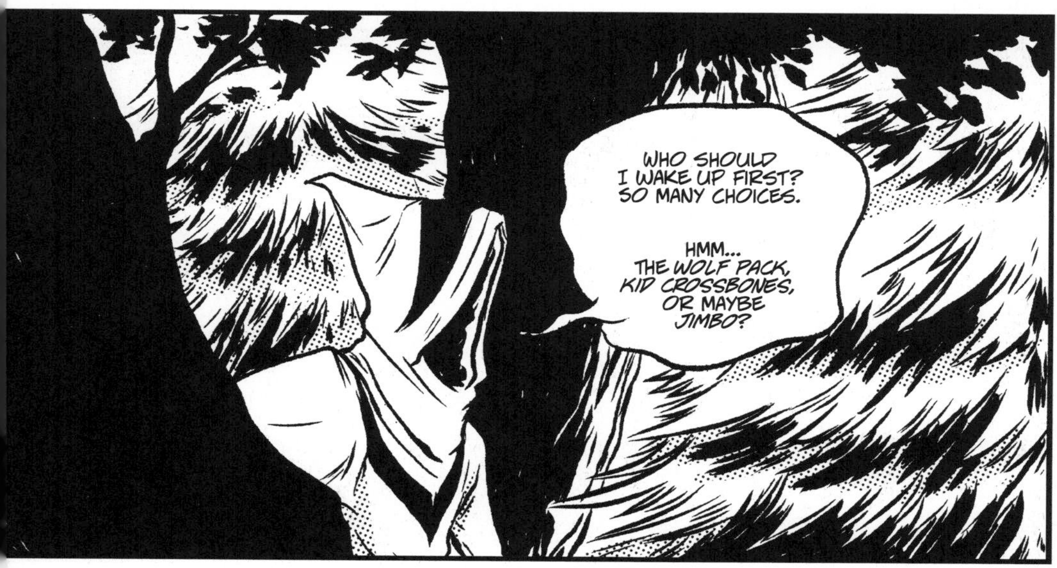
WHO SHOULD I WAKE UP FIRST? SO MANY CHOICES.
HMM... THE WOLF PACK, KID CROSSBONES, OR MAYBE JIMBO?

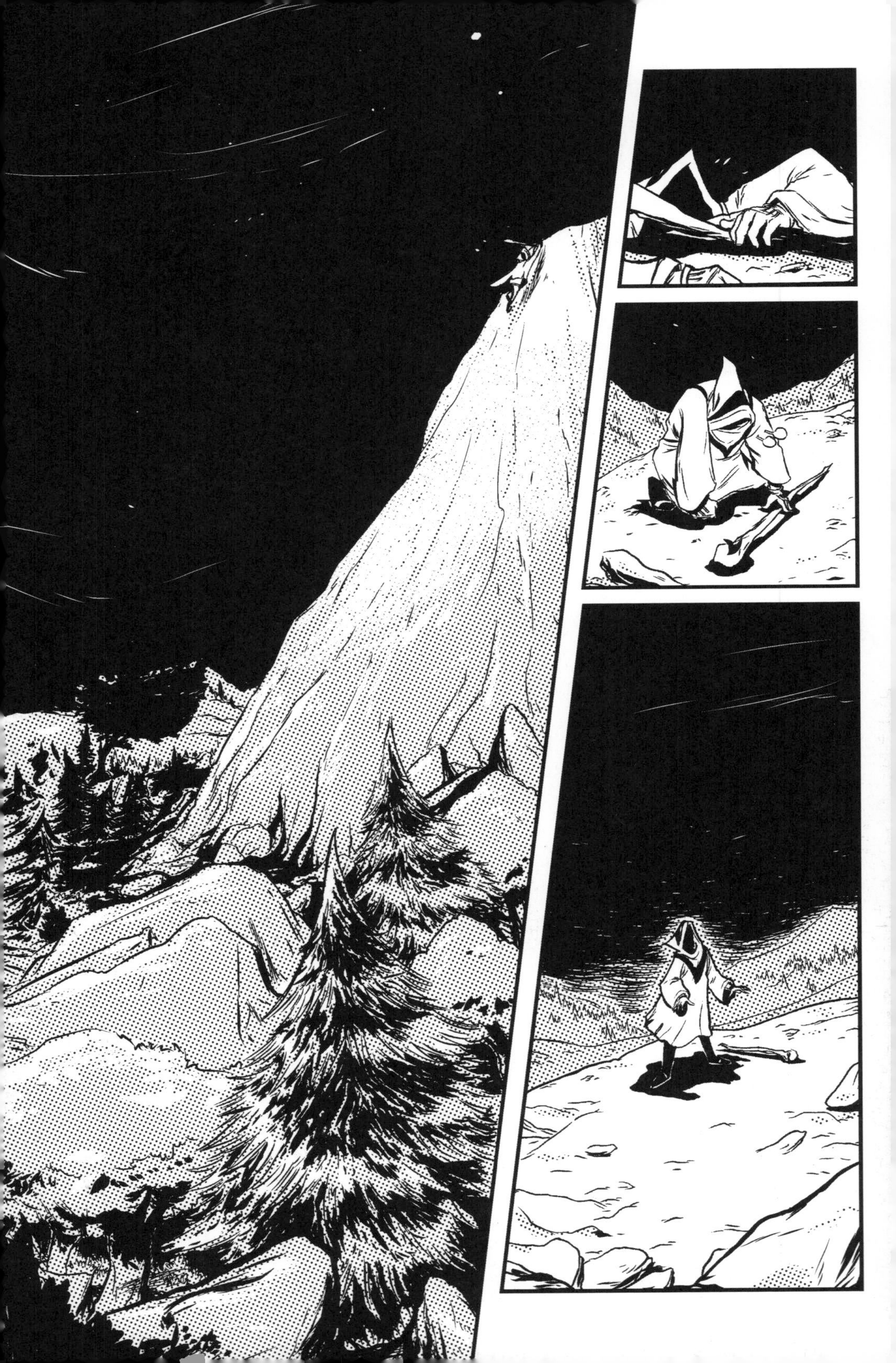

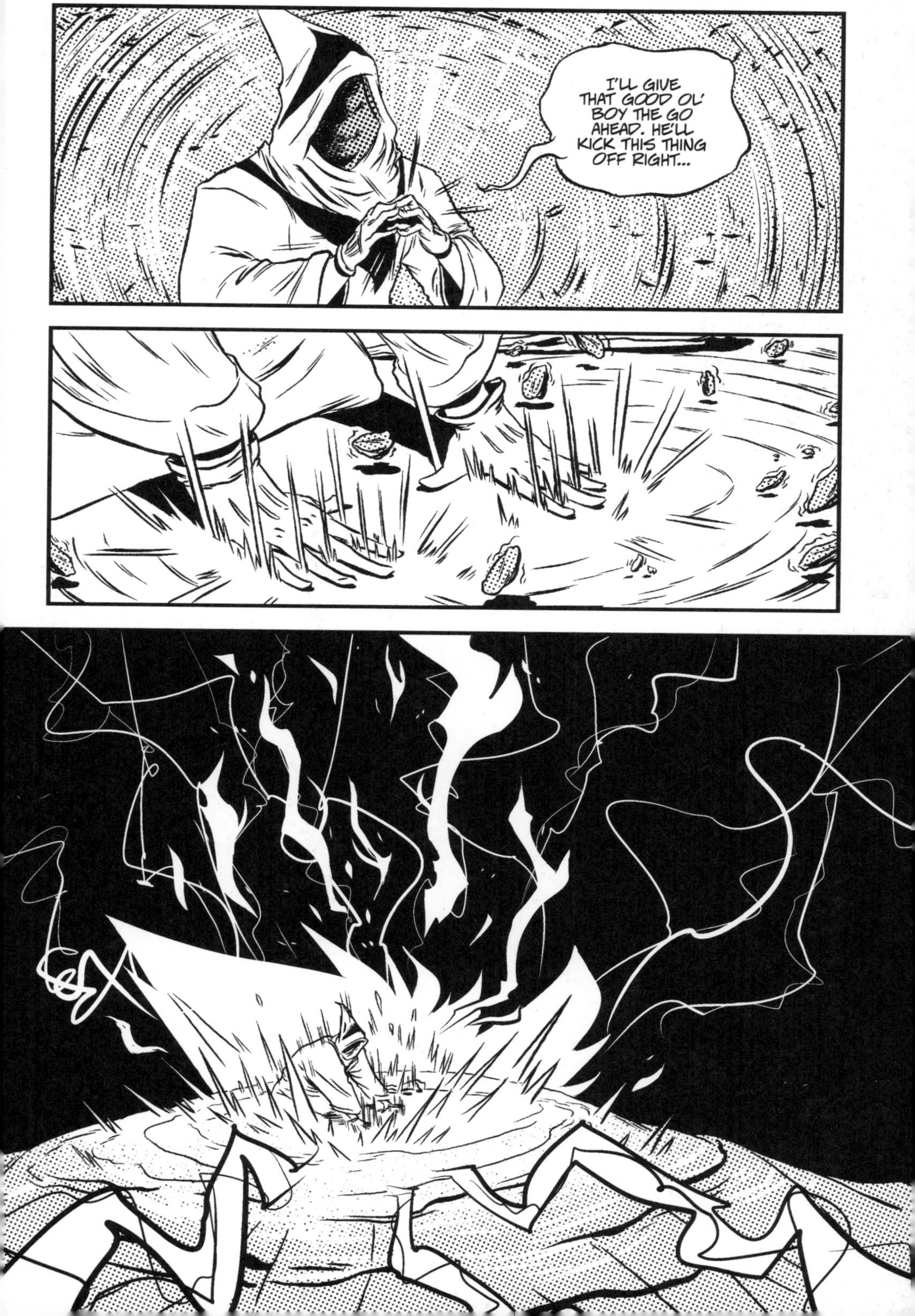
I'LL GIVE THAT GOOD OL' BOY THE GO AHEAD. HE'LL KICK THIS THING OFF RIGHT...

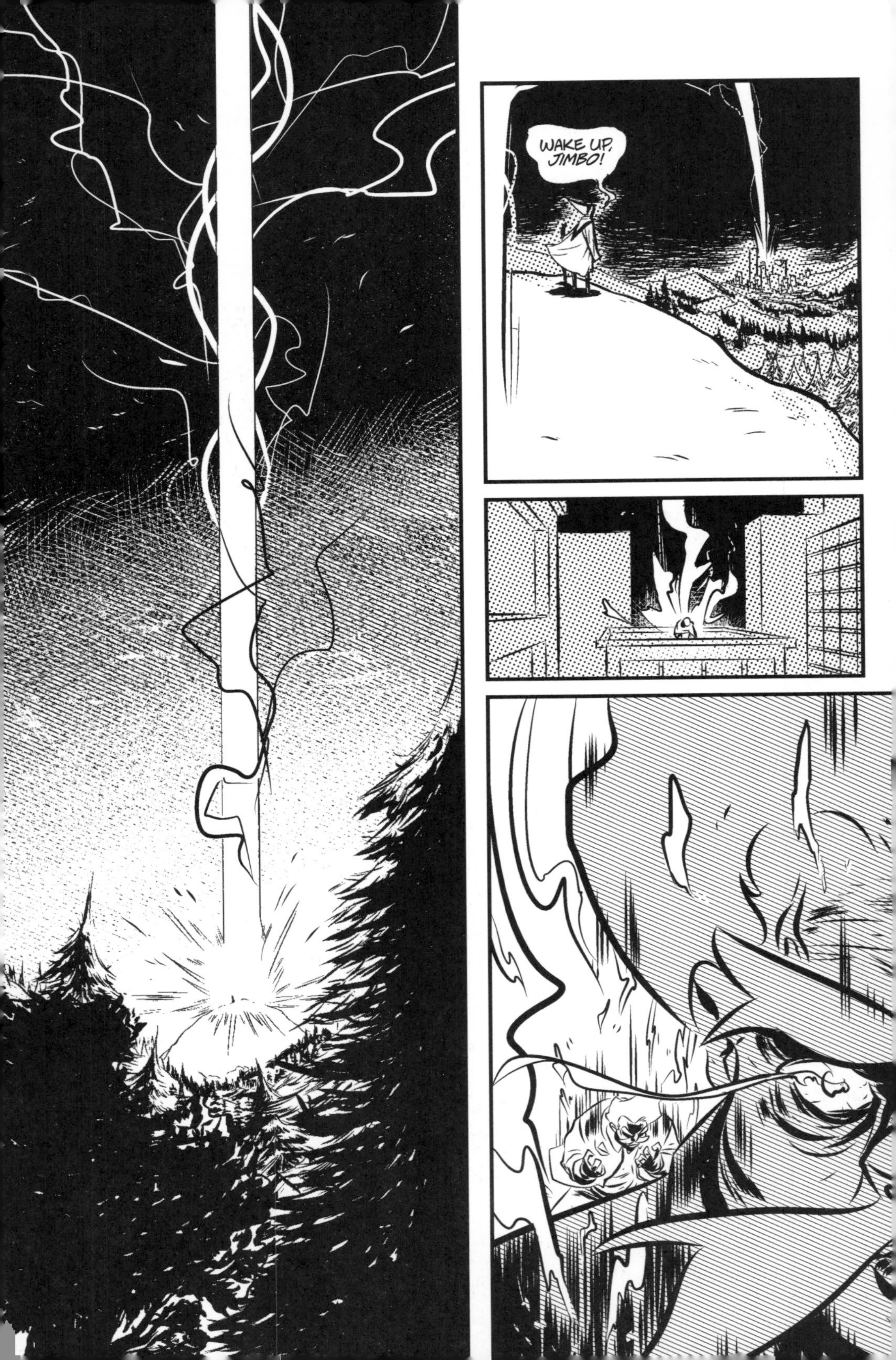
WAKE UP, JIMBO!

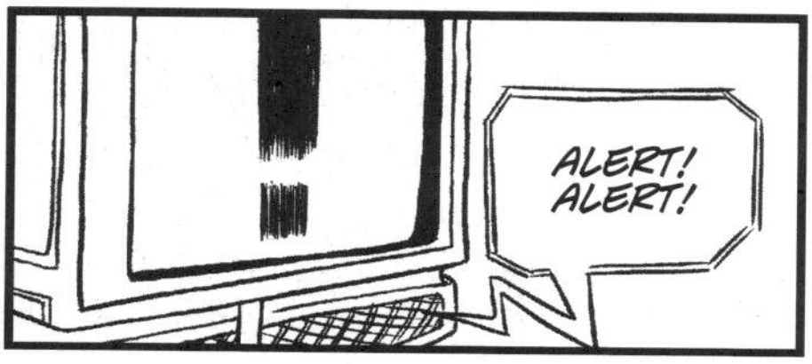
ALERT!
ALERT!

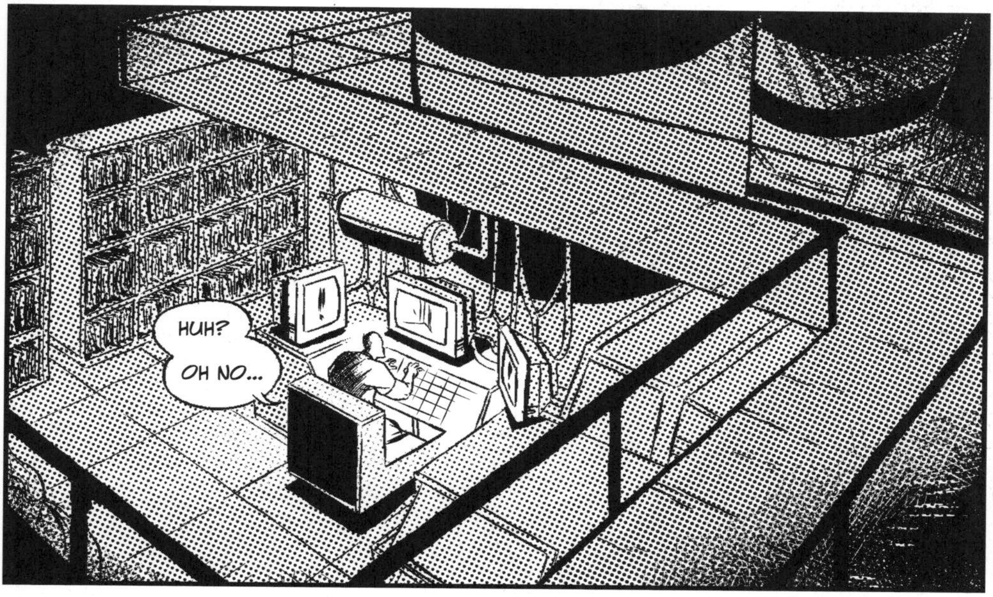
HUH?
OH NO...

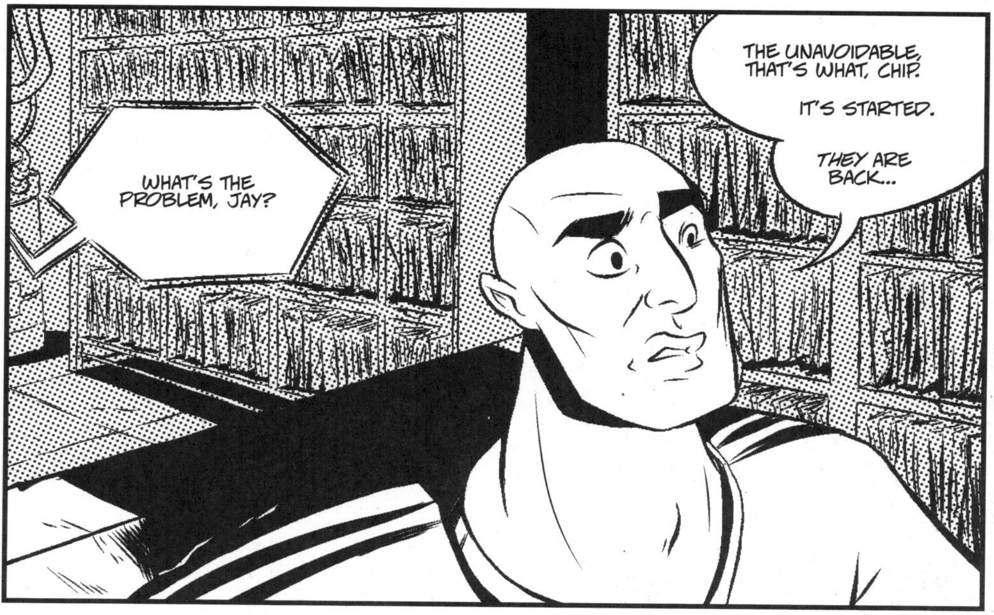
WHAT'S THE PROBLEM, JAY?
THE UNAVOIDABLE, THAT'S WHAT, CHIP.
IT'S STARTED.
THEY ARE BACK...

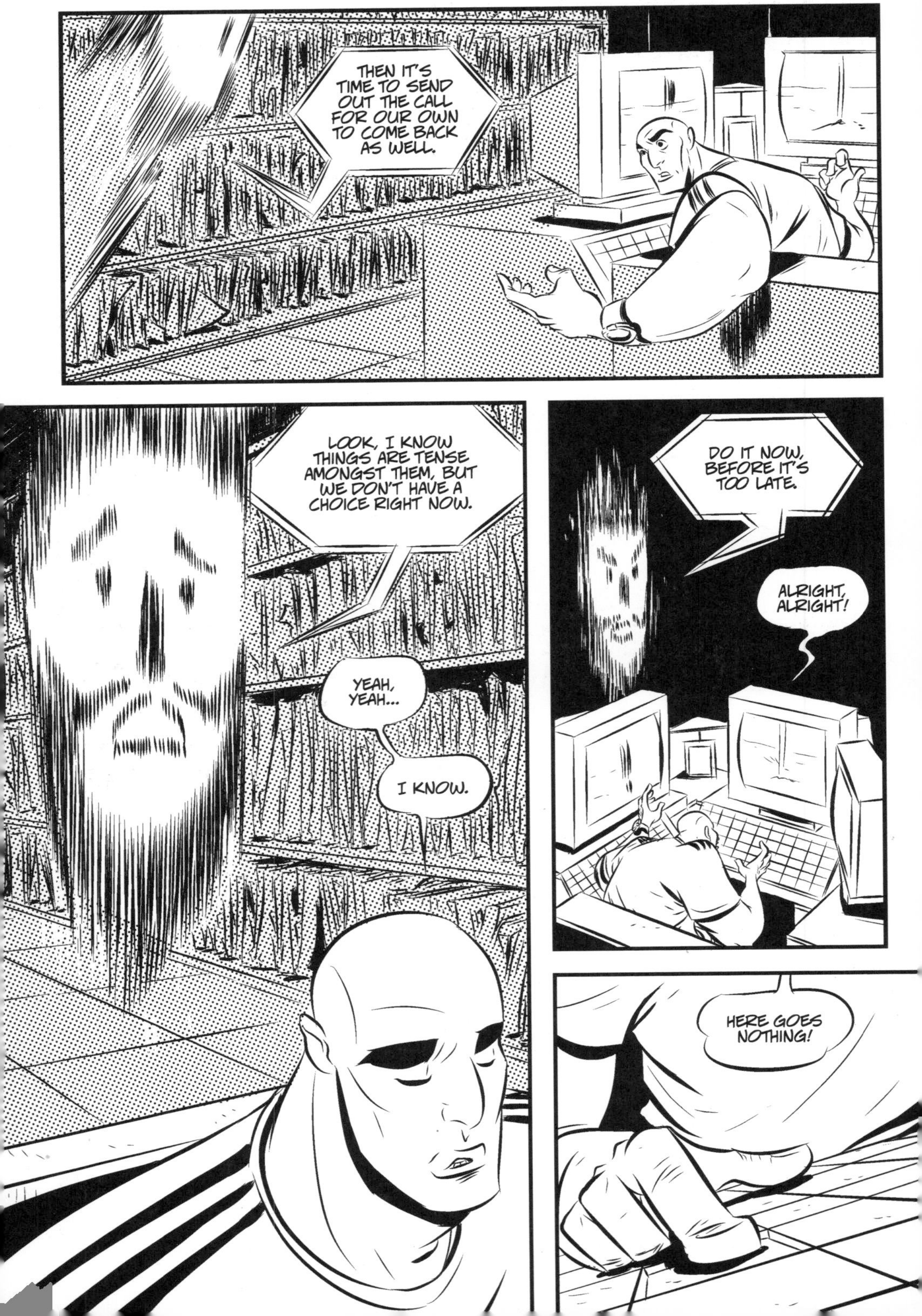
THEN IT'S TIME TO SEND OUT THE CALL FOR OUR OWN TO COME BACK AS WELL.
LOOK, I KNOW THINGS ARE TENSE AMONGST THEM, BUT WE DON'T HAVE A CHOICE RIGHT NOW.
YEAH, YEAH...
I KNOW.
DO IT NOW, BEFORE IT'S TOO LATE.
ALRIGHT, ALRIGHT!
HERE GOES NOTHING!

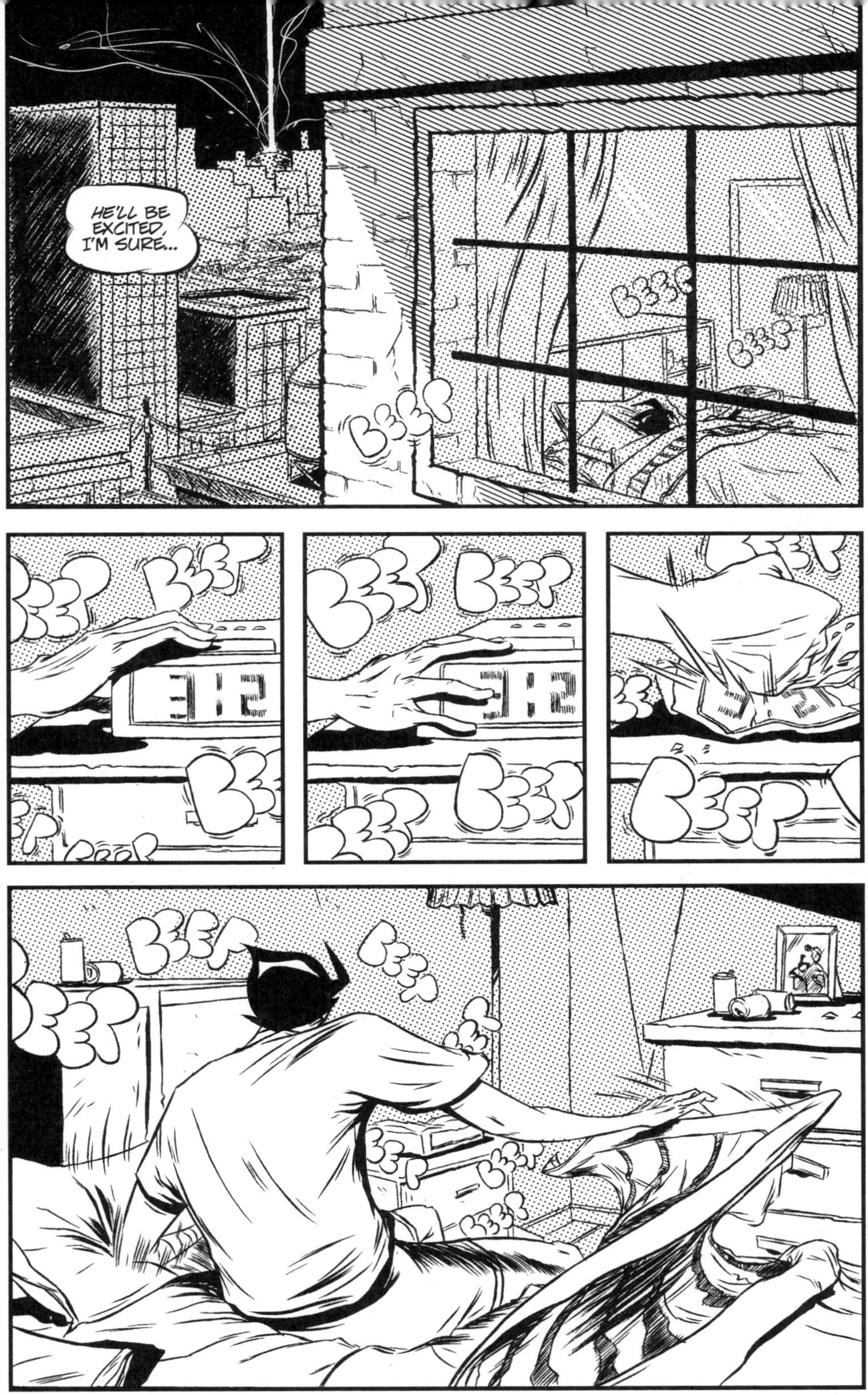
HE'LL BE EXCITED, I'M SURE...
BEEP
BEEP
BEEP
BEEP
BEEP
BEEP
BEEP
BEEP
BEEP
BEEP
BEEP
BEEP
BEEP
BEEP
BEEP

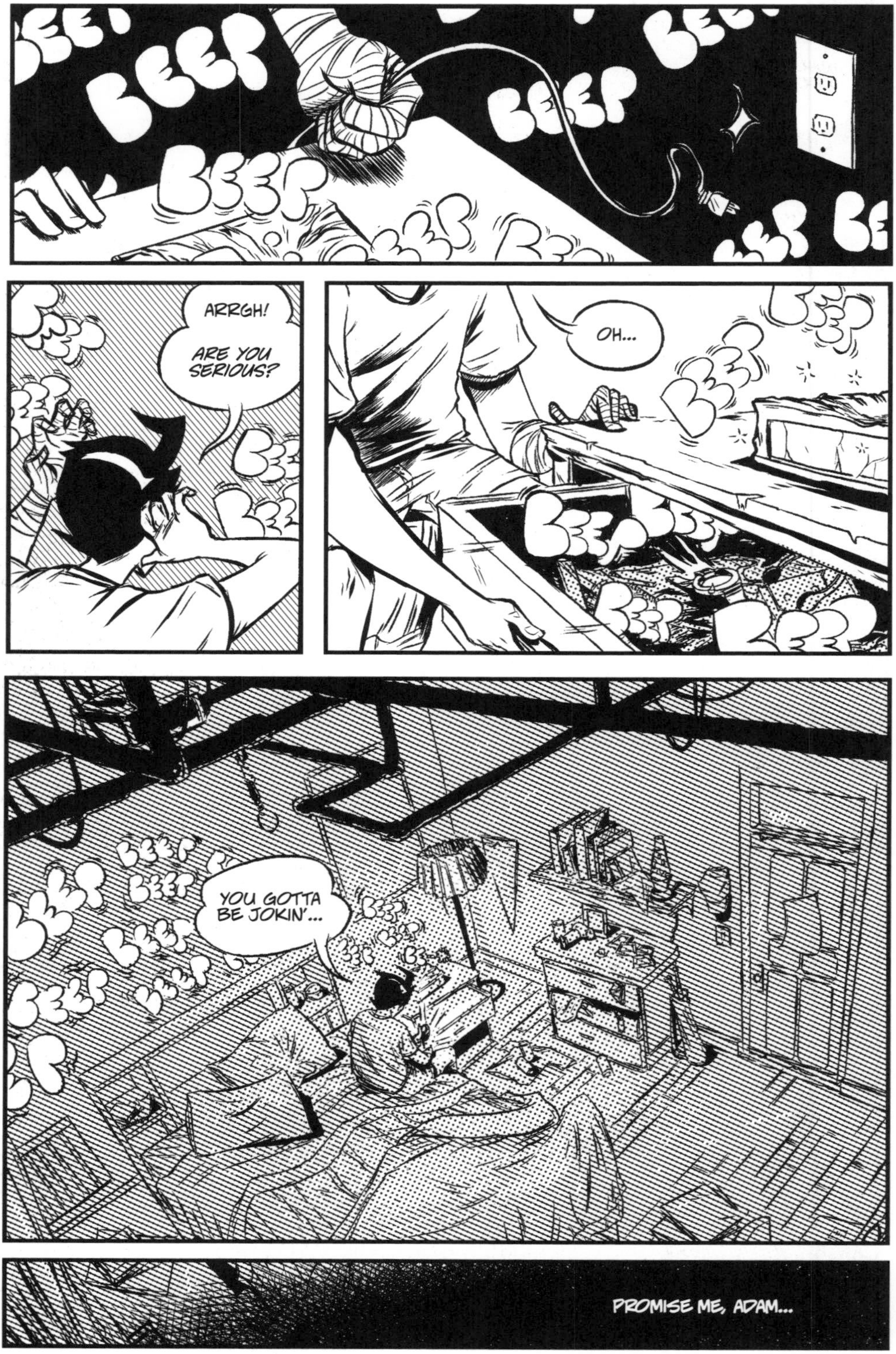
BEEP
BEEP
BEEP
BEEP
ARRGH!
ARE YOU SERIOUS?
OH...
YOU GOTTA BE JOKIN'...
PROMISE ME, ADAM...

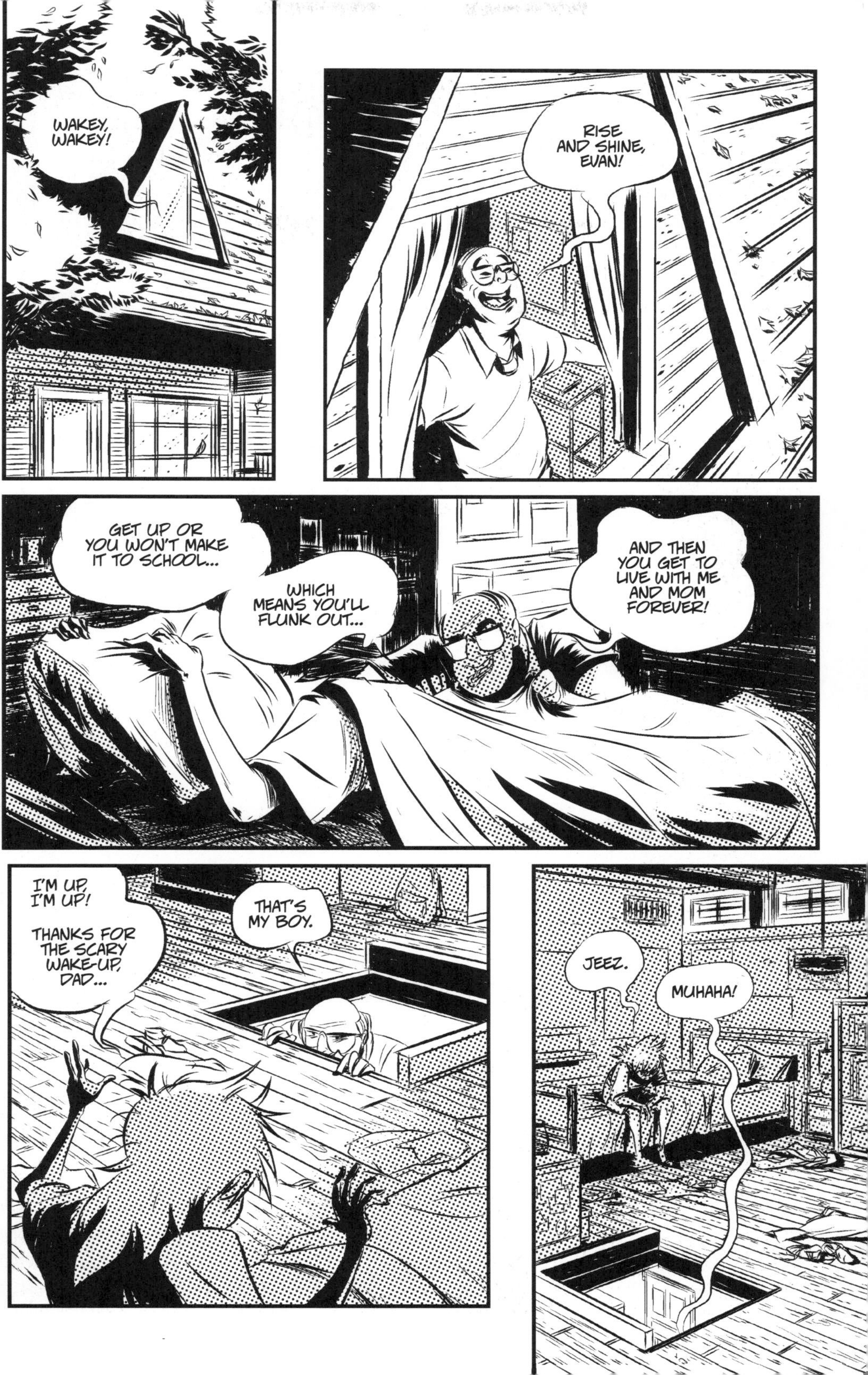
WAKEY, WAKEY!
RISE AND SHINE, EVAN!
GET UP OR YOU WON'T MAKE IT TO SCHOOL...
WHICH MEANS YOU'LL FLUNK OUT...
AND THEN YOU GET TO LIVE WITH ME AND MOM FOREVER!
I'M UP, I'M UP!
THANKS FOR THE SCARY WAKE-UP, DAD...
THAT'S MY BOY.
JEEZ.
MUHAHA!

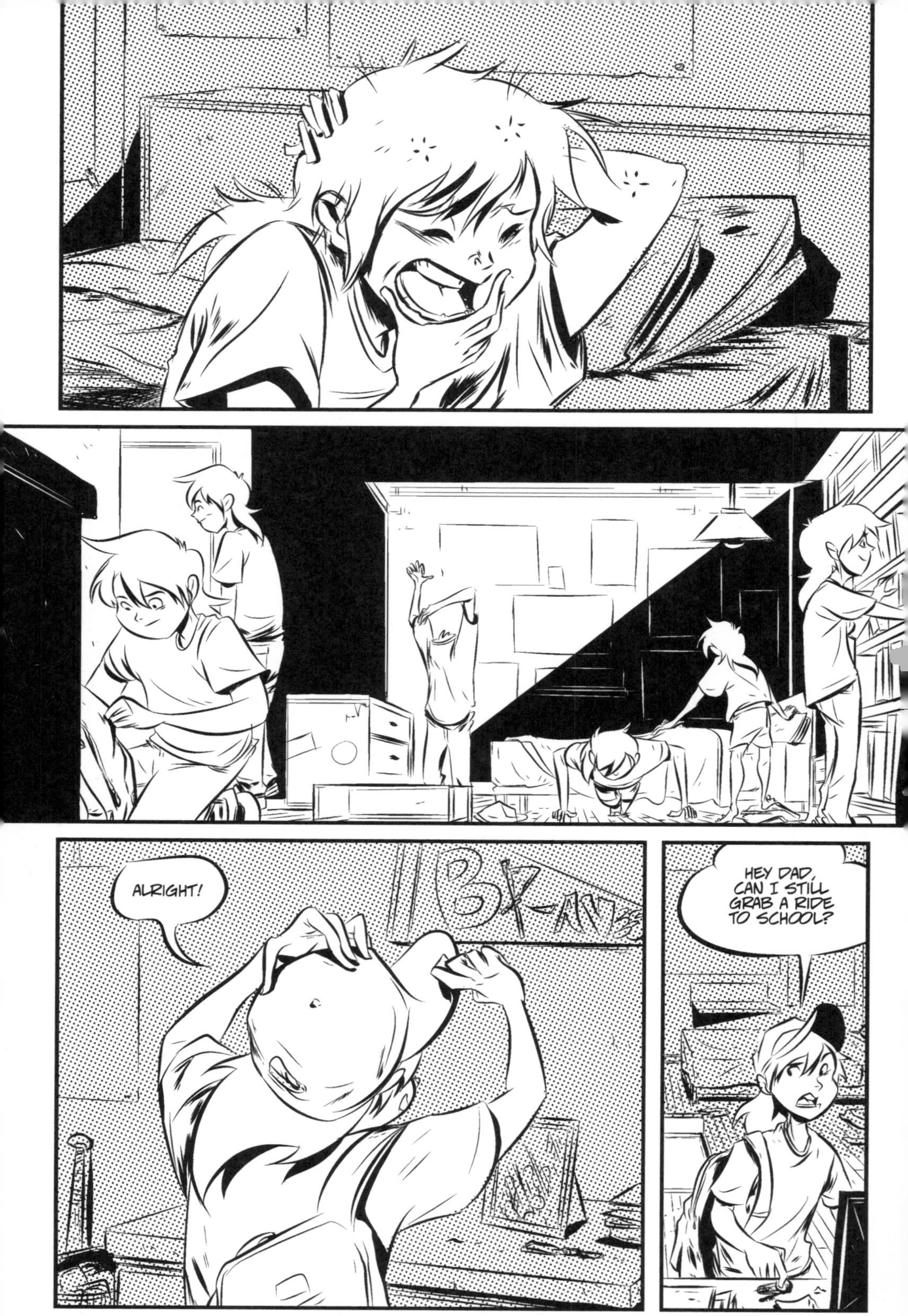
ALRIGHT!
HEY DAD, CAN I STILL GRAB A RIDE TO SCHOOL?

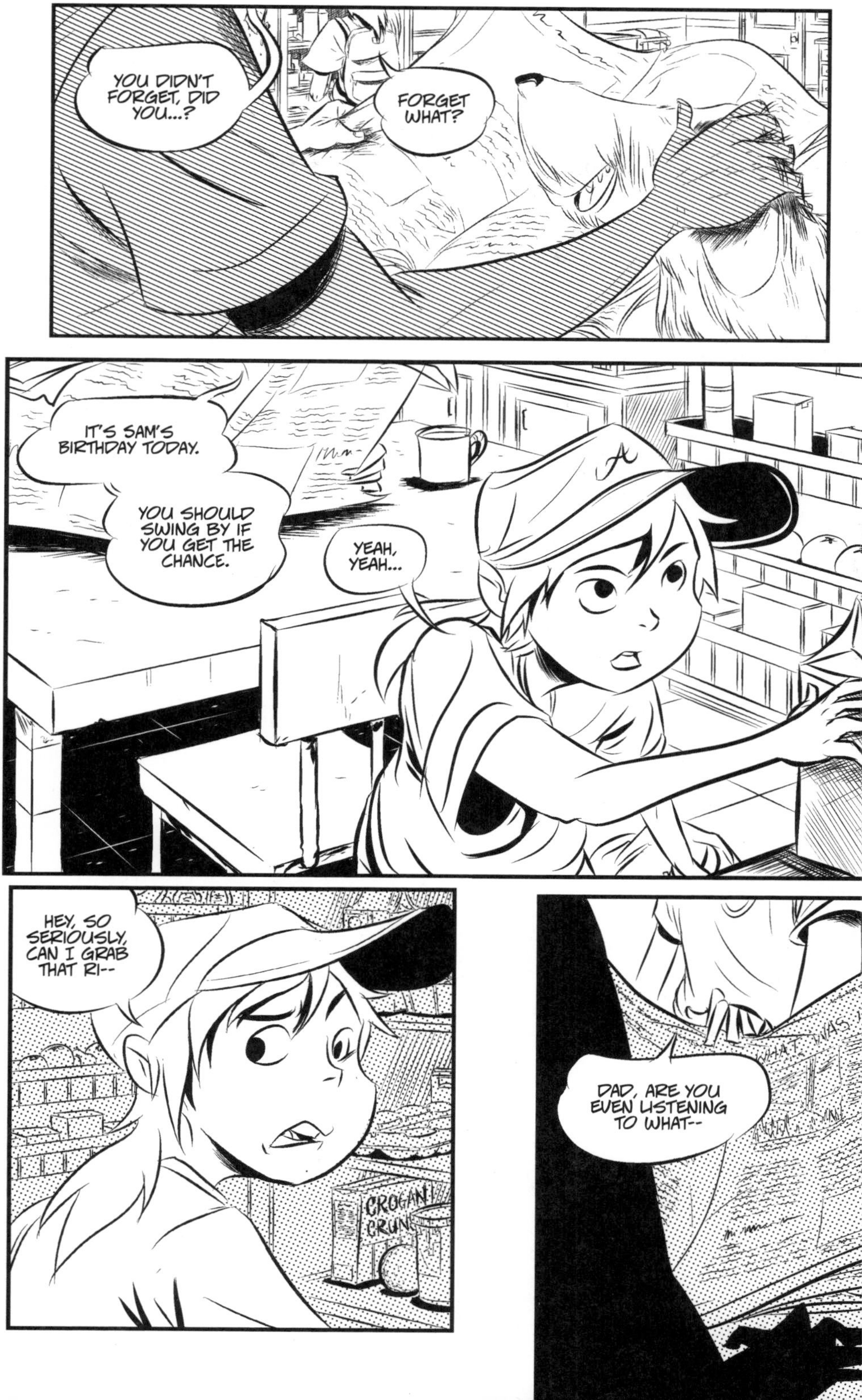
YOU DIDN'T FORGET, DID YOU...?
FORGET WHAT?
IT'S SAM'S BIRTHDAY TODAY.
YOU SHOULD SWING BY IF YOU GET THE CHANCE.
YEAH, YEAH...
HEY, SO SERIOUSLY, CAN I GRAB THAT RI--
DAD, ARE YOU EVEN LISTENING TO WHAT--

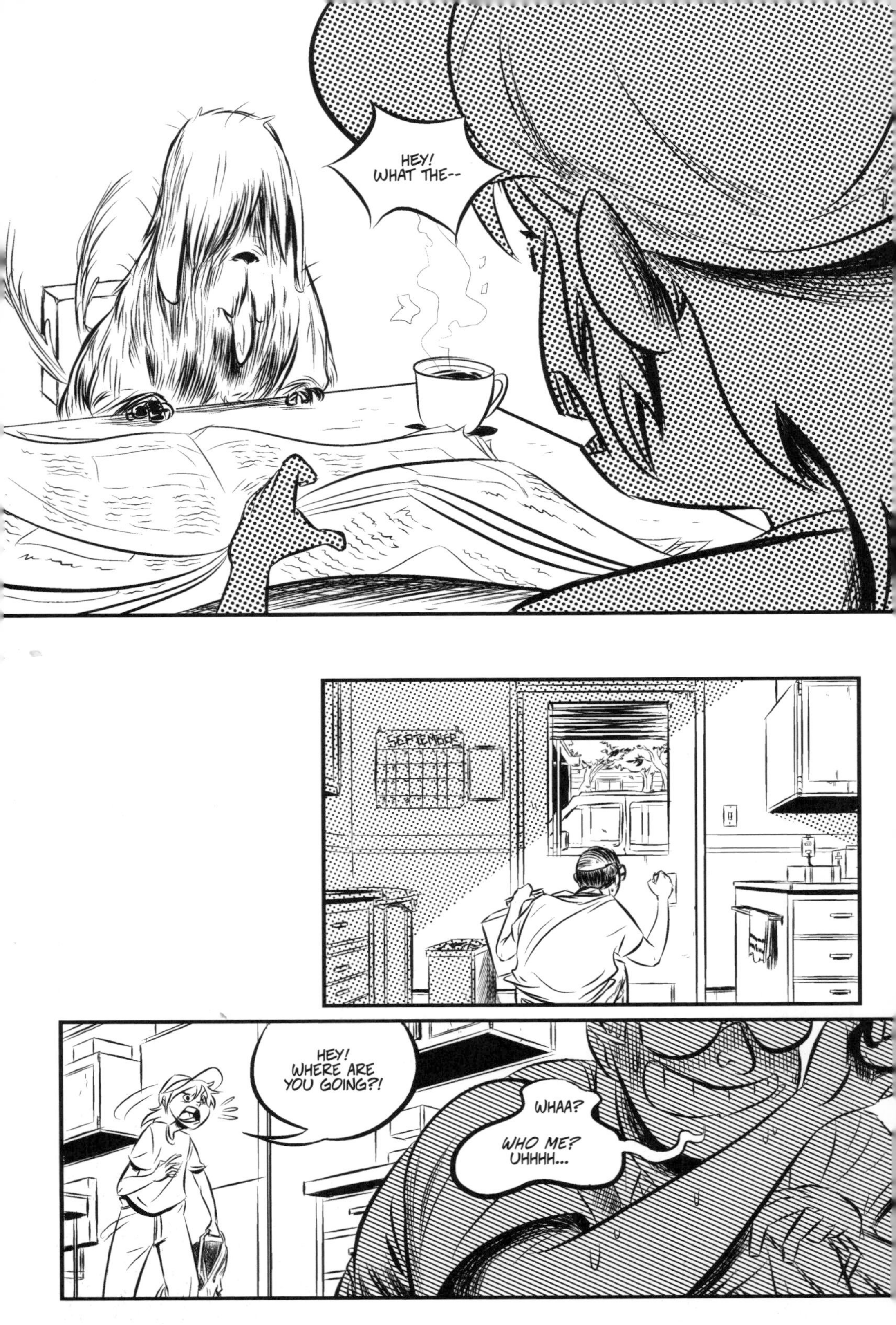
HEY! WHAT THE--
SEPTEMBER
HEY! WHERE ARE YOU GOING?!
WHAA?
WHO ME? UHHHH...

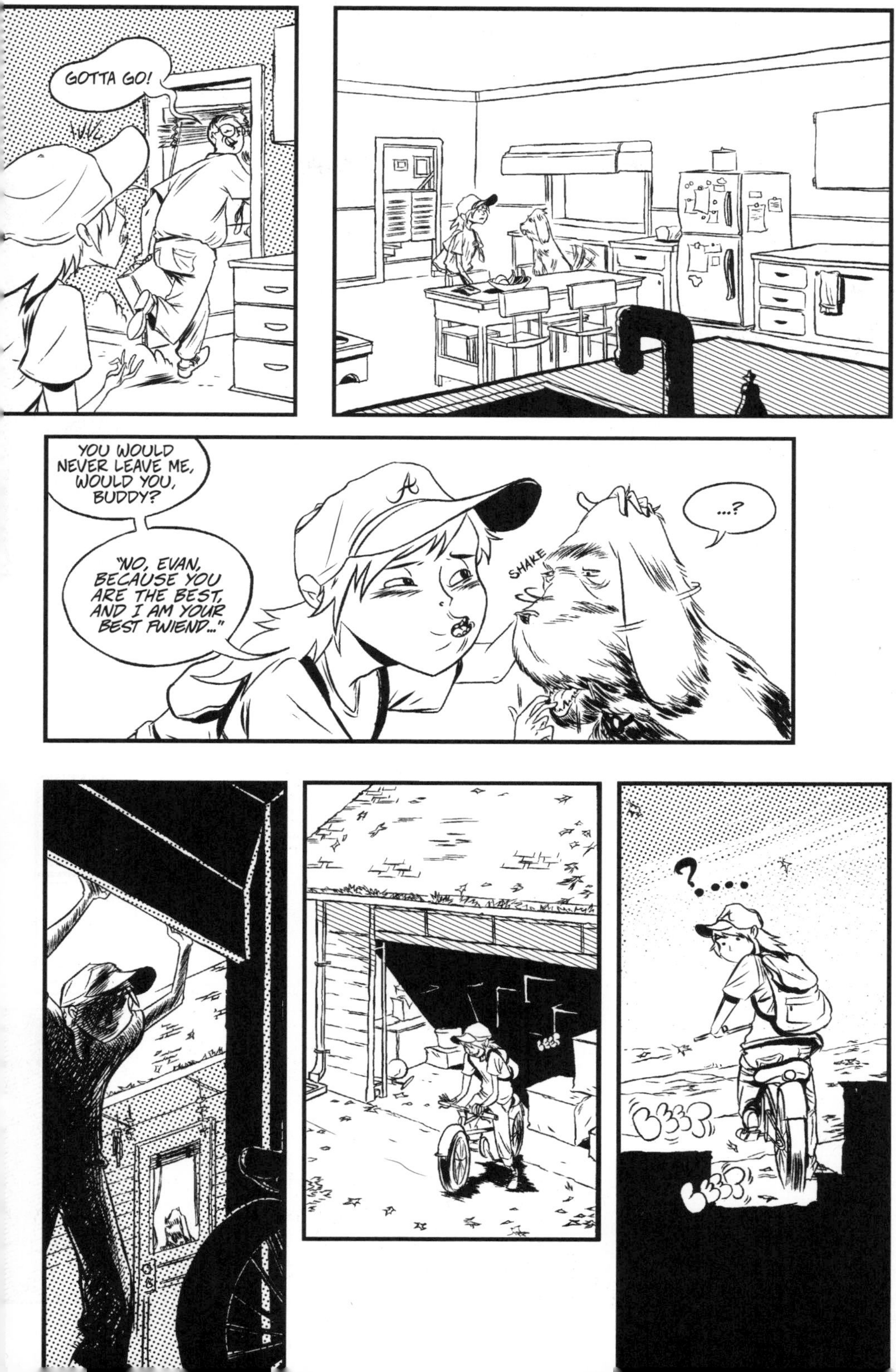
GOTTA GO!
YOU WOULD NEVER LEAVE ME, WOULD YOU, BUDDY?
"NO, EVAN, BECAUSE YOU ARE THE BEST, AND I AM YOUR BEST FWIEND..."
SHAKE
...?
?....

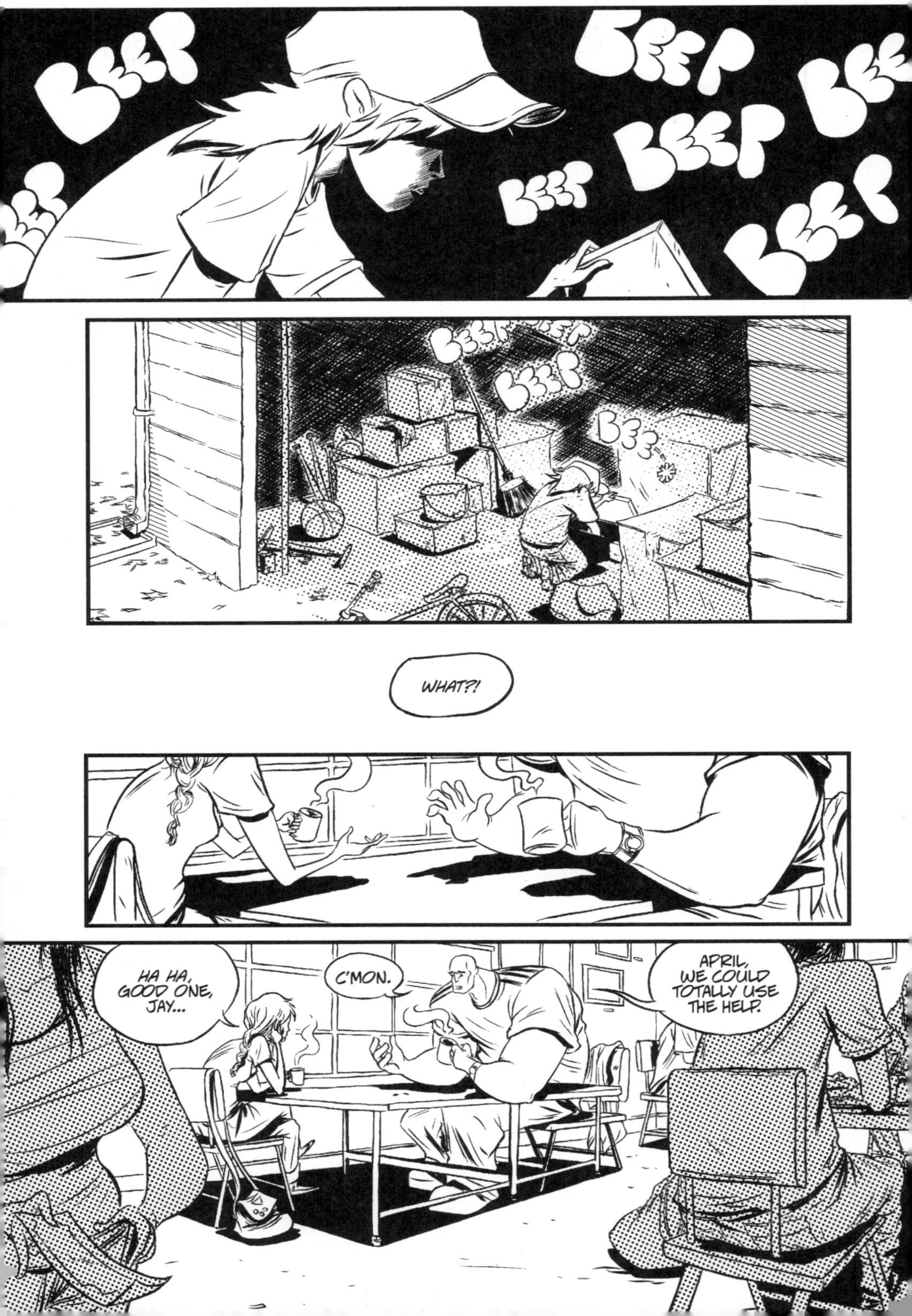
BEEP
BEEP
BEEP
BEEP
BEEP
BEE
BEEP
BEEP
BEEP
BEEP
BEE
WHAT?!
HA HA, GOOD ONE, JAY...
C'MON.
APRIL, WE COULD TOTALLY USE THE HELP.

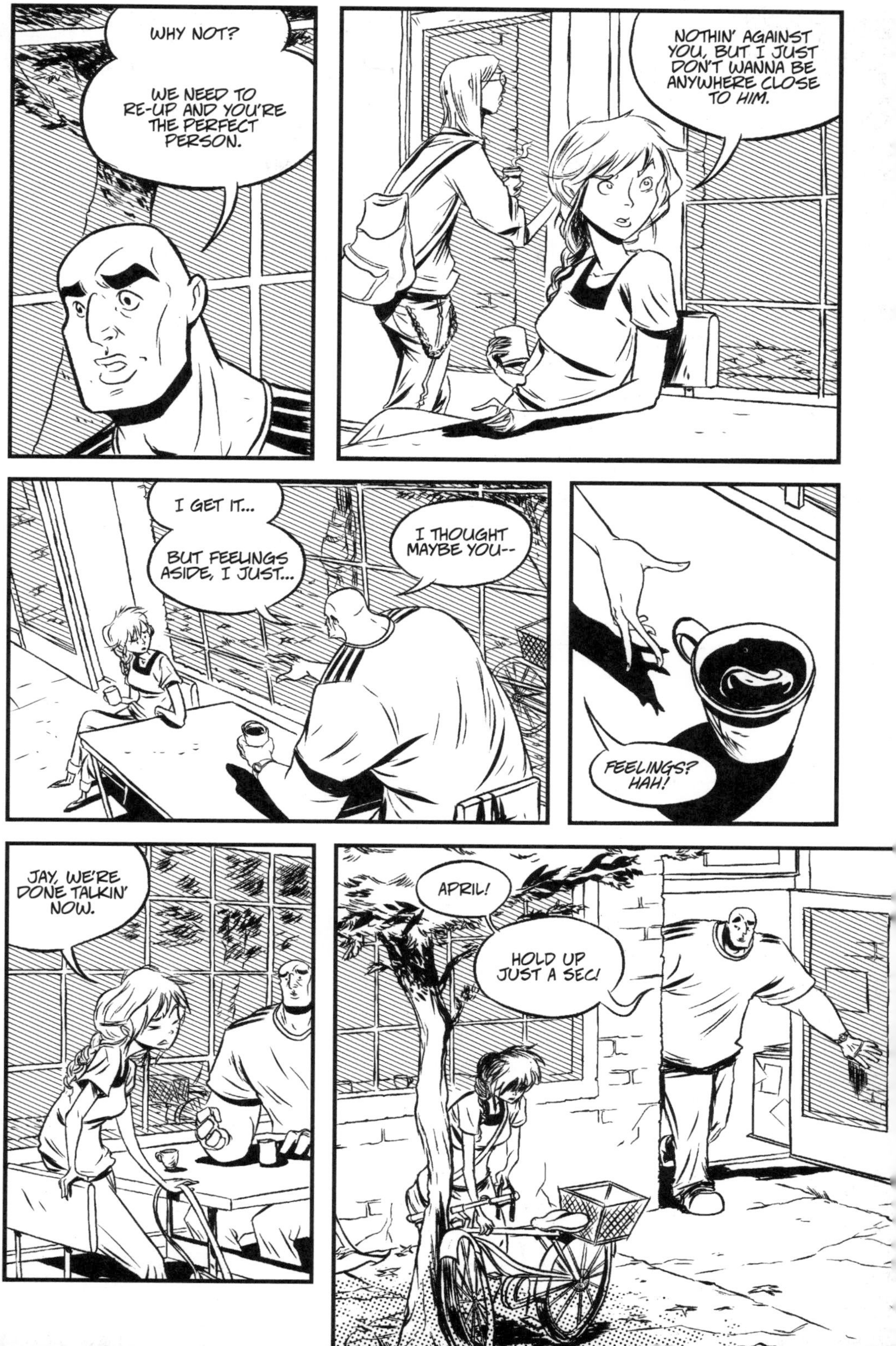
WHY NOT?
WE NEED TO RE-UP AND YOU'RE THE PERFECT PERSON.
NOTHIN' AGAINST YOU, BUT I JUST DON'T WANNA BE ANYWHERE CLOSE TO HIM.
I GET IT...
BUT FEELINGS ASIDE, I JUST...
I THOUGHT MAYBE YOU--
FEELINGS? HAH!
JAY, WE'RE DONE TALKIN' NOW.
APRIL!
HOLD UP JUST A SEC!

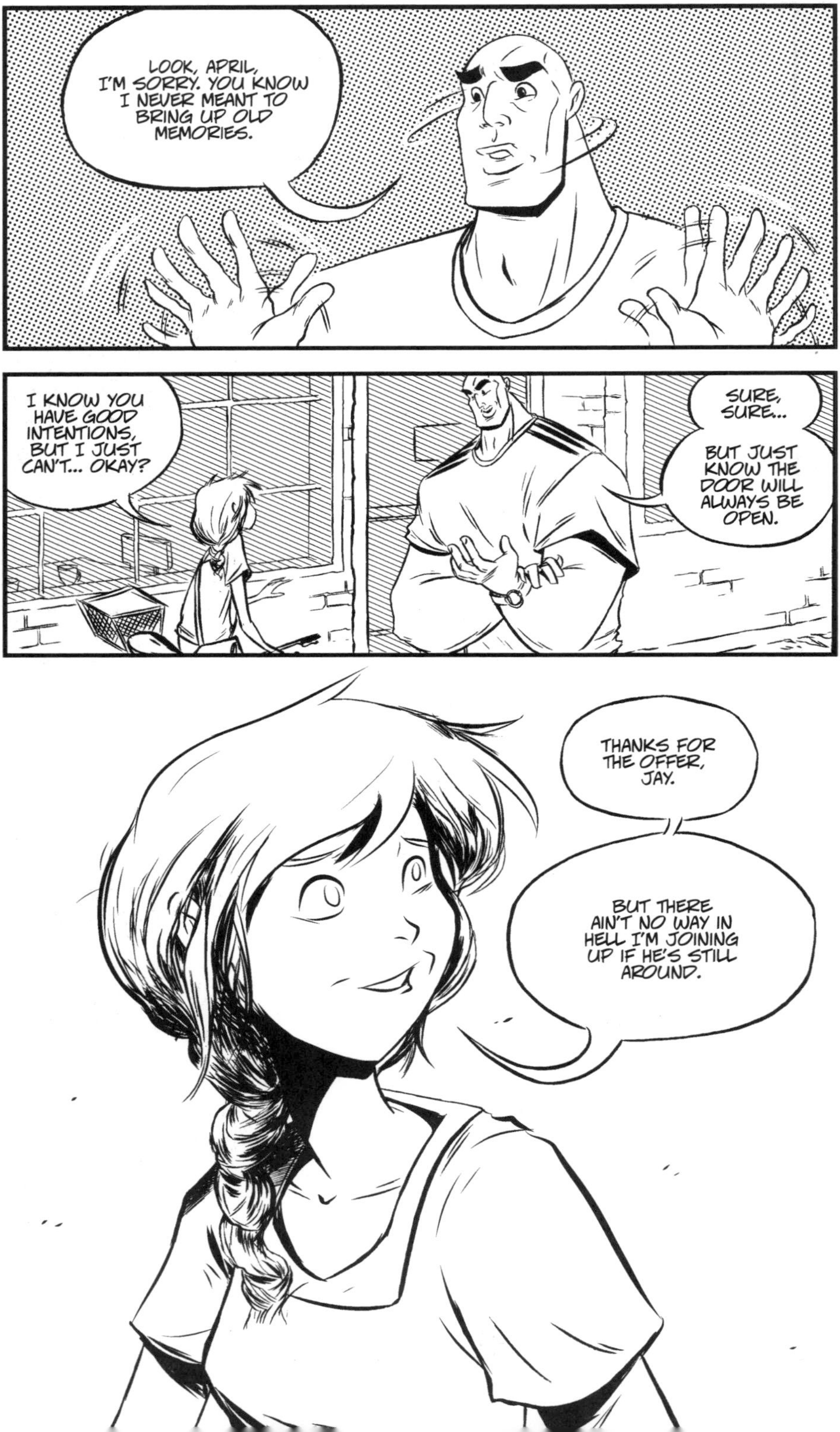
LOOK, APRIL, I'M SORRY. YOU KNOW I NEVER MEANT TO BRING UP OLD MEMORIES.
I KNOW YOU HAVE GOOD INTENTIONS, BUT I JUST CAN'T... OKAY?
SURE, SURE...
BUT JUST KNOW THE DOOR WILL ALWAYS BE OPEN.
THANKS FOR THE OFFER, JAY.
BUT THERE AIN'T NO WAY IN HELL I'M JOINING UP IF HE'S STILL AROUND.

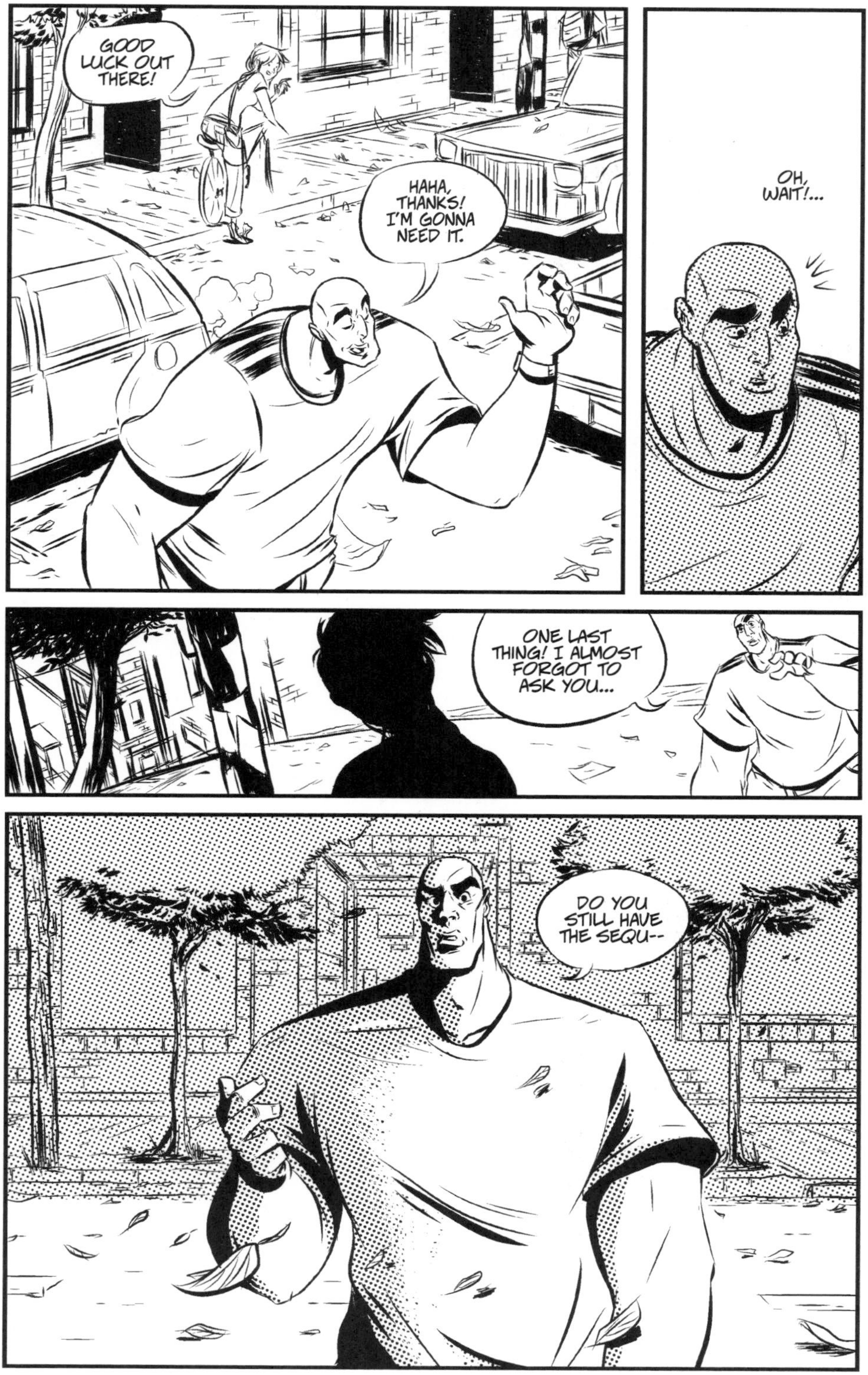
GOOD LUCK OUT THERE!
HAHA, THANKS! I'M GONNA NEED IT.
OH, WAIT!...
ONE LAST THING! I ALMOST FORGOT TO ASK YOU...
DO YOU STILL HAVE THE SEQU--

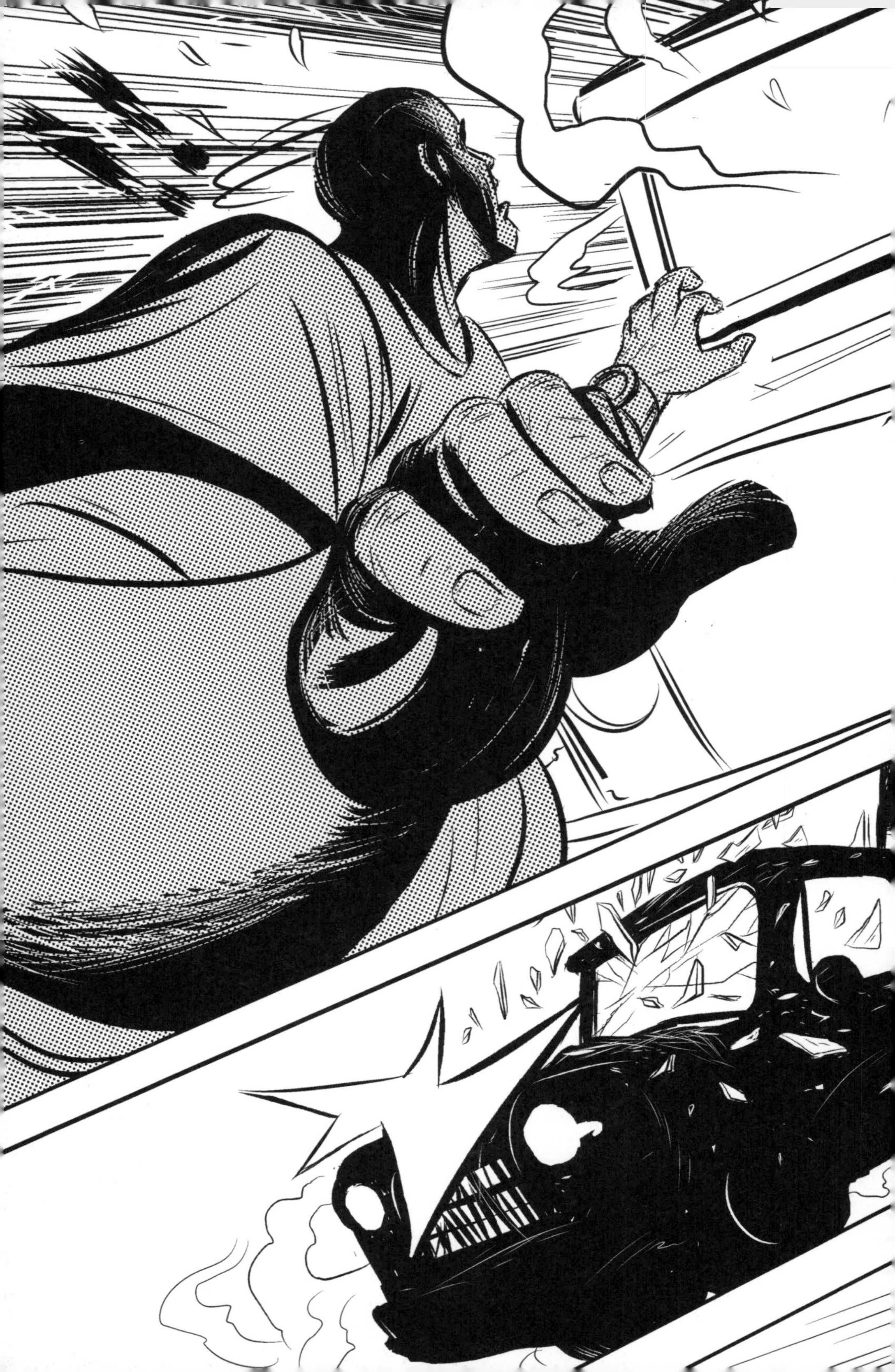

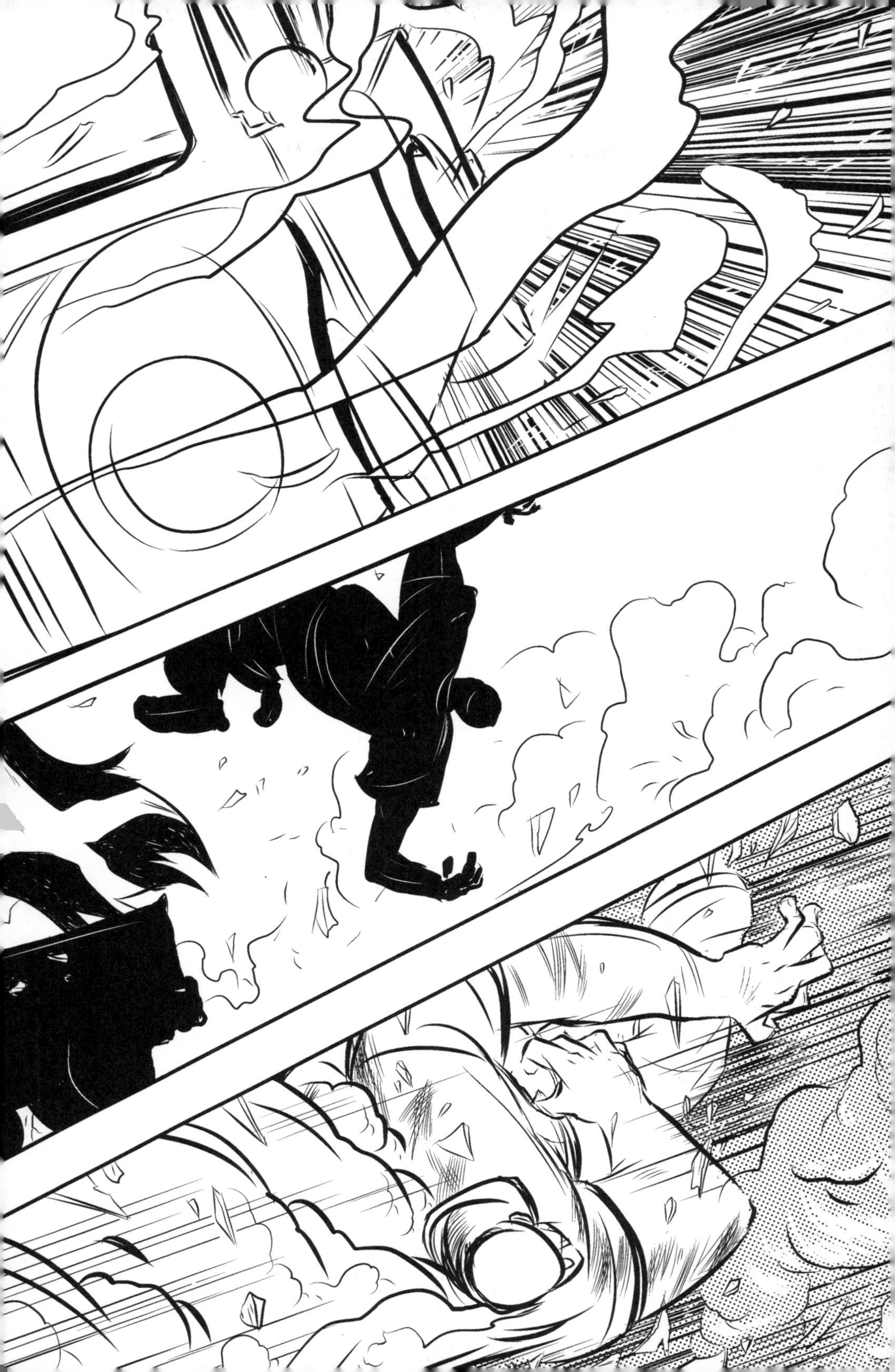

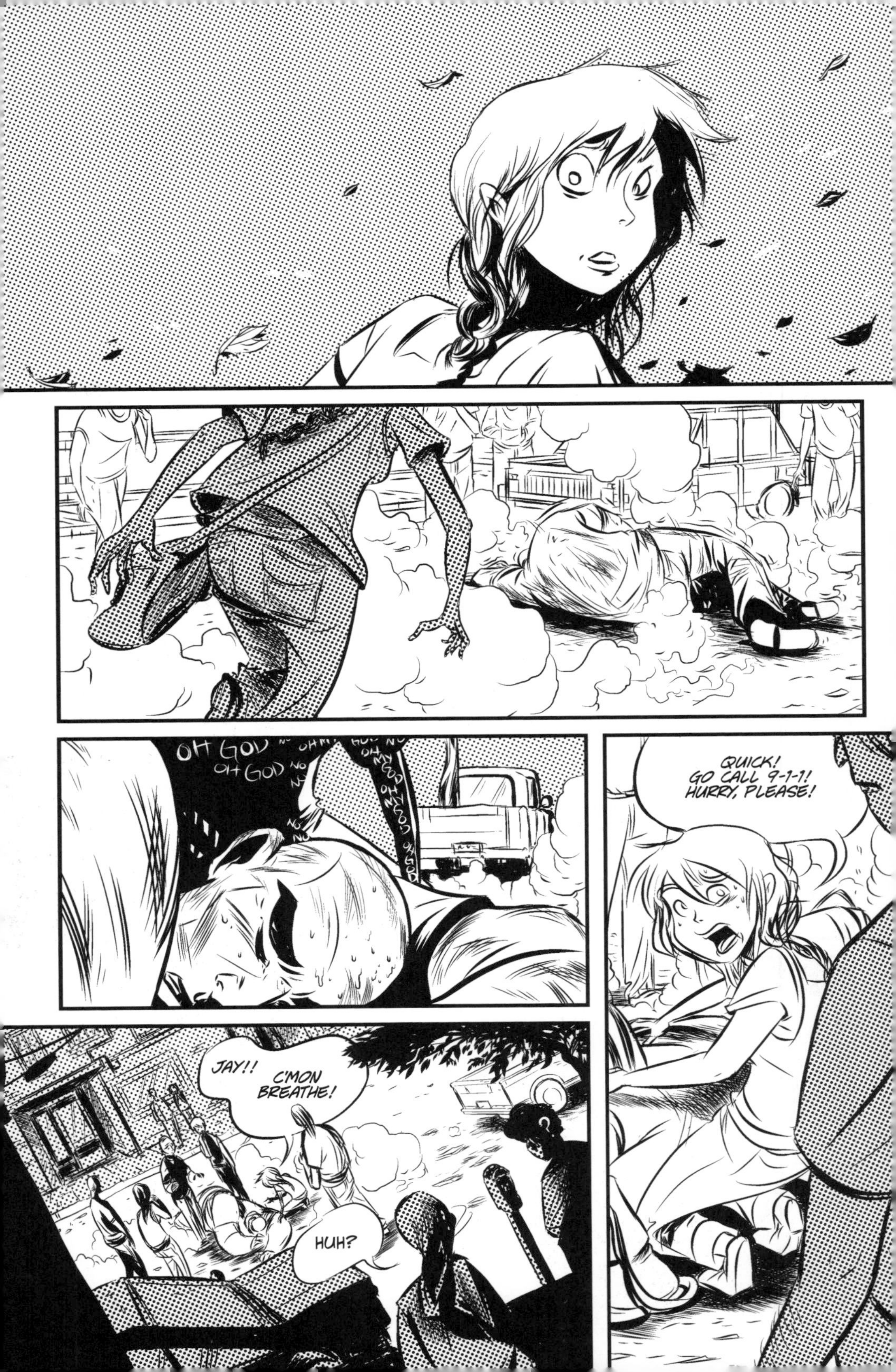

OH GOD
OH GOD
QUICK! GO CALL 9-1-1! HURRY, PLEASE!
JAY!!
C'MON BREATHE!
HUH?

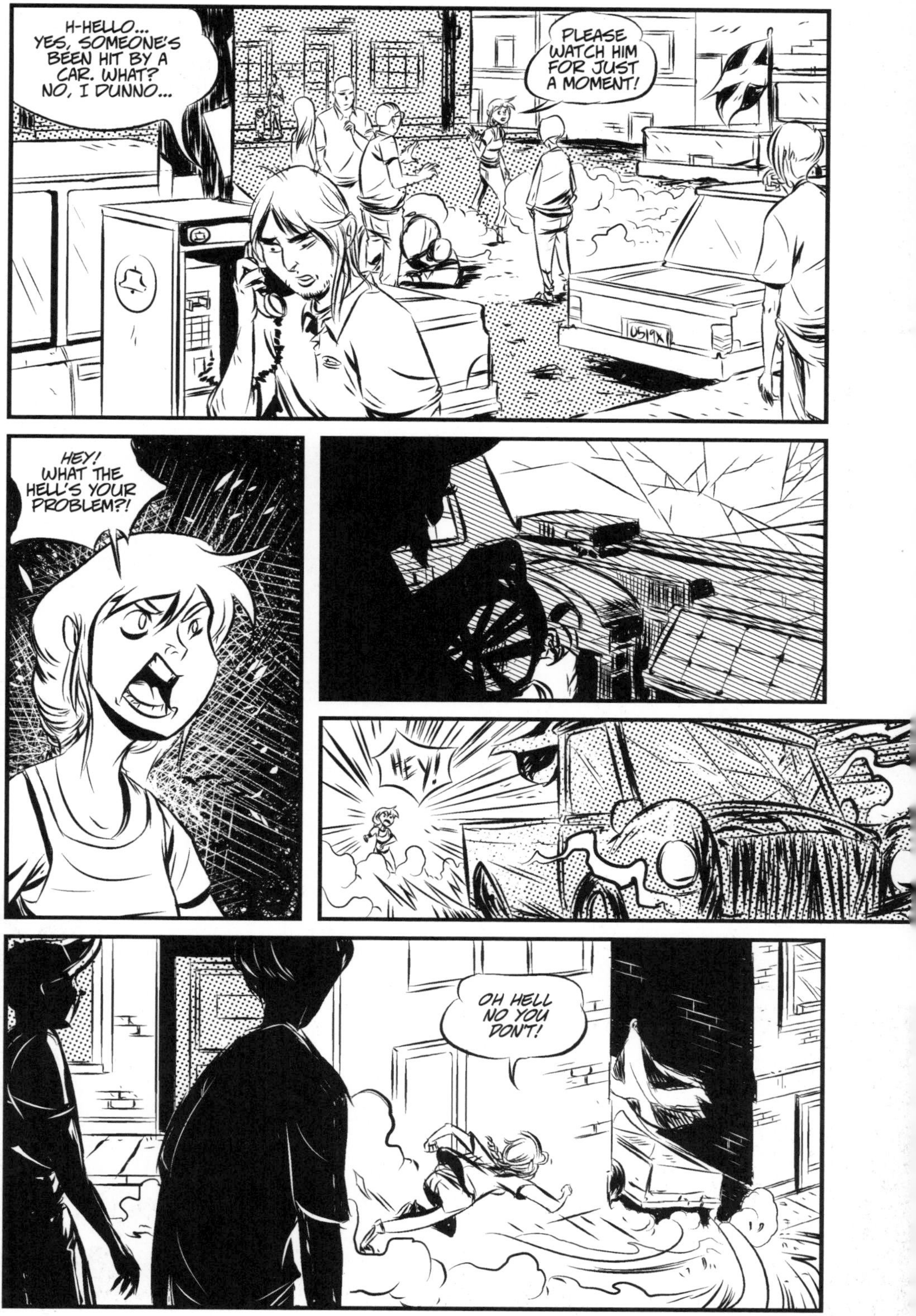
H-HELLO... YES, SOMEONE'S BEEN HIT BY A CAR. WHAT? NO, I DUNNO...
PLEASE WATCH HIM FOR JUST A MOMENT!
U519X
HEY! WHAT THE HELL'S YOUR PROBLEM?!
HEY!
OH HELL NO YOU DON'T!

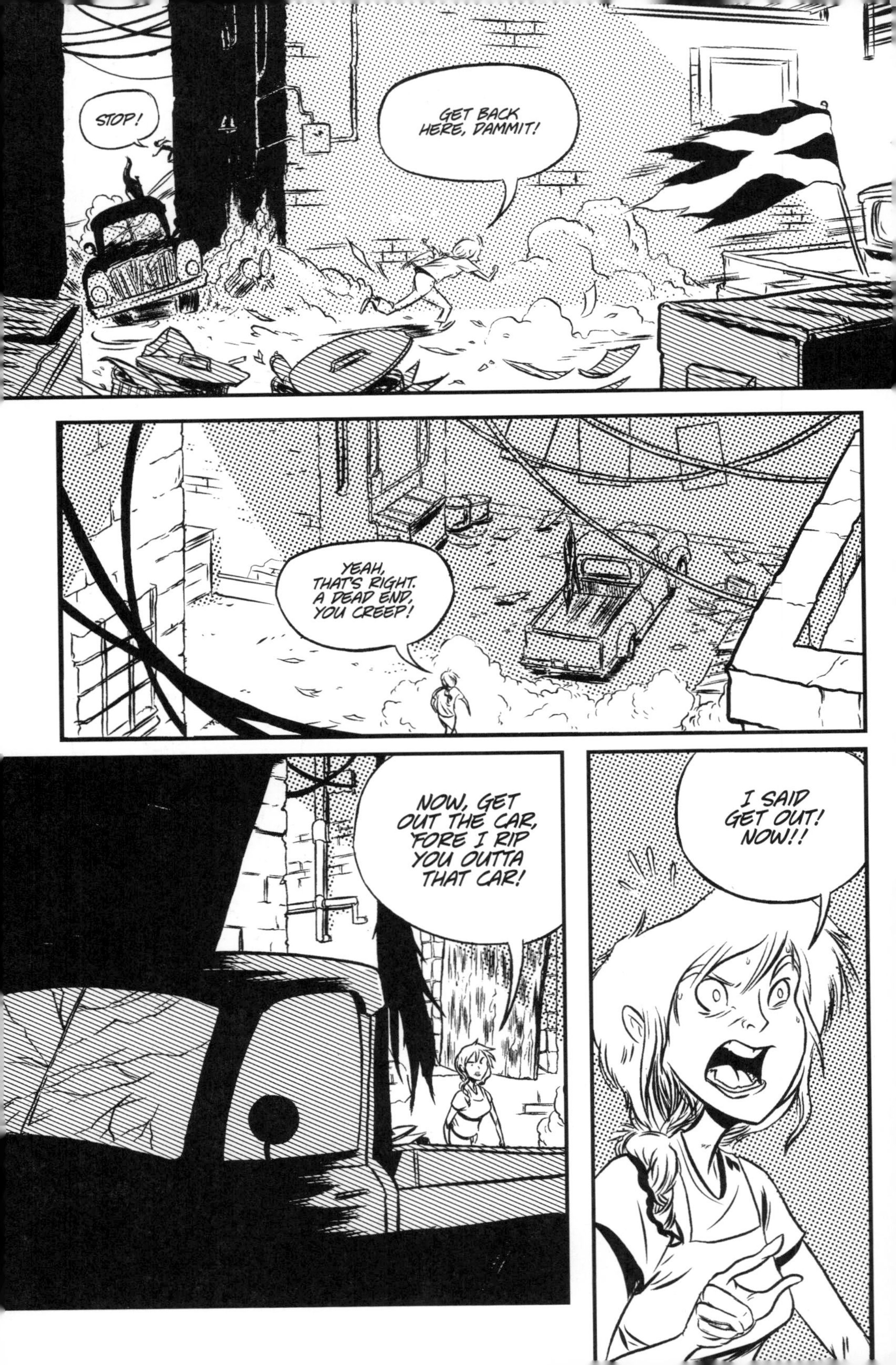
STOP!
GET BACK HERE, DAMMIT!
YEAH, THAT'S RIGHT. A DEAD END, YOU CREEP!
NOW, GET OUT THE CAR, 'FORE I RIP YOU OUTTA THAT CAR!
I SAID GET OUT! NOW!!

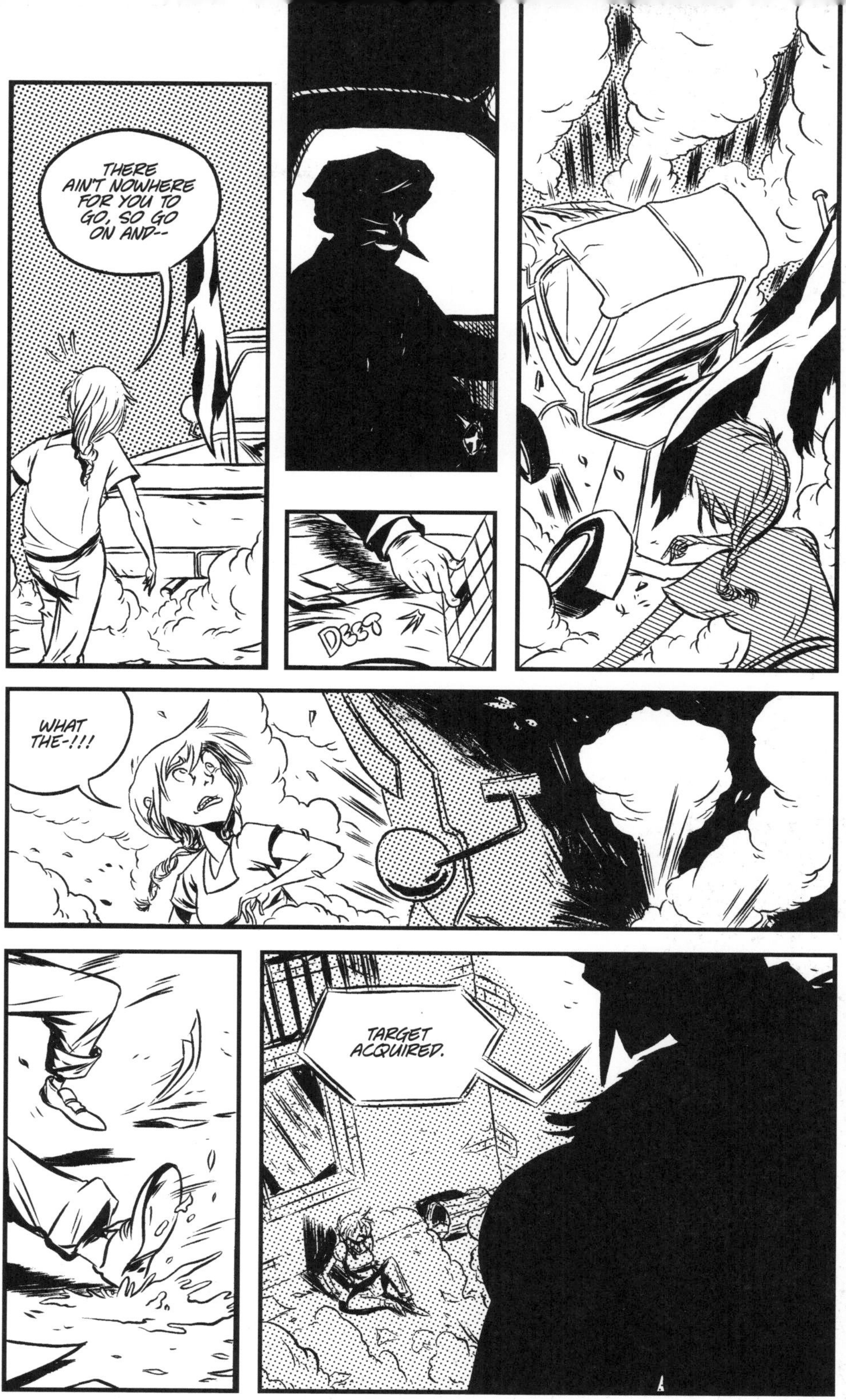
THERE AIN'T NOWHERE FOR YOU TO GO, SO GO ON AND--
DEEP
WHAT THE-!!!
TARGET ACQUIRED.

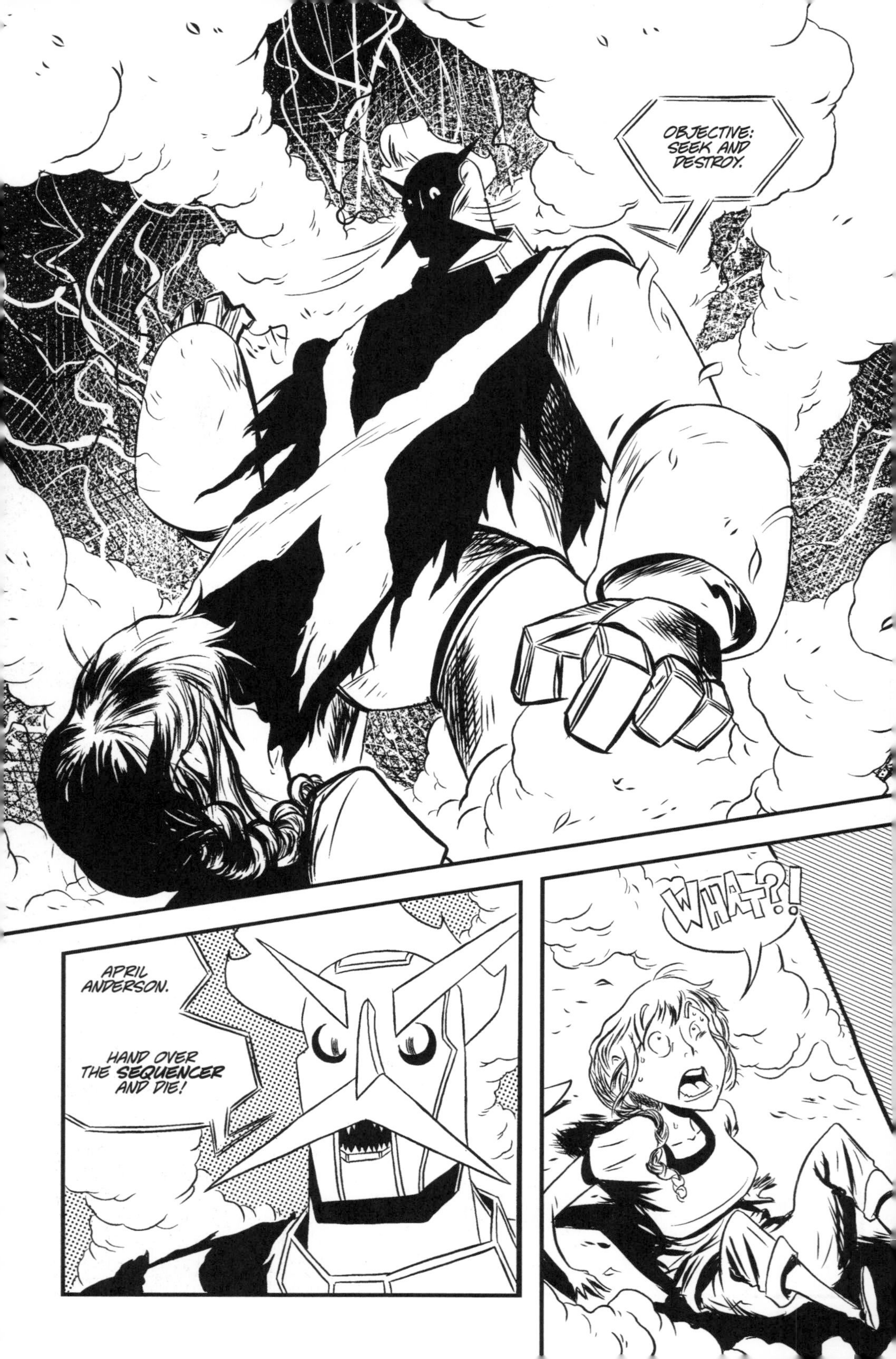
OBJECTIVE: SEEK AND DESTROY.
APRIL ANDERSON.
HAND OVER THE SEQUENCER AND DIE!
WHAT?!

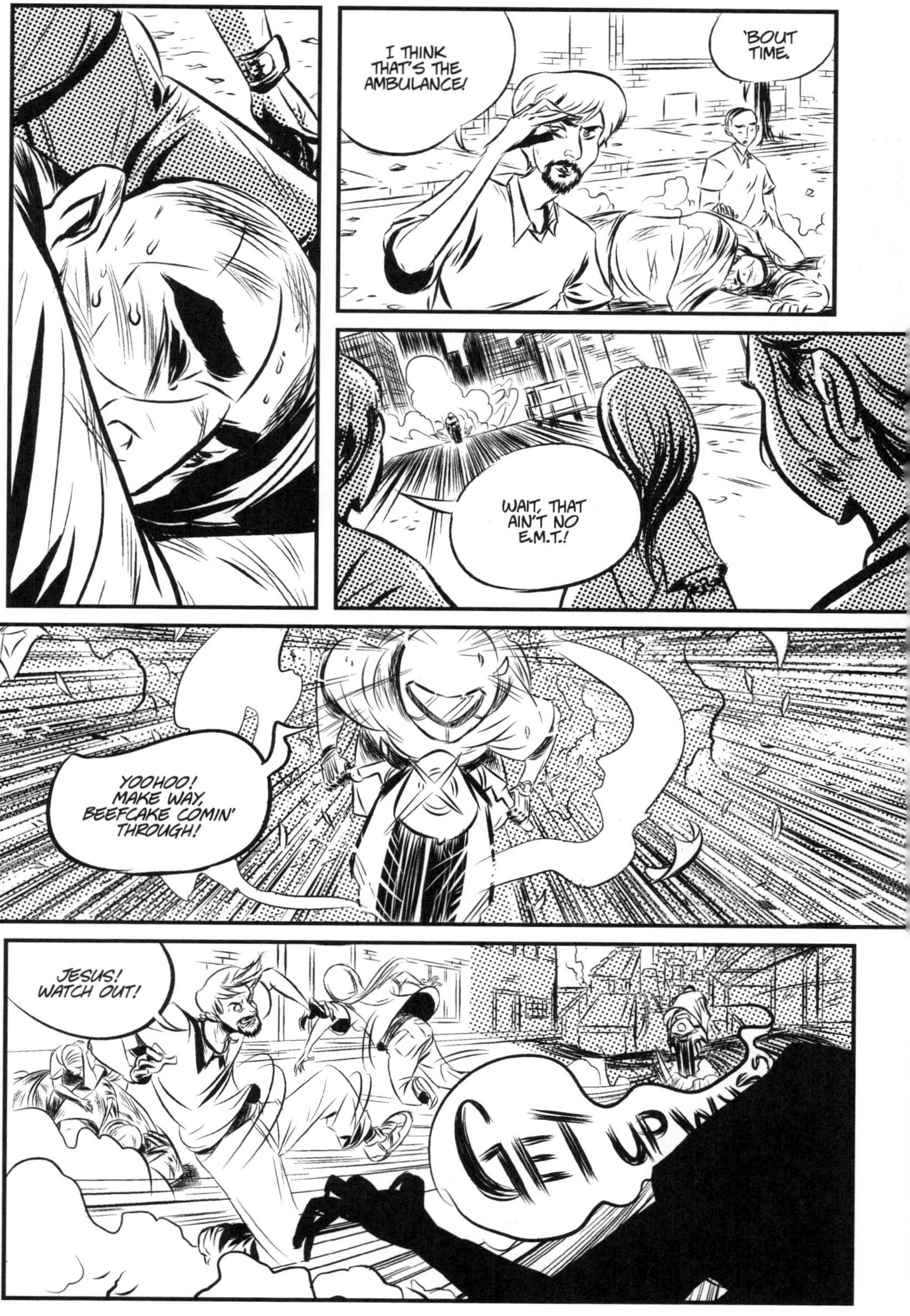
I THINK THAT'S THE AMBULANCE!
'BOUT TIME.
WAIT, THAT AIN'T NO E.M.T.!
YOOHOO! MAKE WAY, BEEFCAKE COMIN' THROUGH!
JESUS! WATCH OUT!
GET UP

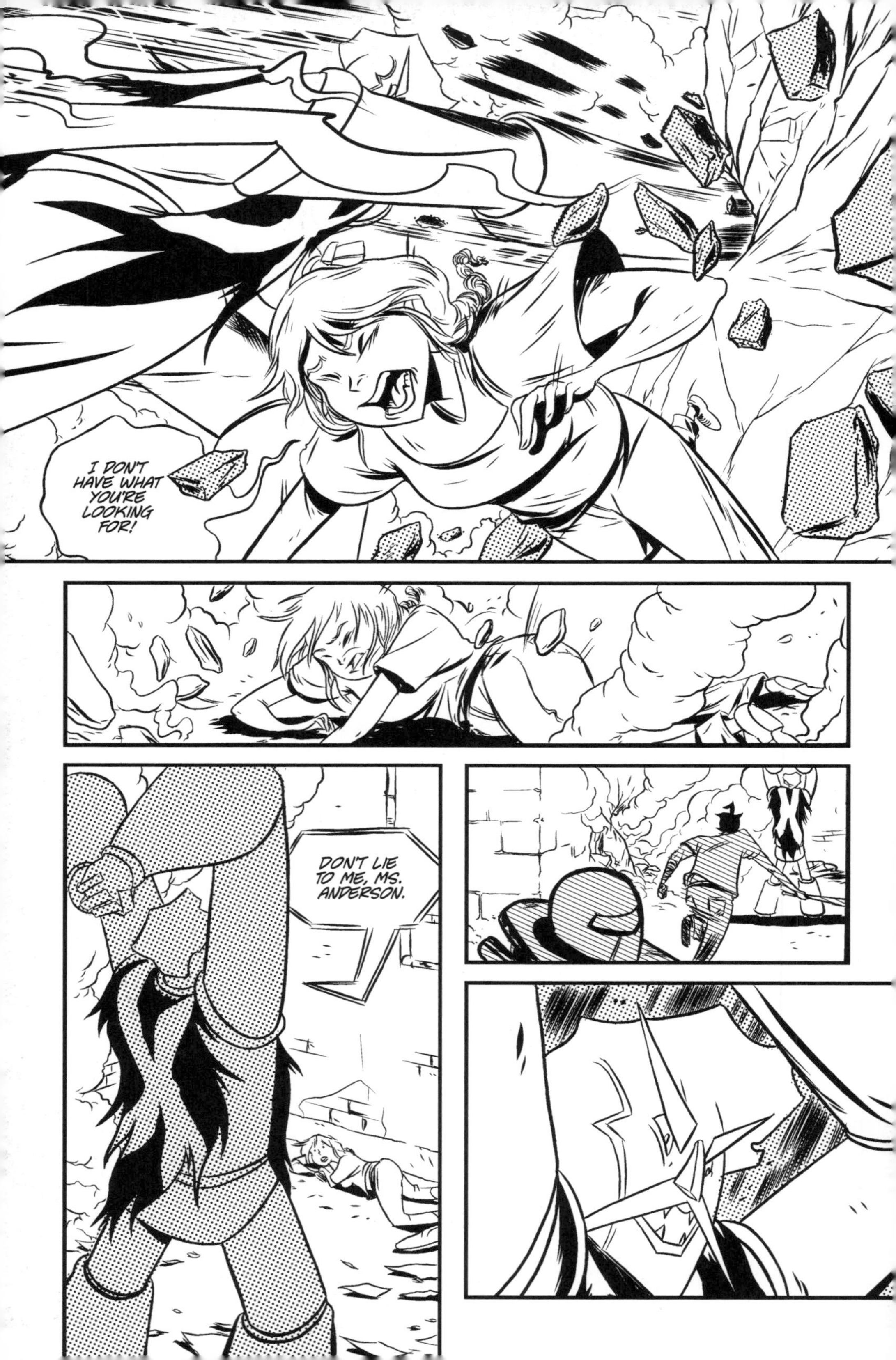
I DON'T HAVE WHAT YOU'RE LOOKING FOR!
DON'T LIE TO ME, MS. ANDERSON.

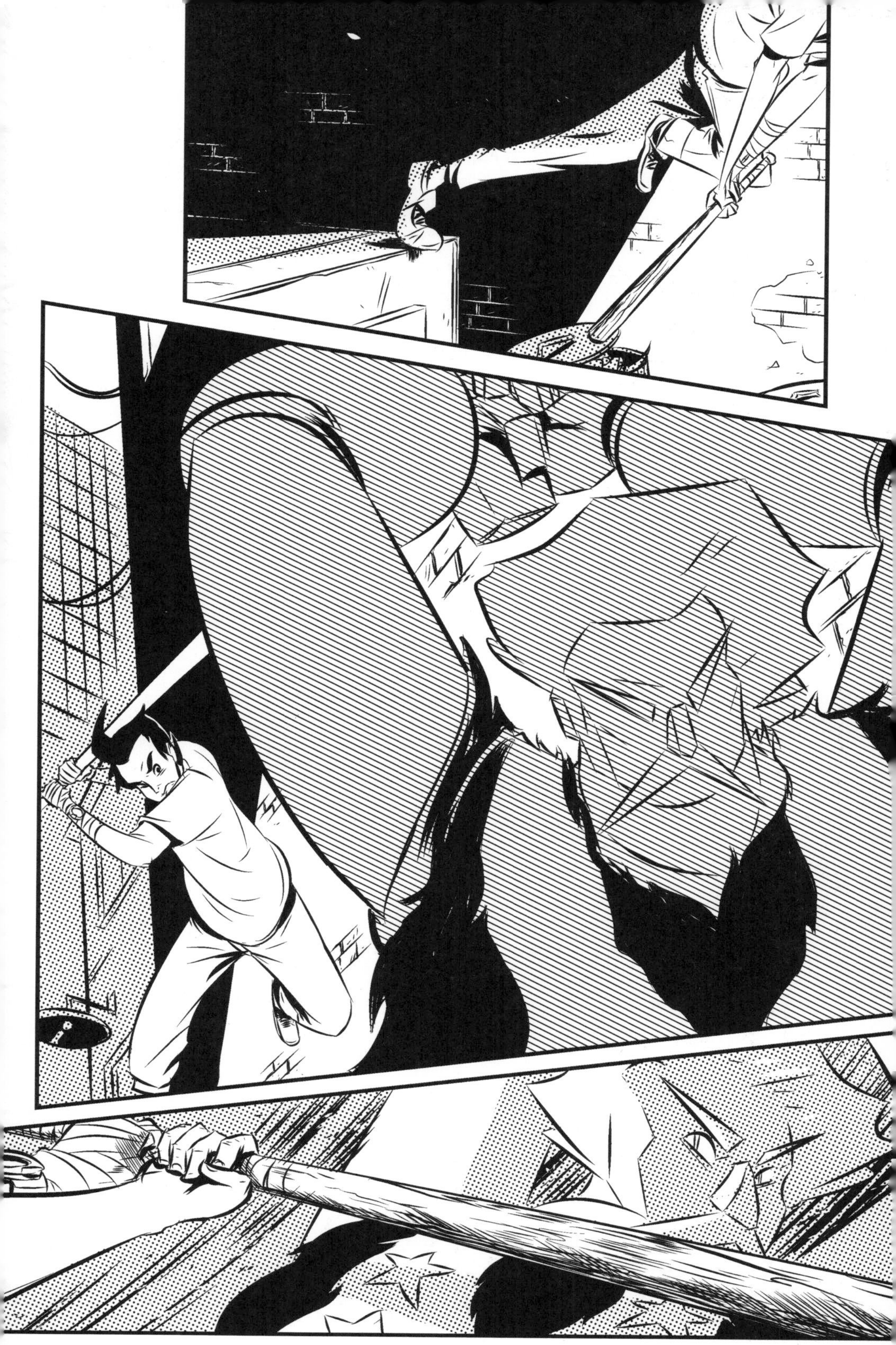

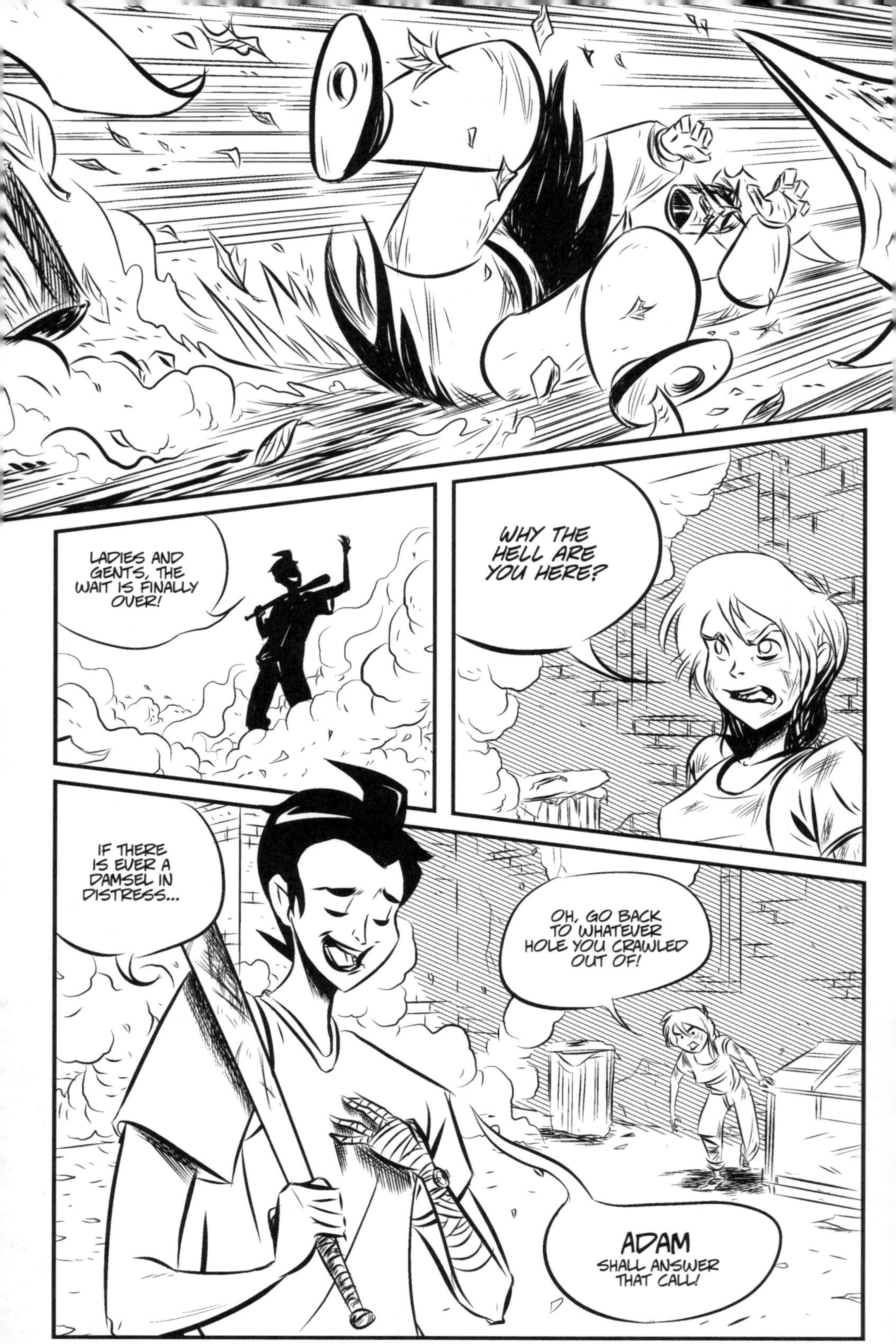
LADIES AND GENTS, THE WAIT IS FINALLY OVER!
WHY THE HELL ARE YOU HERE?
IF THERE IS EVER A DAMSEL IN DISTRESS...
OH, GO BACK TO WHATEVER HOLE YOU CRAWLED OUT OF!
ADAM SHALL ANSWER THAT CALL!

REAWWRR!

SOMEBODY'S IN A MOOD TODAY! HAHA!

OOWWW!

WHAT WAS THAT FOR?

BECAUSE I HATE YOU! THAT'S WHY!

WHY? WHAT DID I EV--

WHY? ...WHY?! REALLY YOU'RE ASKING ME WHY?!

AARGH!

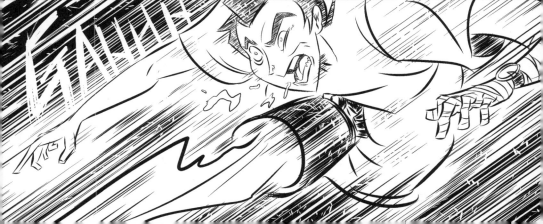

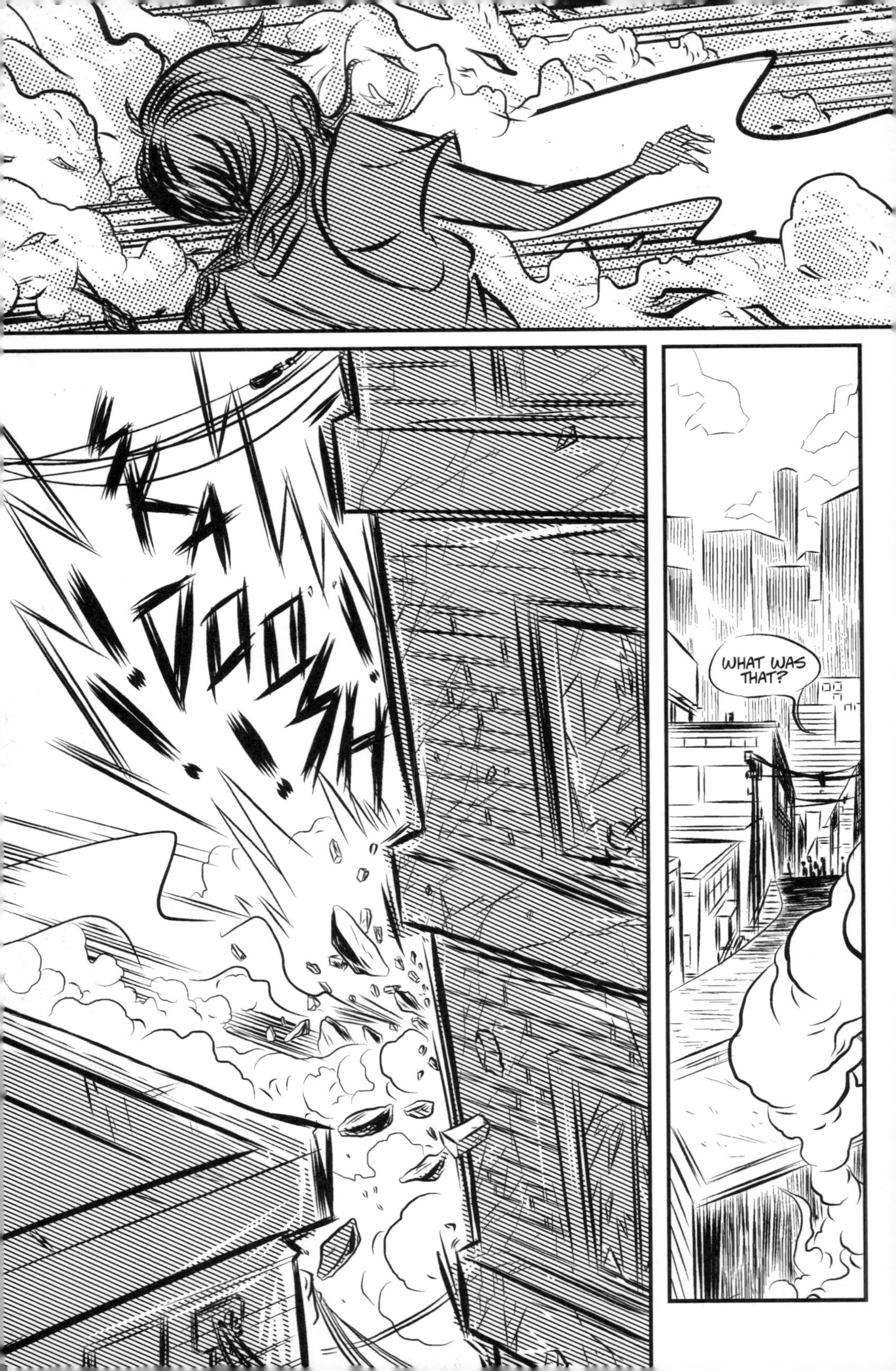
KA-DOOSH!!!
WHAT WAS THAT?

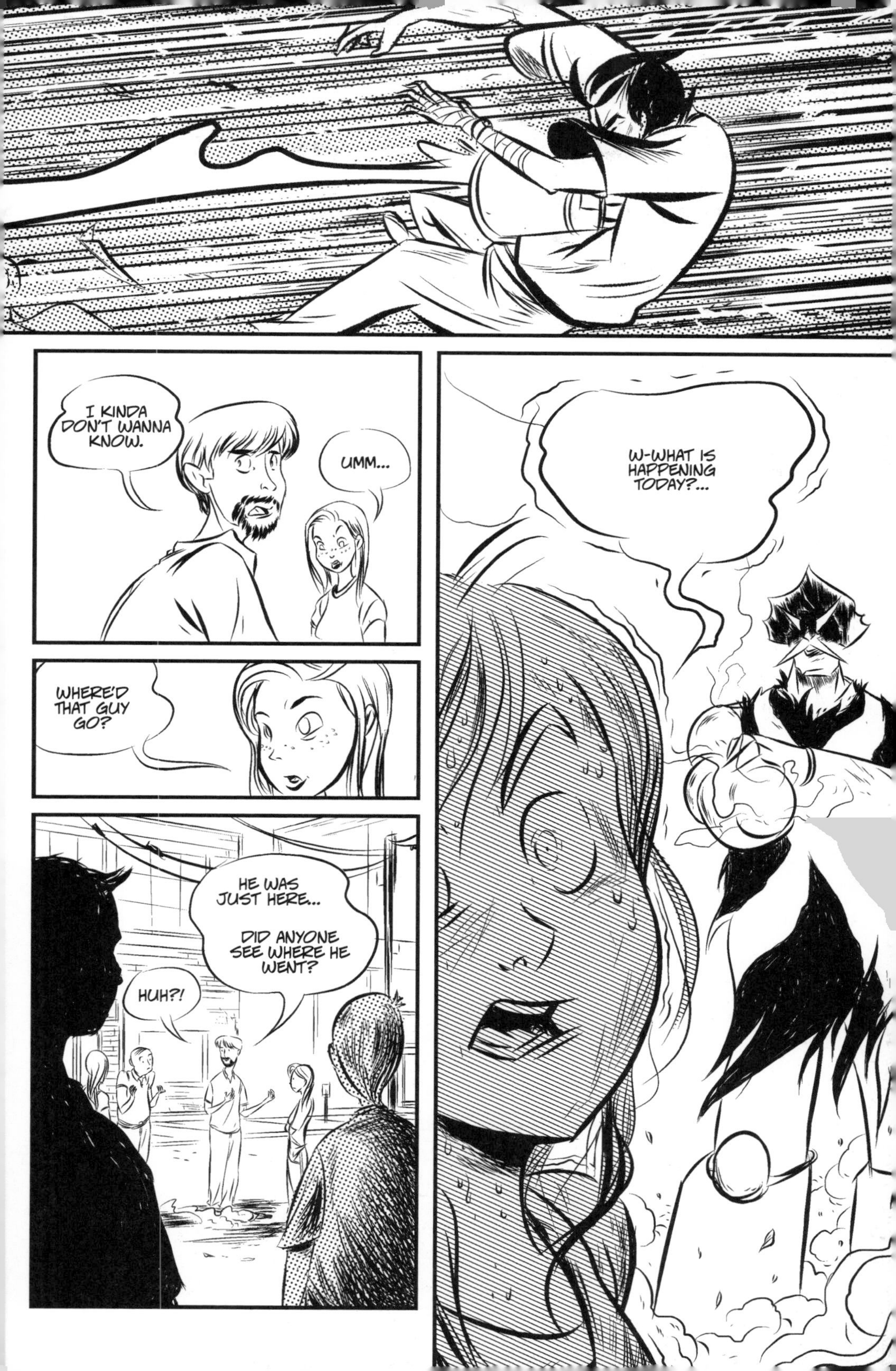
I KINDA DON'T WANNA KNOW.
UMM...
WHERE'D THAT GUY GO?
HE WAS JUST HERE...
DID ANYONE SEE WHERE HE WENT?
HUH?!
W-WHAT IS HAPPENING TODAY?...

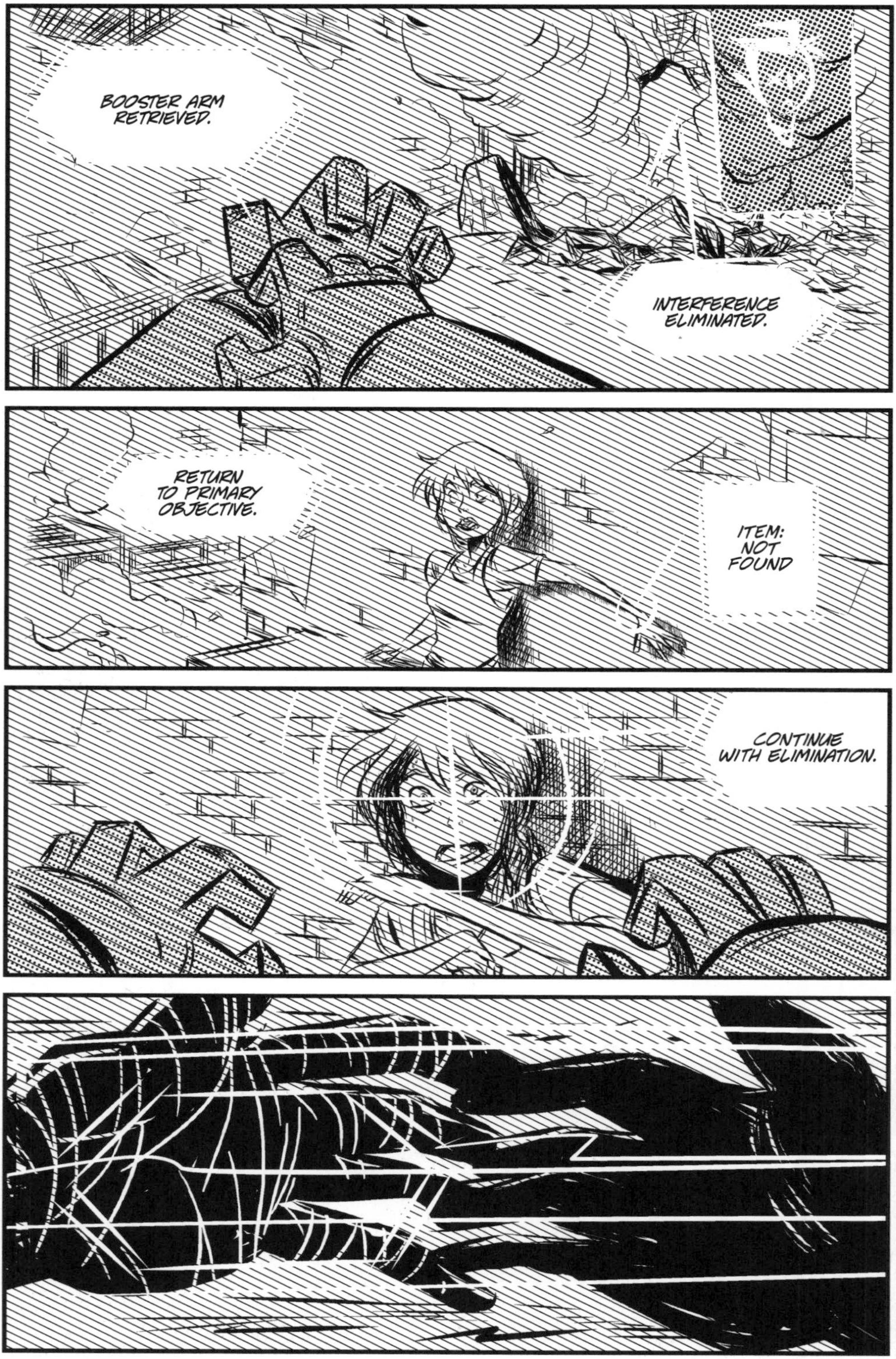
BOOSTER ARM RETRIEVED.
INTERFERENCE ELIMINATED.
RETURN TO PRIMARY OBJECTIVE.
ITEM: NOT FOUND
CONTINUE WITH ELIMINATION.

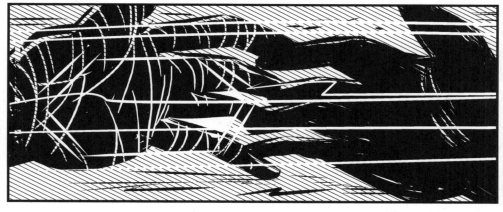

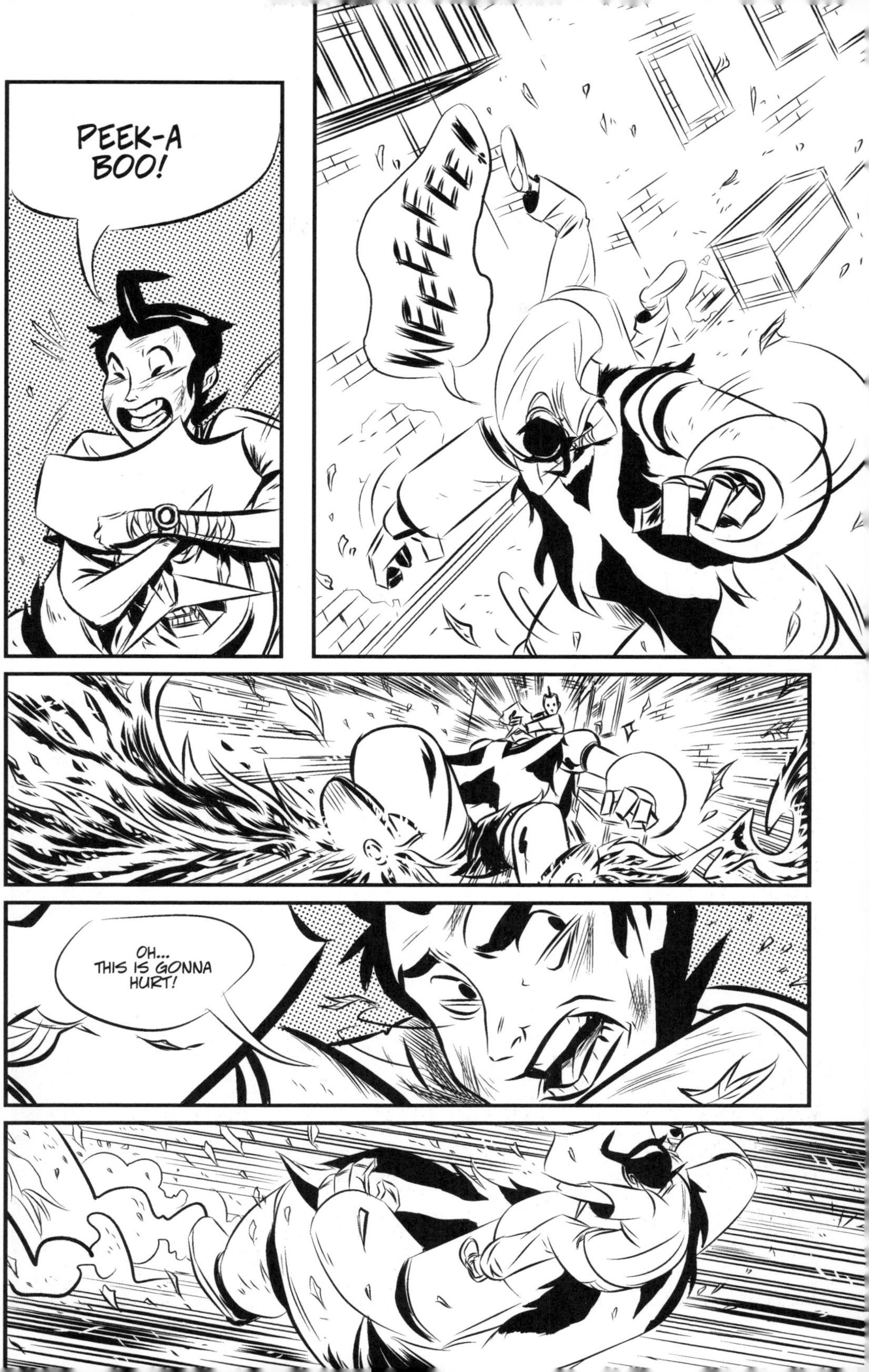
PEEK-A
BOO!
WEEEEEE!
OH...
THIS IS GONNA
HURT!

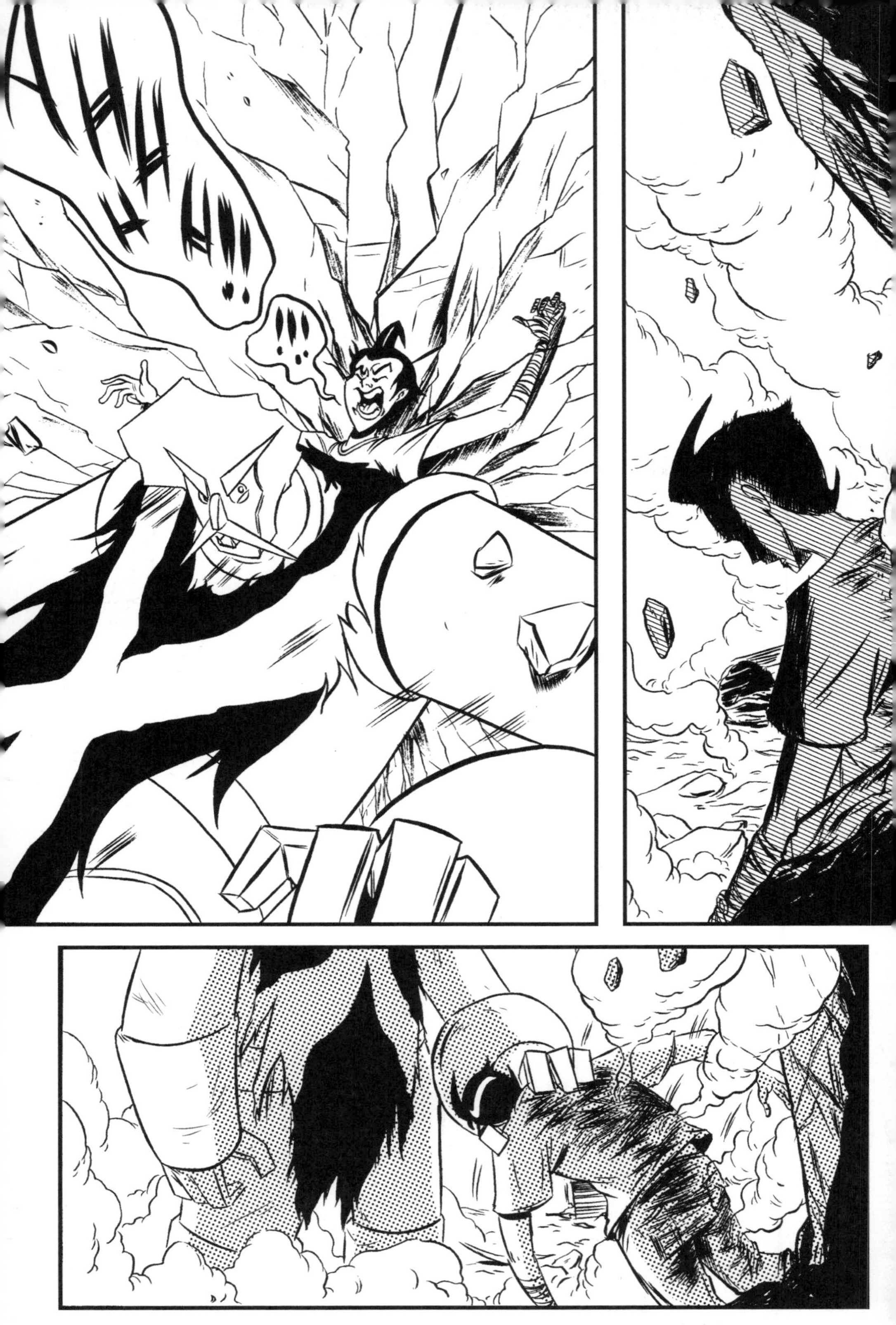
AHHHH!!
!!!

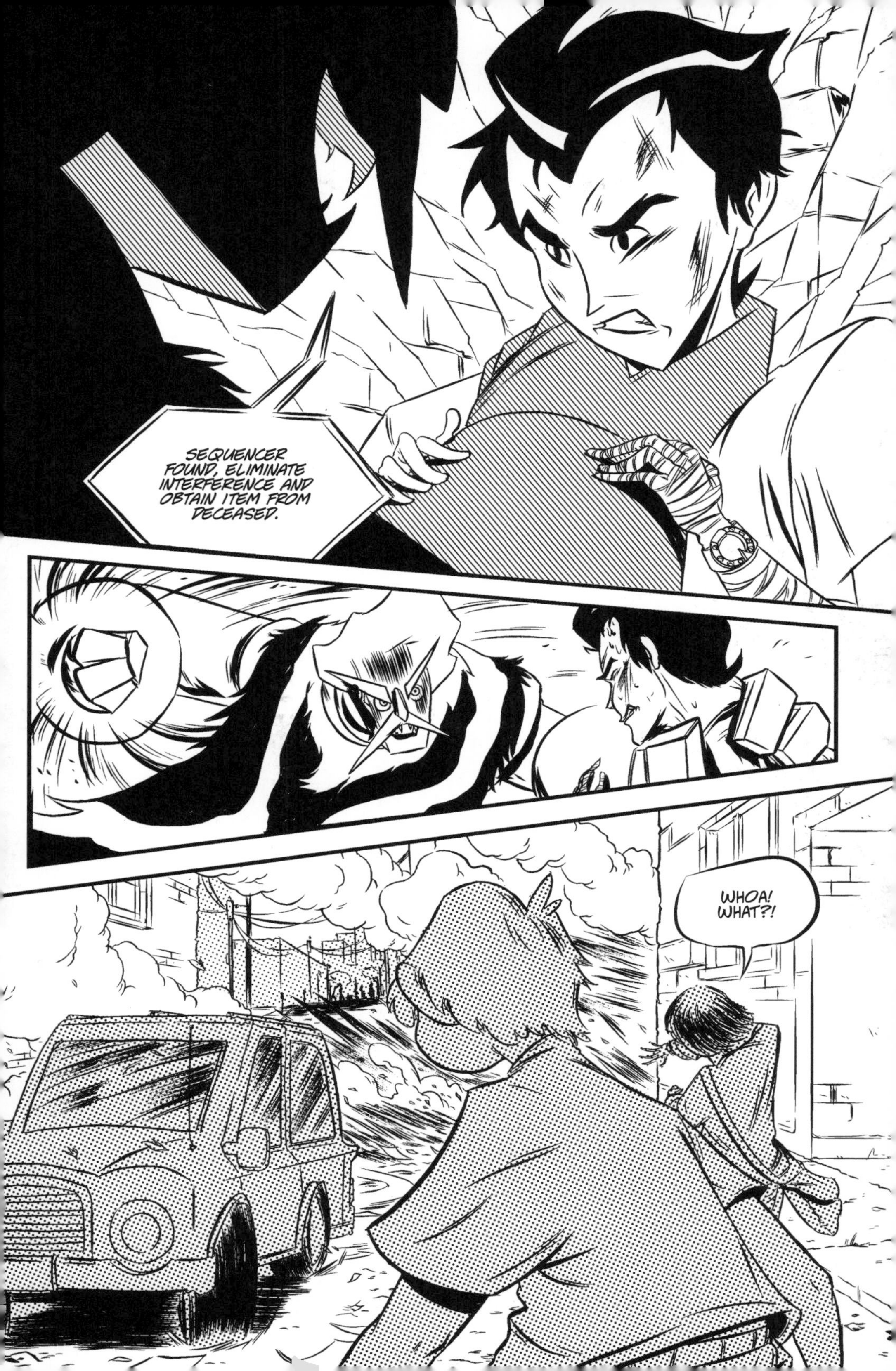

SEQUENCER FOUND, ELIMINATE INTERFERENCE AND OBTAIN ITEM FROM DECEASED.
WHOA! WHAT?!

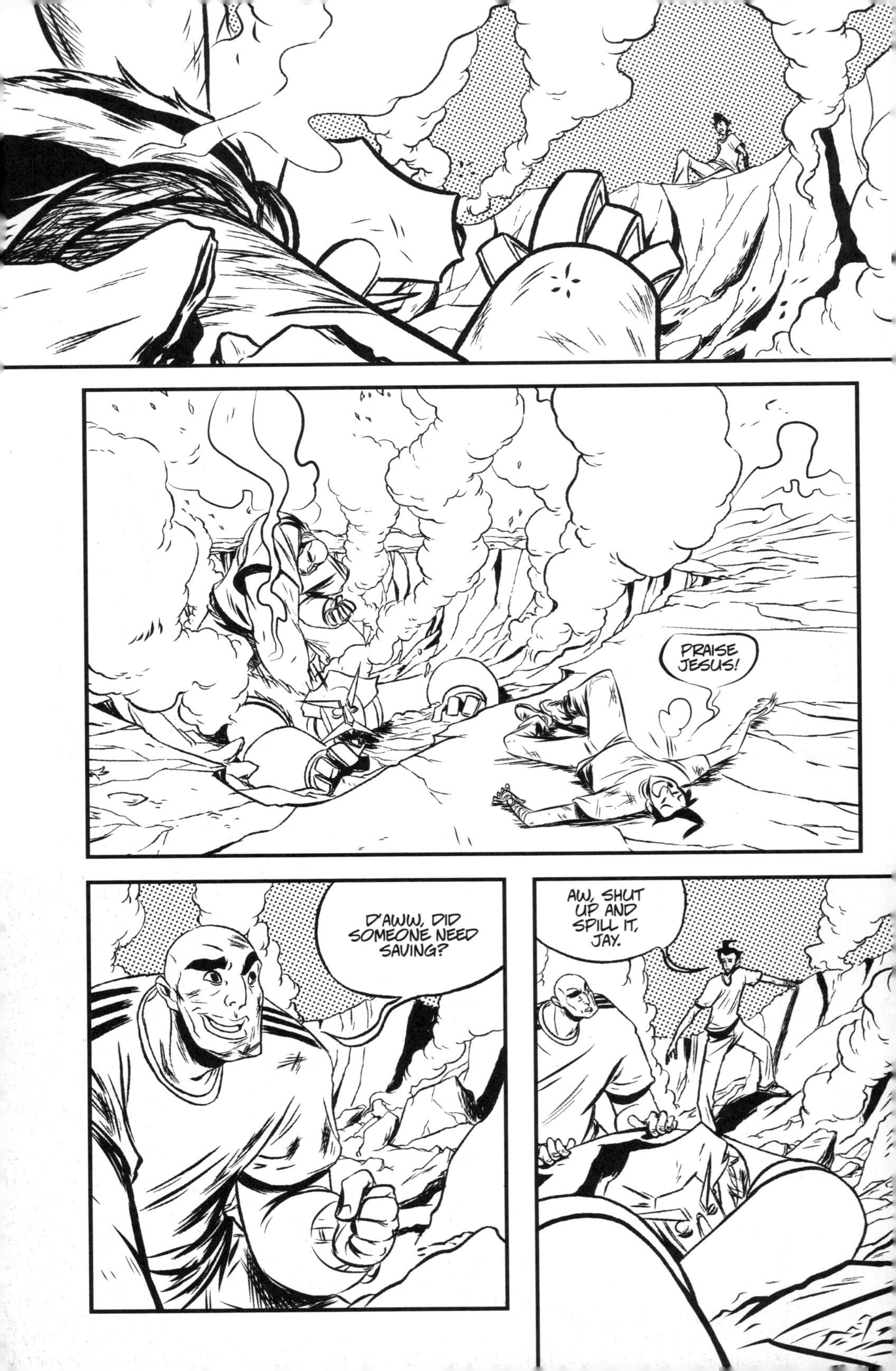
PRAISE JESUS!
D'AWW, DID SOMEONE NEED SAVING?
AW, SHUT UP AND SPILL IT, JAY.

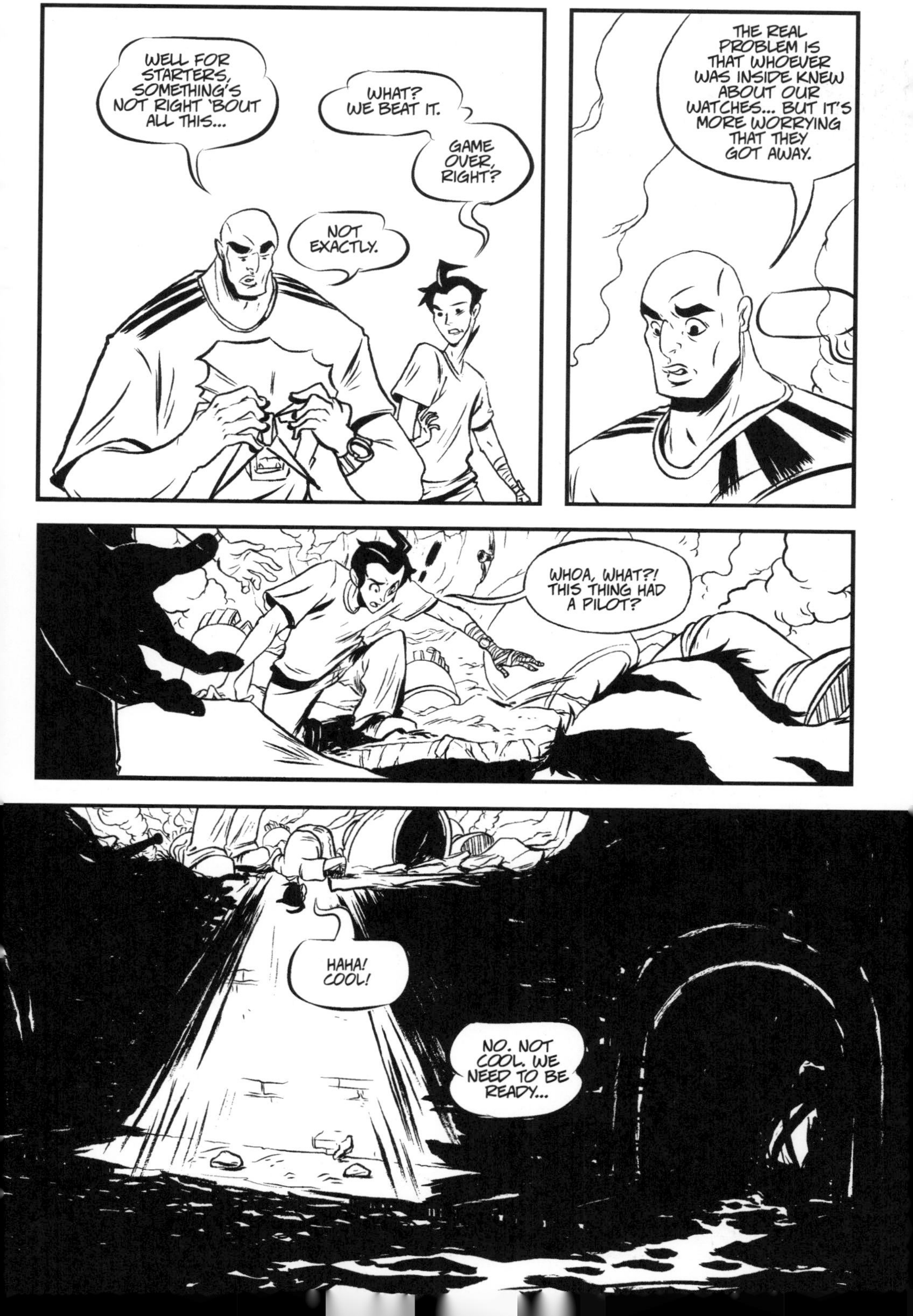
WELL FOR STARTERS, SOMETHING'S NOT RIGHT 'BOUT ALL THIS...
WHAT? WE BEAT IT.
GAME OVER, RIGHT?
NOT EXACTLY.
THE REAL PROBLEM IS THAT WHOEVER WAS INSIDE KNEW ABOUT OUR WATCHES... BUT IT'S MORE WORRYING THAT THEY GOT AWAY.
WHOA, WHAT?! THIS THING HAD A PILOT?
HAHA! COOL!
NO. NOT COOL. WE NEED TO BE READY...

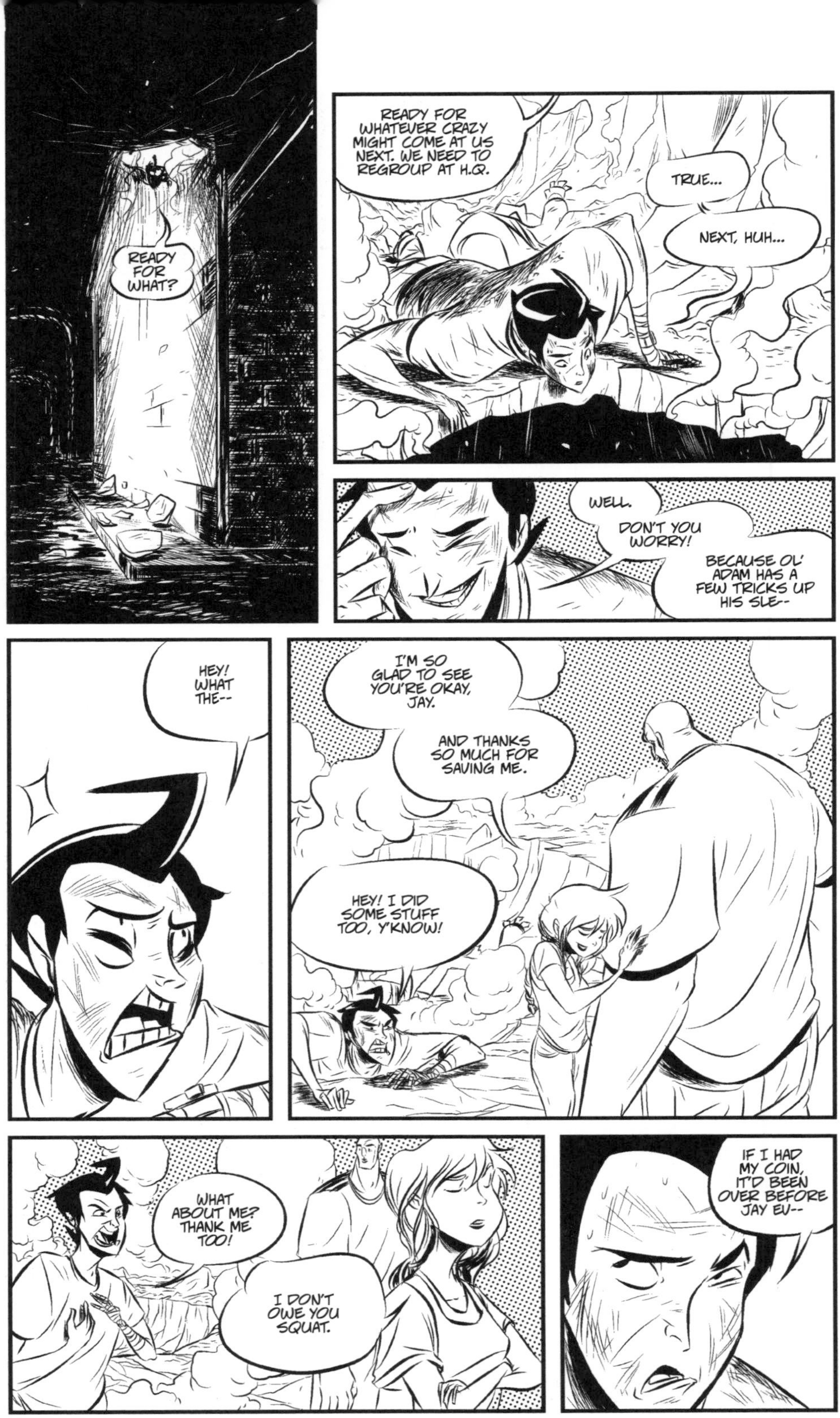
READY FOR WHAT?
READY FOR WHATEVER CRAZY MIGHT COME AT US NEXT. WE NEED TO REGROUP AT H.Q.
TRUE...
NEXT, HUH...
WELL.
DON'T YOU WORRY!
BECAUSE OL' ADAM HAS A FEW TRICKS UP HIS SLE--
HEY! WHAT THE--
I'M SO GLAD TO SEE YOU'RE OKAY, JAY.
AND THANKS SO MUCH FOR SAVING ME.
HEY! I DID SOME STUFF TOO, Y'KNOW!
WHAT ABOUT ME? THANK ME TOO!
I DON'T OWE YOU SQUAT.
IF I HAD MY COIN, IT'D BEEN OVER BEFORE JAY EV--

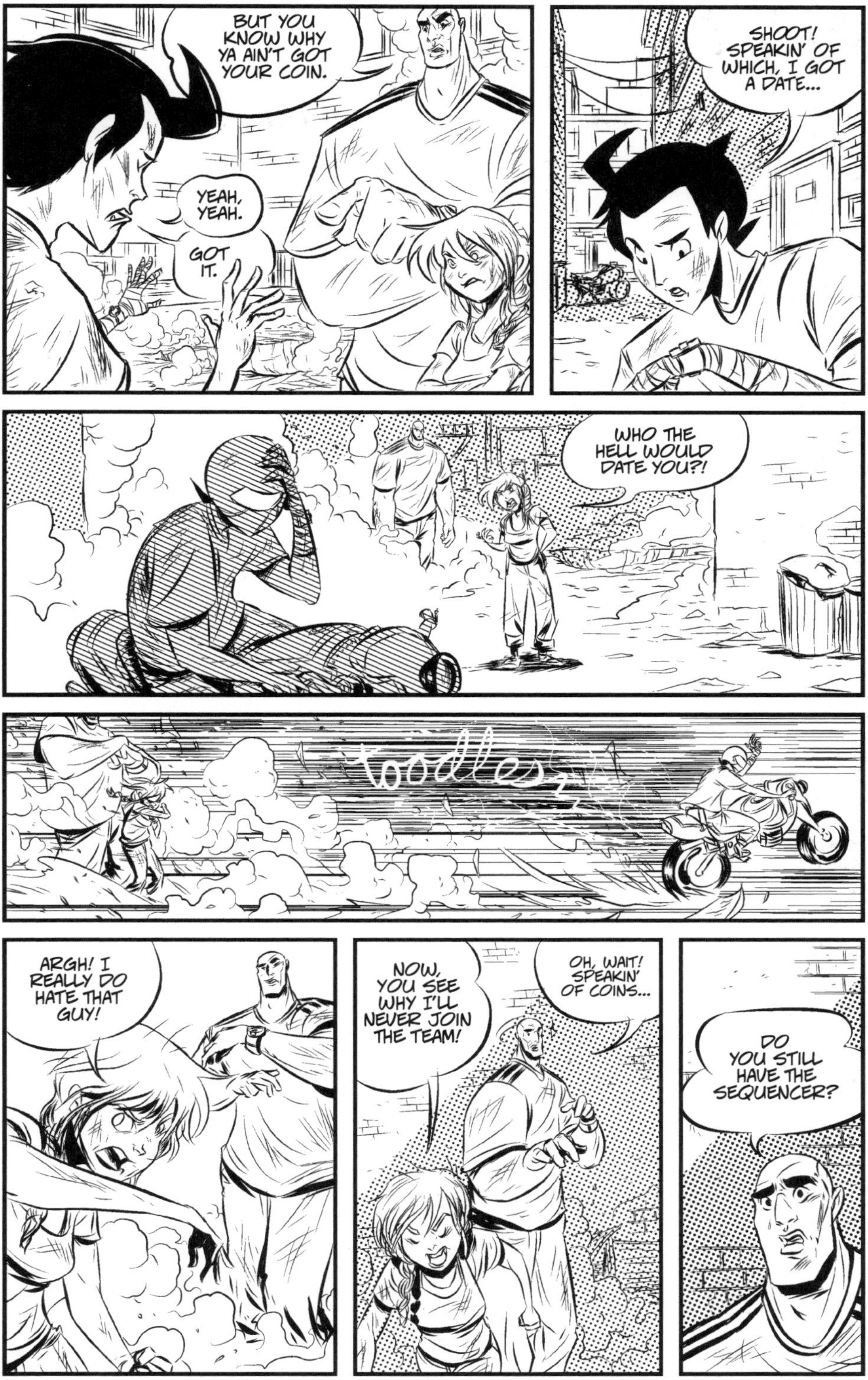
BUT YOU KNOW WHY YA AIN'T GOT YOUR COIN.
YEAH, YEAH.
GOT IT.
SHOOT! SPEAKIN' OF WHICH, I GOT A DATE...
WHO THE HELL WOULD DATE YOU?!
toodles
ARGH! I REALLY DO HATE THAT GUY!
NOW, YOU SEE WHY I'LL NEVER JOIN THE TEAM!
OH, WAIT! SPEAKIN' OF COINS...
DO YOU STILL HAVE THE SEQUENCER?

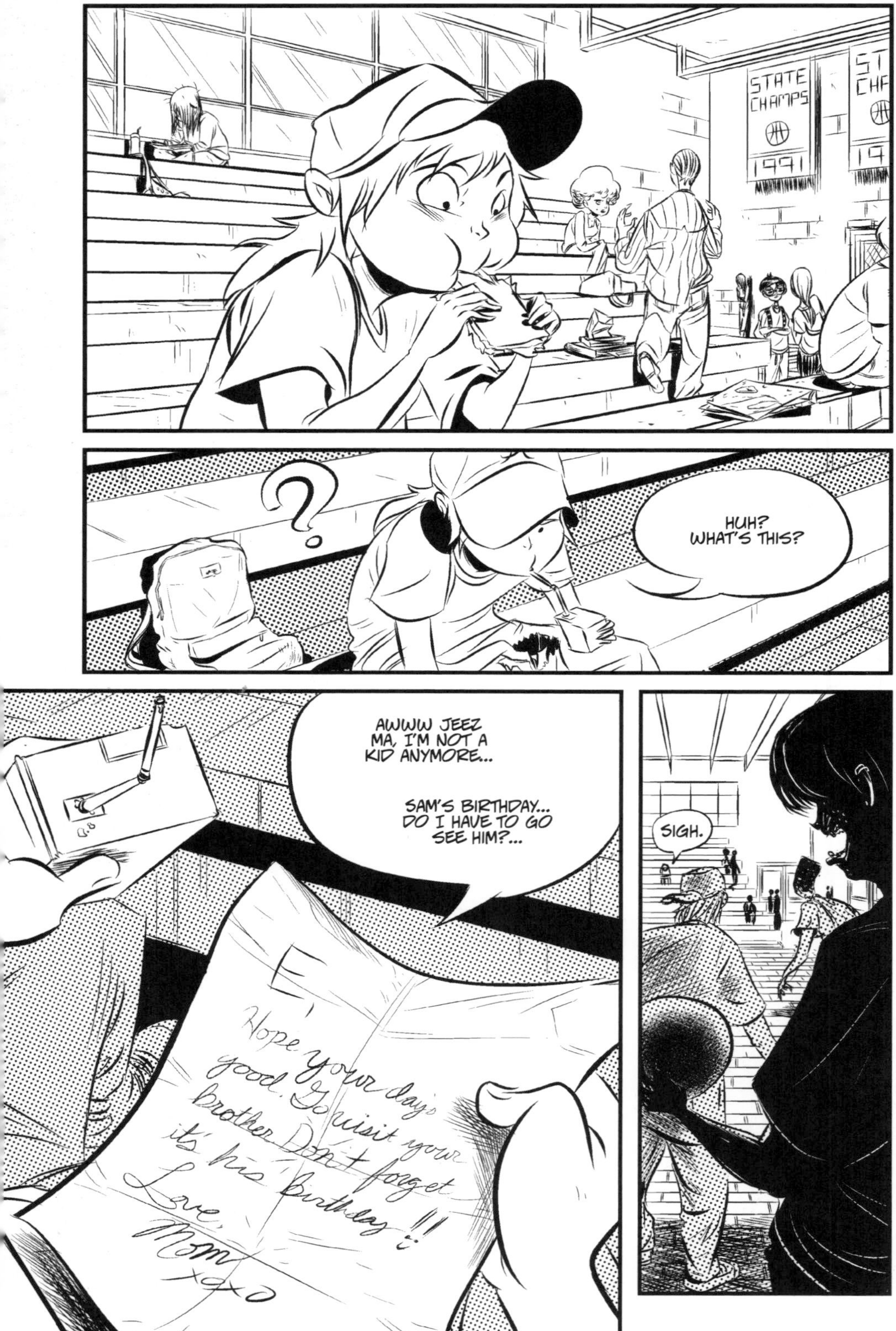
STATE CHAMPS 1991
HUH? WHAT'S THIS?
AWWW JEEZ MA, I'M NOT A KID ANYMORE...
SAM'S BIRTHDAY... DO I HAVE TO GO SEE HIM?...
Hope your day's good. Go visit your brother. Don't forget it's his Birthday!!
Love, Mom
xoxo
SIGH.

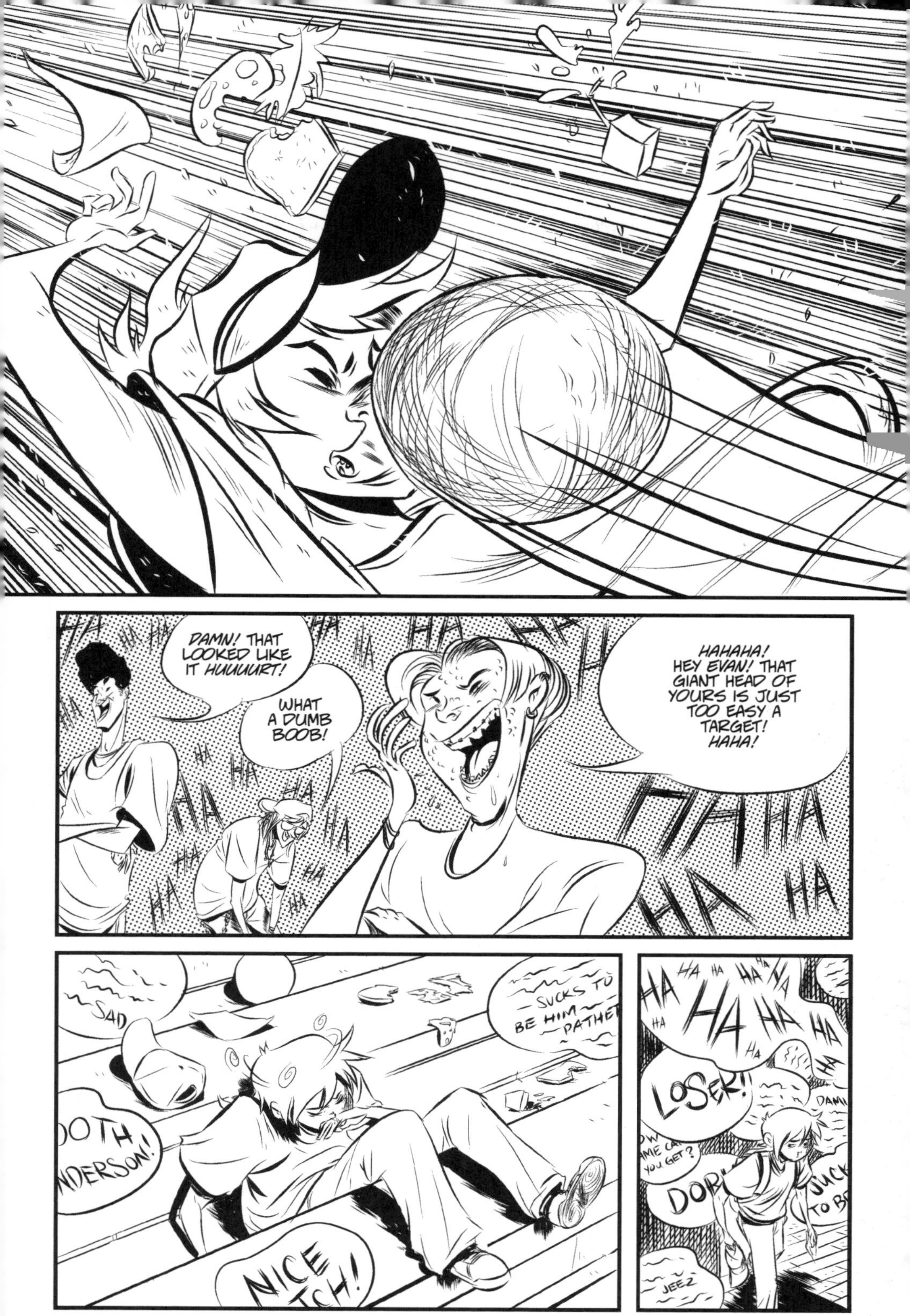
DAMN! THAT LOOKED LIKE IT HUUUURT!
WHAT A DUMB BOOB!
HAHAHA! HEY EVAN! THAT GIANT HEAD OF YOURS IS JUST TOO EASY A TARGET! HAHA!
HA HA HA HA
SAD
SUCKS TO BE HIM
HA HA HA HA
LOSER!
JEEZ

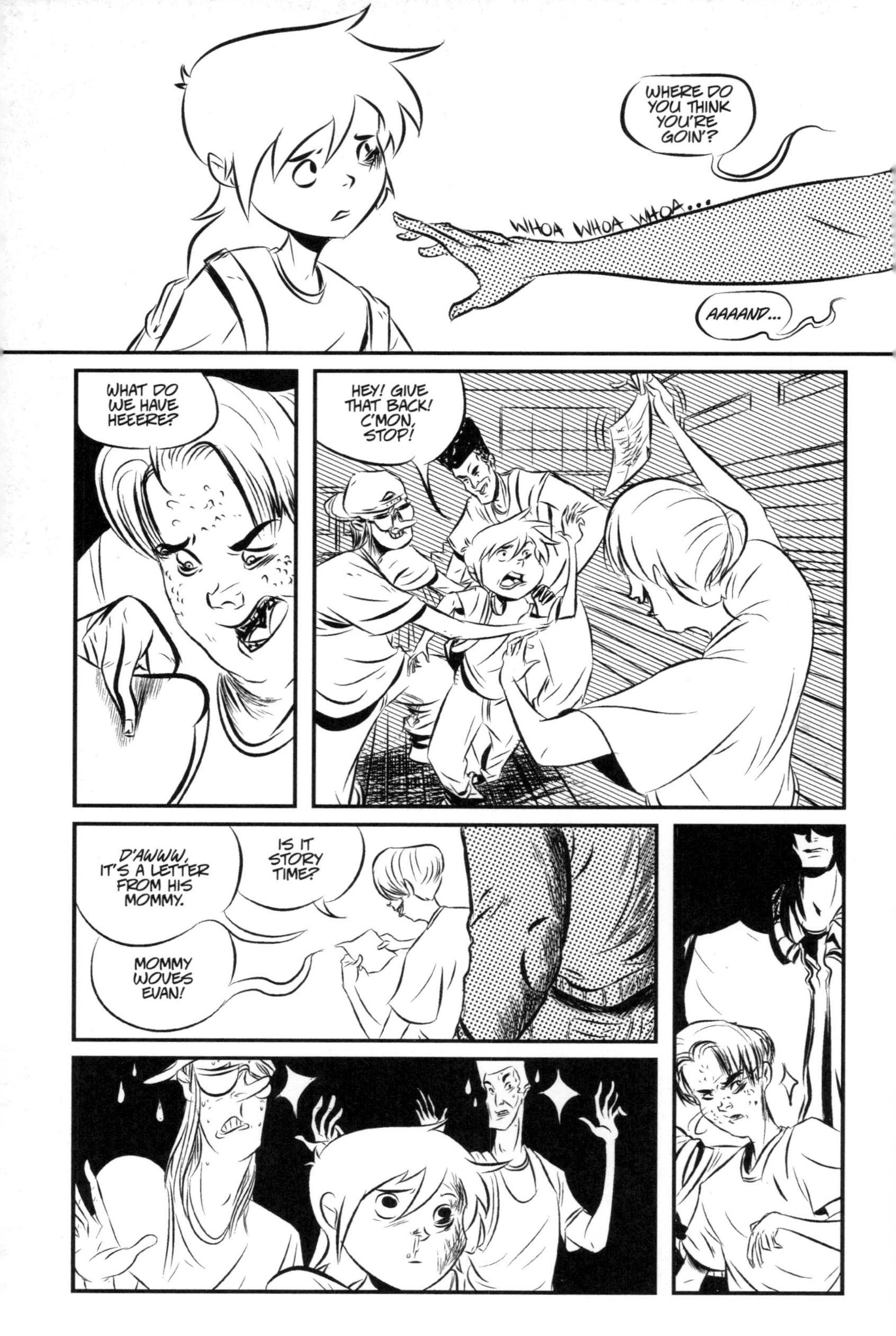
WHERE DO YOU THINK YOU'RE GOIN'?
WHOA WHOA WHOA...
AAAAND...
WHAT DO WE HAVE HEEERE?
HEY! GIVE THAT BACK! C'MON, STOP!
D'AWWW, IT'S A LETTER FROM HIS MOMMY.
IS IT STORY TIME?
MOMMY WOVES EVAN!

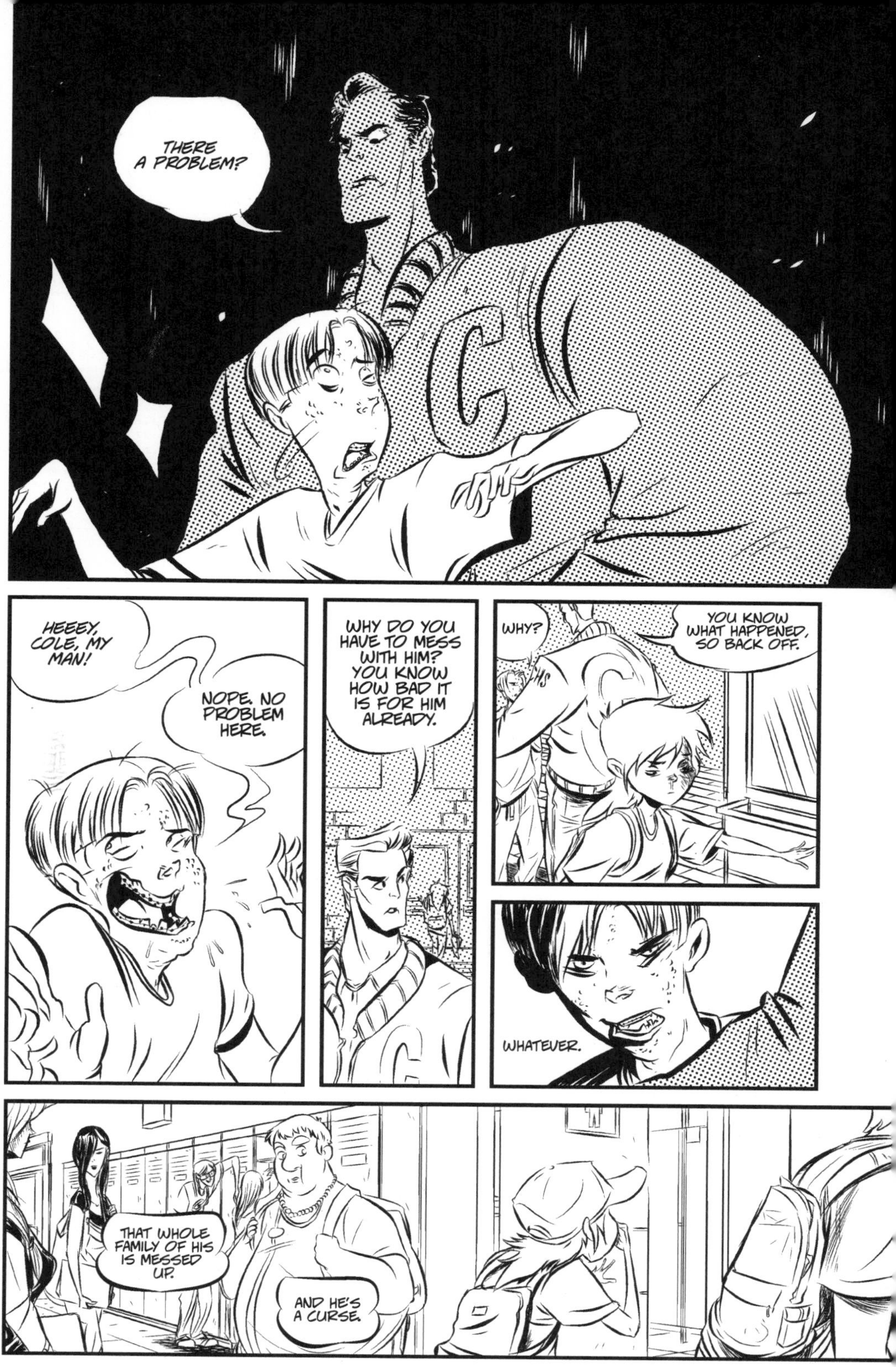
THERE A PROBLEM?
HEEEY, COLE, MY MAN!
NOPE. NO PROBLEM HERE.
WHY DO YOU HAVE TO MESS WITH HIM? YOU KNOW HOW BAD IT IS FOR HIM ALREADY.
WHY?
YOU KNOW WHAT HAPPENED, SO BACK OFF.
WHATEVER.
THAT WHOLE FAMILY OF HIS IS MESSED UP.
AND HE'S A CURSE.

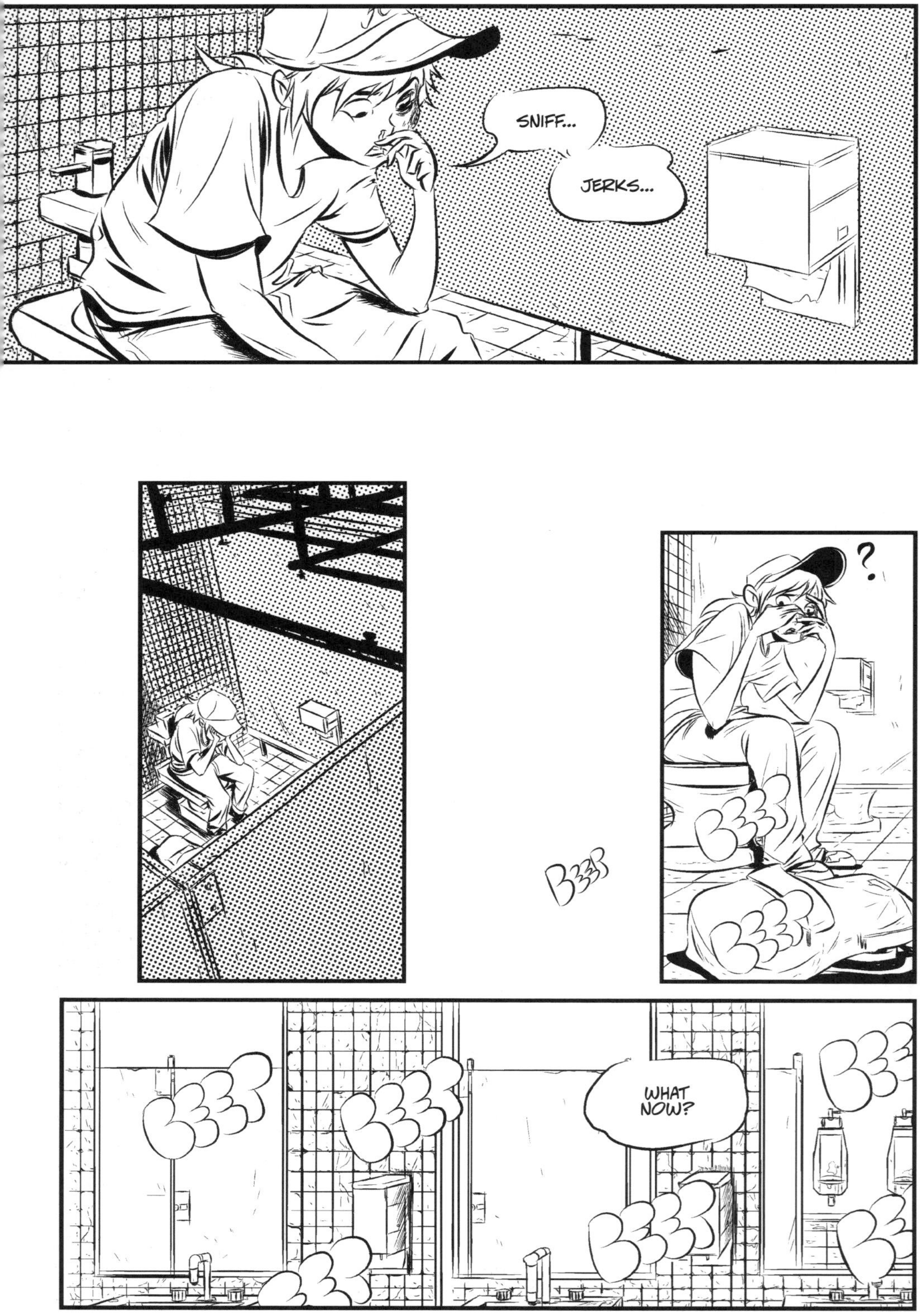
SNIFF...
JERKS...
?
WHAT NOW?

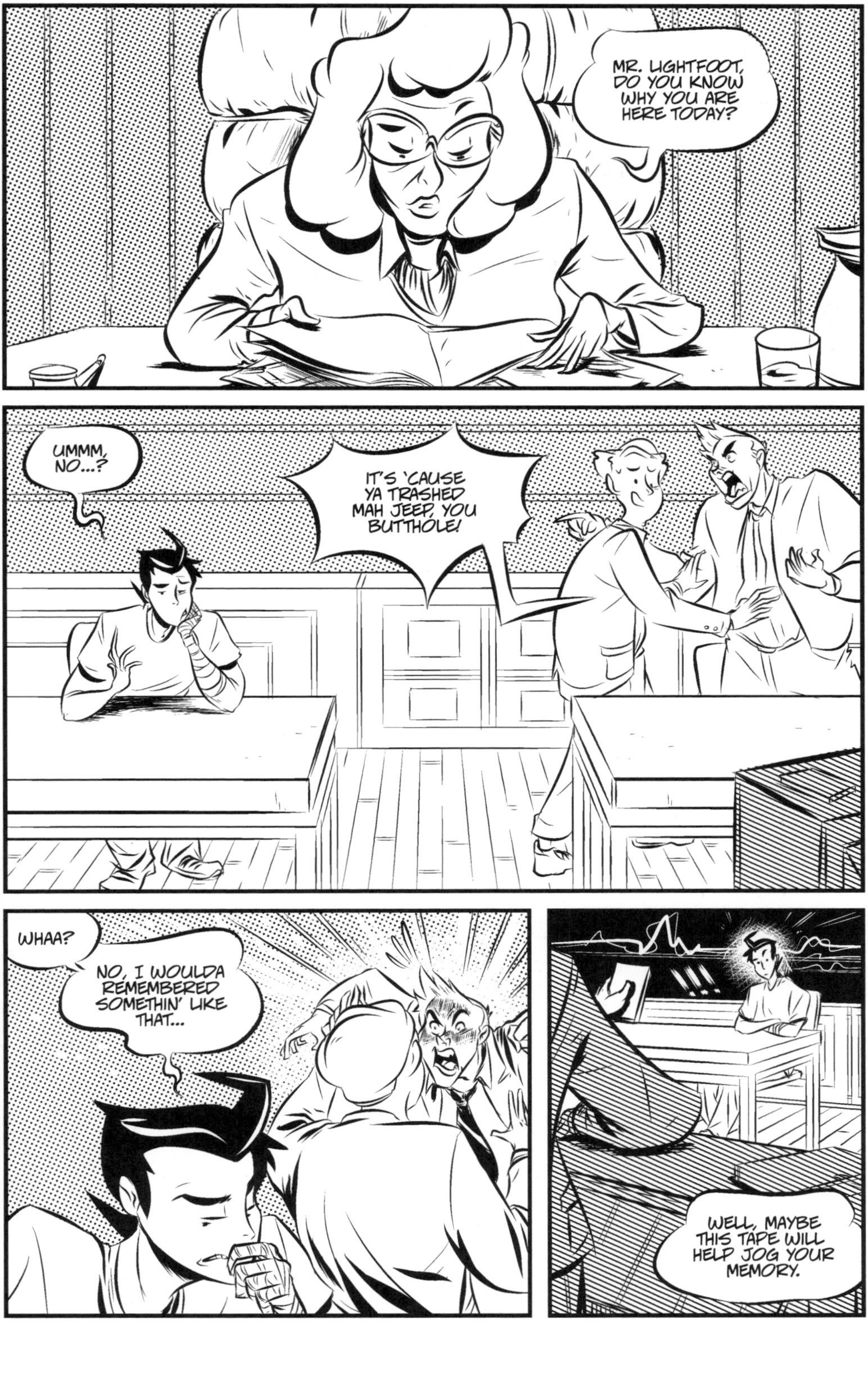
MR. LIGHTFOOT, DO YOU KNOW WHY YOU ARE HERE TODAY?
UMMM, NO...?
IT'S 'CAUSE YA TRASHED MAH JEEP, YOU BUTTHOLE!
WHAA?
NO, I WOULDA REMEMBERED SOMETHIN' LIKE THAT...
WELL, MAYBE THIS TAPE WILL HELP JOG YOUR MEMORY.

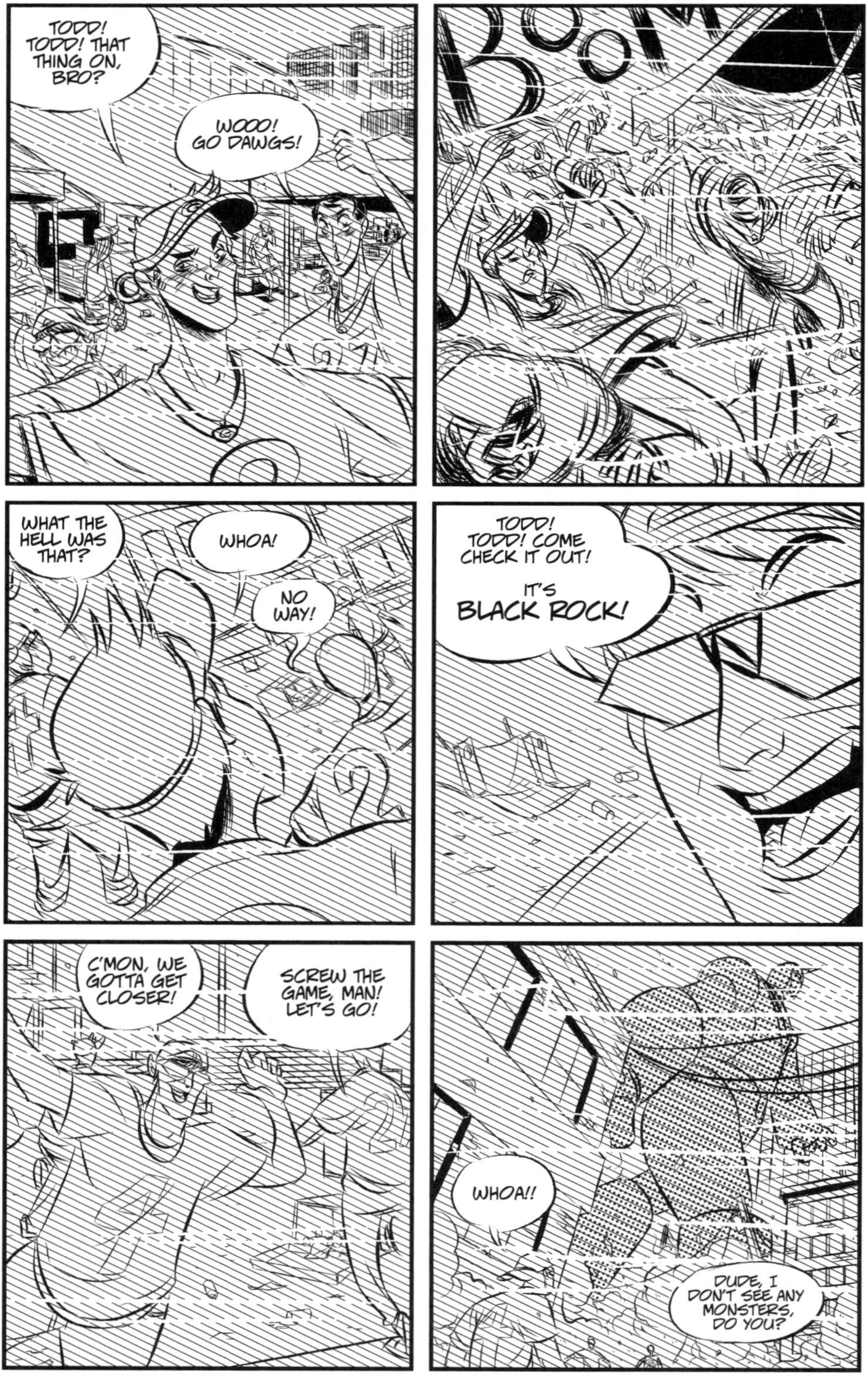

TODD! TODD! THAT THING ON, BRO?
WOOO! GO DAWGS!
BOOM
WHAT THE HELL WAS THAT?
WHOA!
NO WAY!
TODD! TODD! COME CHECK IT OUT!
IT'S BLACK ROCK!
C'MON, WE GOTTA GET CLOSER!
SCREW THE GAME, MAN! LET'S GO!
WHOA!!
DUDE, I DON'T SEE ANY MONSTERS, DO YOU?

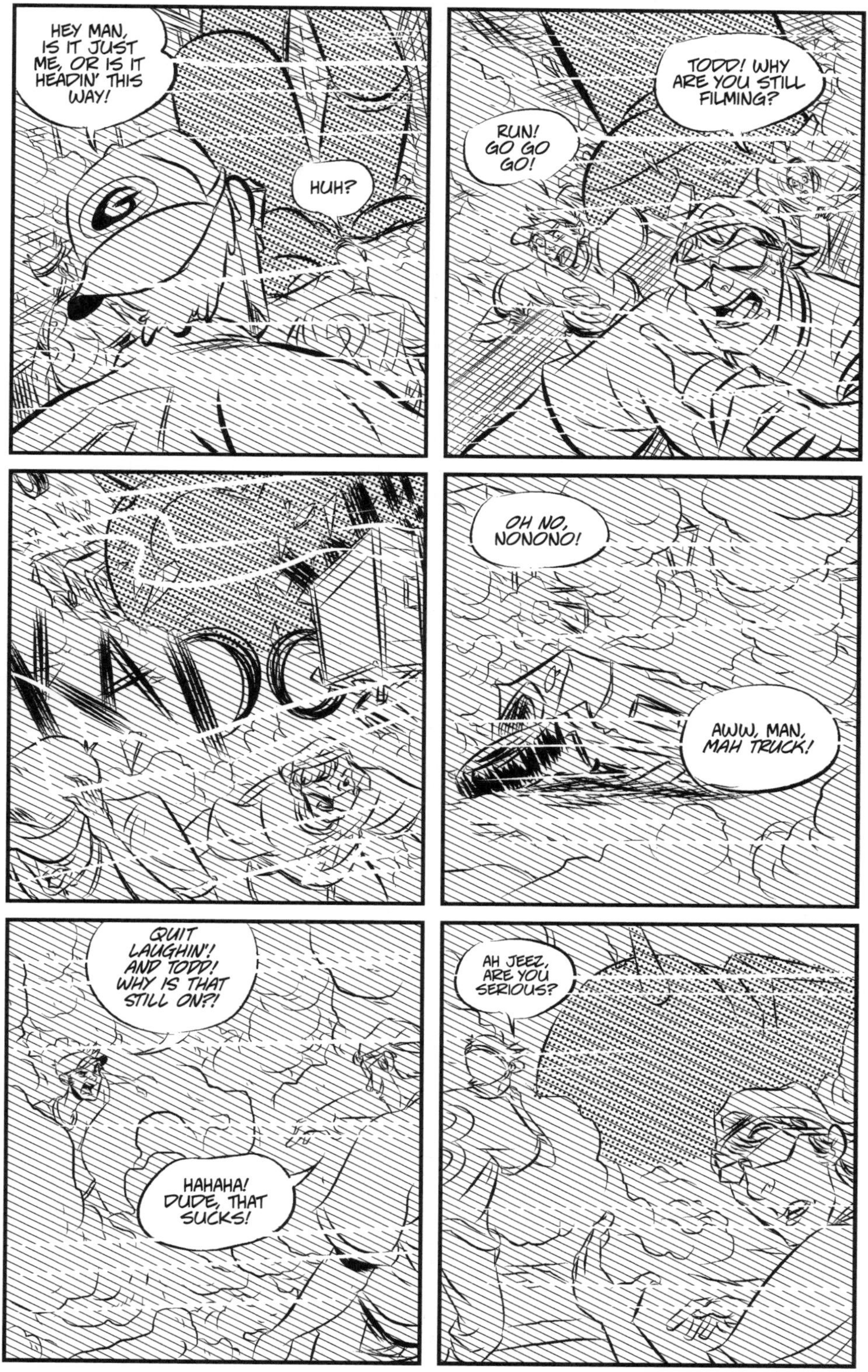
HEY MAN, IS IT JUST ME, OR IS IT HEADIN' THIS WAY!
HUH?
TODD! WHY ARE YOU STILL FILMING?
RUN! GO GO GO!
OH NO, NONONO!
AWW, MAN, MAH TRUCK!
QUIT LAUGHIN'! AND TODD! WHY IS THAT STILL ON?!
HAHAHA! DUDE, THAT SUCKS!
AH JEEZ, ARE YOU SERIOUS?

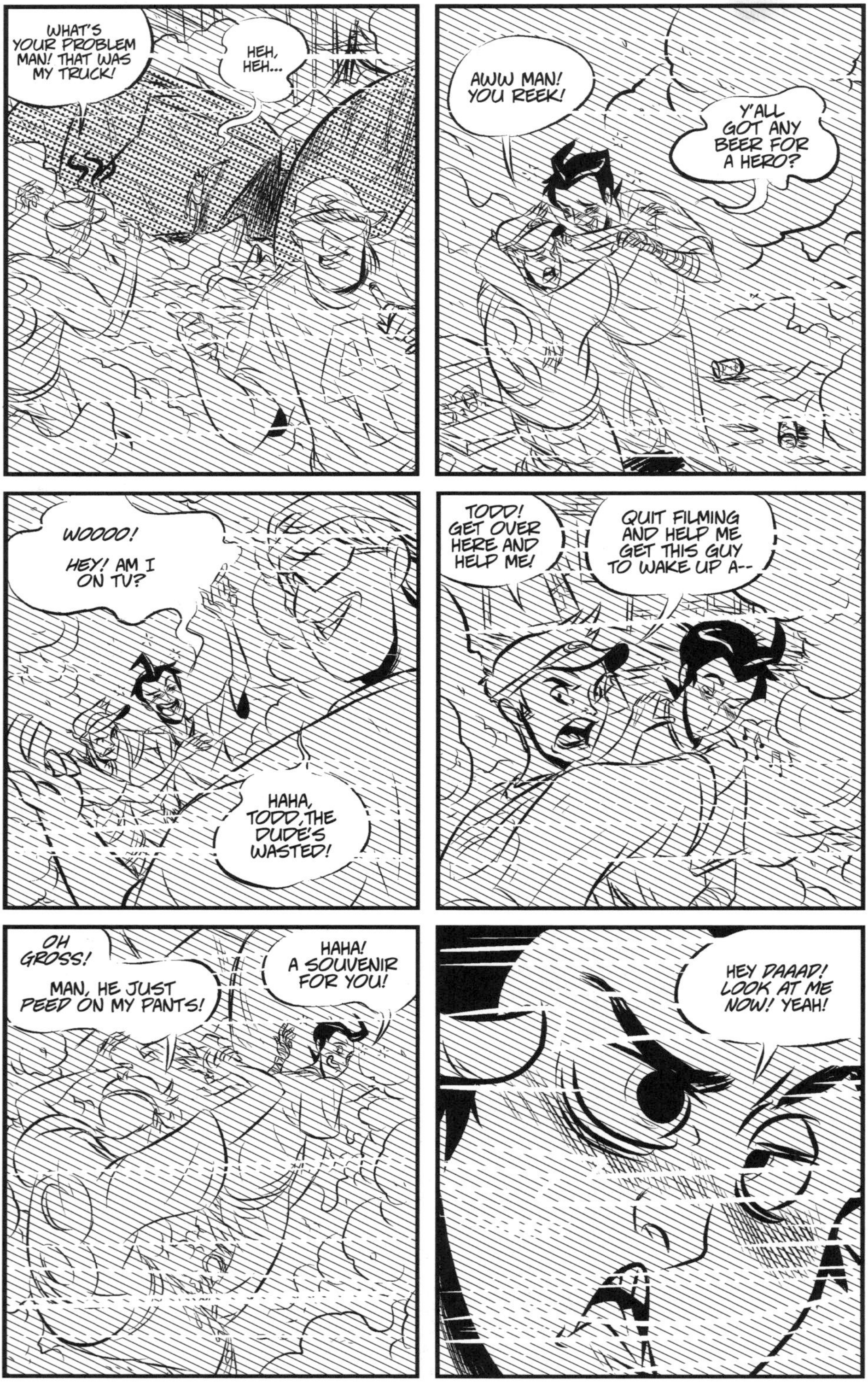
WHAT'S YOUR PROBLEM MAN! THAT WAS MY TRUCK!
HEH, HEH...
AWW MAN! YOU REEK!
Y'ALL GOT ANY BEER FOR A HERO?
WOOOO!
HEY! AM I ON TV?
HAHA, TODD, THE DUDE'S WASTED!
TODD! GET OVER HERE AND HELP ME!
QUIT FILMING AND HELP ME GET THIS GUY TO WAKE UP A--
OH GROSS!
MAN, HE JUST PEED ON MY PANTS!
HAHA! A SOUVENIR FOR YOU!
HEY DAAAD! LOOK AT ME NOW! YEAH!

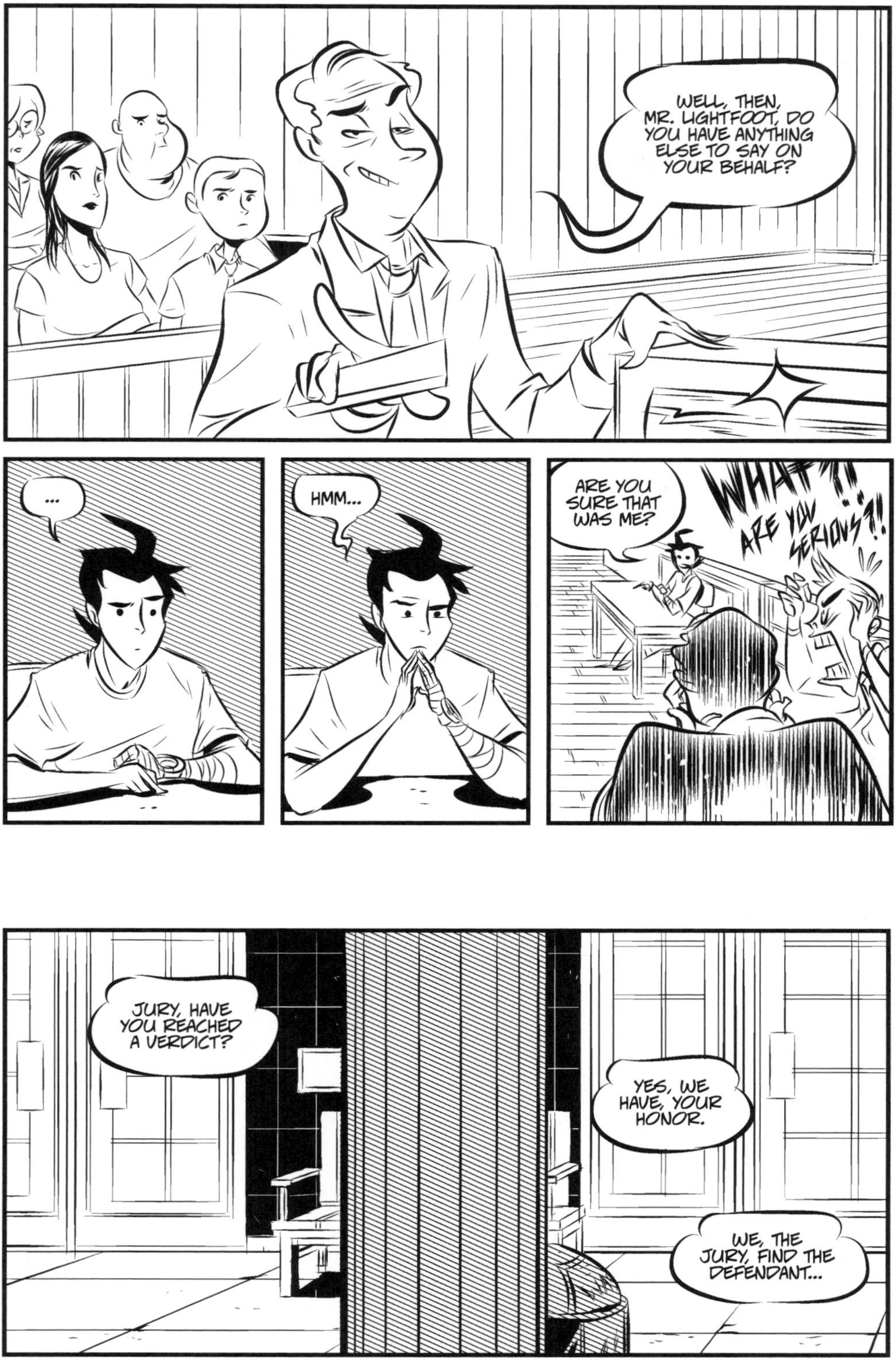
WELL, THEN, MR. LIGHTFOOT, DO YOU HAVE ANYTHING ELSE TO SAY ON YOUR BEHALF?
...
HMM...
ARE YOU SURE THAT WAS ME?
WHAT?!
ARE YOU SERIOUS?!!
JURY, HAVE YOU REACHED A VERDICT?
YES, WE HAVE, YOUR HONOR.
WE, THE JURY, FIND THE DEFENDANT...

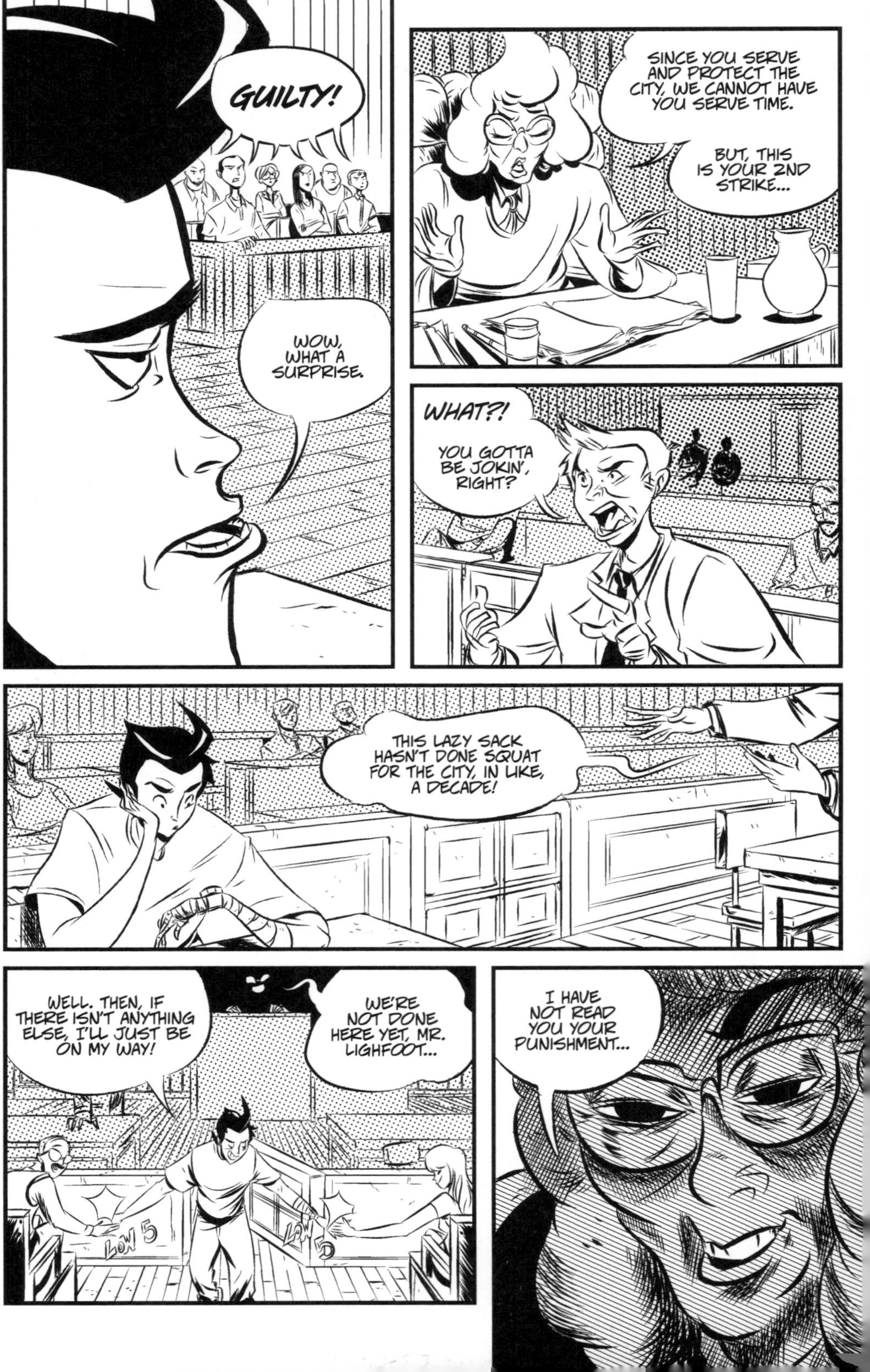
GUILTY!
WOW, WHAT A SURPRISE.
SINCE YOU SERVE AND PROTECT THE CITY, WE CANNOT HAVE YOU SERVE TIME.
BUT, THIS IS YOUR 2ND STRIKE...
WHAT?!
YOU GOTTA BE JOKIN', RIGHT?
THIS LAZY SACK HASN'T DONE SQUAT FOR THE CITY, IN LIKE, A DECADE!
WELL. THEN, IF THERE ISN'T ANYTHING ELSE, I'LL JUST BE ON MY WAY!
LOW 5
LOW 5
WE'RE NOT DONE HERE YET, MR. LIGHFOOT...
I HAVE NOT READ YOU YOUR PUNISHMENT...

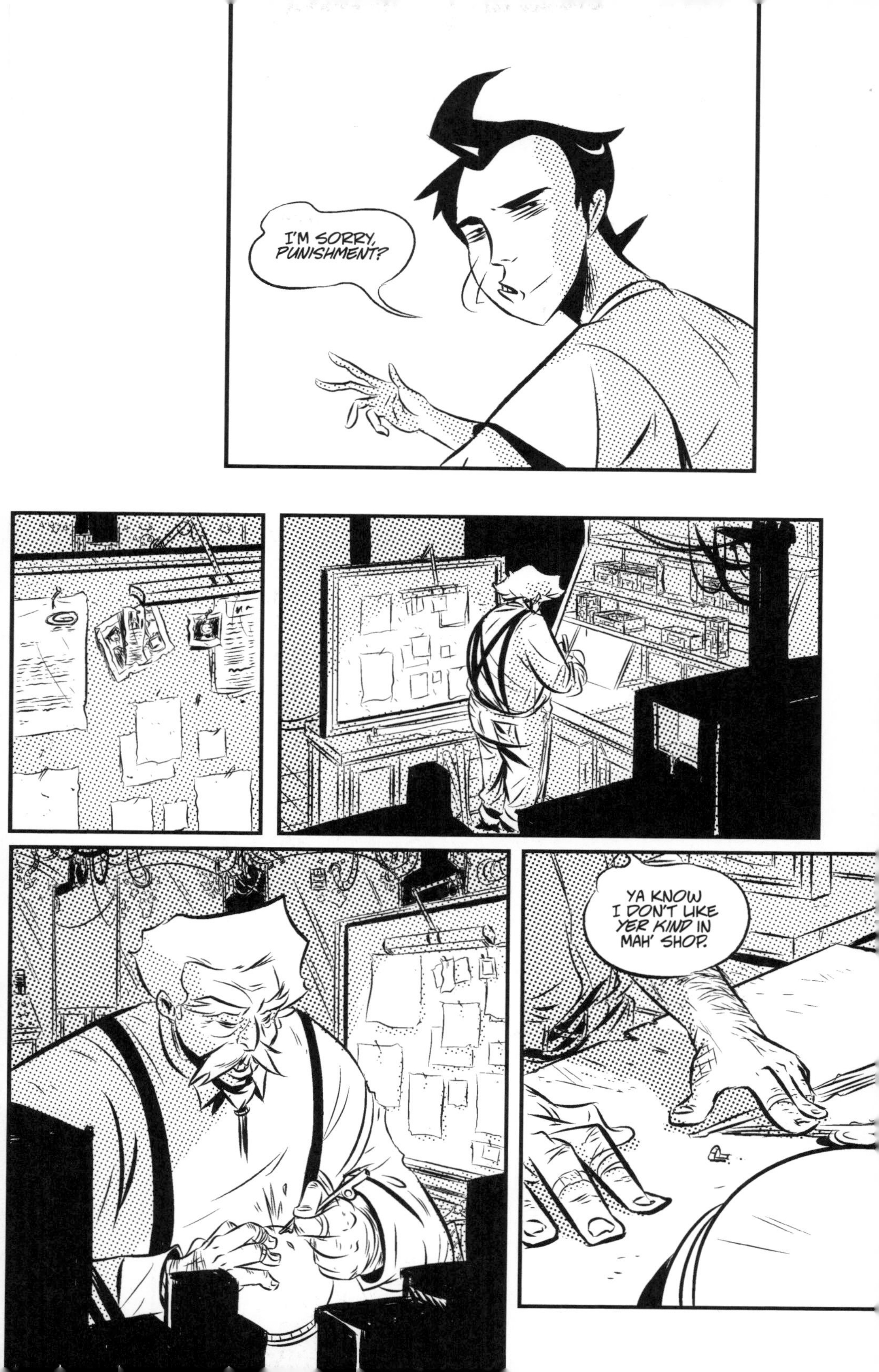
I'M SORRY, PUNISHMENT?
YA KNOW I DON'T LIKE YER KIND IN MAH' SHOP.

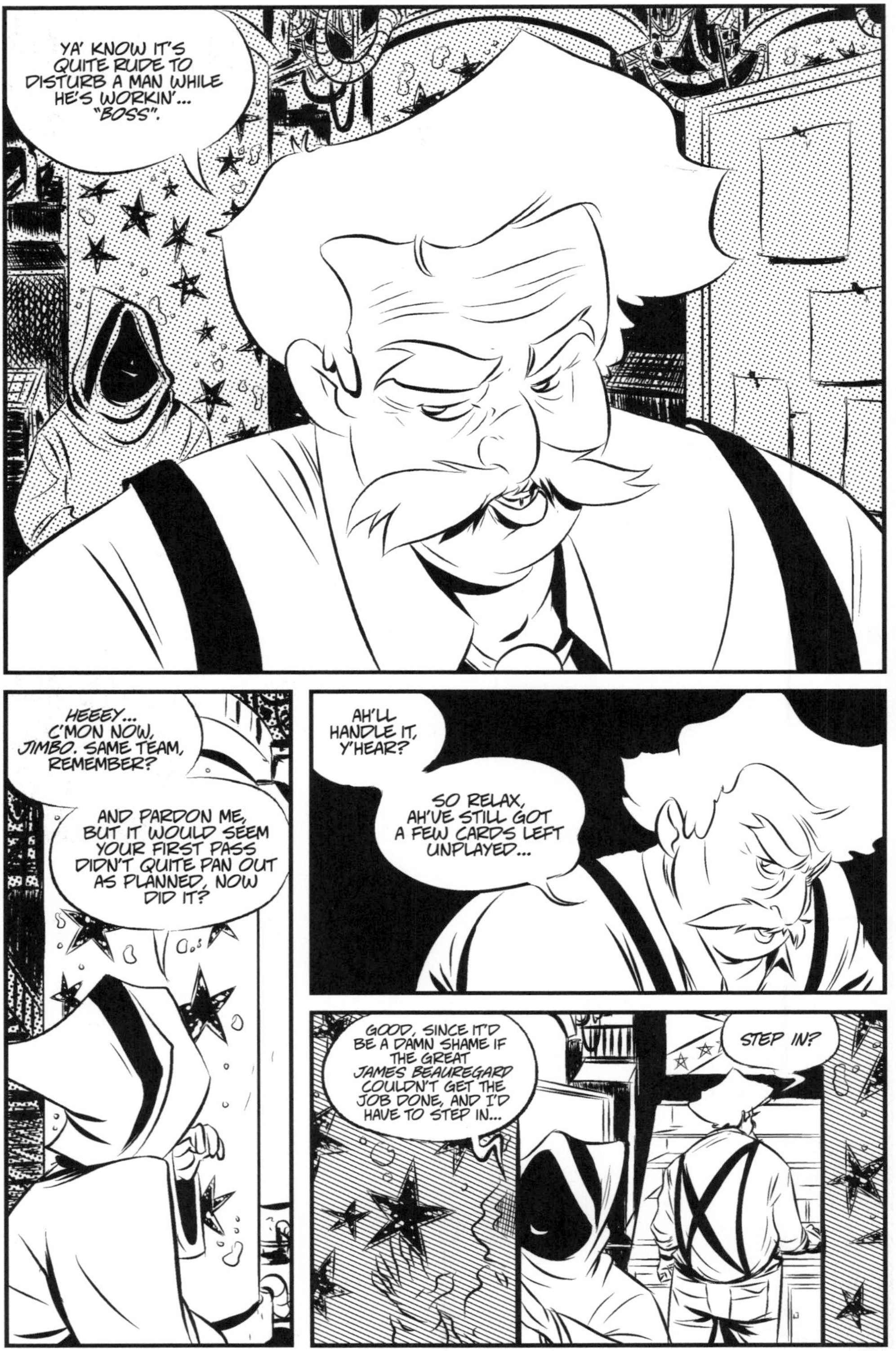
YA' KNOW IT'S QUITE RUDE TO DISTURB A MAN WHILE HE'S WORKIN'... "BOSS".
HEEEY... C'MON NOW, JIMBO. SAME TEAM, REMEMBER?
AND PARDON ME, BUT IT WOULD SEEM YOUR FIRST PASS DIDN'T QUITE PAN OUT AS PLANNED, NOW DID IT?
AH'LL HANDLE IT, Y'HEAR?
SO RELAX, AH'VE STILL GOT A FEW CARDS LEFT UNPLAYED...
GOOD, SINCE IT'D BE A DAMN SHAME IF THE GREAT JAMES BEAUREGARD COULDN'T GET THE JOB DONE, AND I'D HAVE TO STEP IN...
STEP IN?

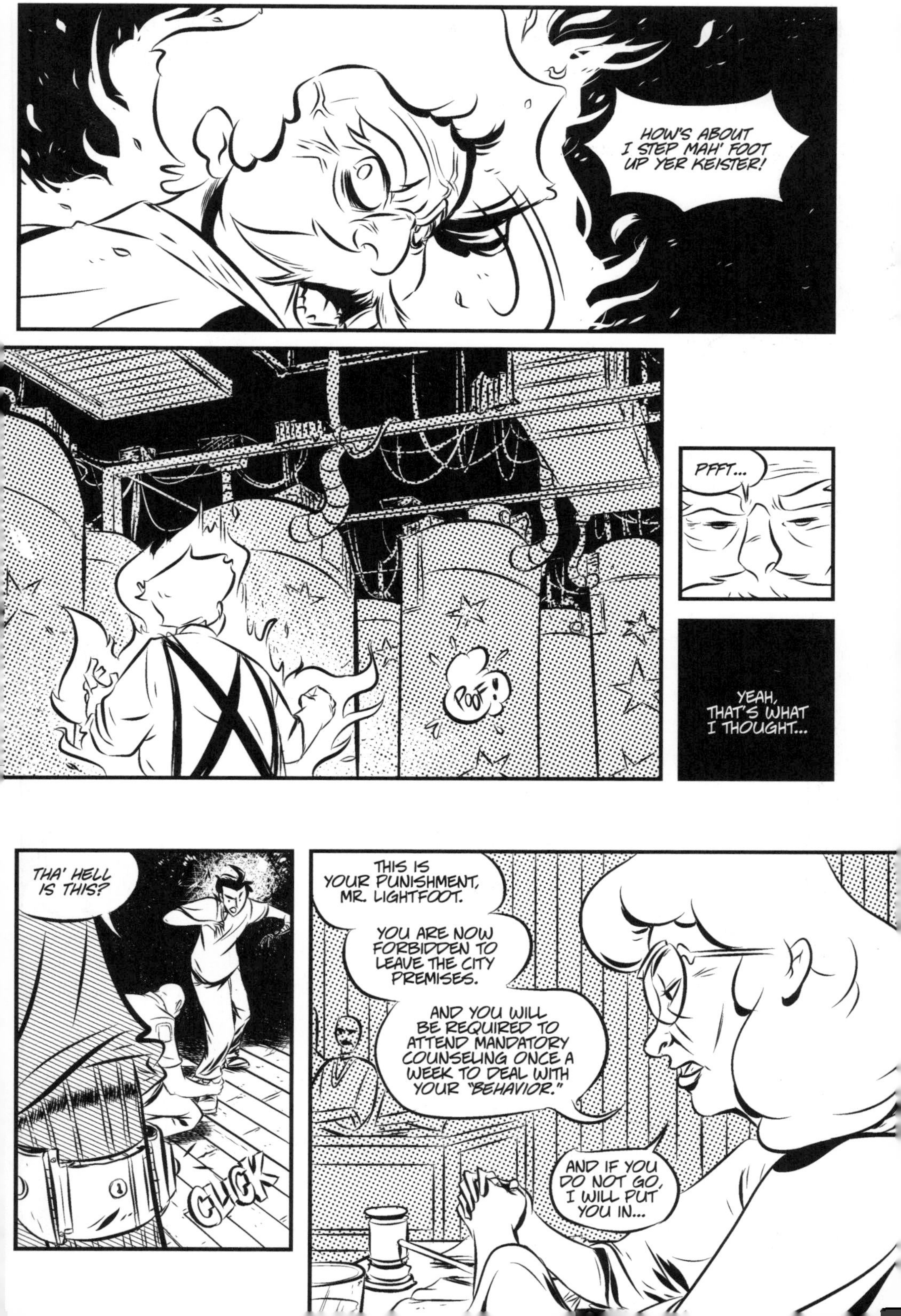
HOW'S ABOUT I STEP MAH' FOOT UP YER KEISTER!
POOF!
PFFT...
YEAH, THAT'S WHAT I THOUGHT...
THA' HELL IS THIS?
CLICK
THIS IS YOUR PUNISHMENT, MR. LIGHTFOOT.
YOU ARE NOW FORBIDDEN TO LEAVE THE CITY PREMISES.
AND YOU WILL BE REQUIRED TO ATTEND MANDATORY COUNSELING ONCE A WEEK TO DEAL WITH YOUR "BEHAVIOR."
AND IF YOU DO NOT GO, I WILL PUT YOU IN...

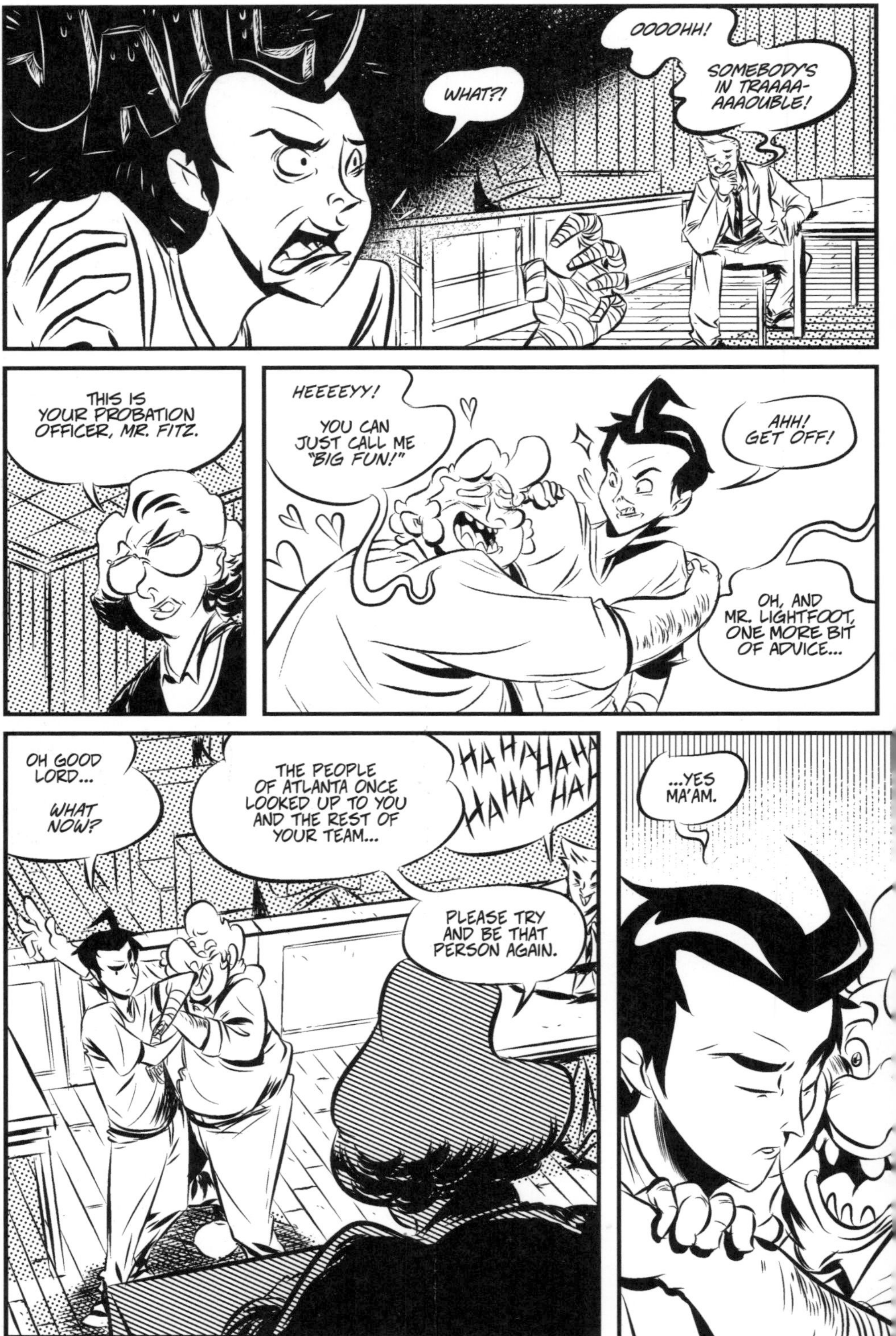
JAIL
WHAT?!
OOOOHH!
SOMEBODY'S IN TRAAAA-AAAOUBLE!
THIS IS YOUR PROBATION OFFICER, MR. FITZ.
HEEEEYY!
YOU CAN JUST CALL ME "BIG FUN!"
AHH! GET OFF!
OH, AND MR. LIGHTFOOT, ONE MORE BIT OF ADVICE...
OH GOOD LORD...
WHAT NOW?
THE PEOPLE OF ATLANTA ONCE LOOKED UP TO YOU AND THE REST OF YOUR TEAM...
PLEASE TRY AND BE THAT PERSON AGAIN.
...YES MA'AM.

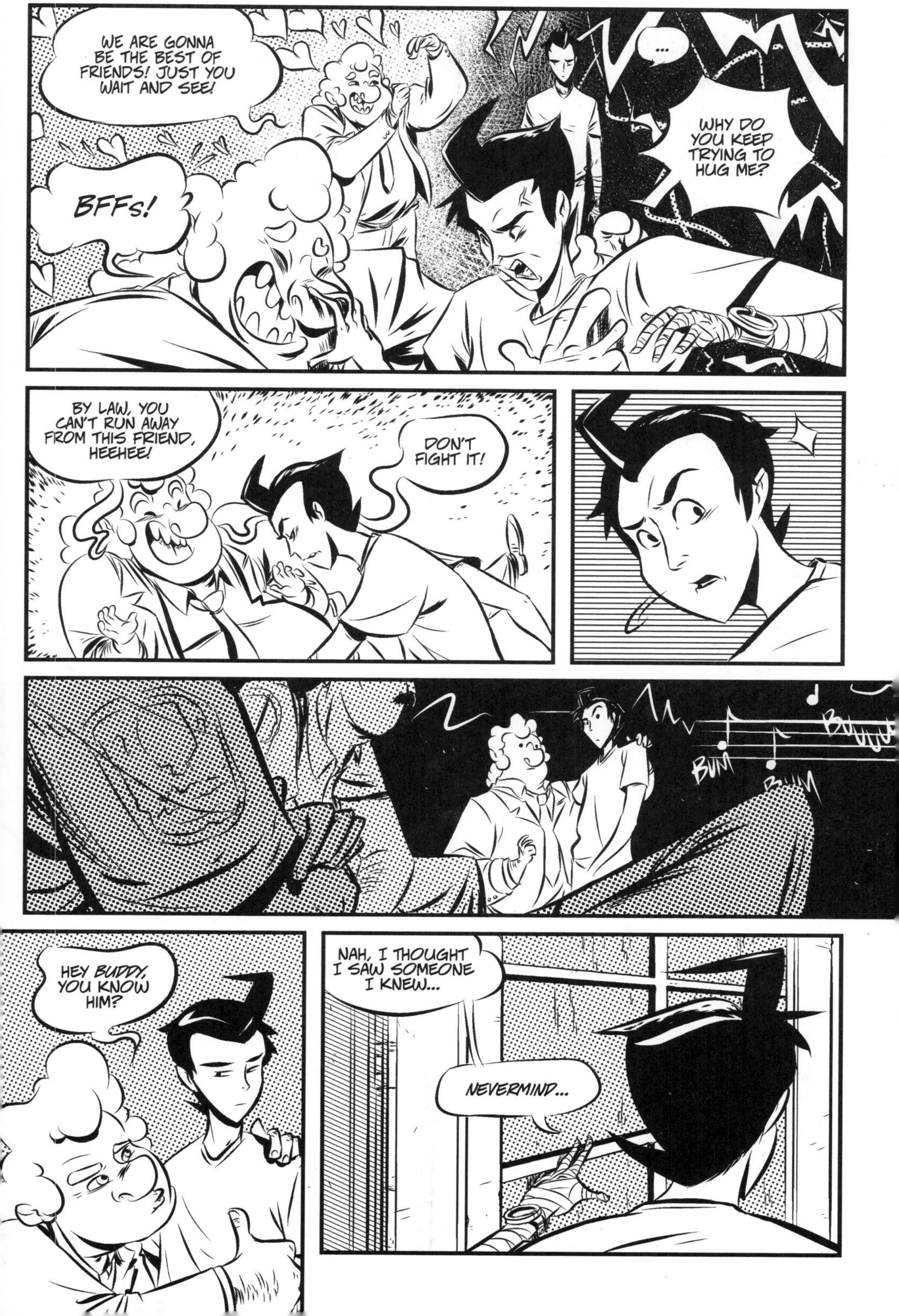
WE ARE GONNA BE THE BEST OF FRIENDS! JUST YOU WAIT AND SEE!
BFFs!
...
WHY DO YOU KEEP TRYING TO HUG ME?
BY LAW, YOU CAN'T RUN AWAY FROM THIS FRIEND, HEEHEE!
DON'T FIGHT IT!
BUM
BUM
HEY BUDDY, YOU KNOW HIM?
NAH, I THOUGHT I SAW SOMEONE I KNEW...
NEVERMIND...

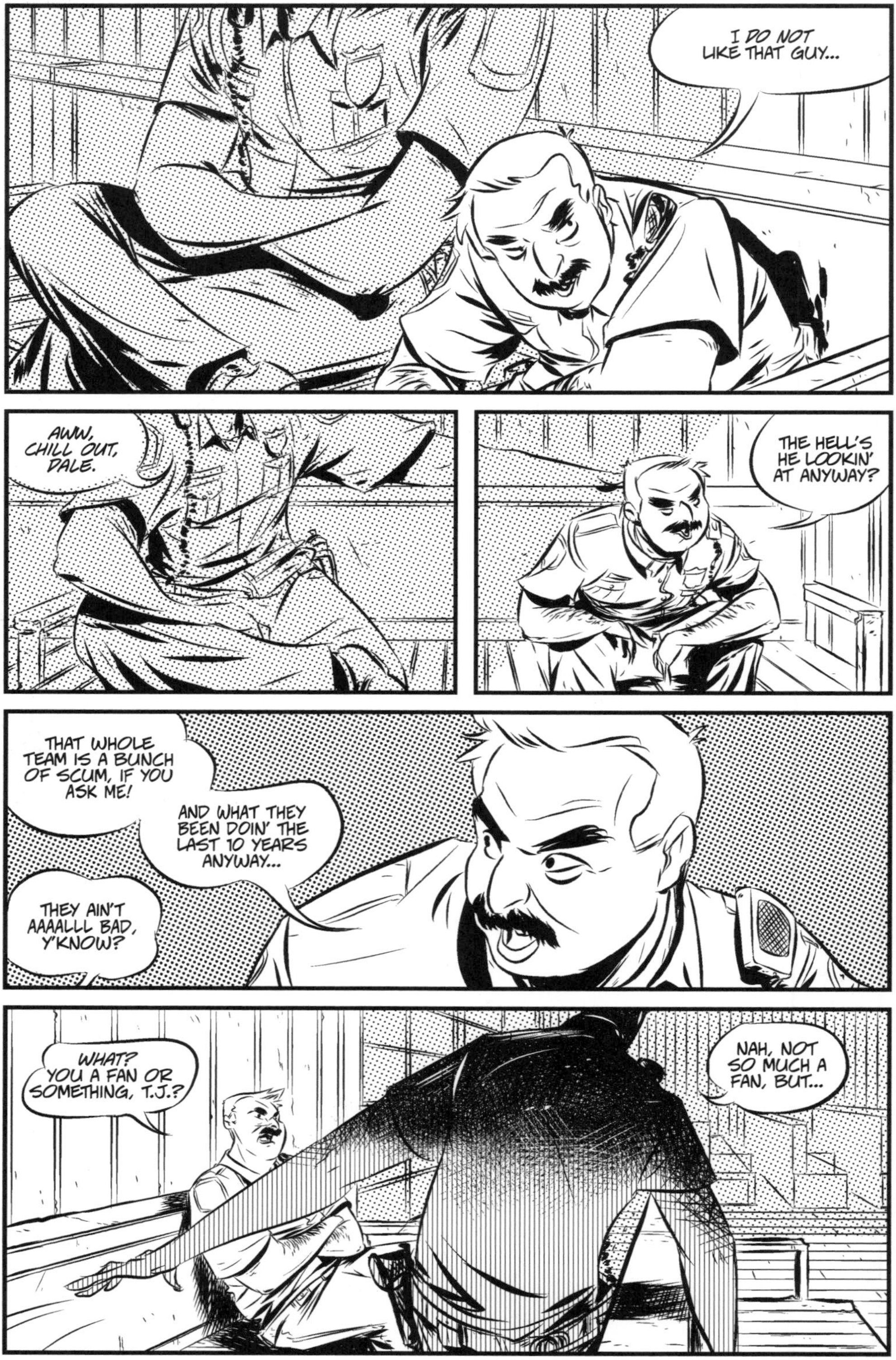
I DO NOT LIKE THAT GUY...
AWW, CHILL OUT, DALE.
THE HELL'S HE LOOKIN' AT ANYWAY?
THAT WHOLE TEAM IS A BUNCH OF SCUM, IF YOU ASK ME!
AND WHAT THEY BEEN DOIN' THE LAST 10 YEARS ANYWAY...
THEY AIN'T AAAALLL BAD, Y'KNOW?
WHAT? YOU A FAN OR SOMETHING, T.J.?
NAH, NOT SO MUCH A FAN, BUT...

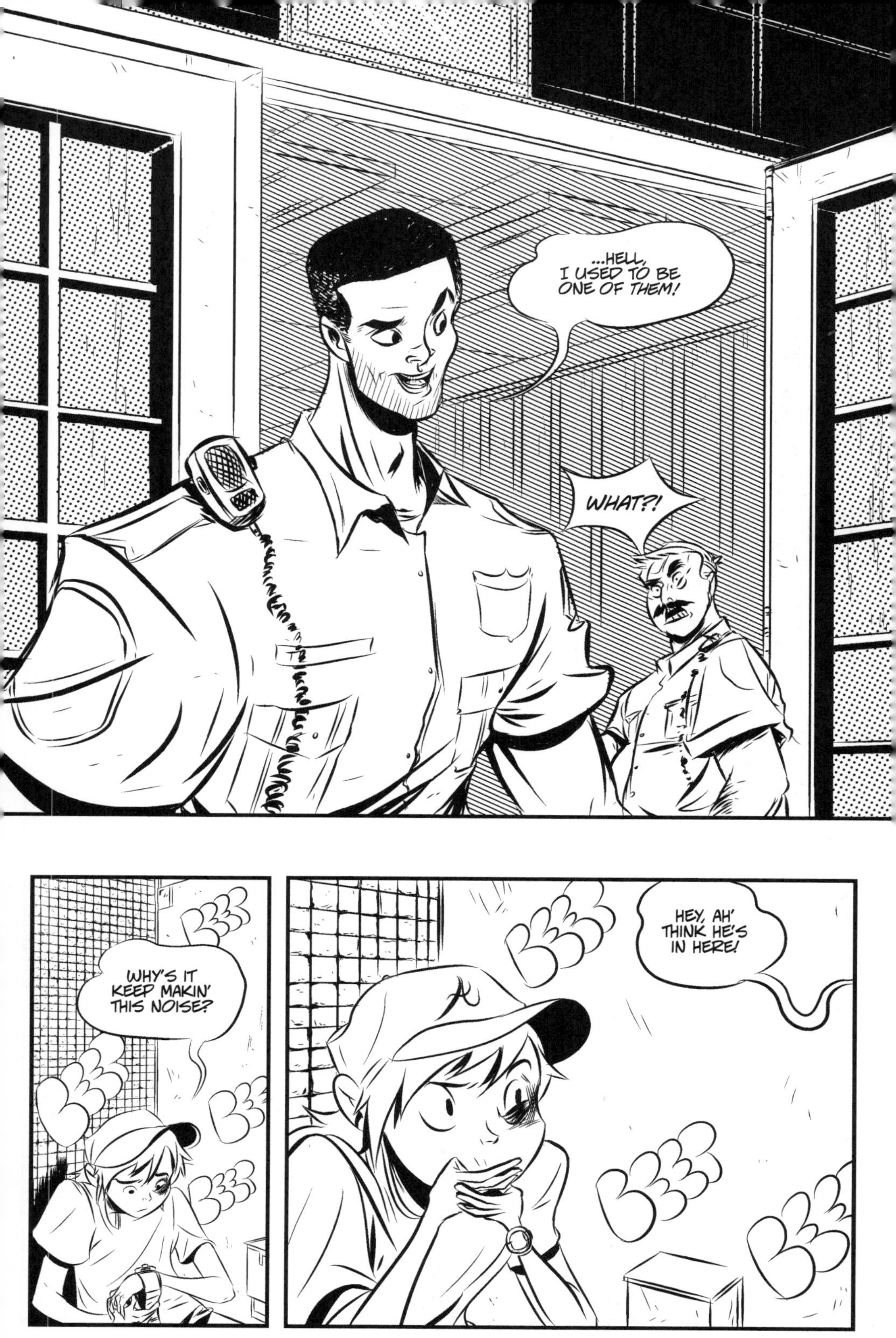
...HELL, I USED TO BE ONE OF THEM!
WHAT?!
WHY'S IT KEEP MAKIN' THIS NOISE?
HEY, AH' THINK HE'S IN HERE!

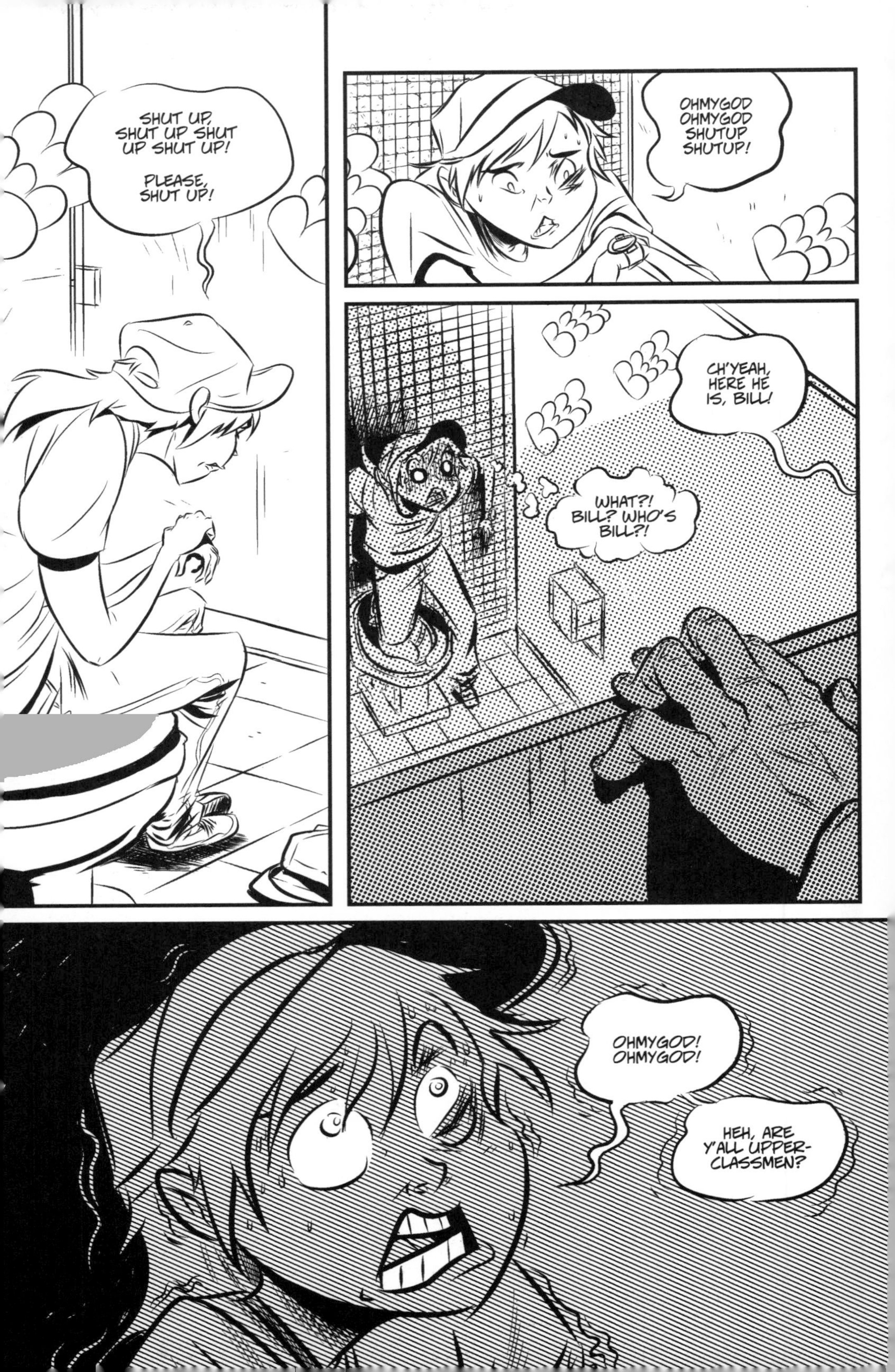
SHUT UP, SHUT UP SHUT UP SHUT UP!
PLEASE, SHUT UP!
OHMYGOD OHMYGOD SHUTUP SHUTUP!
CH'YEAH, HERE HE IS, BILL!
WHAT?! BILL? WHO'S BILL?!
OHMYGOD! OHMYGOD!
HEH, ARE Y'ALL UPPER-CLASSMEN?

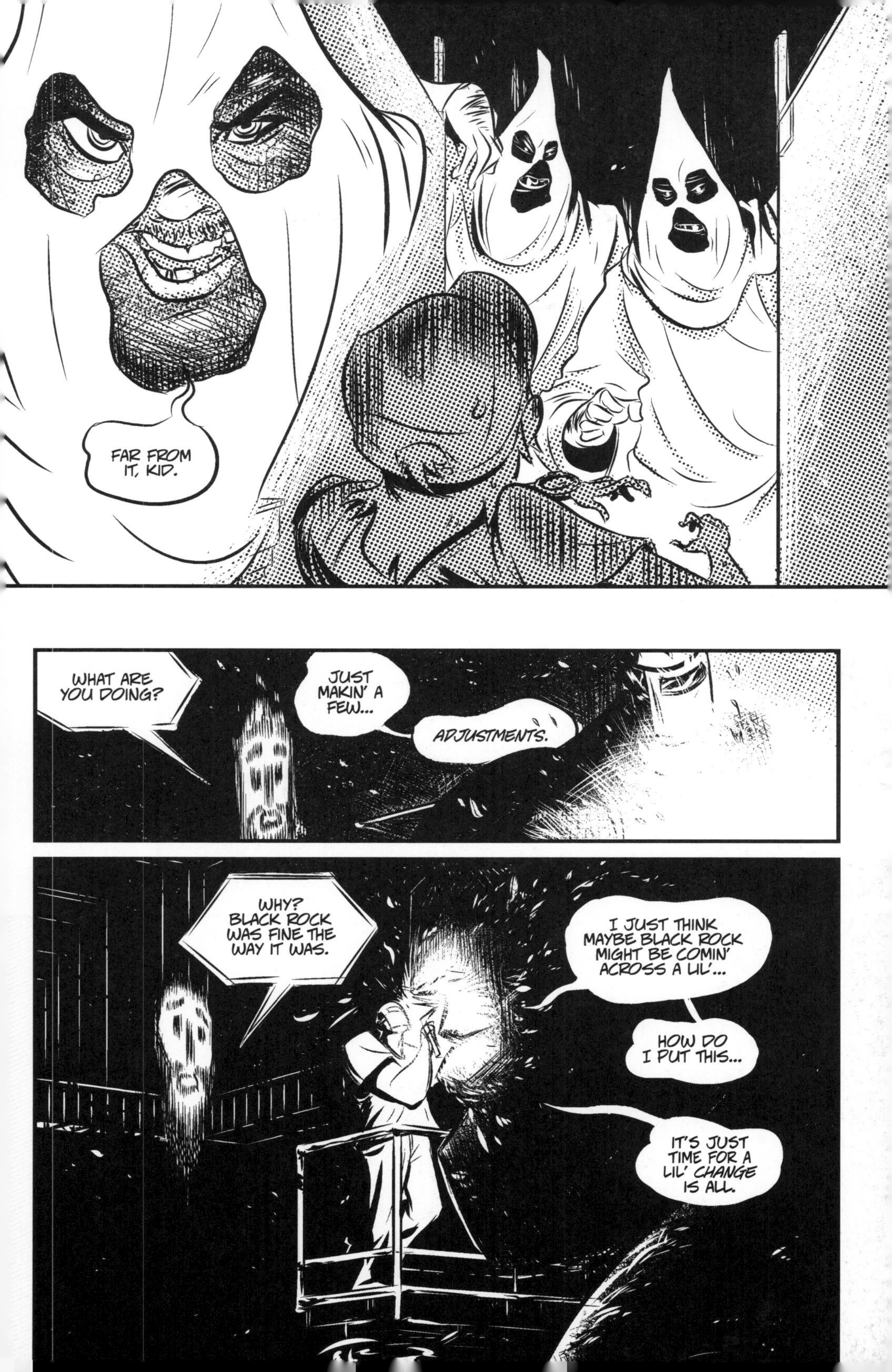
FAR FROM IT, KID.
WHAT ARE YOU DOING?
JUST MAKIN' A FEW...
ADJUSTMENTS.
WHY? BLACK ROCK WAS FINE THE WAY IT WAS.
I JUST THINK MAYBE BLACK ROCK MIGHT BE COMIN' ACROSS A LIL'...
HOW DO I PUT THIS...
IT'S JUST TIME FOR A LIL' CHANGE IS ALL.

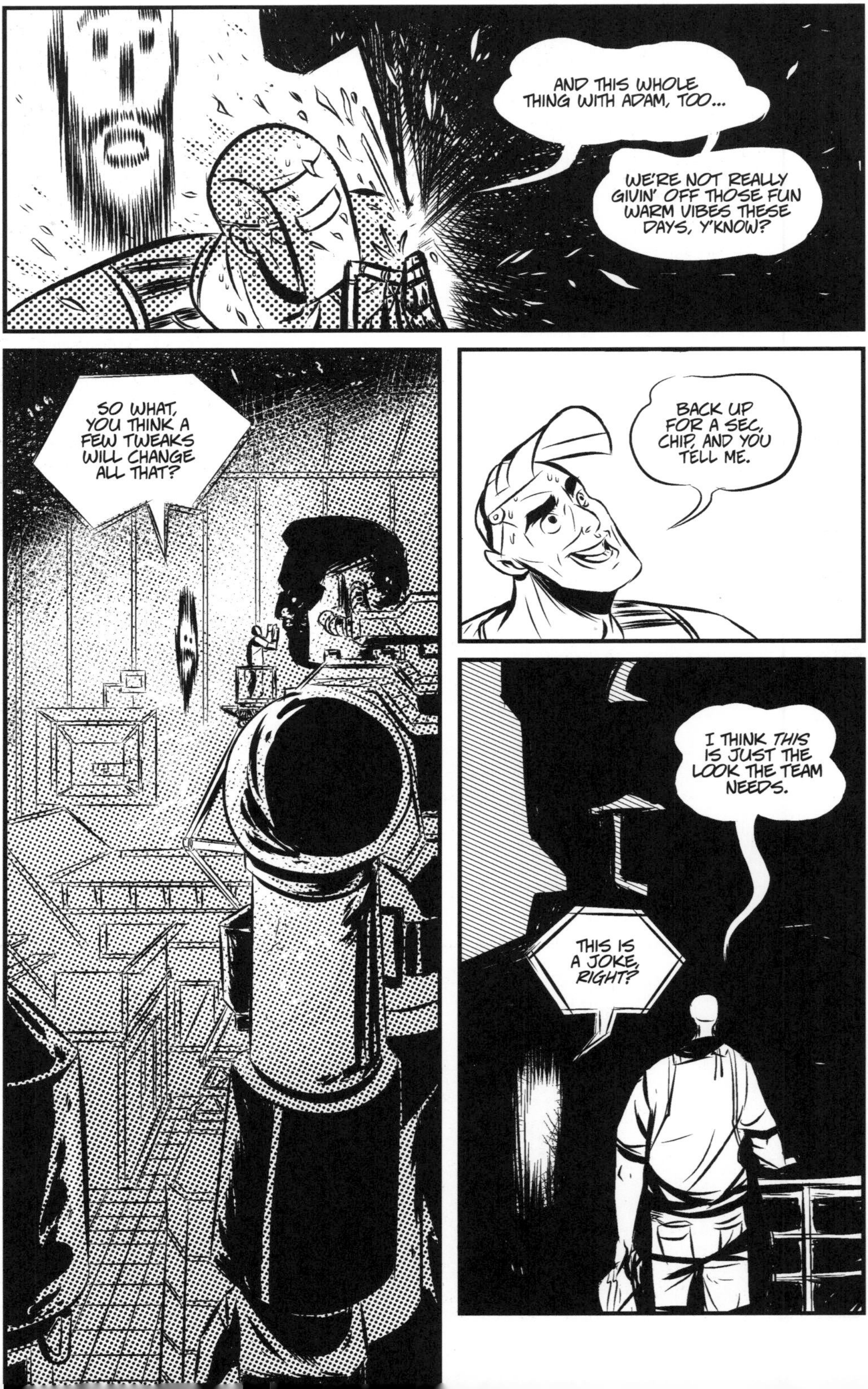
AND THIS WHOLE THING WITH ADAM, TOO...
WE'RE NOT REALLY GIVIN' OFF THOSE FUN WARM VIBES THESE DAYS, Y'KNOW?
SO WHAT, YOU THINK A FEW TWEAKS WILL CHANGE ALL THAT?
BACK UP FOR A SEC, CHIP, AND YOU TELL ME.
I THINK *THIS* IS JUST THE LOOK THE TEAM NEEDS.
THIS IS A JOKE, *RIGHT?*

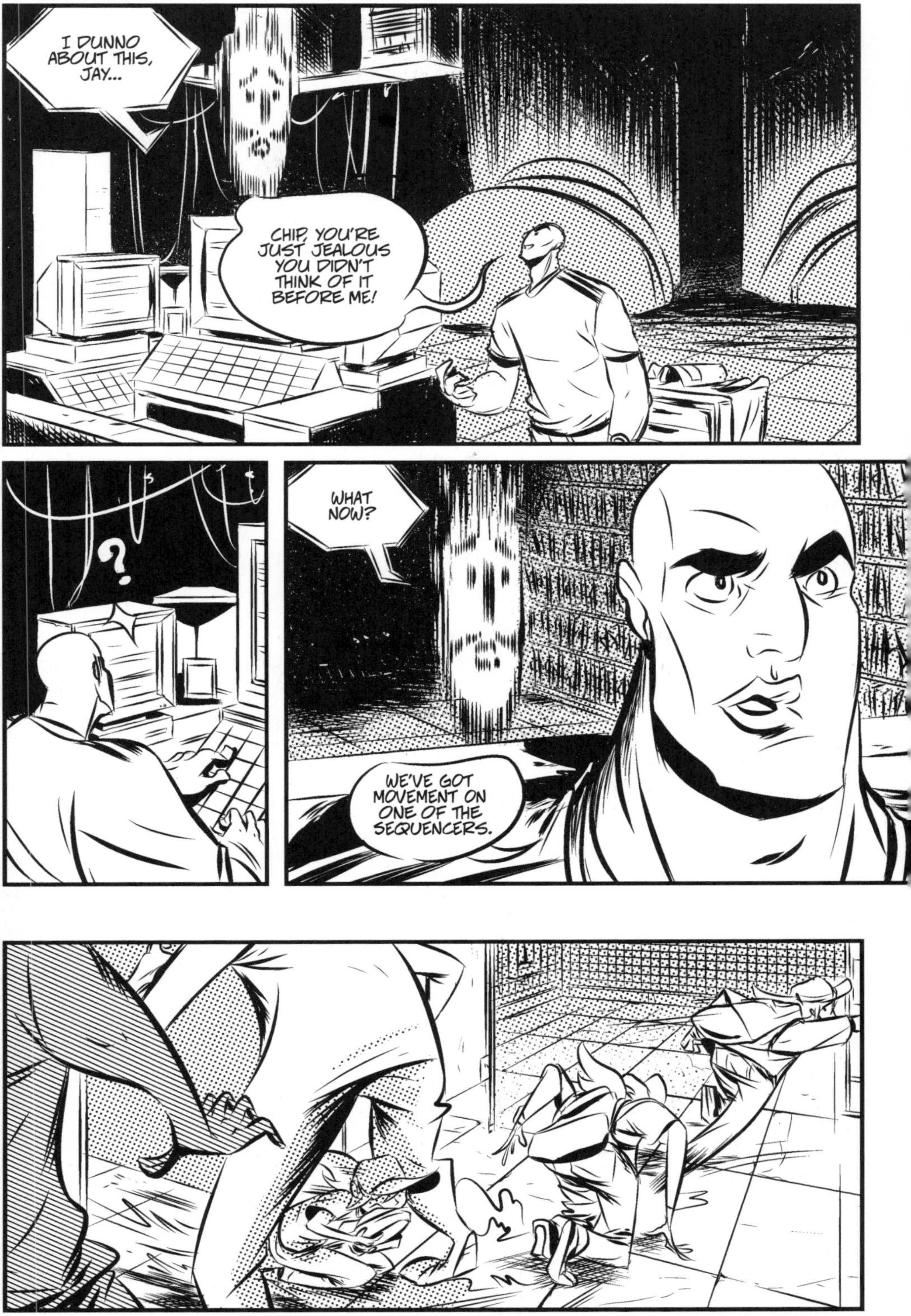
I DUNNO ABOUT THIS, JAY...
CHIP, YOU'RE JUST JEALOUS YOU DIDN'T THINK OF IT BEFORE ME!
WHAT NOW?
WE'VE GOT MOVEMENT ON ONE OF THE SEQUENCERS.

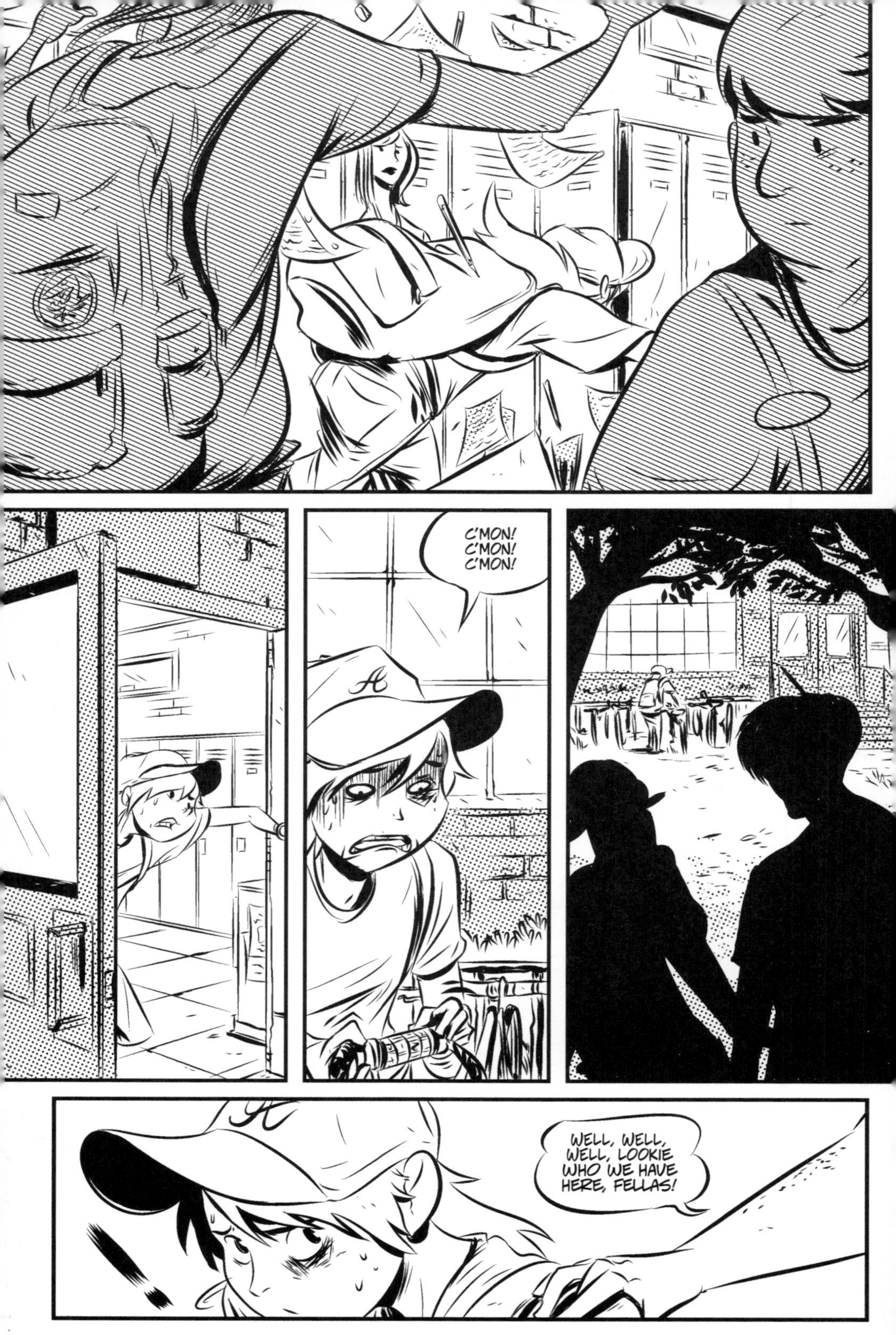
C'MON! C'MON! C'MON!
WELL, WELL, WELL, LOOKIE WHO WE HAVE HERE, FELLAS!

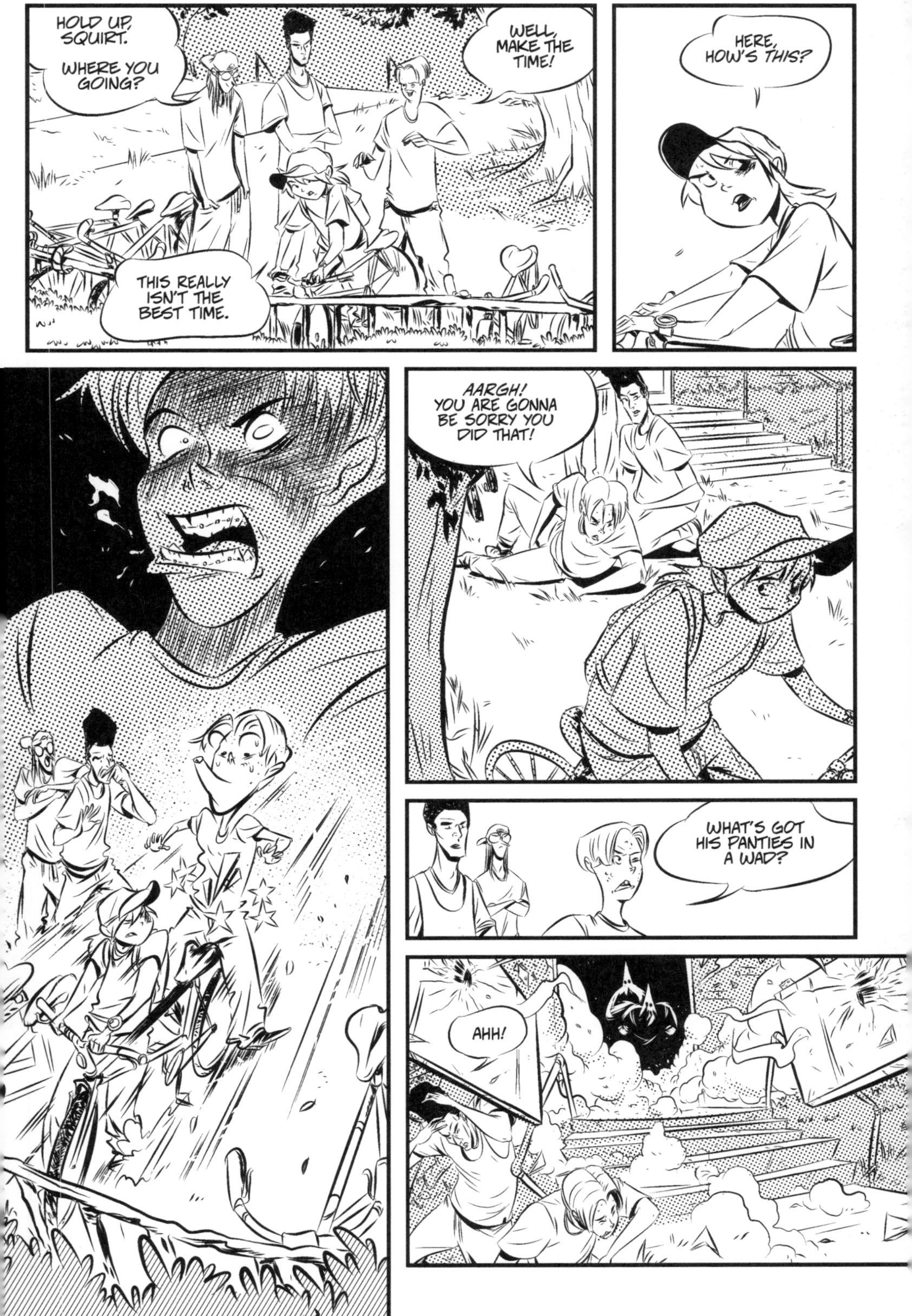
HOLD UP, SQUIRT.
WHERE YOU GOING?
WELL, MAKE THE TIME!
THIS REALLY ISN'T THE BEST TIME.
HERE, HOW'S THIS?
AARGH! YOU ARE GONNA BE SORRY YOU DID THAT!
WHAT'S GOT HIS PANTIES IN A WAD?
AHH!

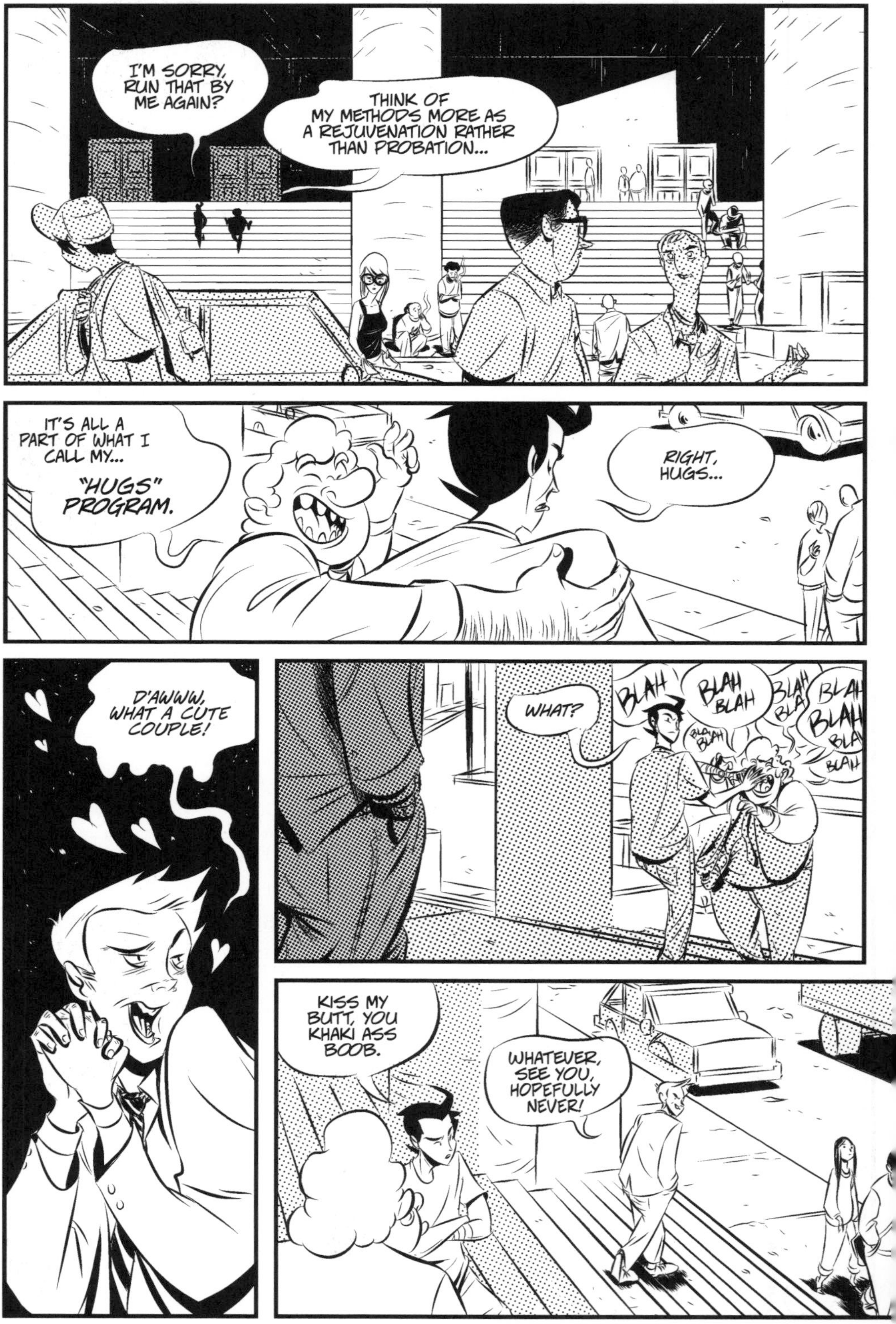
I'M SORRY, RUN THAT BY ME AGAIN?
THINK OF MY METHODS MORE AS A REJUVENATION RATHER THAN PROBATION...
IT'S ALL A PART OF WHAT I CALL MY... "HUGS" PROGRAM.
RIGHT, HUGS...
D'AWWW, WHAT A CUTE COUPLE!
WHAT?
BLAH BLAH BLAH BLAH BLAH BLAH BLAH BLAH BLAH BLAH BLAH
KISS MY BUTT, YOU KHAKI ASS BOOB.
WHATEVER, SEE YOU, HOPEFULLY NEVER!

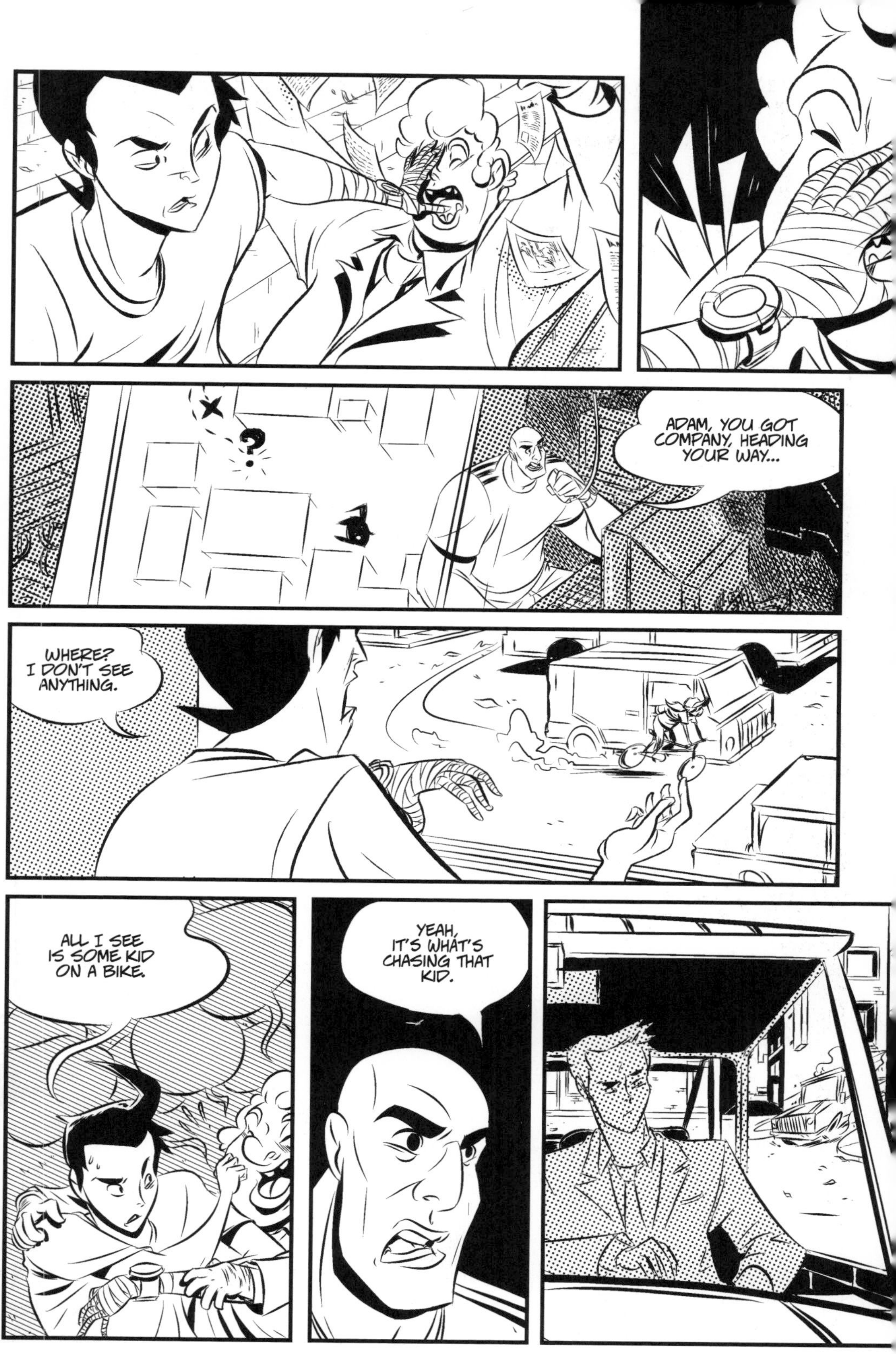
ADAM, YOU GOT COMPANY, HEADING YOUR WAY...
WHERE? I DON'T SEE ANYTHING.
ALL I SEE IS SOME KID ON A BIKE.
YEAH, IT'S WHAT'S CHASING THAT KID.

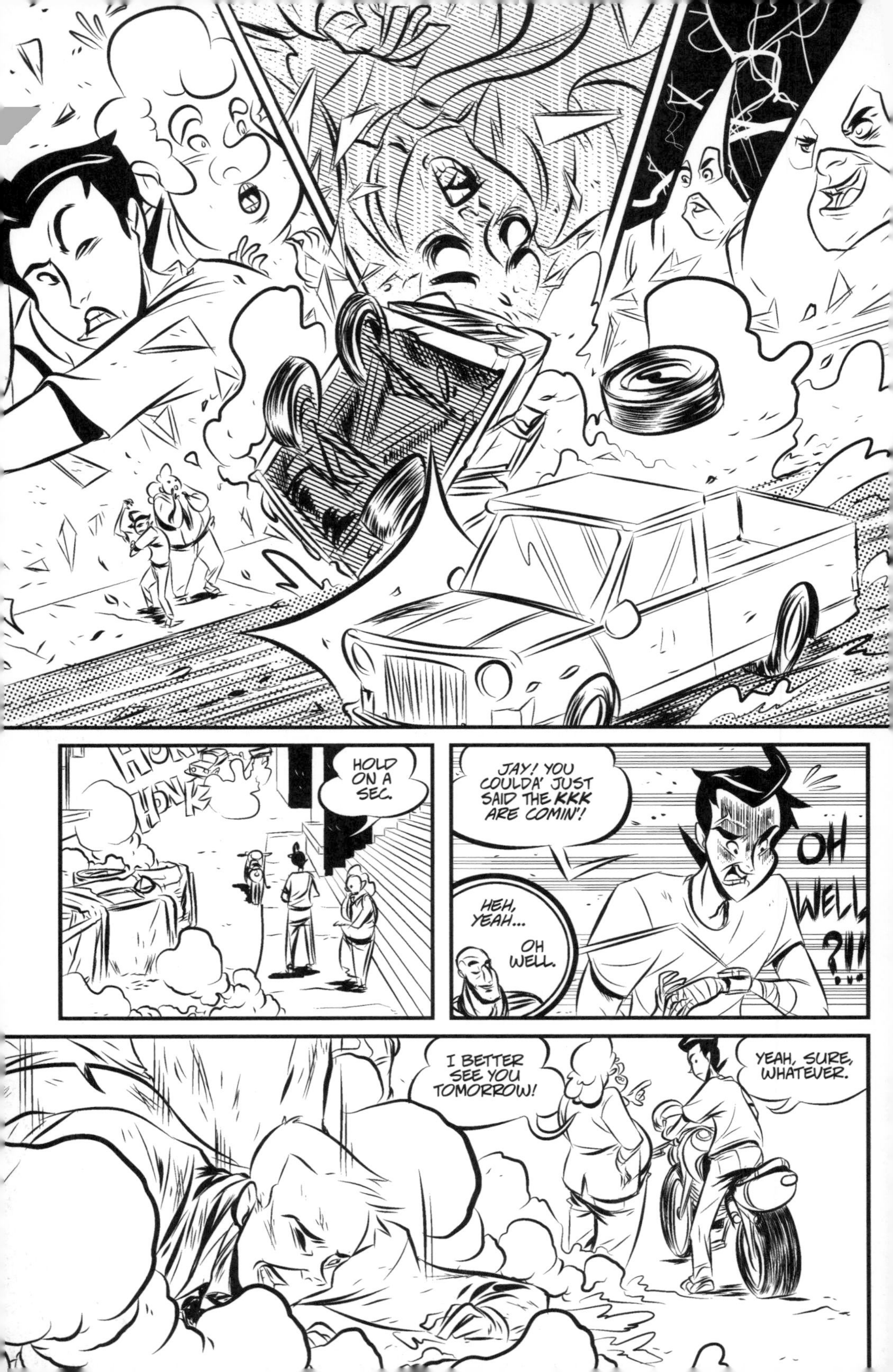
HONK
HONK
HOLD ON A SEC.
JAY! YOU COULDA' JUST SAID THE KKK ARE COMIN'!
OH WELL?!!
HEH, YEAH... OH WELL.
I BETTER SEE YOU TOMORROW!
YEAH, SURE, WHATEVER.

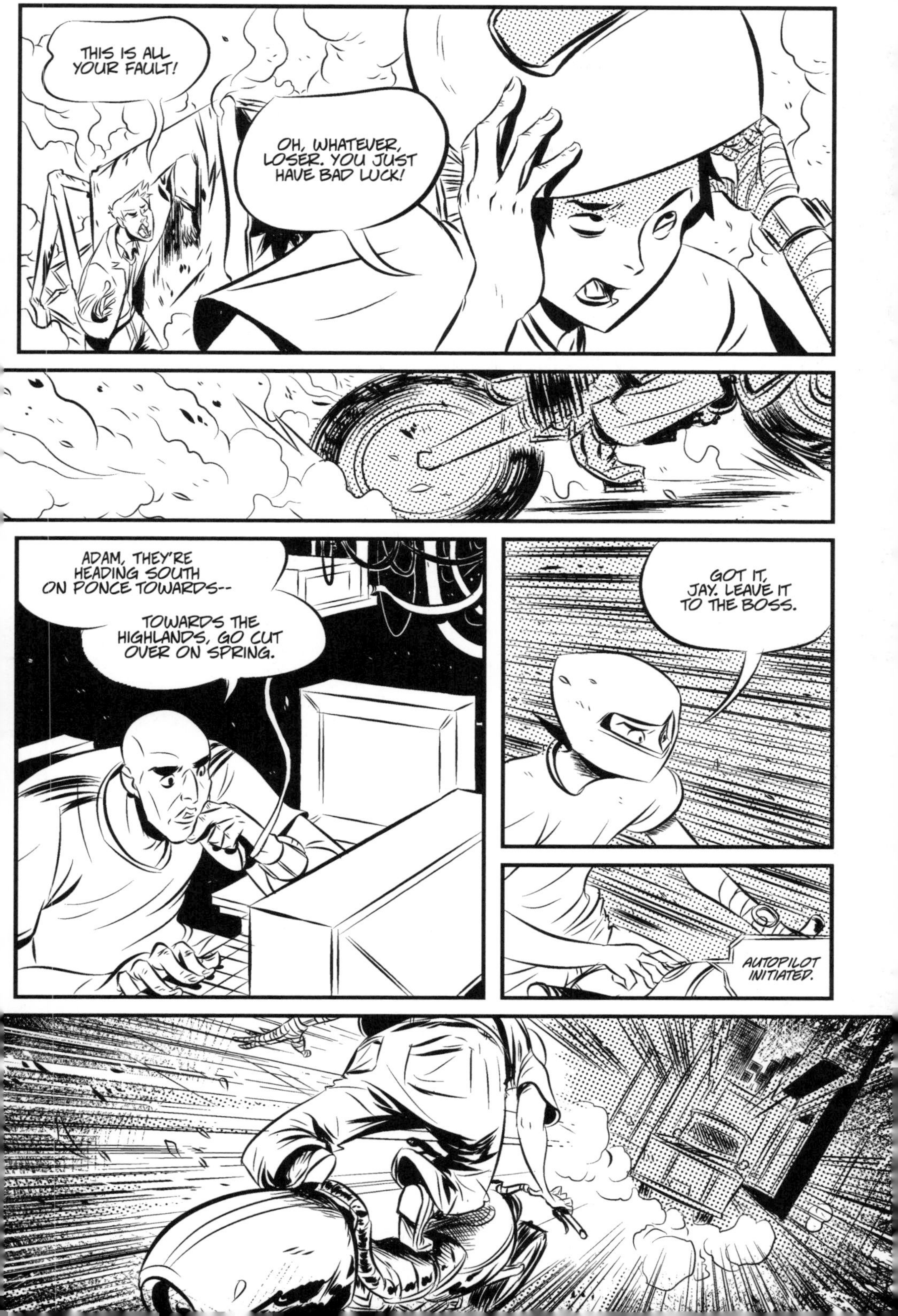
THIS IS ALL YOUR FAULT!
OH, WHATEVER, LOSER. YOU JUST HAVE BAD LUCK!
ADAM, THEY'RE HEADING SOUTH ON PONCE TOWARDS--
TOWARDS THE HIGHLANDS, GO CUT OVER ON SPRING.
GOT IT, JAY. LEAVE IT TO THE BOSS.
AUTOPILOT INITIATED.

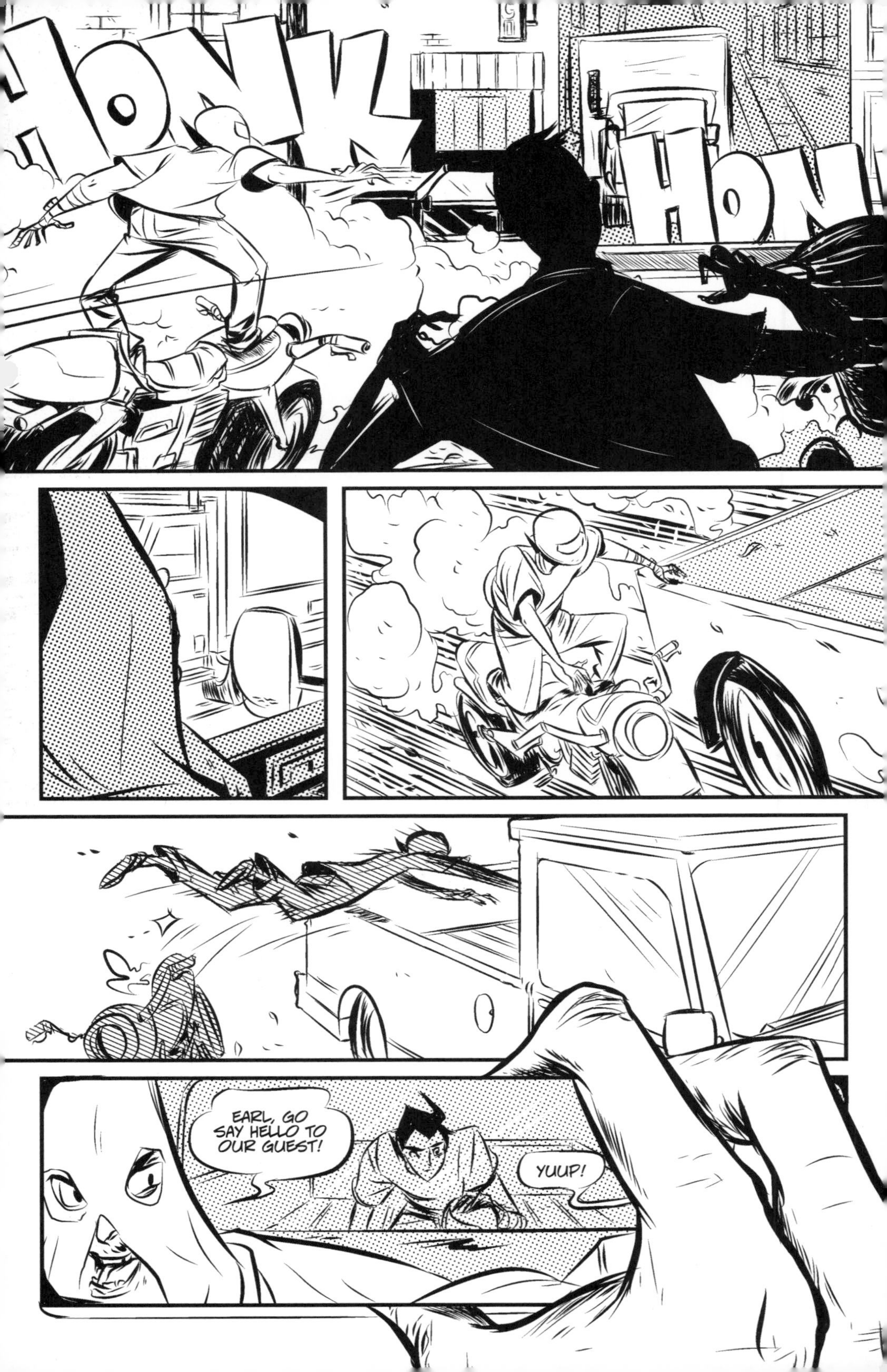
HONK
HONK
EARL, GO SAY HELLO TO OUR GUEST!
YUUP!

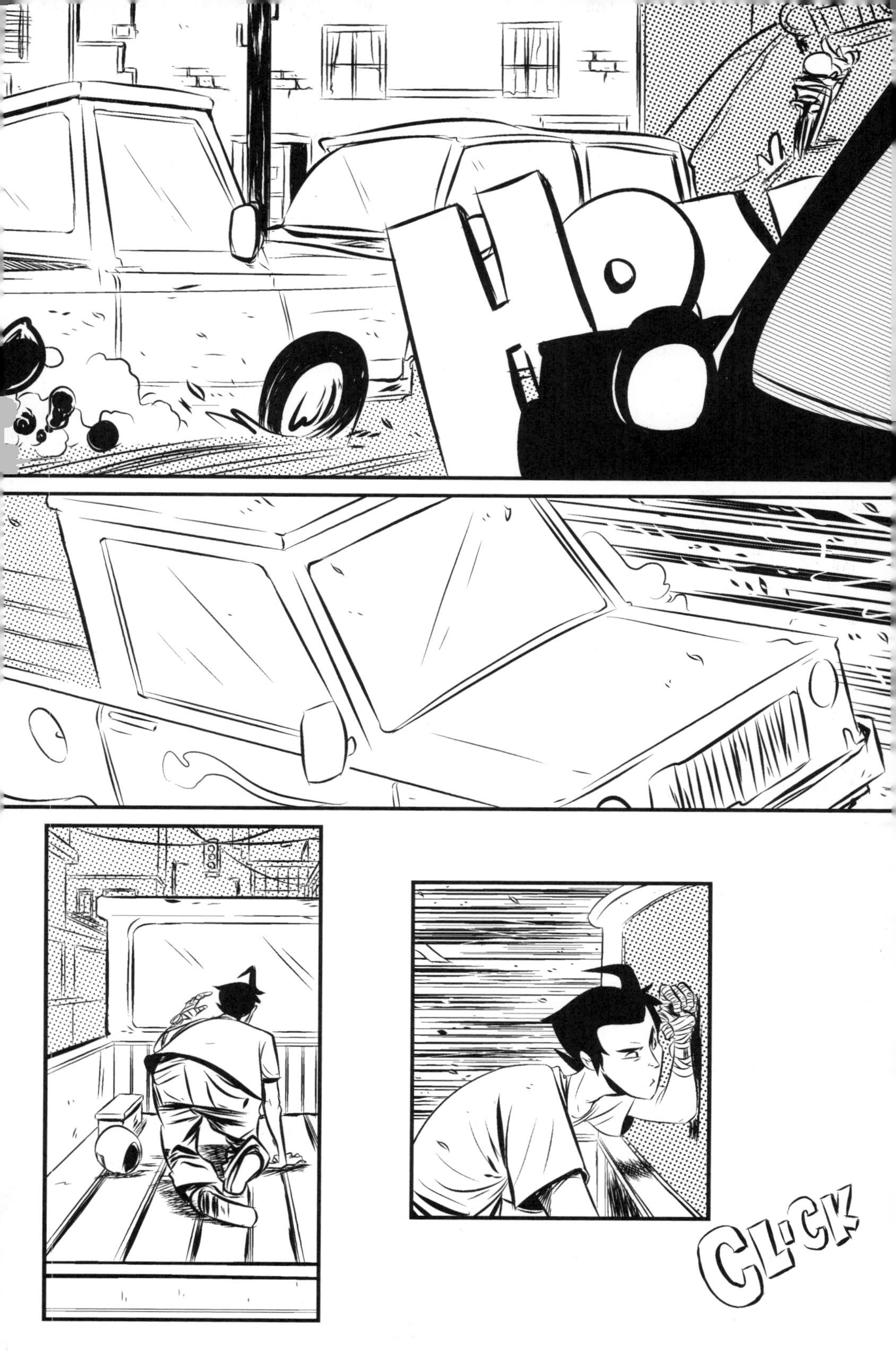
CLICK

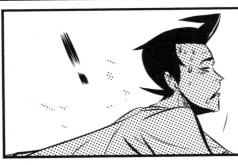

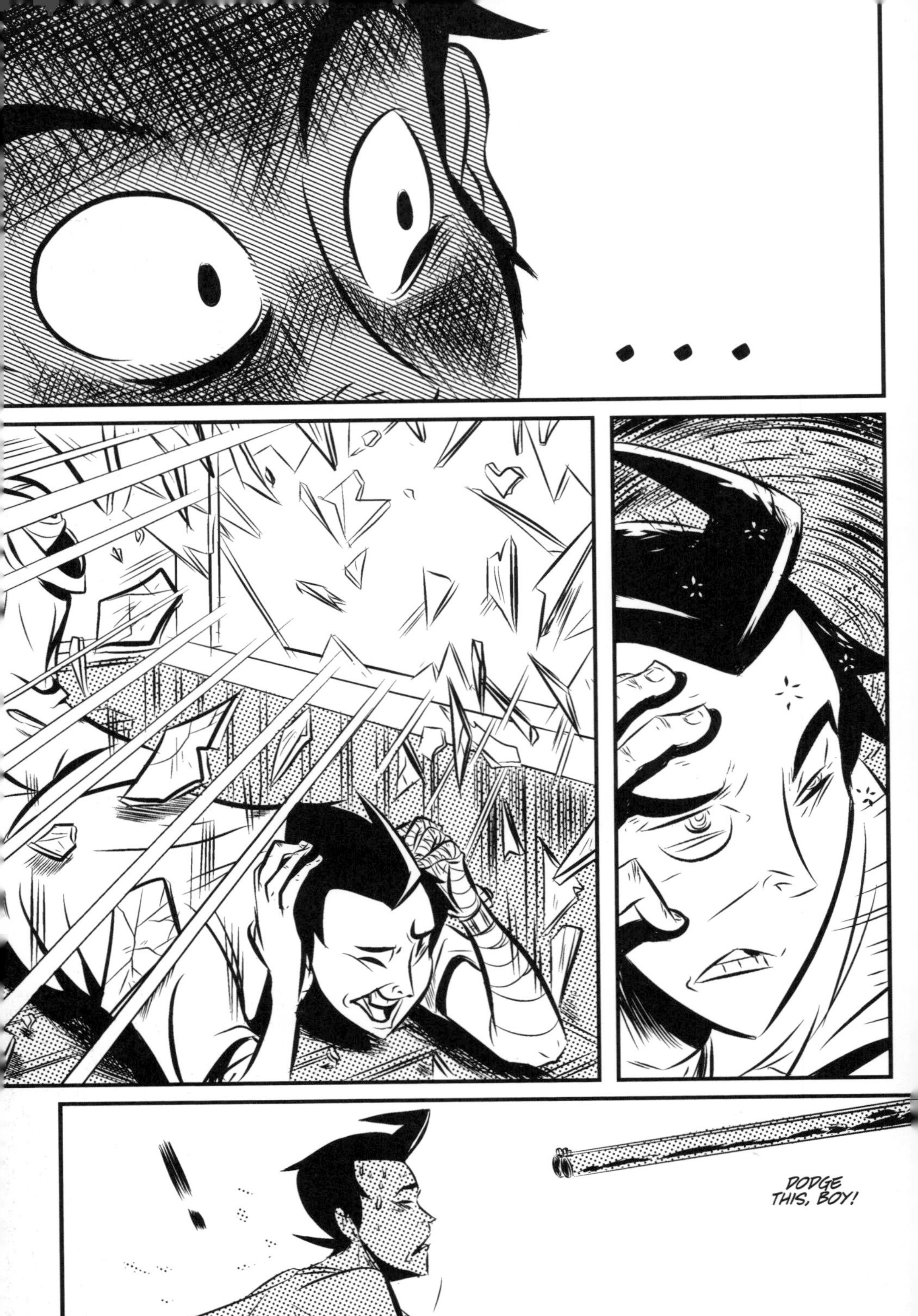
...
DODGE THIS, BOY!

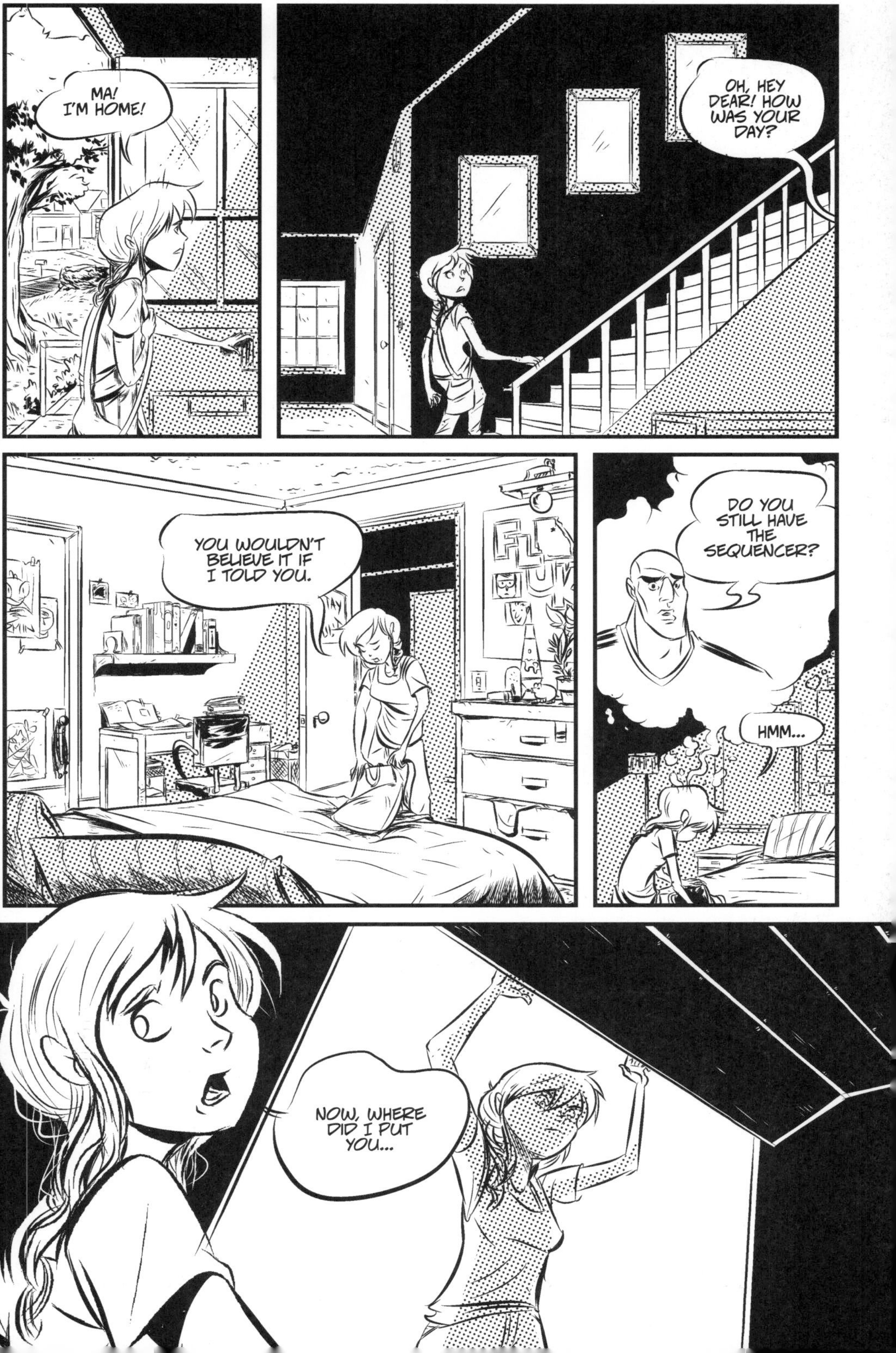
MA! I'M HOME!
OH, HEY DEAR! HOW WAS YOUR DAY?
YOU WOULDN'T BELIEVE IT IF I TOLD YOU.
DO YOU STILL HAVE THE SEQUENCER?
HMM...
NOW, WHERE DID I PUT YOU...

AH HA, JACKPOT!

I KNOW I PUT IT HERE...

...

EVAN!!

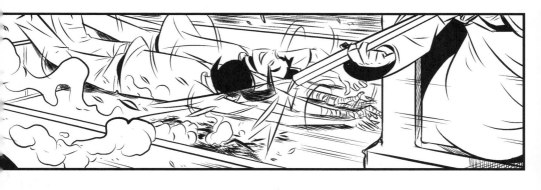

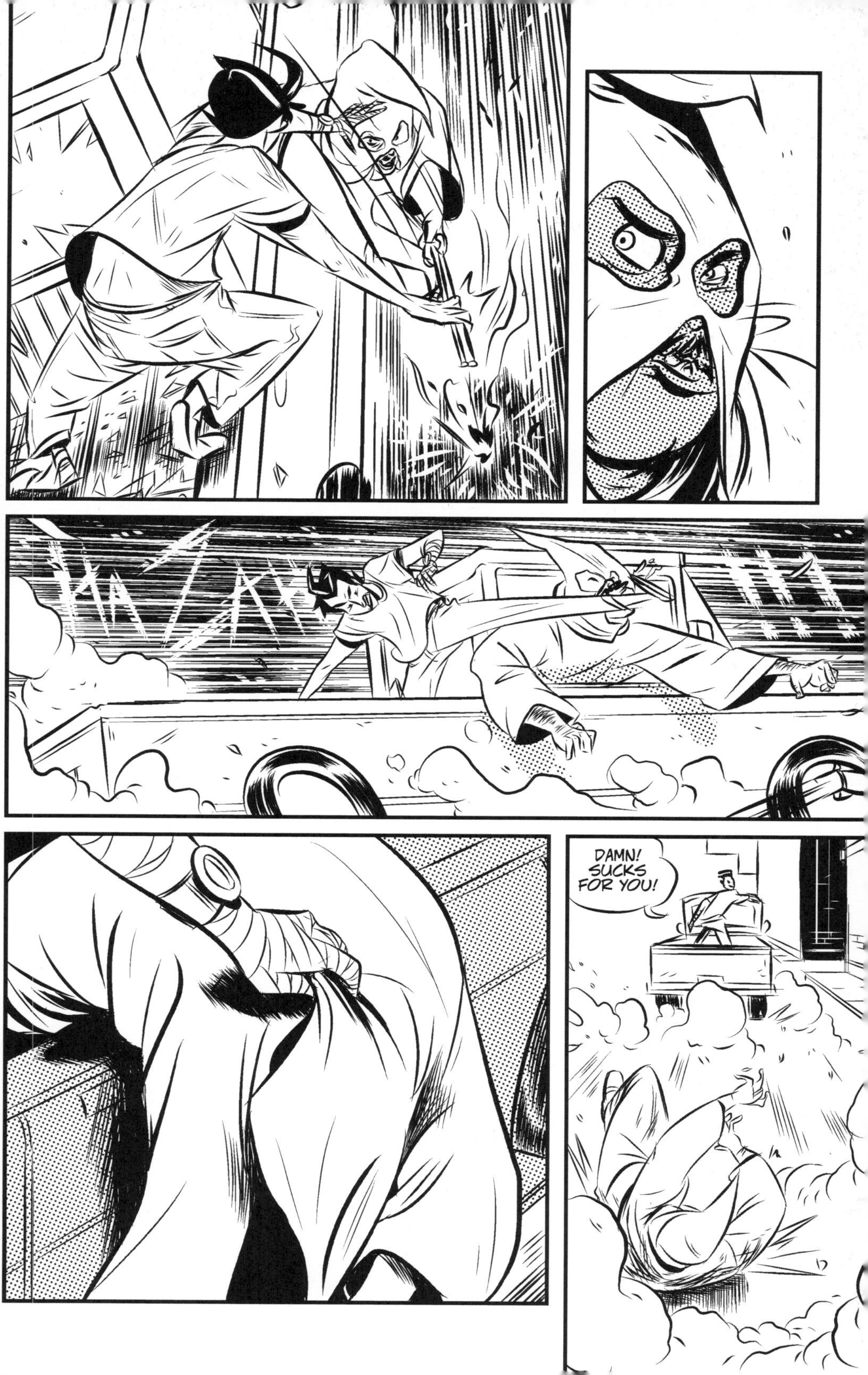
DAMN! SUCKS FOR YOU!

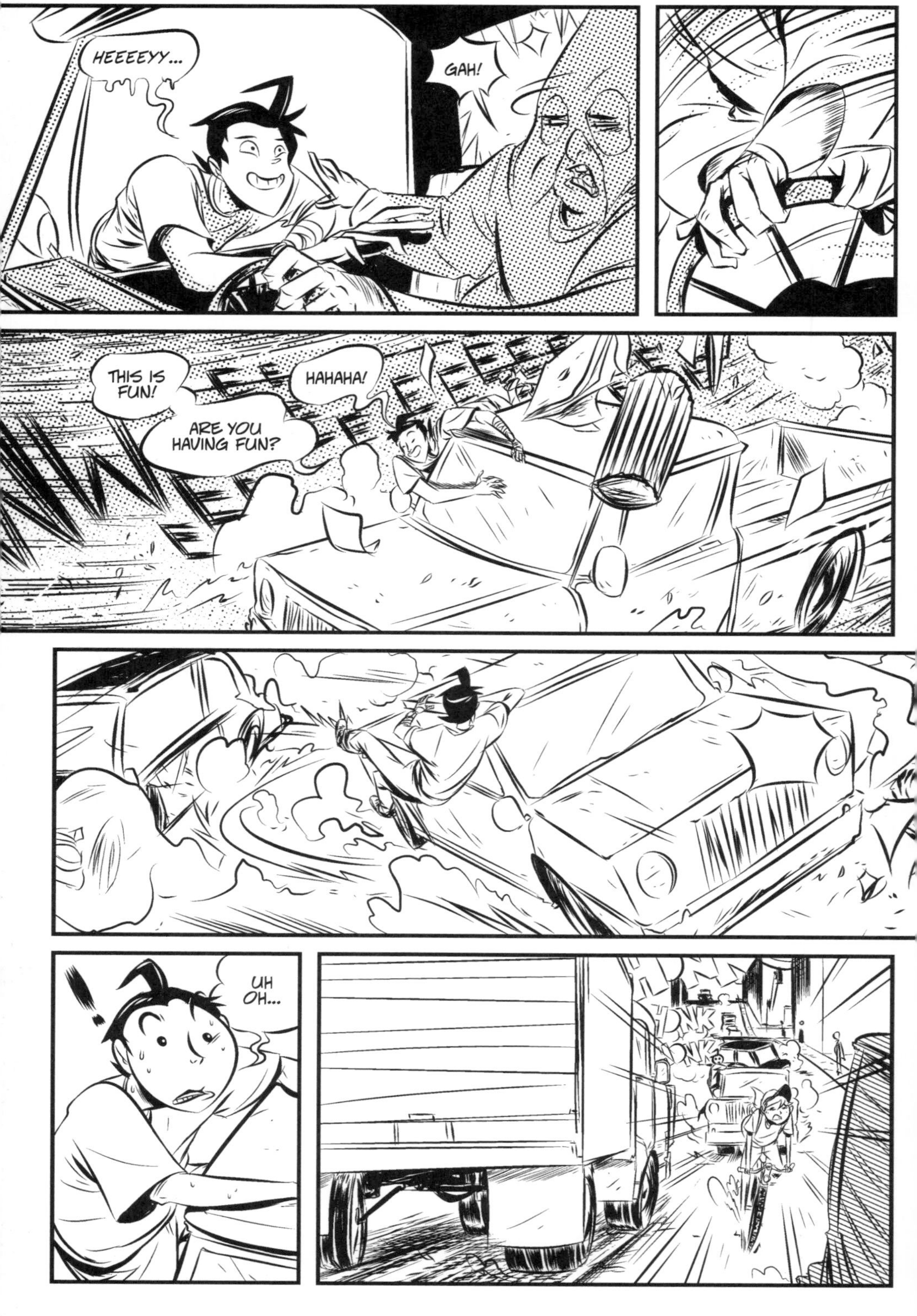
HEEEEYY...
GAH!
THIS IS FUN!
HAHAHA!
ARE YOU HAVING FUN?
UH OH...
HONK
HONK

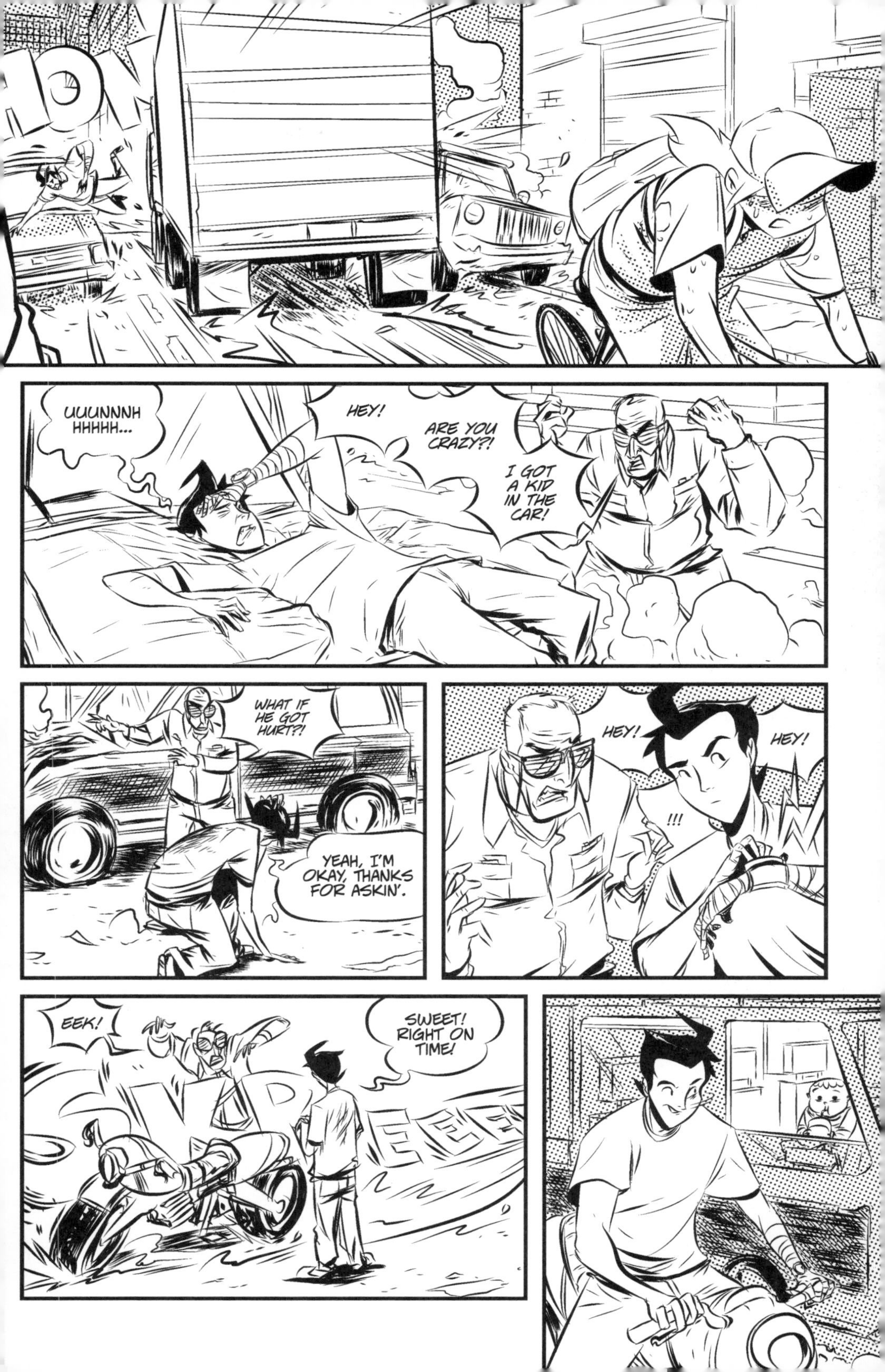
HON
UUUNNNH HHHHH...
HEY!
ARE YOU CRAZY?!
I GOT A KID IN THE CAR!
WHAT IF HE GOT HURT?!
YEAH, I'M OKAY, THANKS FOR ASKIN'.
HEY!
!!!
HEY!
EEK!
SWEET! RIGHT ON TIME!
VRREEEE

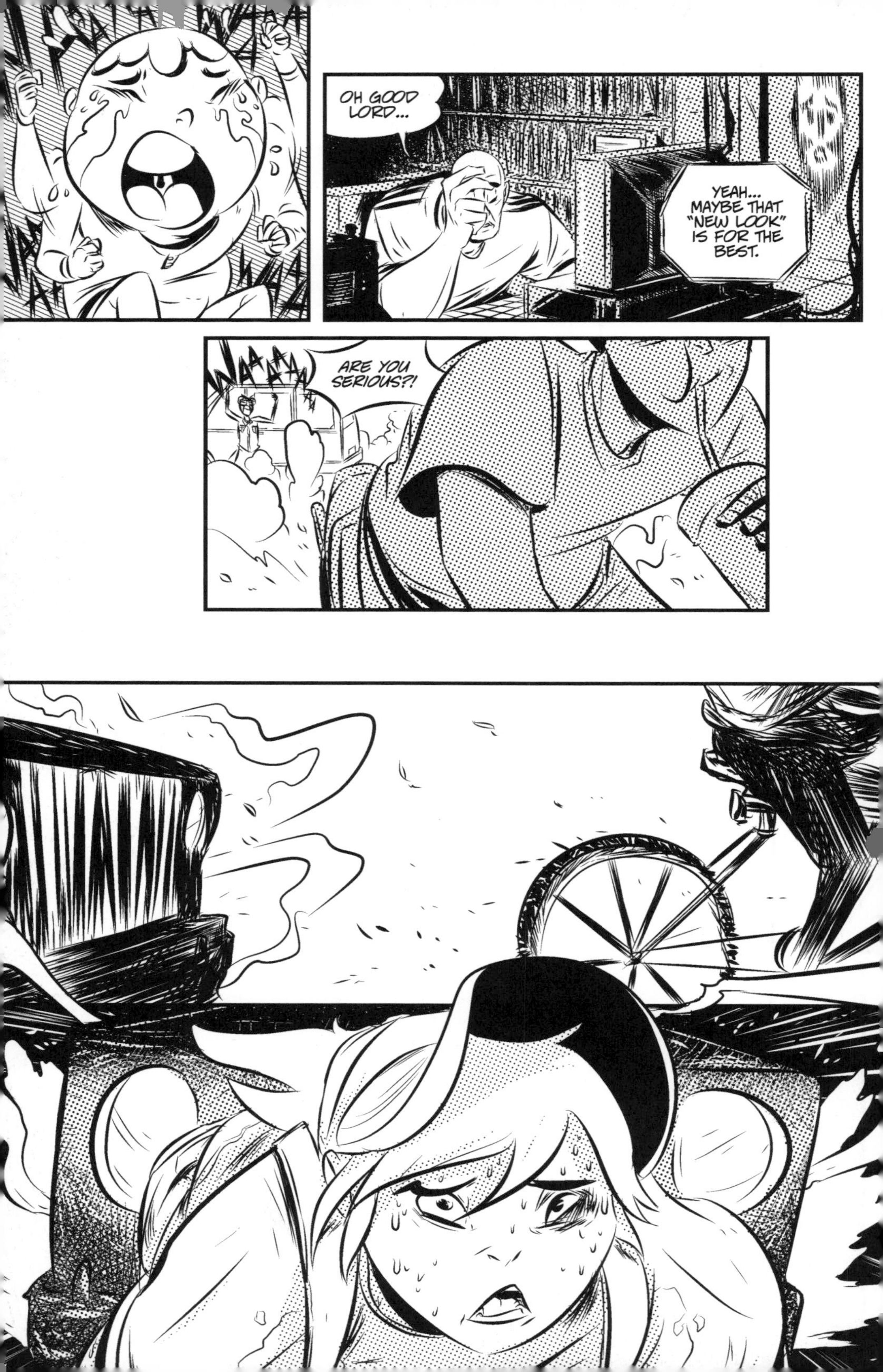
OH GOOD LORD...
YEAH... MAYBE THAT "NEW LOOK" IS FOR THE BEST.
ARE YOU SERIOUS?!

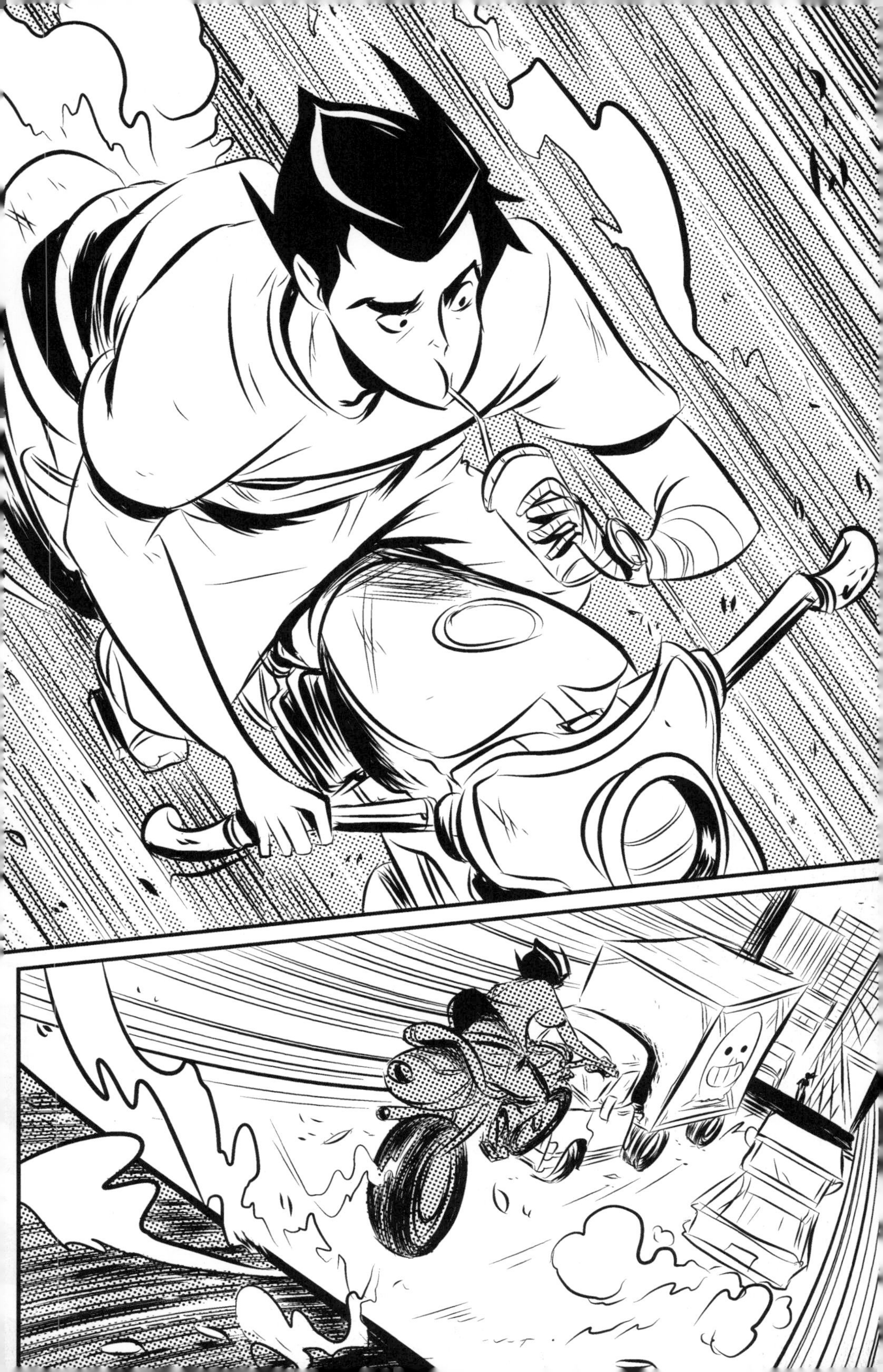

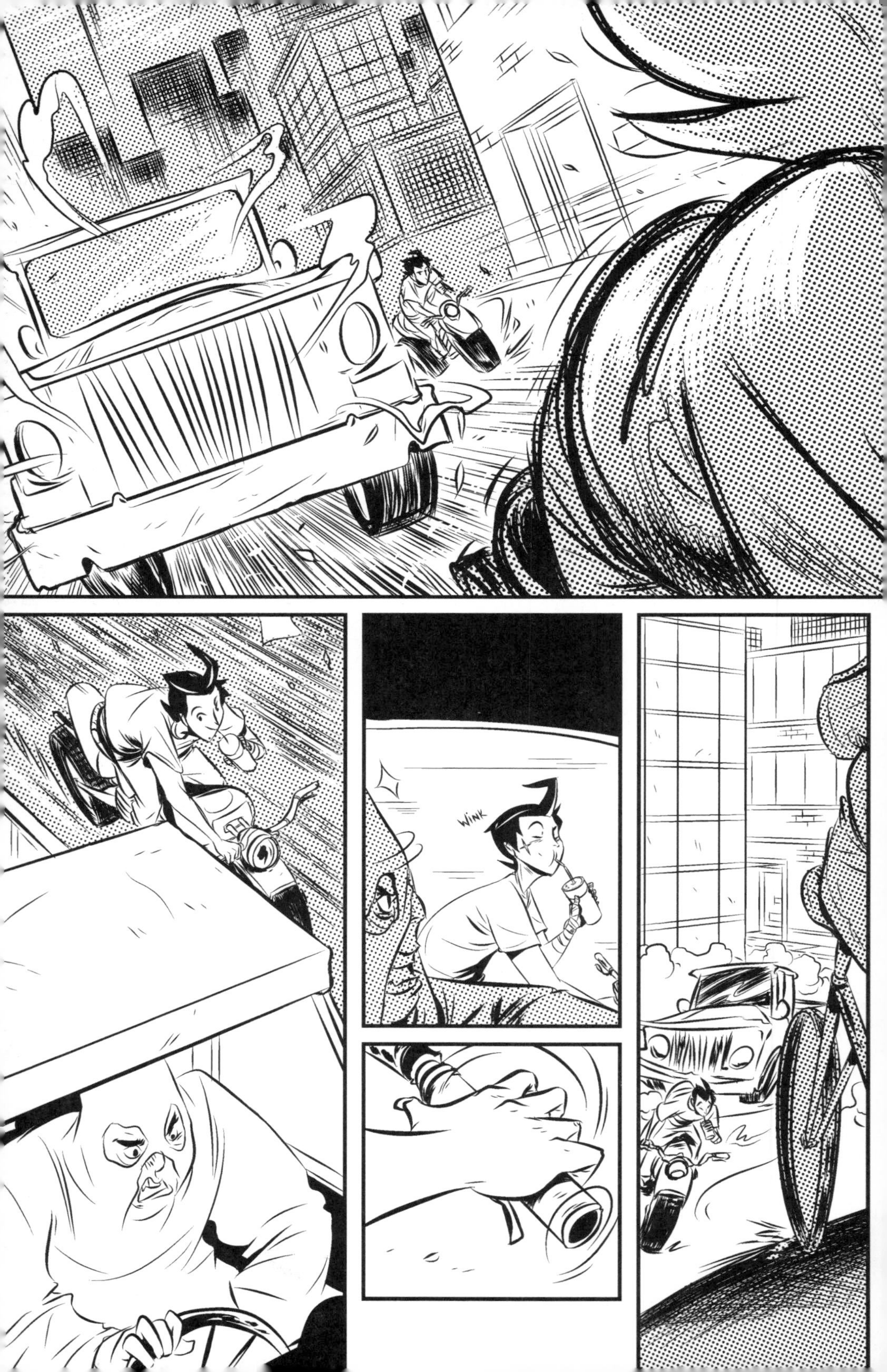
WINK

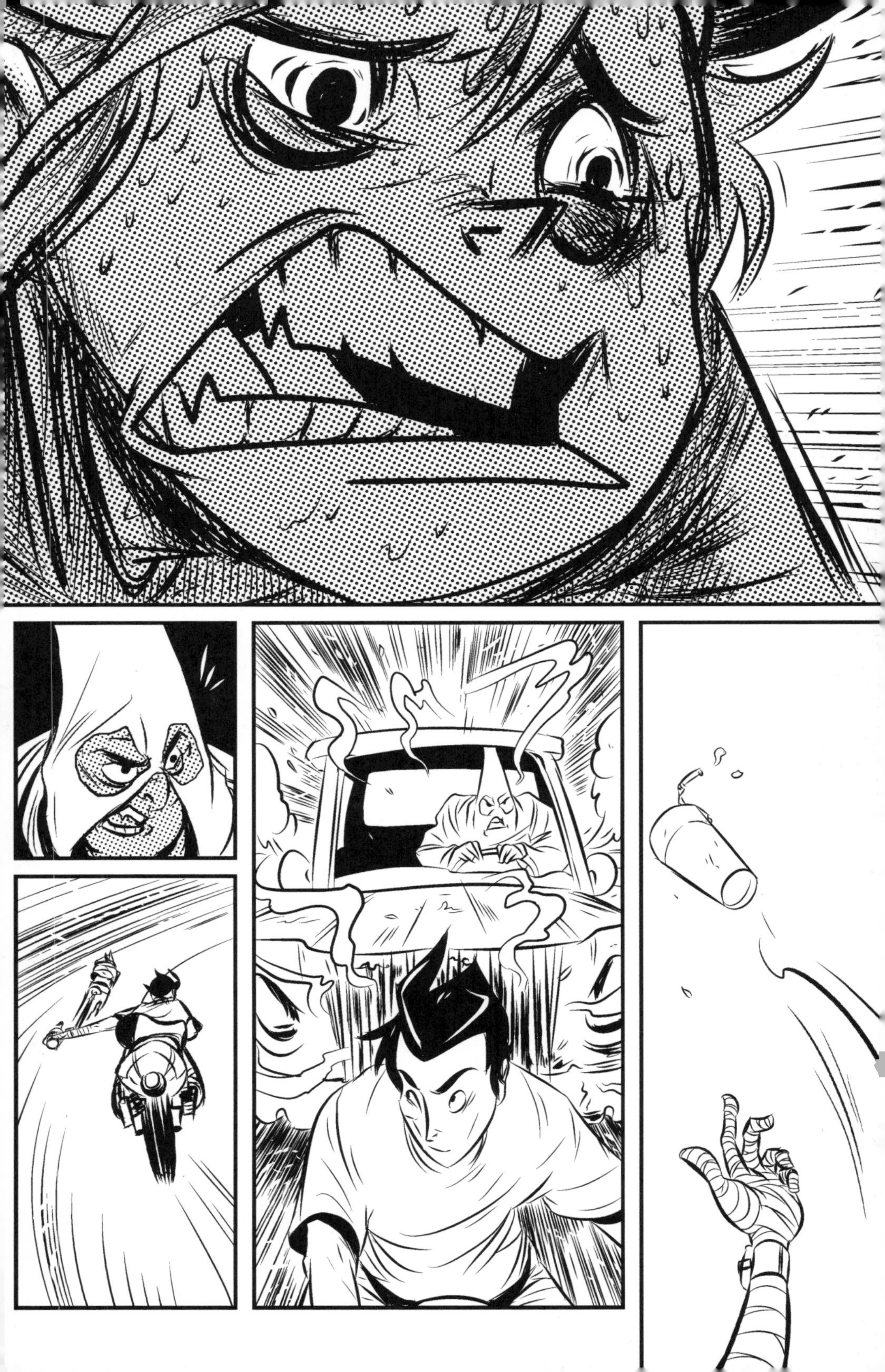

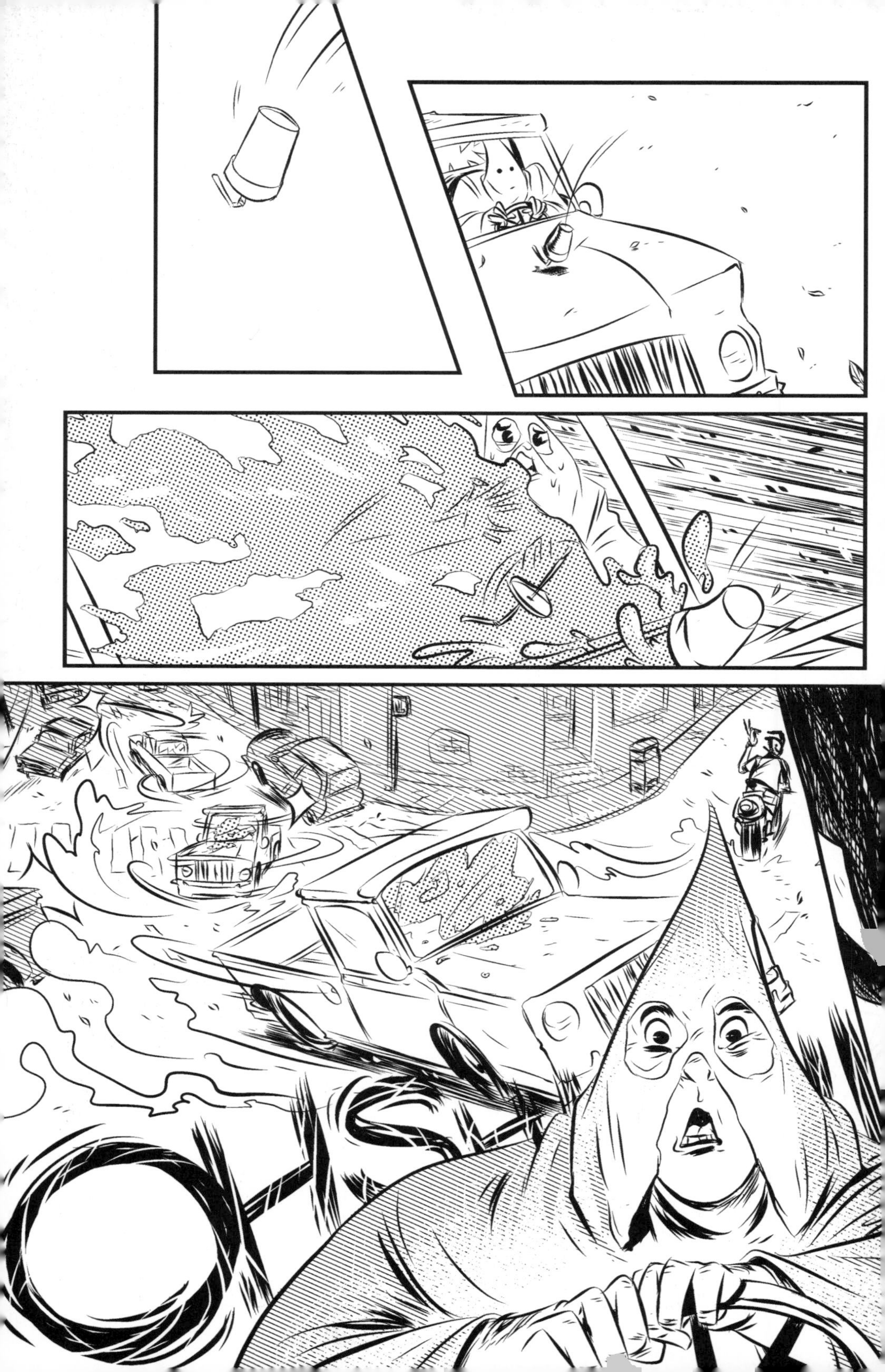

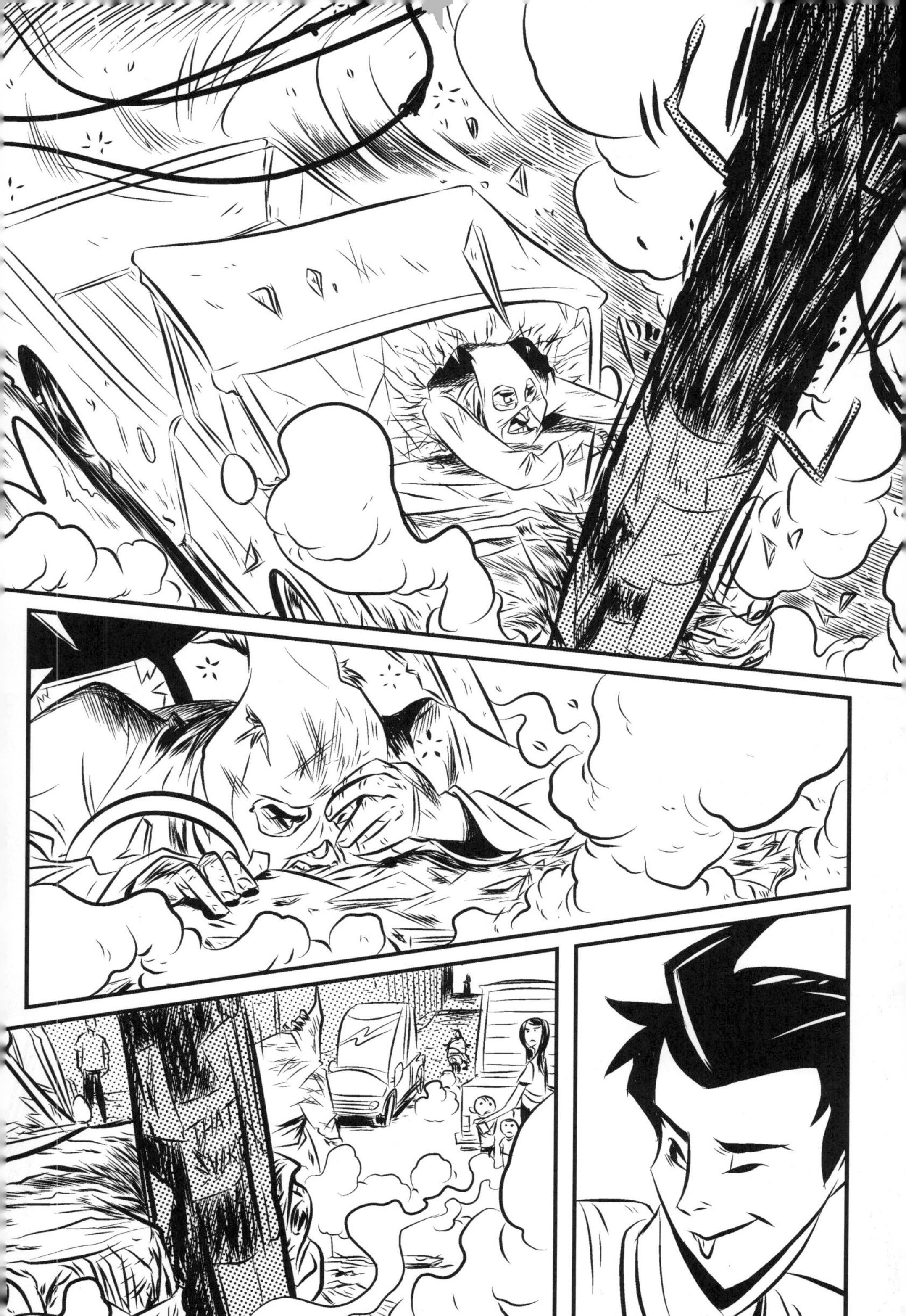

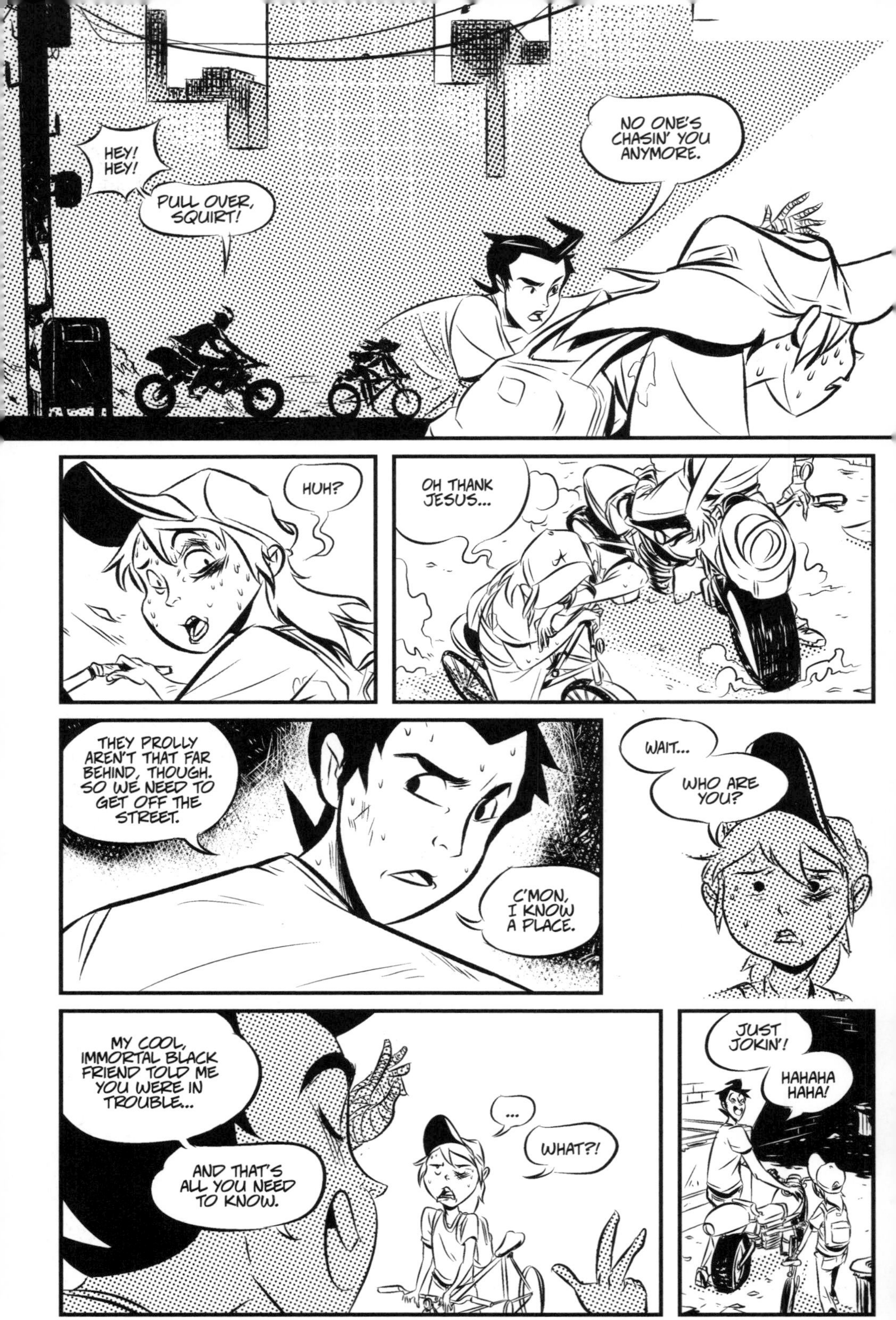
HEY! HEY!
PULL OVER, SQUIRT!
NO ONE'S CHASIN' YOU ANYMORE.
HUH?
OH THANK JESUS...
THEY PROLLY AREN'T THAT FAR BEHIND, THOUGH. SO WE NEED TO GET OFF THE STREET.
C'MON, I KNOW A PLACE.
WAIT...
WHO ARE YOU?
MY COOL, IMMORTAL BLACK FRIEND TOLD ME YOU WERE IN TROUBLE...
AND THAT'S ALL YOU NEED TO KNOW.
...
WHAT?!
JUST JOKIN'!
HAHAHA HAHA!

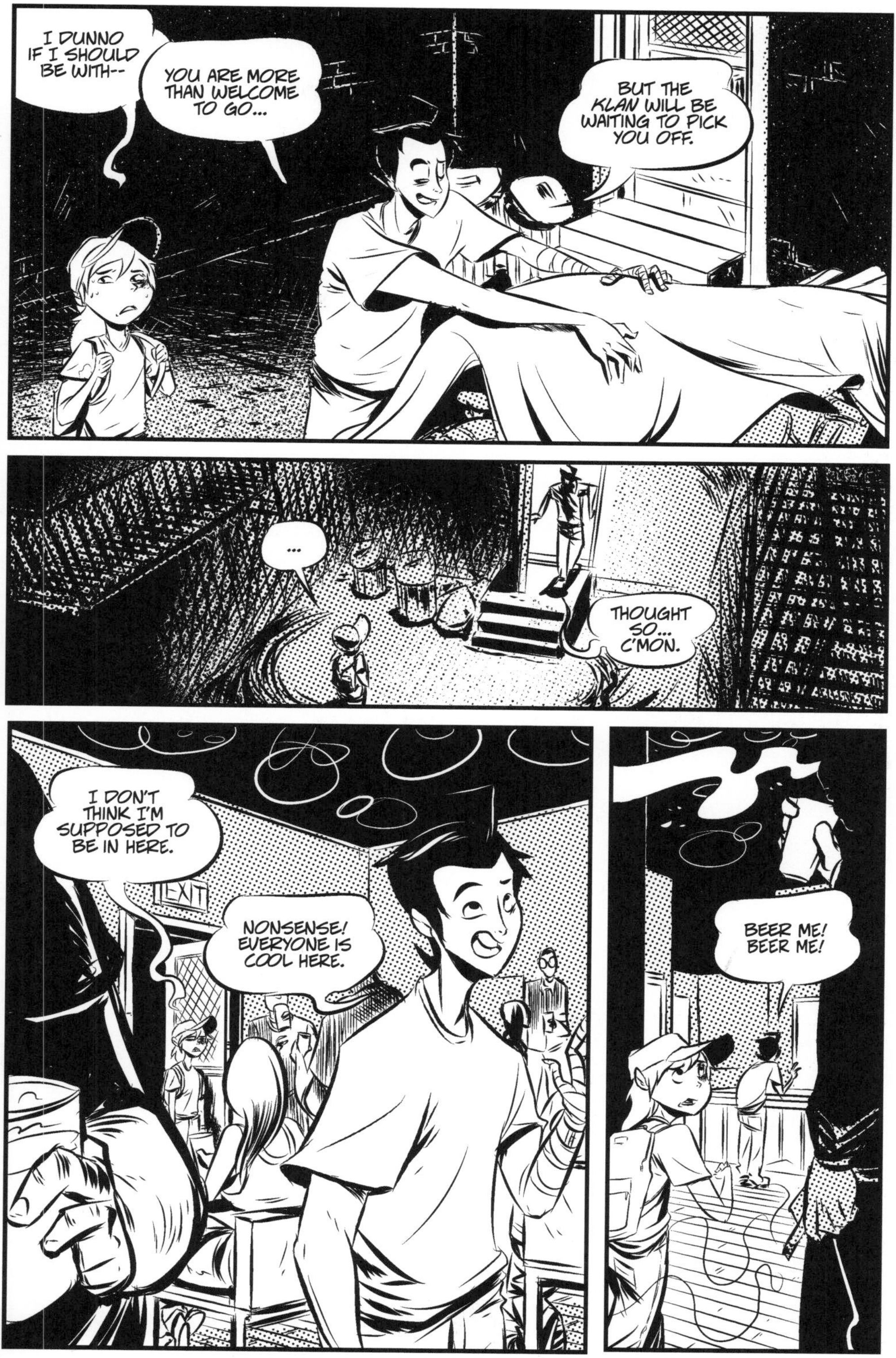
I DUNNO IF I SHOULD BE WITH--
YOU ARE MORE THAN WELCOME TO GO...
BUT THE *KLAN* WILL BE WAITING TO PICK YOU OFF.
...
THOUGHT SO... C'MON.
I DON'T THINK I'M SUPPOSED TO BE IN HERE.
EXIT
NONSENSE! EVERYONE IS COOL HERE.
BEER ME! BEER ME!

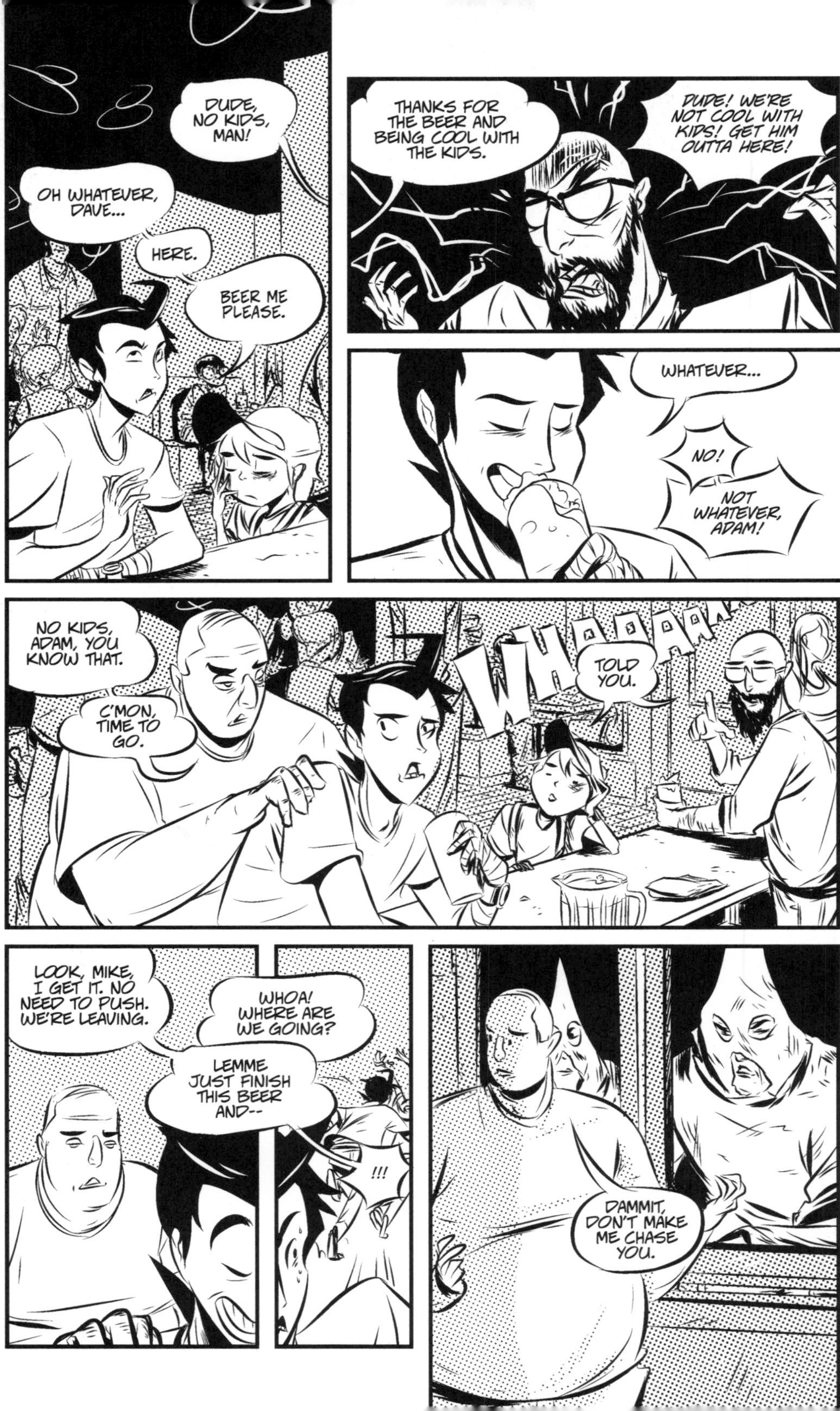
DUDE, NO KIDS, MAN!
OH WHATEVER, DAVE...
HERE.
BEER ME PLEASE.
THANKS FOR THE BEER AND BEING COOL WITH THE KIDS.
DUDE! WE'RE NOT COOL WITH KIDS! GET HIM OUTTA HERE!
WHATEVER...
NO!
NOT WHATEVER, ADAM!
NO KIDS, ADAM, YOU KNOW THAT.
C'MON, TIME TO GO.
WHAAAA
TOLD YOU.
LOOK, MIKE, I GET IT. NO NEED TO PUSH. WE'RE LEAVING.
WHOA! WHERE ARE WE GOING?
LEMME JUST FINISH THIS BEER AND--
!!!
DAMMIT, DON'T MAKE ME CHASE YOU.

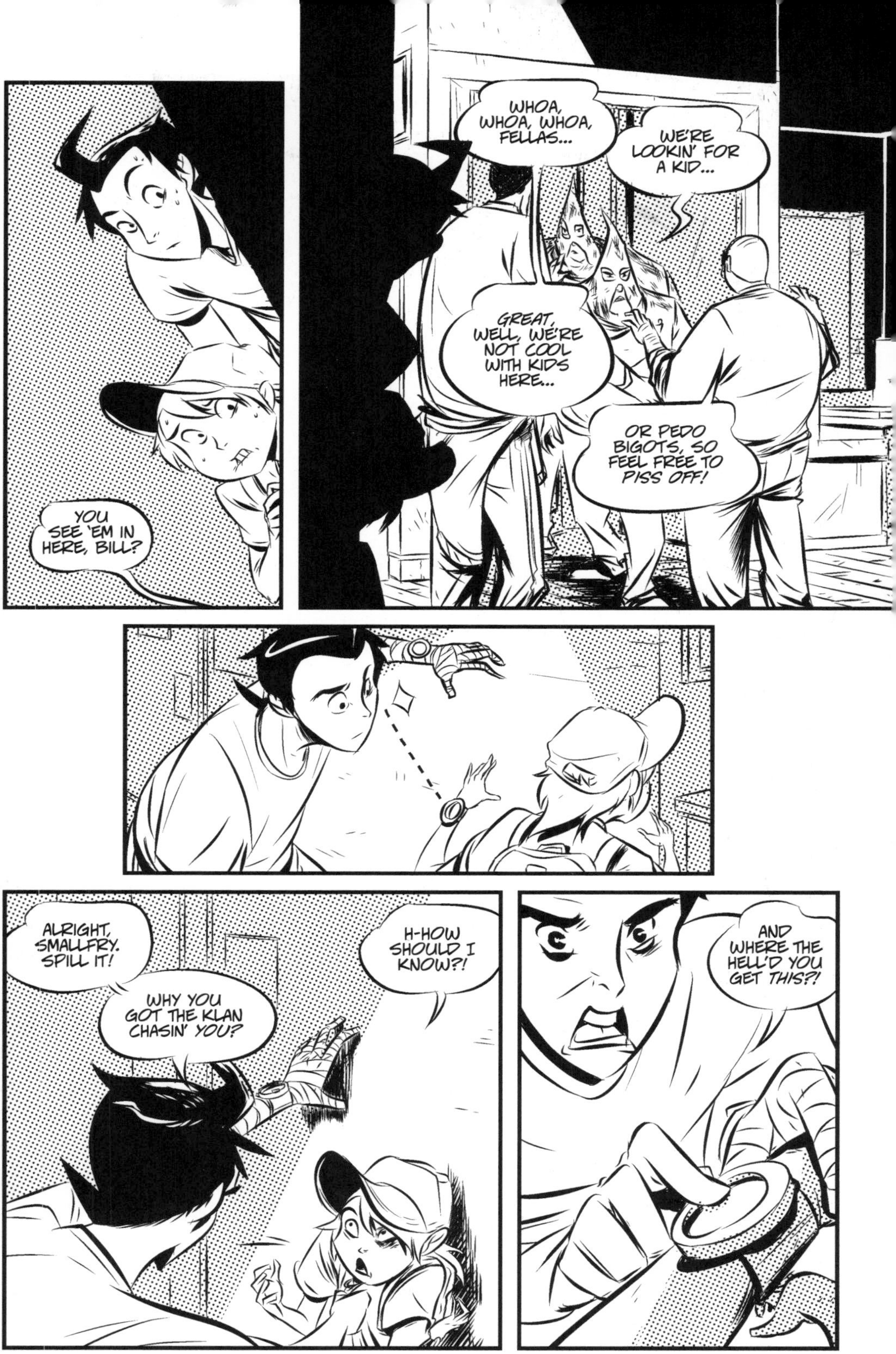
YOU SEE 'EM IN HERE, BILL?
WHOA, WHOA, WHOA, FELLAS...
WE'RE LOOKIN' FOR A KID...
GREAT, WELL, WE'RE NOT COOL WITH KIDS HERE...
OR PEDO BIGOTS, SO FEEL FREE TO PISS OFF!
ALRIGHT, SMALLFRY. SPILL IT!
WHY YOU GOT THE KLAN CHASIN' YOU?
H-HOW SHOULD I KNOW?!
AND WHERE THE HELL'D YOU GET THIS?!

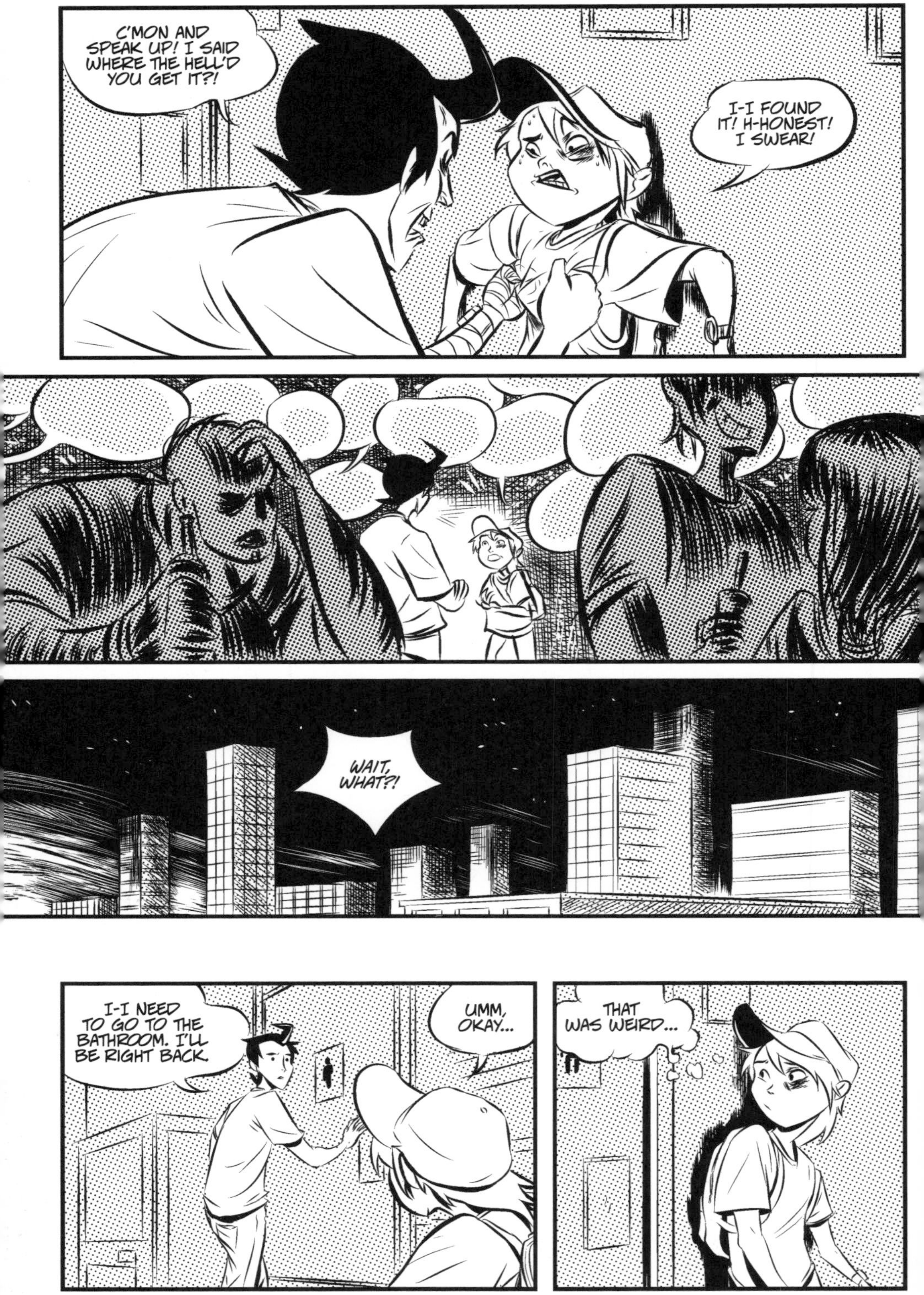
C'MON AND SPEAK UP! I SAID WHERE THE HELL'D YOU GET IT?!
I-I FOUND IT! H-HONEST! I SWEAR!
WAIT, WHAT?!
I-I NEED TO GO TO THE BATHROOM. I'LL BE RIGHT BACK.
UMM, OKAY...
THAT WAS WEIRD...

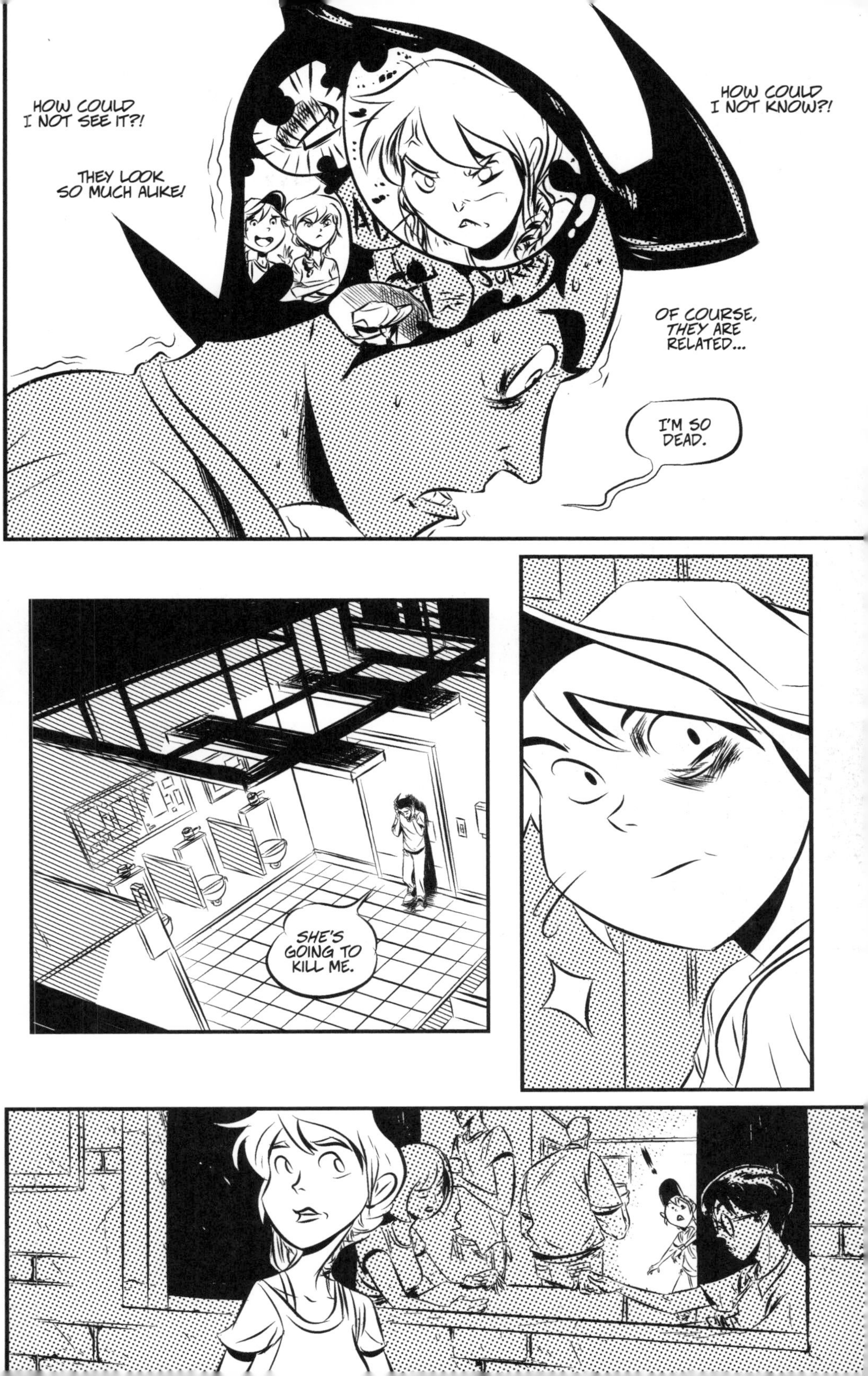

HOW COULD I NOT SEE IT?!
THEY LOOK SO MUCH ALIKE!
HOW COULD I NOT KNOW?!
OF COURSE, THEY ARE RELATED...
I'M SO DEAD.
SHE'S GOING TO KILL ME.

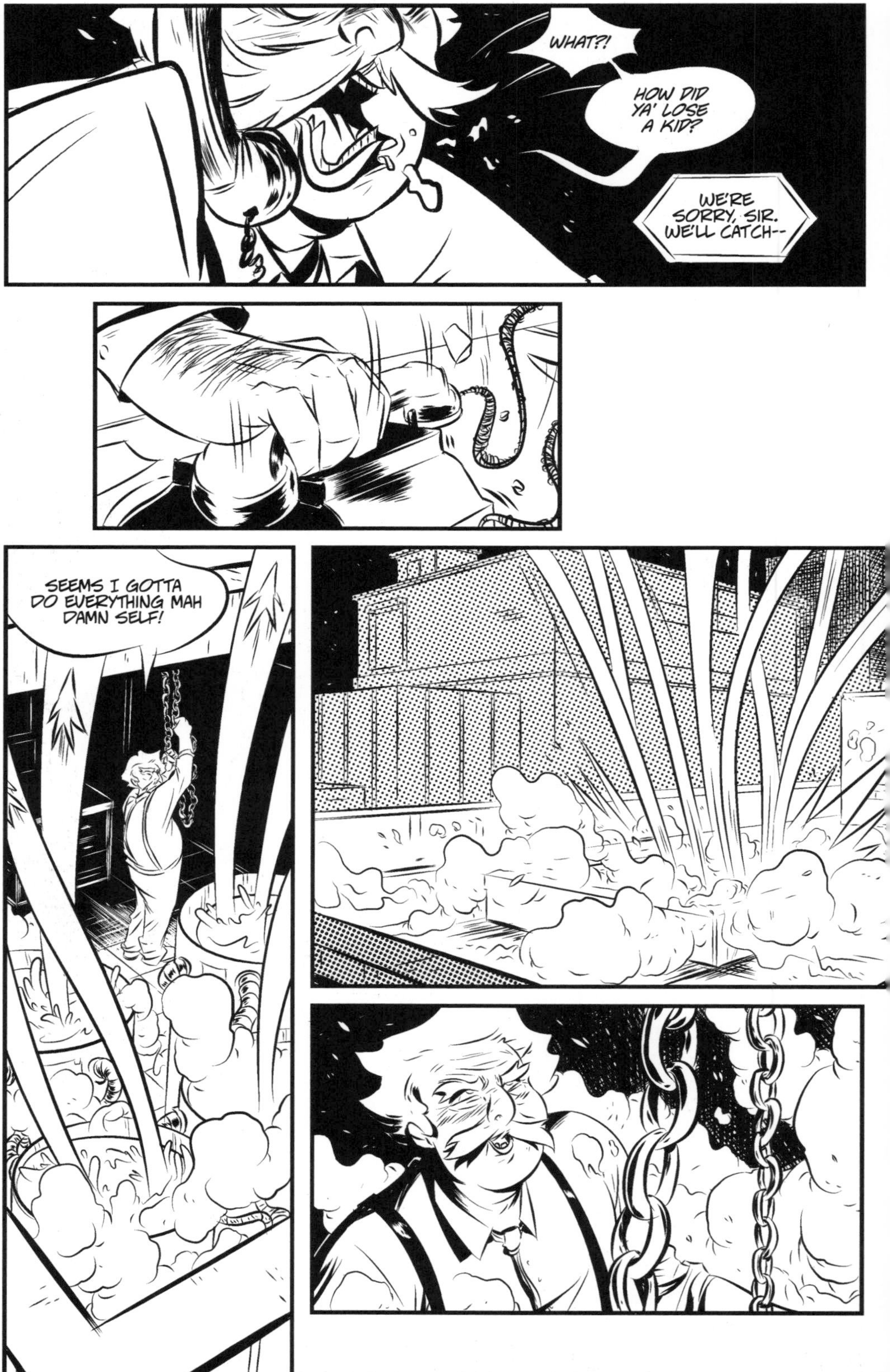
WHAT?!
HOW DID YA' LOSE A KID?
WE'RE SORRY, SIR. WE'LL CATCH--
SEEMS I GOTTA DO EVERYTHING MAH DAMN SELF!

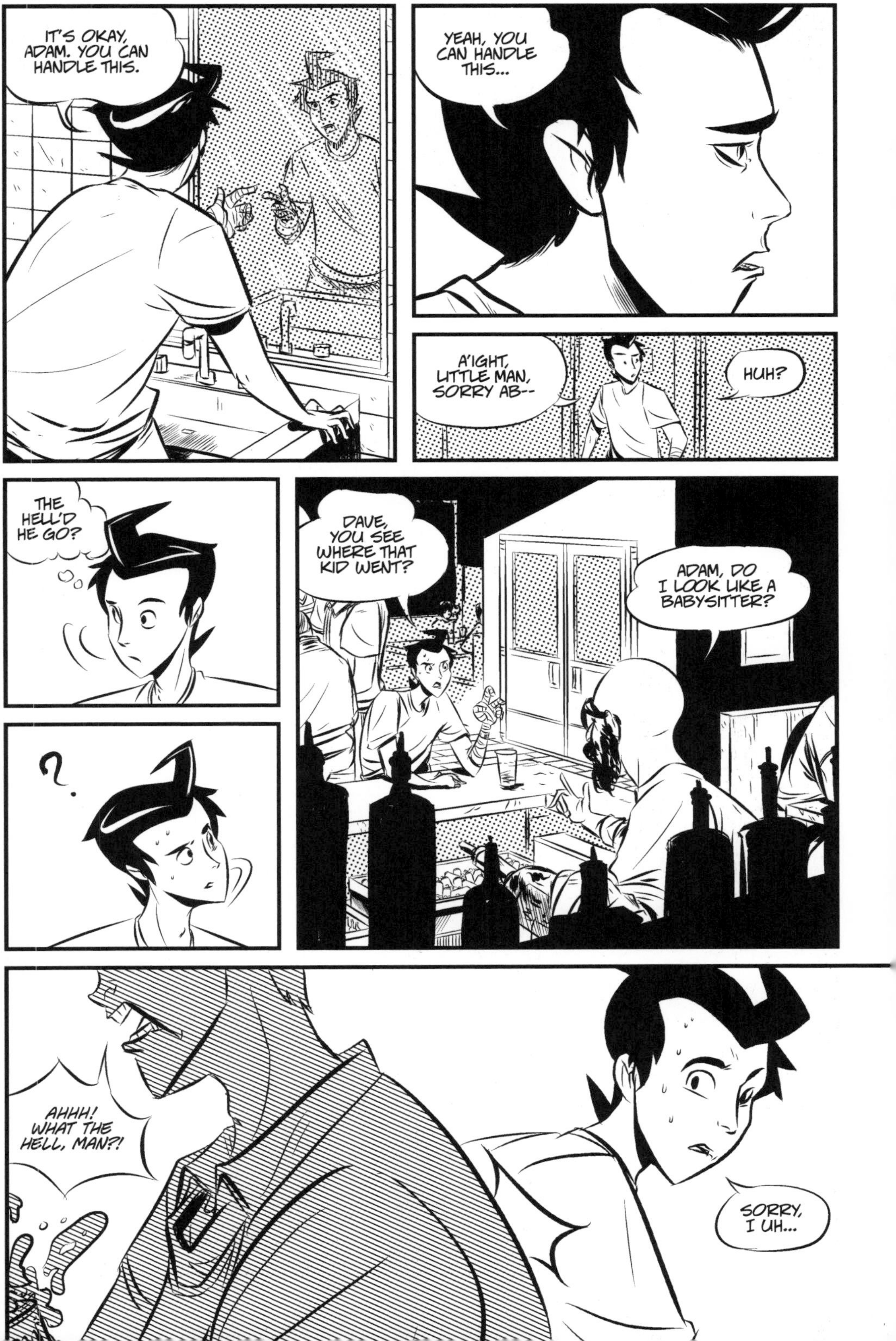
IT'S OKAY, ADAM. YOU CAN HANDLE THIS.
YEAH, YOU CAN HANDLE THIS...
A'IGHT, LITTLE MAN, SORRY AB--
HUH?
THE HELL'D HE GO?
?
DAVE, YOU SEE WHERE THAT KID WENT?
ADAM, DO I LOOK LIKE A BABYSITTER?
AHHH! WHAT THE HELL, MAN?!
SORRY, I UH...

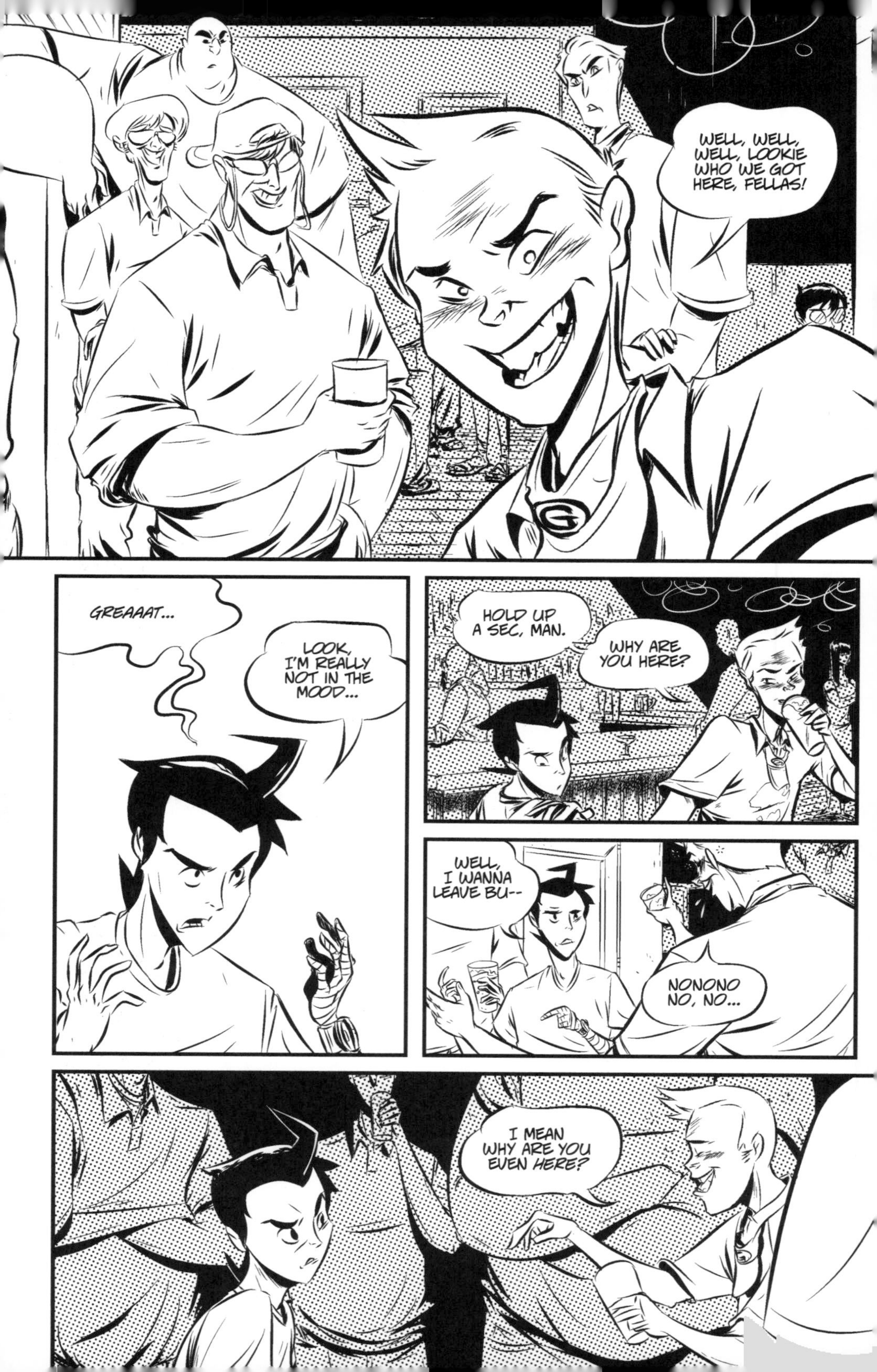
WELL, WELL, WELL, LOOKIE WHO WE GOT HERE, FELLAS!
GREAAAT...
LOOK, I'M REALLY NOT IN THE MOOD...
HOLD UP A SEC, MAN.
WHY ARE YOU HERE?
WELL, I WANNA LEAVE BU--
NONONO NO, NO...
I MEAN WHY ARE YOU EVEN HERE?

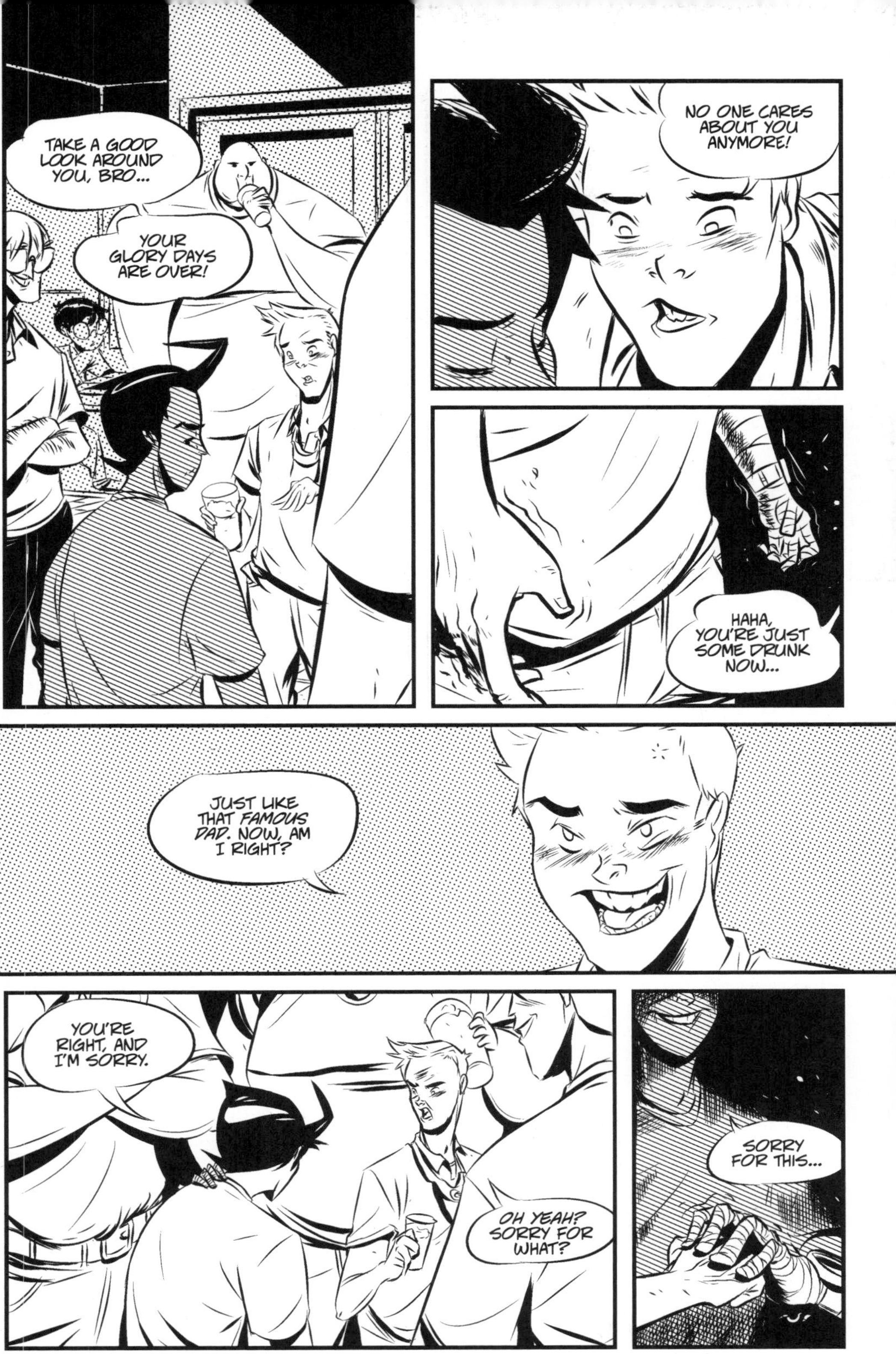
TAKE A GOOD LOOK AROUND YOU, BRO...
YOUR GLORY DAYS ARE OVER!
NO ONE CARES ABOUT YOU ANYMORE!
HAHA, YOU'RE JUST SOME DRUNK NOW...
JUST LIKE THAT *FAMOUS DAD*. NOW, AM I RIGHT?
YOU'RE RIGHT, AND I'M SORRY.
OH YEAH? SORRY FOR WHAT?
SORRY FOR THIS...

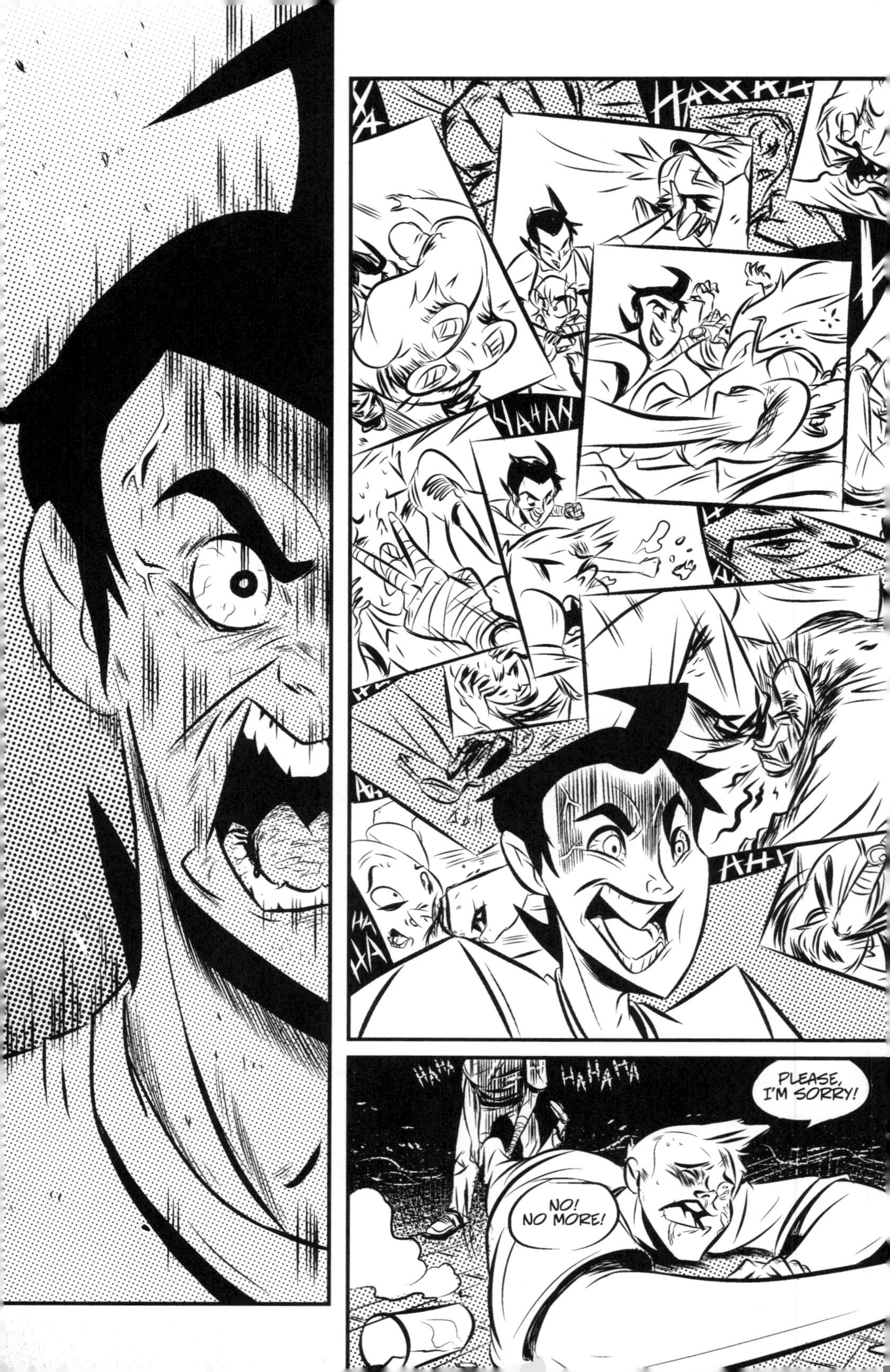
HAHAHA
PLEASE, I'M SORRY!
NO! NO MORE!

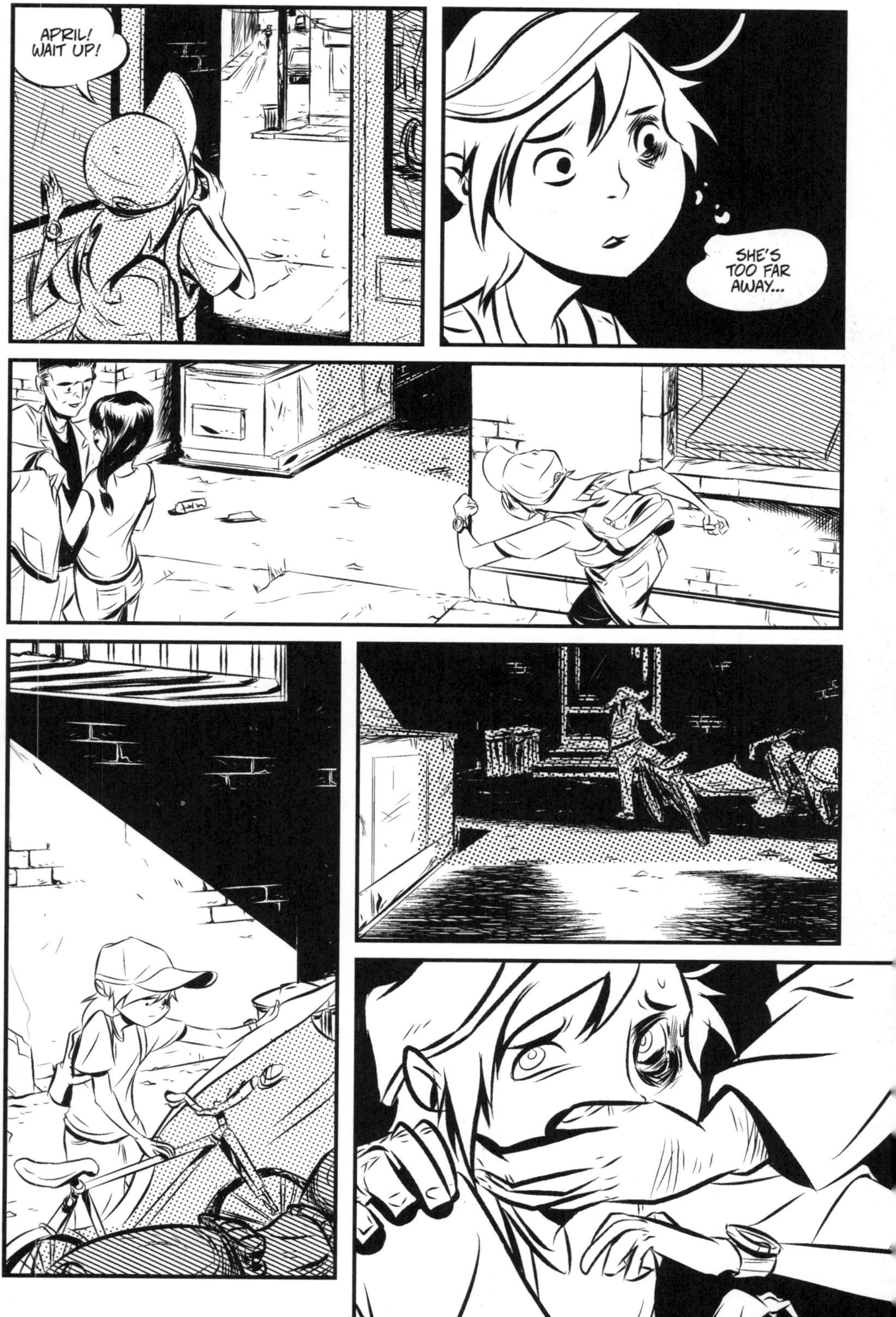
APRIL! WAIT UP!
SHE'S TOO FAR AWAY...

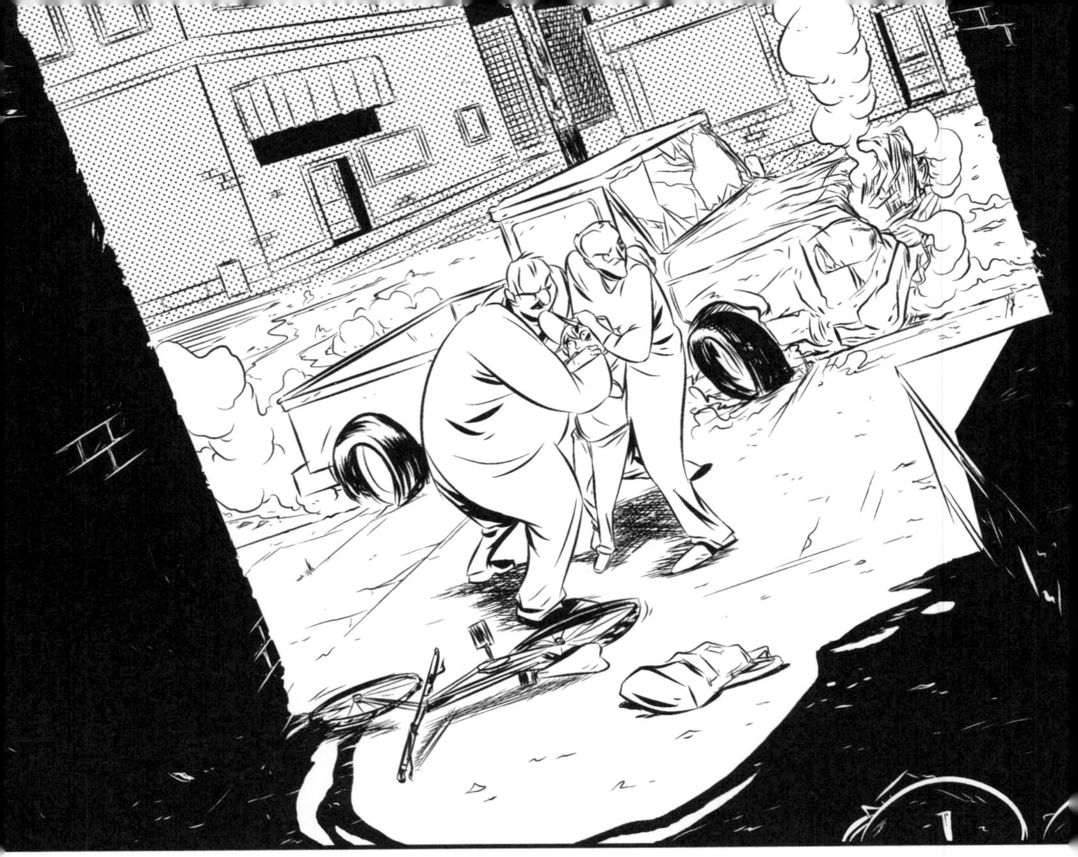

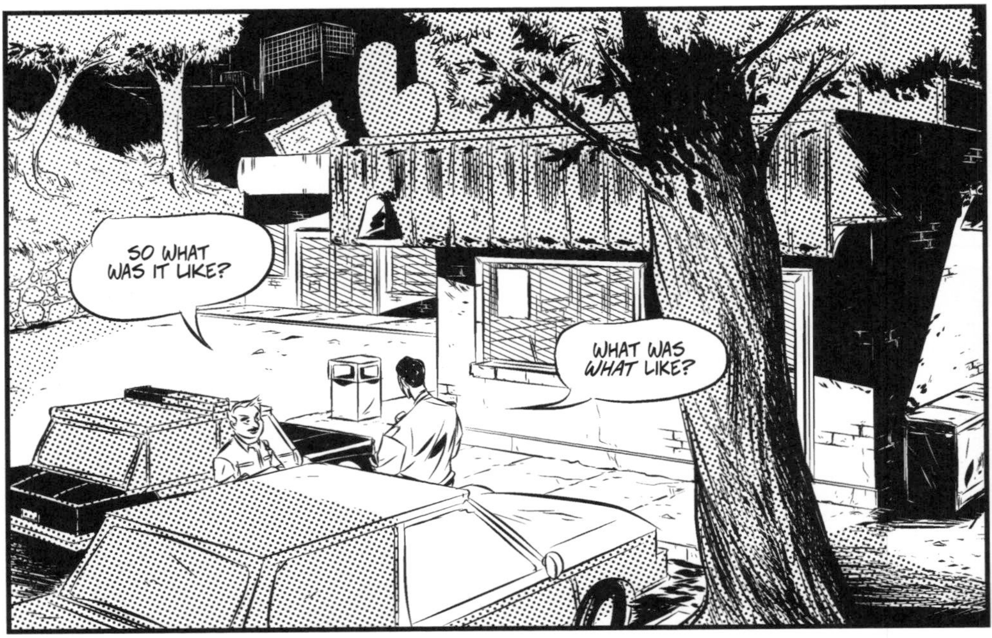
SO WHAT WAS IT LIKE?
WHAT WAS WHAT LIKE?

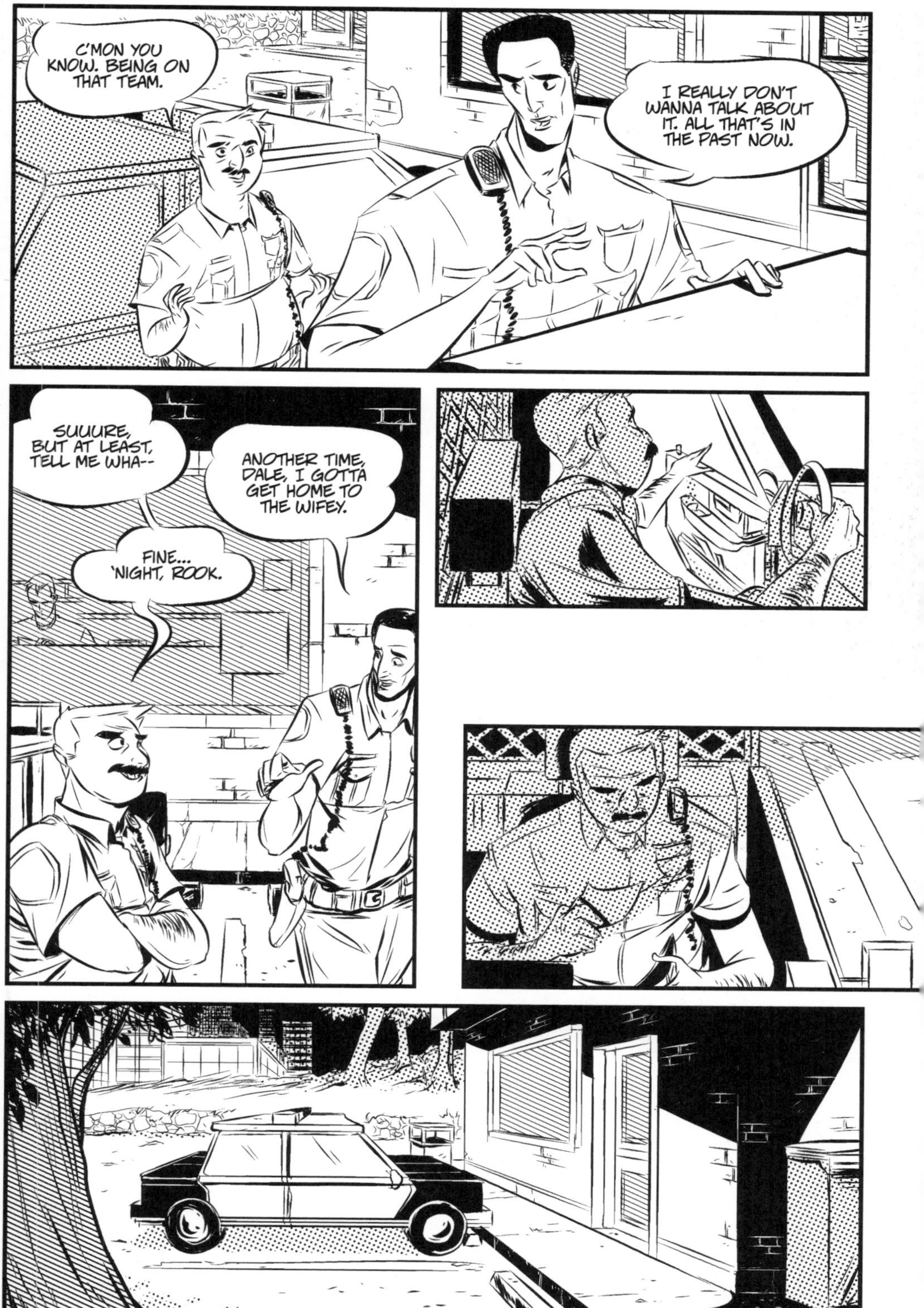
C'MON YOU KNOW. BEING ON THAT TEAM.
I REALLY DON'T WANNA TALK ABOUT IT. ALL THAT'S IN THE PAST NOW.
SUUURE, BUT AT LEAST, TELL ME WHA--
ANOTHER TIME, DALE, I GOTTA GET HOME TO THE WIFEY.
FINE... 'NIGHT, ROOK.

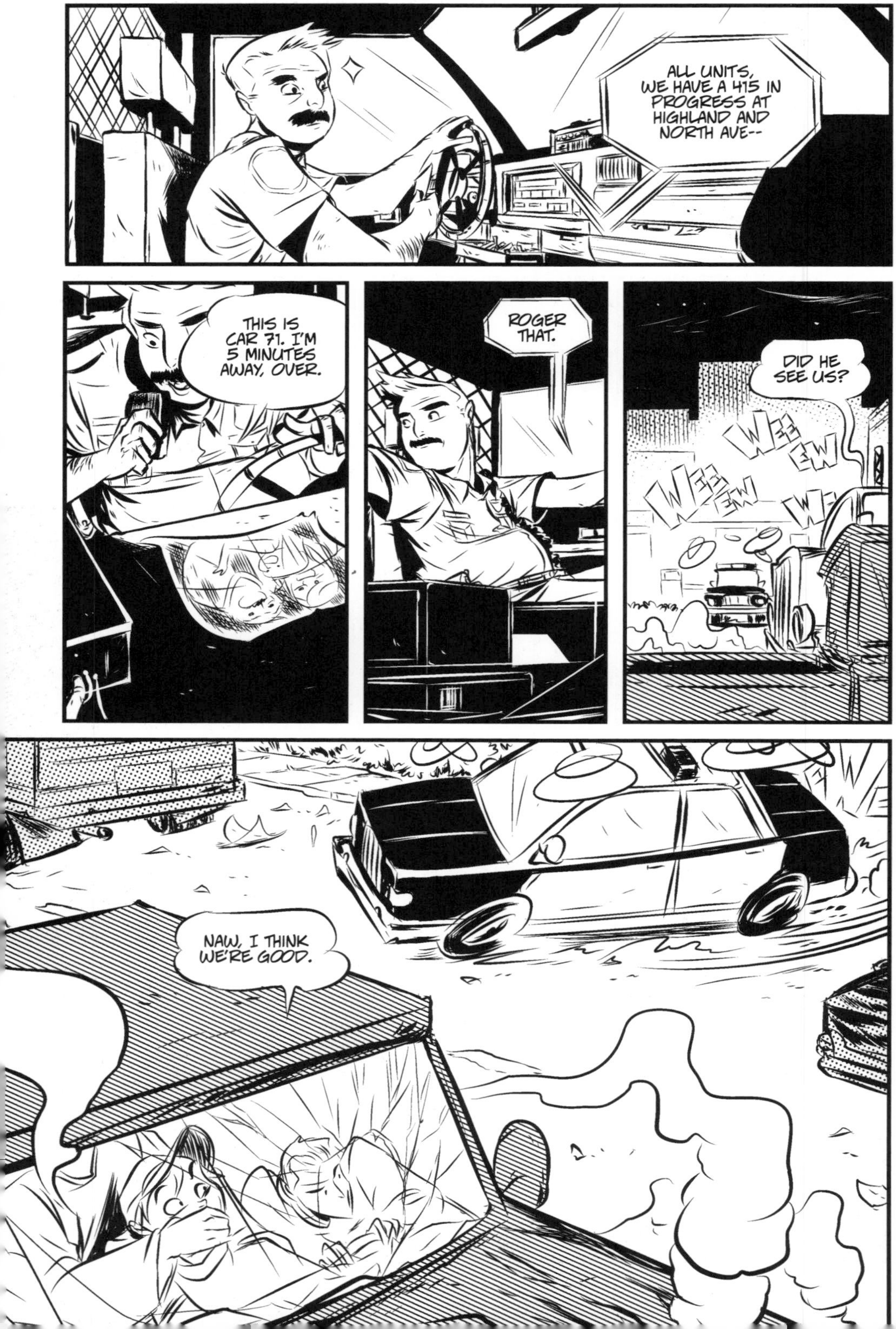
ALL UNITS, WE HAVE A 415 IN PROGRESS AT HIGHLAND AND NORTH AVE--
THIS IS CAR 71. I'M 5 MINUTES AWAY, OVER.
ROGER THAT.
DID HE SEE US?
NAW, I THINK WE'RE GOOD.

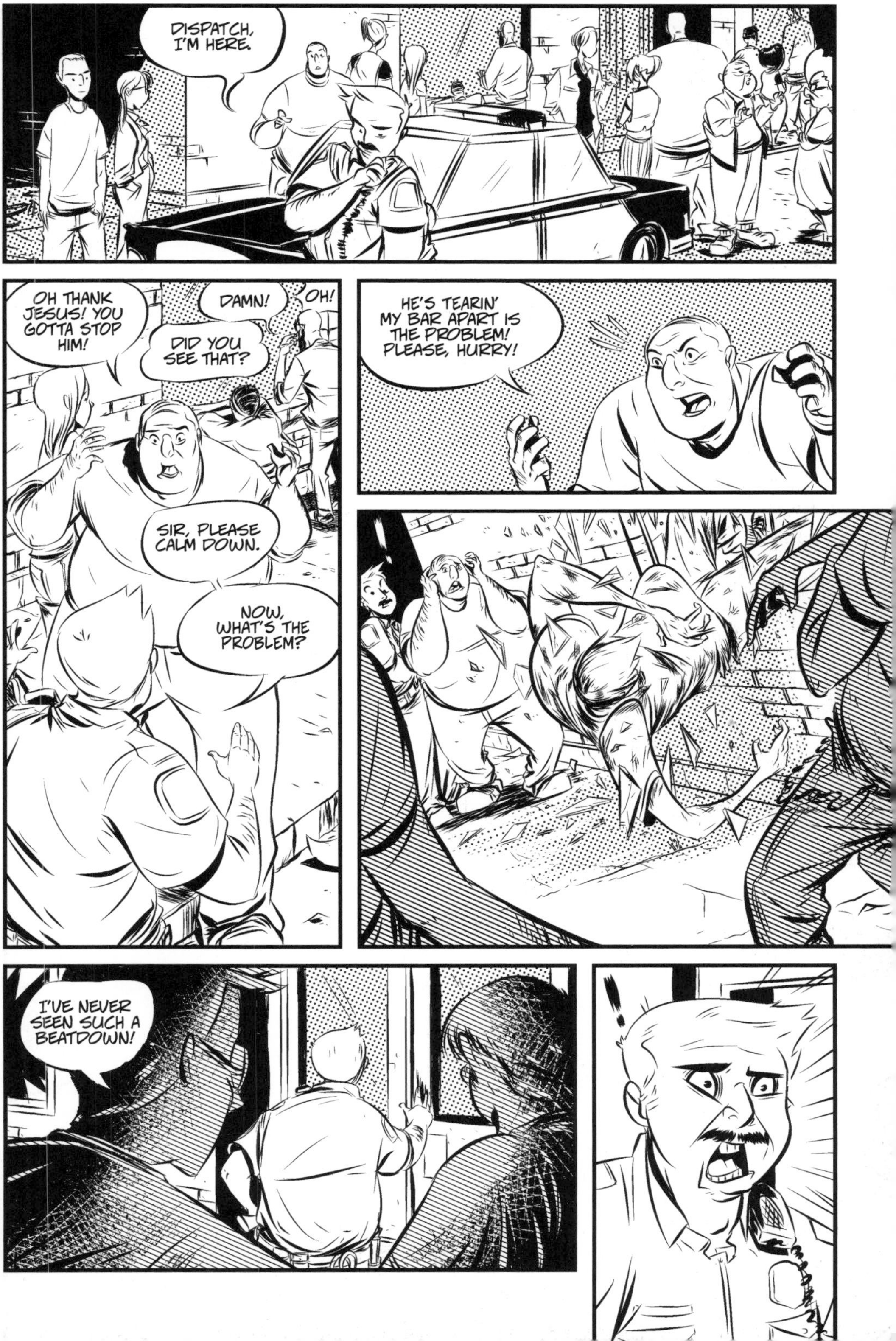
DISPATCH, I'M HERE.
OH THANK JESUS! YOU GOTTA STOP HIM!
DAMN!
OH!
DID YOU SEE THAT?
SIR, PLEASE CALM DOWN.
NOW, WHAT'S THE PROBLEM?
HE'S TEARIN' MY BAR APART IS THE PROBLEM! PLEASE, HURRY!
I'VE NEVER SEEN SUCH A BEATDOWN!

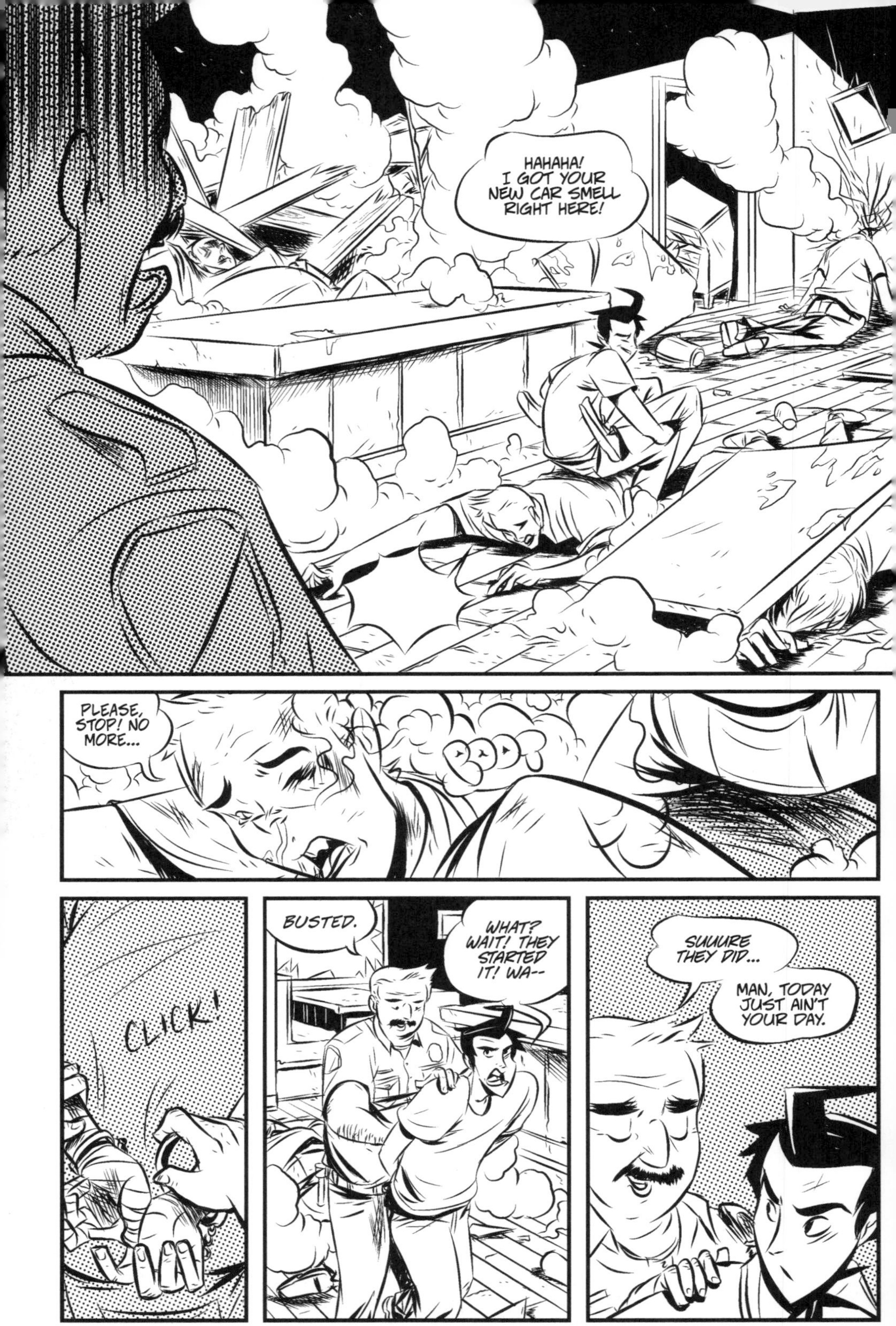
HAHAHA! I GOT YOUR NEW CAR SMELL RIGHT HERE!
PLEASE, STOP! NO MORE...
BRAAP
CLICK!
BUSTED.
WHAT? WAIT! THEY STARTED IT! WA--
SUUURE THEY DID...
MAN, TODAY JUST AIN'T YOUR DAY.

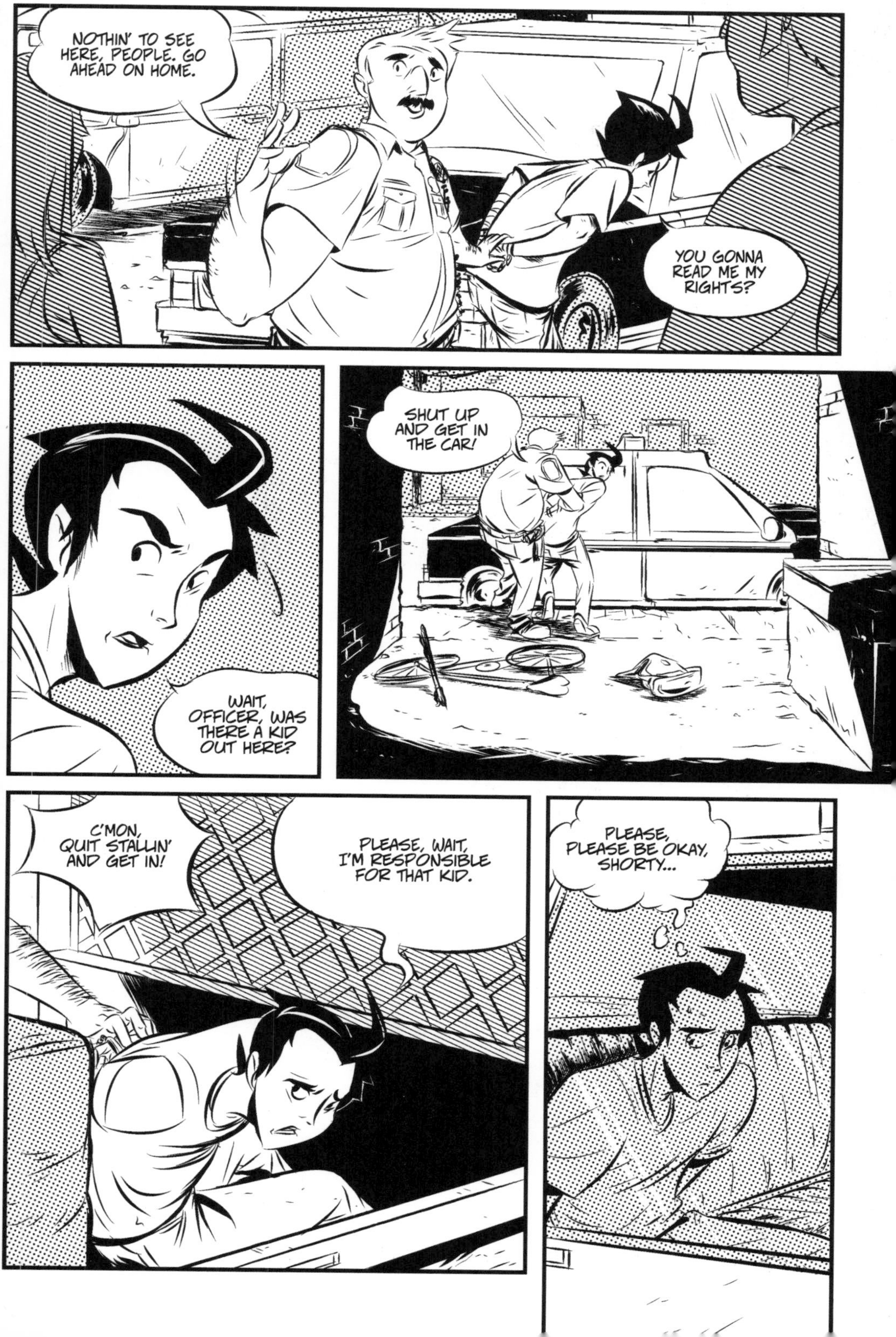
NOTHIN' TO SEE HERE, PEOPLE. GO AHEAD ON HOME.
YOU GONNA READ ME MY RIGHTS?
WAIT, OFFICER, WAS THERE A KID OUT HERE?
SHUT UP AND GET IN THE CAR!
C'MON, QUIT STALLIN' AND GET IN!
PLEASE, WAIT, I'M RESPONSIBLE FOR THAT KID.
PLEASE, PLEASE BE OKAY, SHORTY...

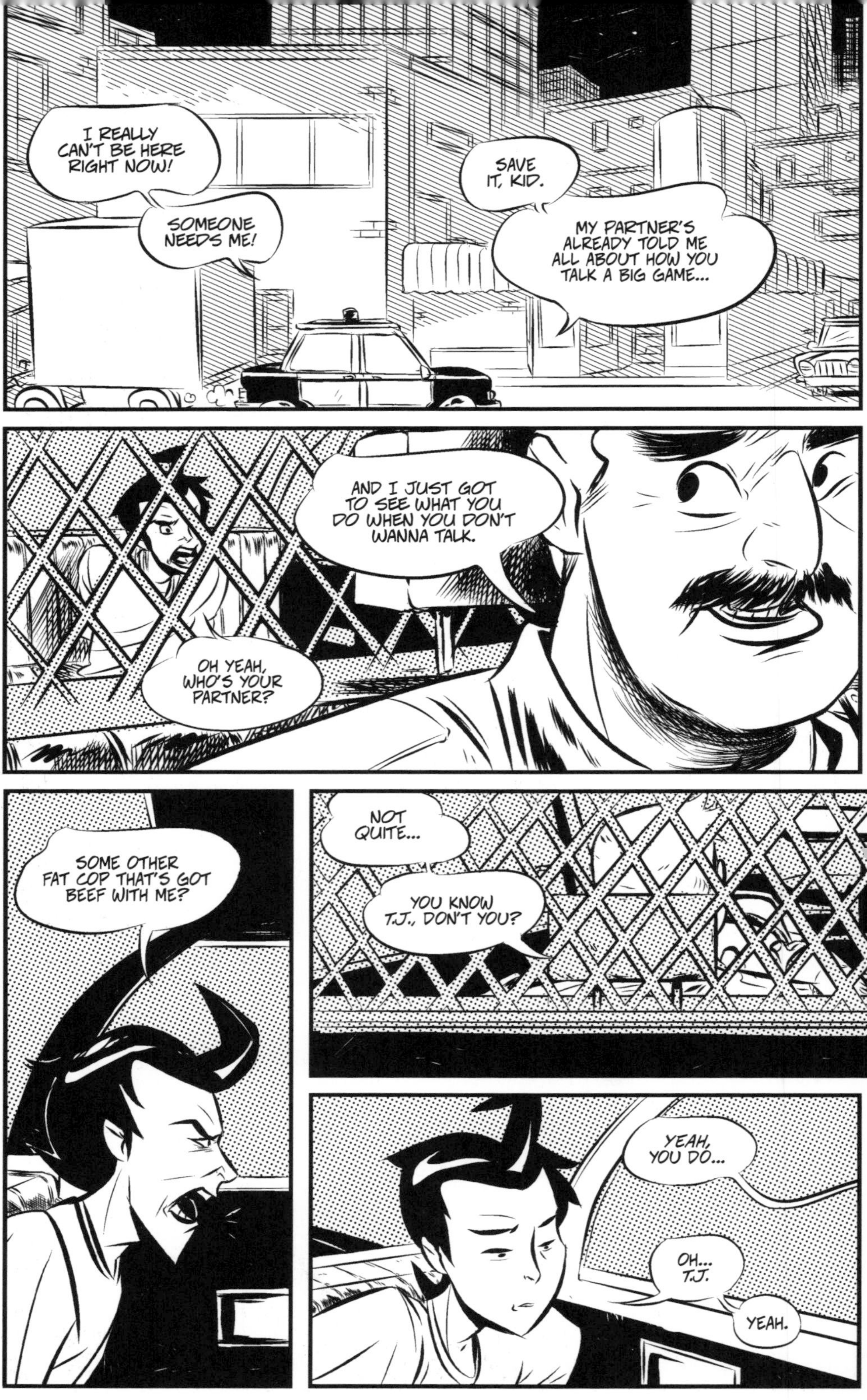
I REALLY CAN'T BE HERE RIGHT NOW!
SOMEONE NEEDS ME!
SAVE IT, KID.
MY PARTNER'S ALREADY TOLD ME ALL ABOUT HOW YOU TALK A BIG GAME...
AND I JUST GOT TO SEE WHAT YOU DO WHEN YOU DON'T WANNA TALK.
OH YEAH, WHO'S YOUR PARTNER?
SOME OTHER FAT COP THAT'S GOT BEEF WITH ME?
NOT QUITE...
YOU KNOW T.J., DON'T YOU?
YEAH, YOU DO...
OH... T.J.
YEAH.

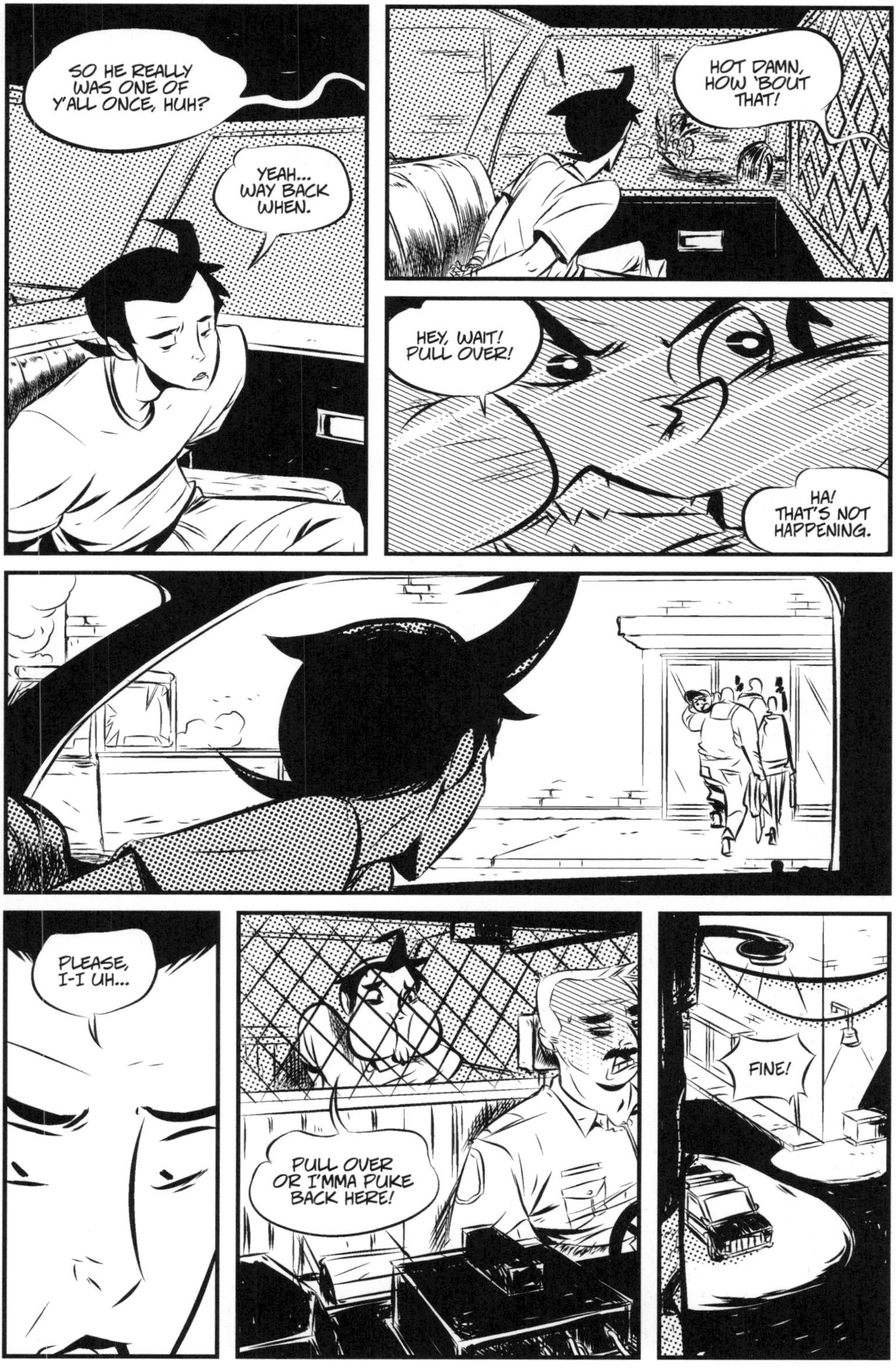
SO HE REALLY WAS ONE OF Y'ALL ONCE, HUH?
YEAH... WAY BACK WHEN.
HOT DAMN, HOW 'BOUT THAT!
HEY, WAIT! PULL OVER!
HA! THAT'S NOT HAPPENING.
PLEASE, I-I UH...
PULL OVER OR I'MMA PUKE BACK HERE!
FINE!

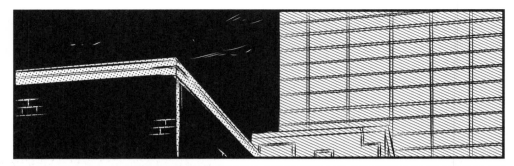

C'MON NOW...

CAN'T BELIEVE I'M DOING THIS.

A'IGHT, NO FUNNY BUSINESS.

THANKS, THIS'LL ONLY TAKE A SEC.

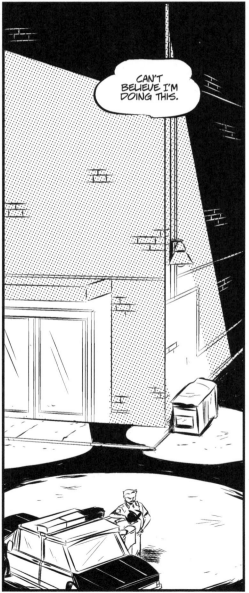

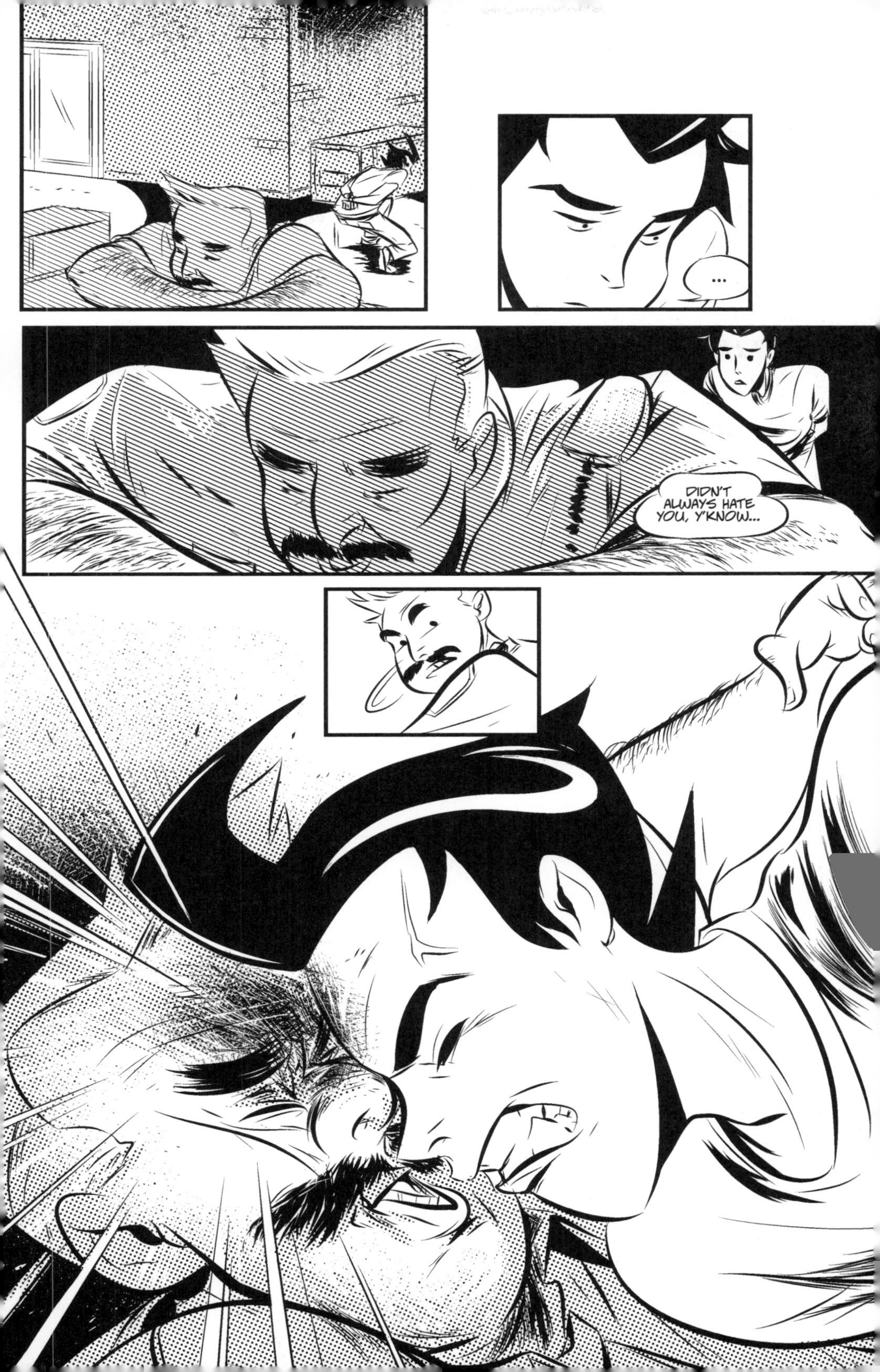
...
DIDN'T ALWAYS HATE YOU, Y'KNOW...

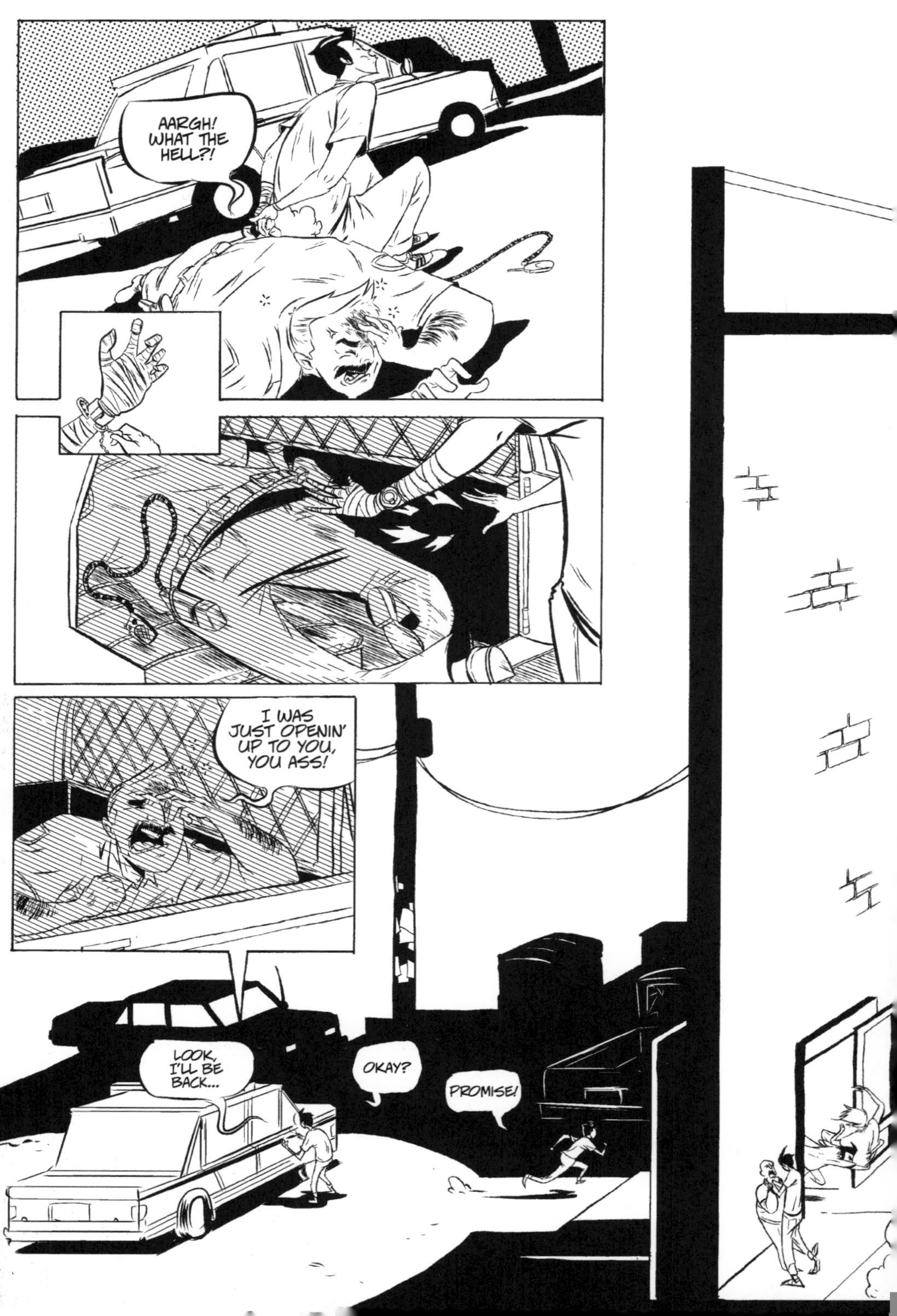
AARGH! WHAT THE HELL?!
I WAS JUST OPENIN' UP TO YOU, YOU ASS!
LOOK, I'LL BE BACK...
OKAY?
PROMISE!

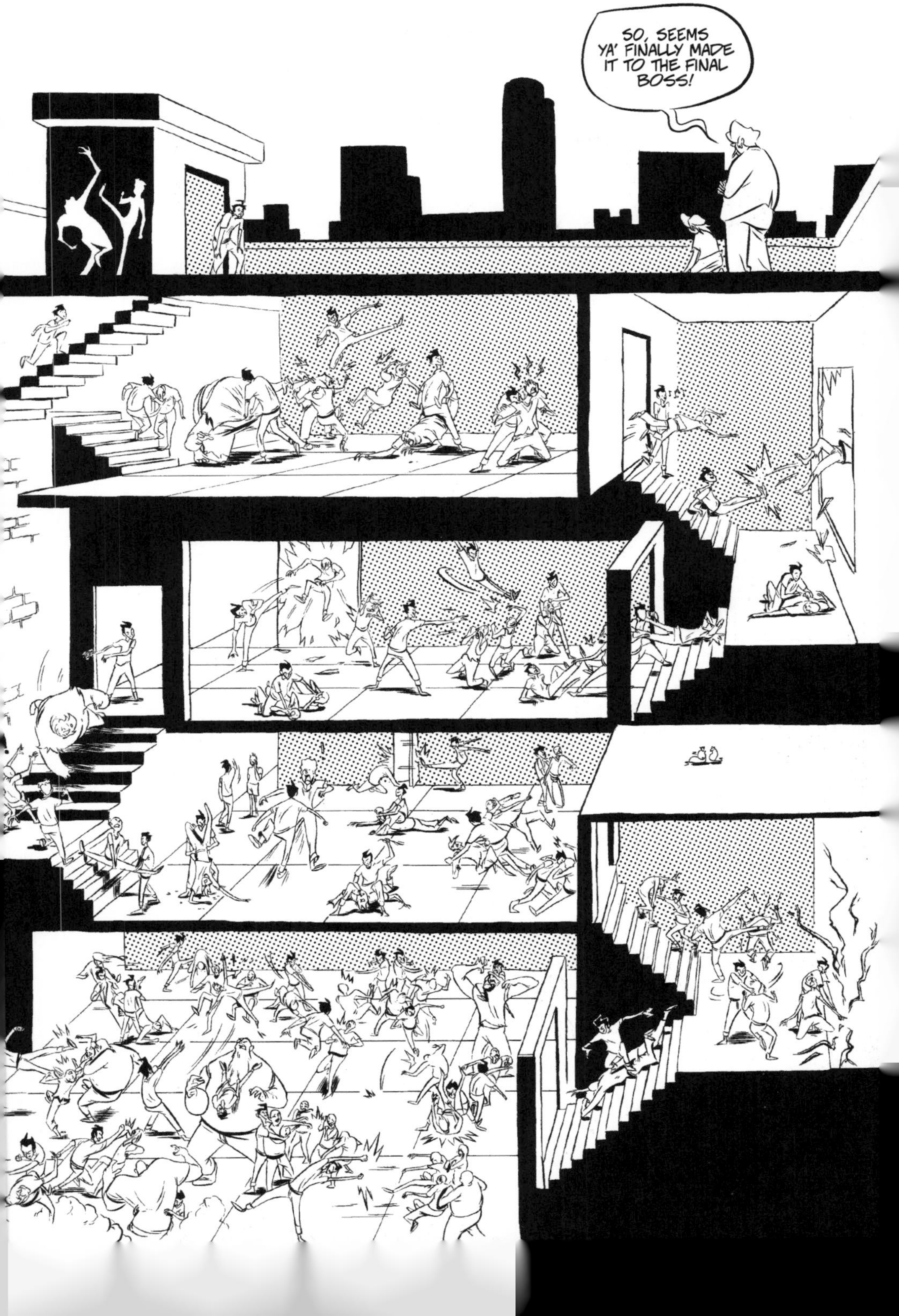
SO, SEEMS YA' FINALLY MADE IT TO THE FINAL BOSS!

NOW, WHY AIN'T YOU DEAD YET, BOY?

HA! I THINK I CAN HANDLE A FEW DOZEN REDNECKS!

HAWHAW! NOW NOW, THAT WAS JUST THE OPENING ACT, SON.

WHAAT?!

WHERE? I DON'T SEE ANYONE ELSE HERE?

LOOK UP. SECOND ROUND'S COMING...

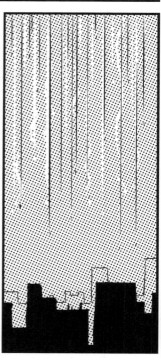

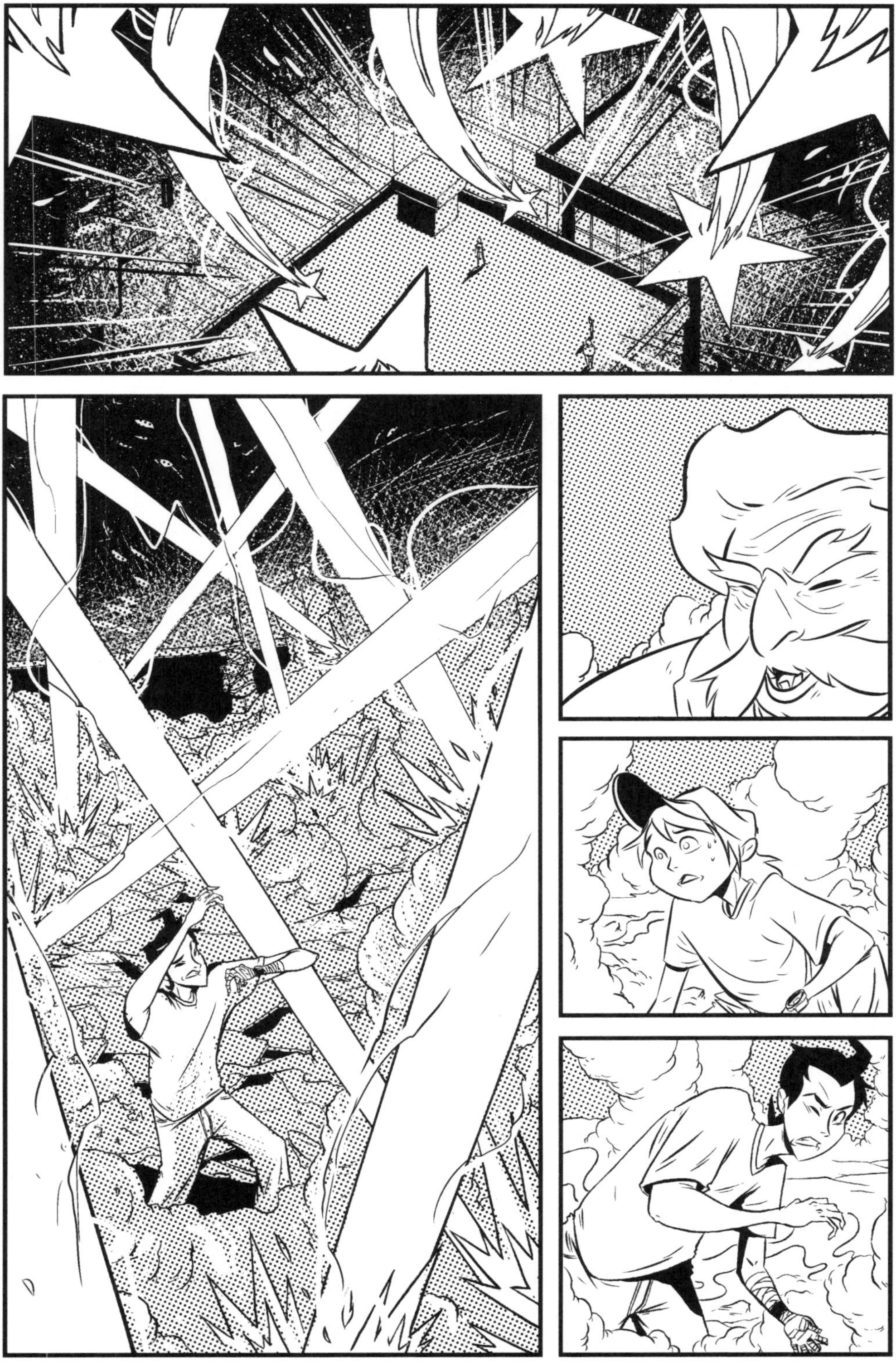

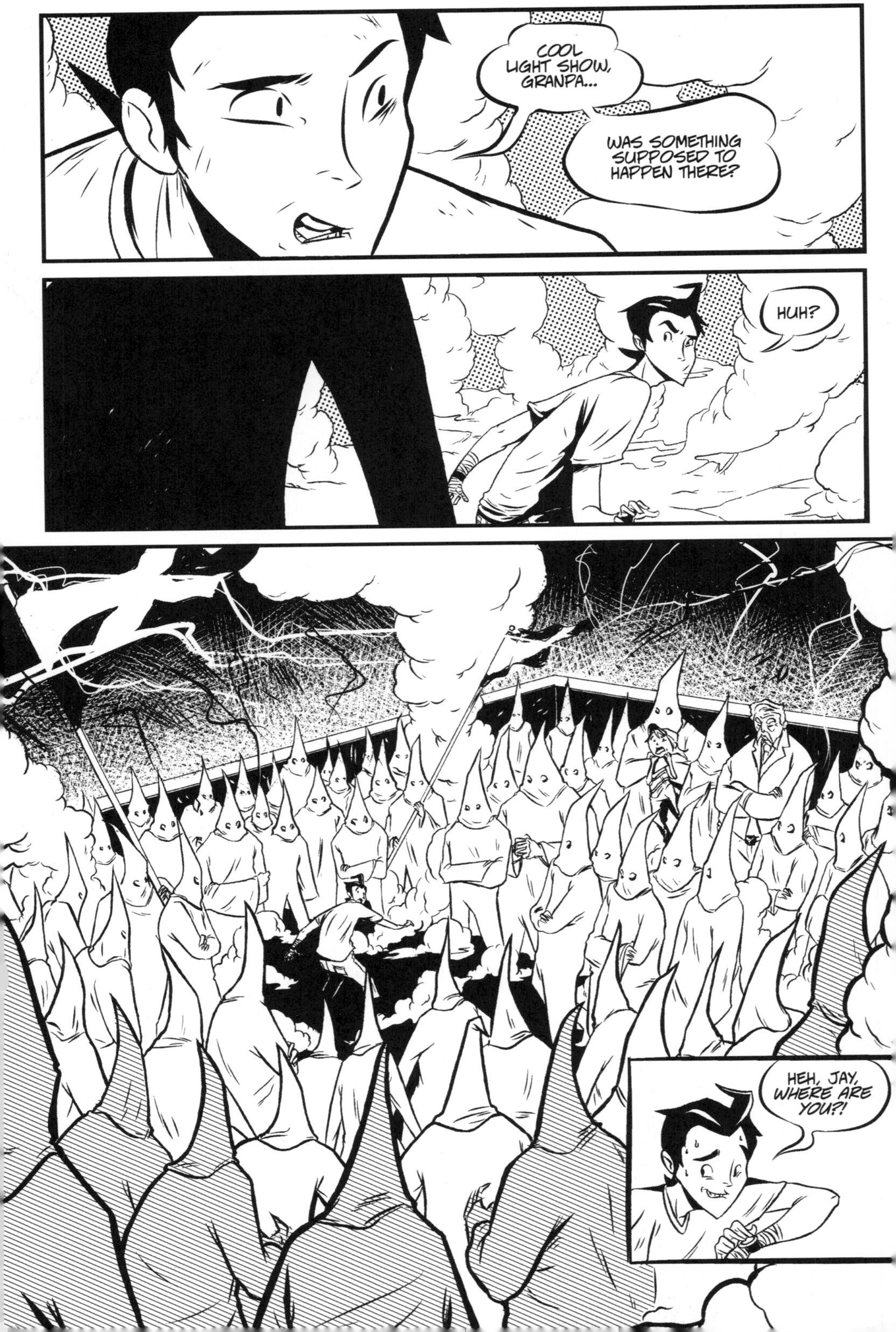
COOL LIGHT SHOW, GRANPA...
WAS SOMETHING SUPPOSED TO HAPPEN THERE?
HUH?
HEH, JAY, WHERE ARE YOU?!

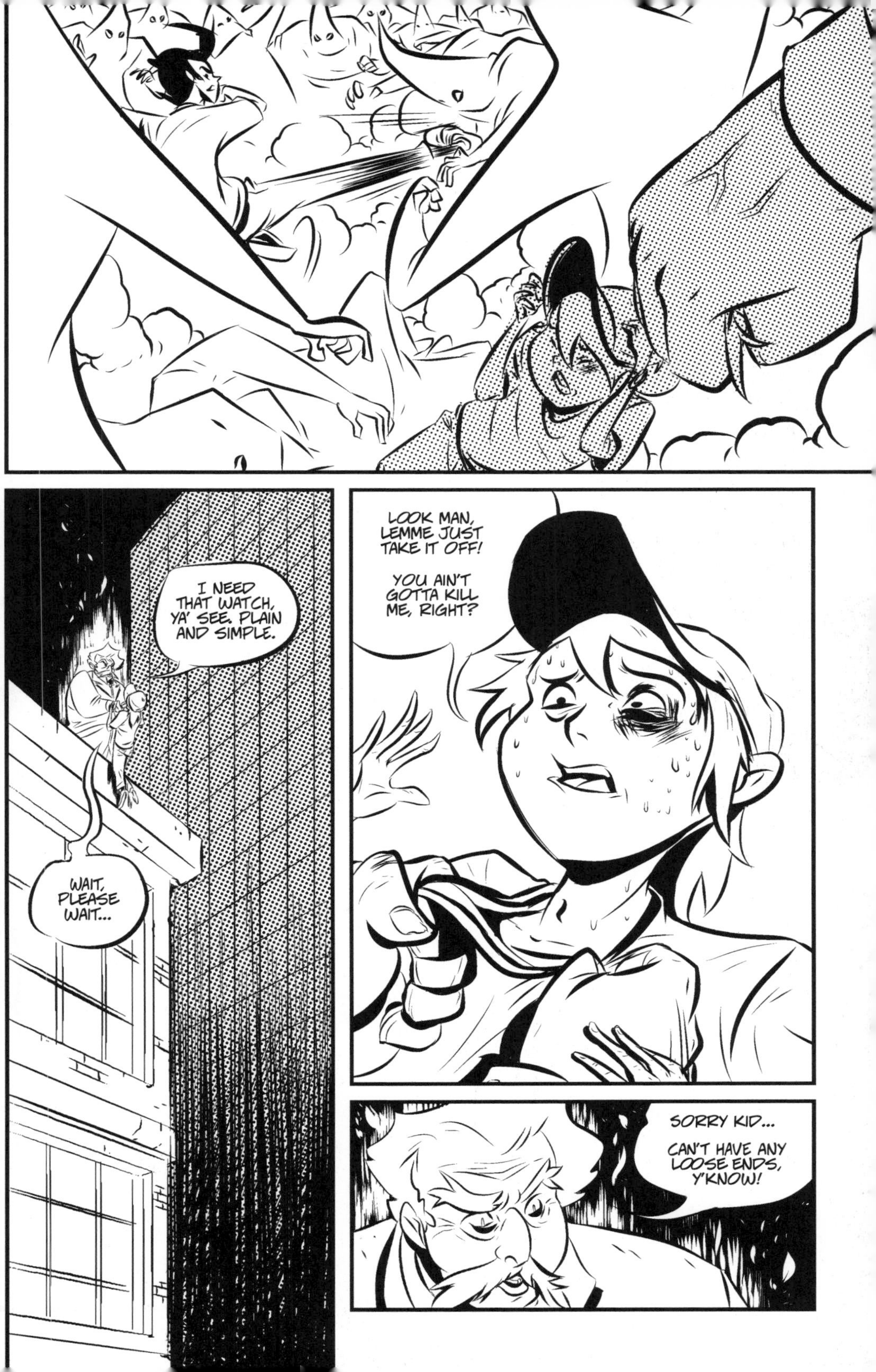
I NEED THAT WATCH, YA' SEE. PLAIN AND SIMPLE.
WAIT, PLEASE WAIT...
LOOK MAN, LEMME JUST TAKE IT OFF!
YOU AIN'T GOTTA KILL ME, RIGHT?
SORRY KID...
CAN'T HAVE ANY LOOSE ENDS, Y'KNOW!

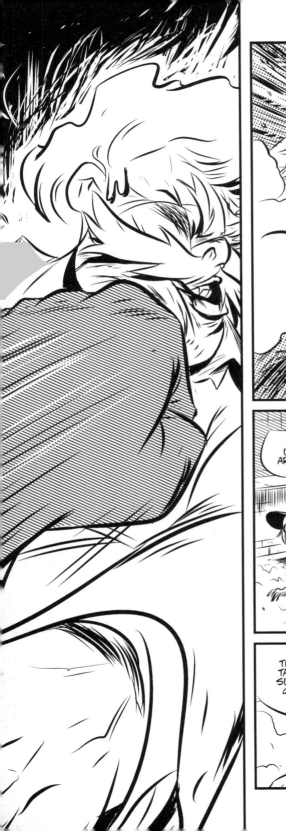

HUH? W-WHO ARE YOU?

THAT'S FOR HITTIN' ME WITH YOUR DAMN TRUCK, FOOL!

THANKS FOR TAKIN' YOUR SWEET TIME, OLD MAN!

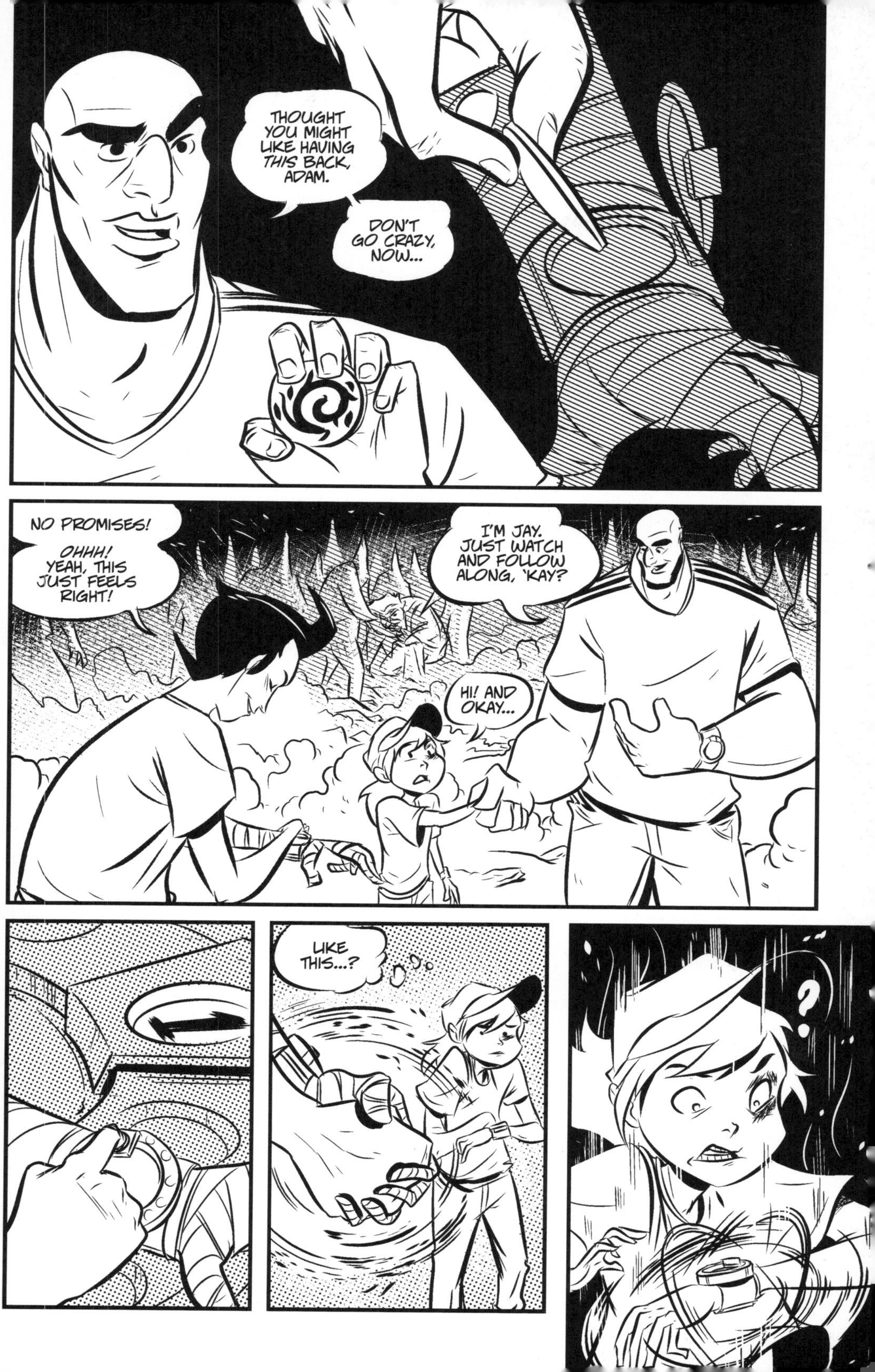
THOUGHT YOU MIGHT LIKE HAVING THIS BACK, ADAM.
DON'T GO CRAZY, NOW...
NO PROMISES!
OHHH! YEAH, THIS JUST FEELS RIGHT!
I'M JAY. JUST WATCH AND FOLLOW ALONG, 'KAY?
HI! AND OKAY...
LIKE THIS...?
?

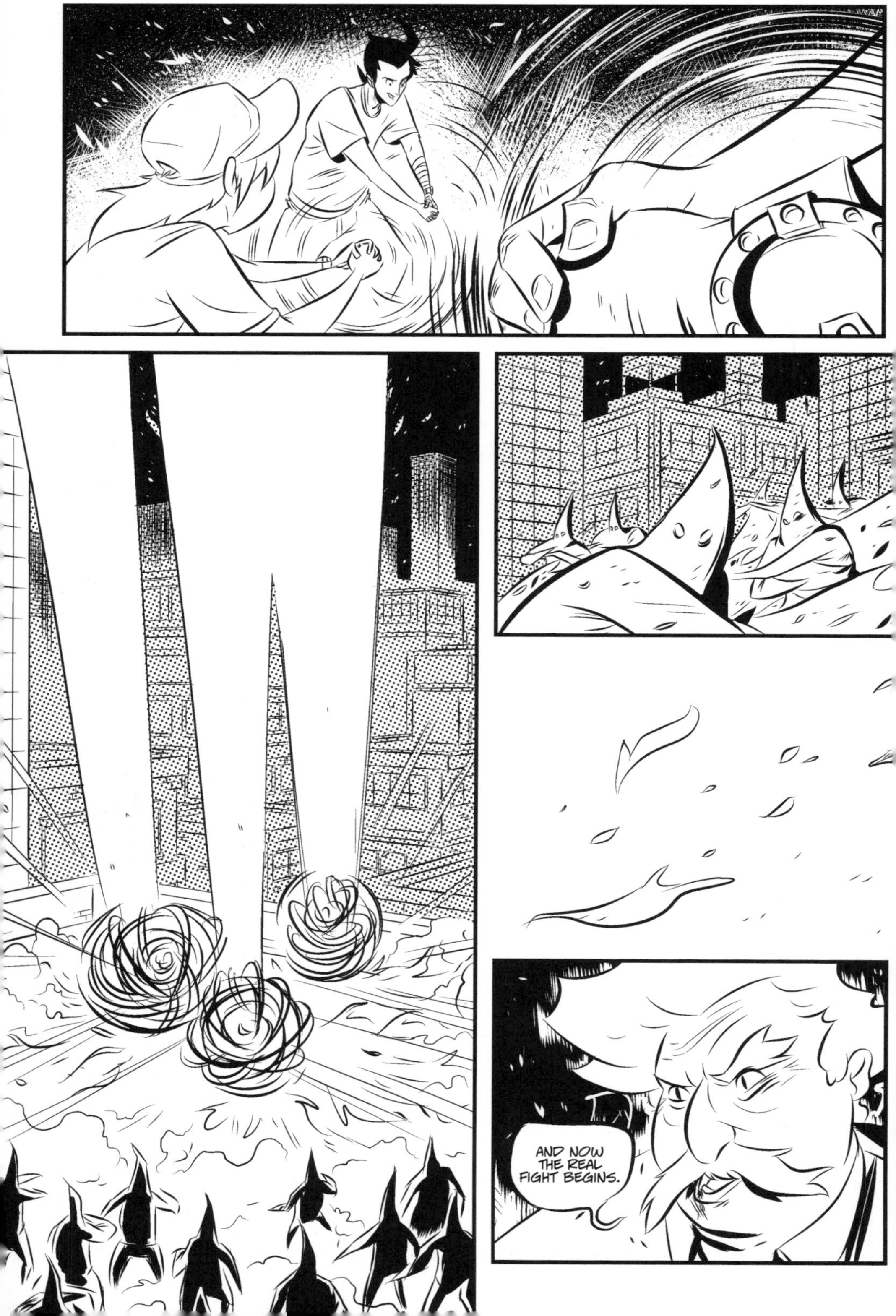
AND NOW THE REAL FIGHT BEGINS.

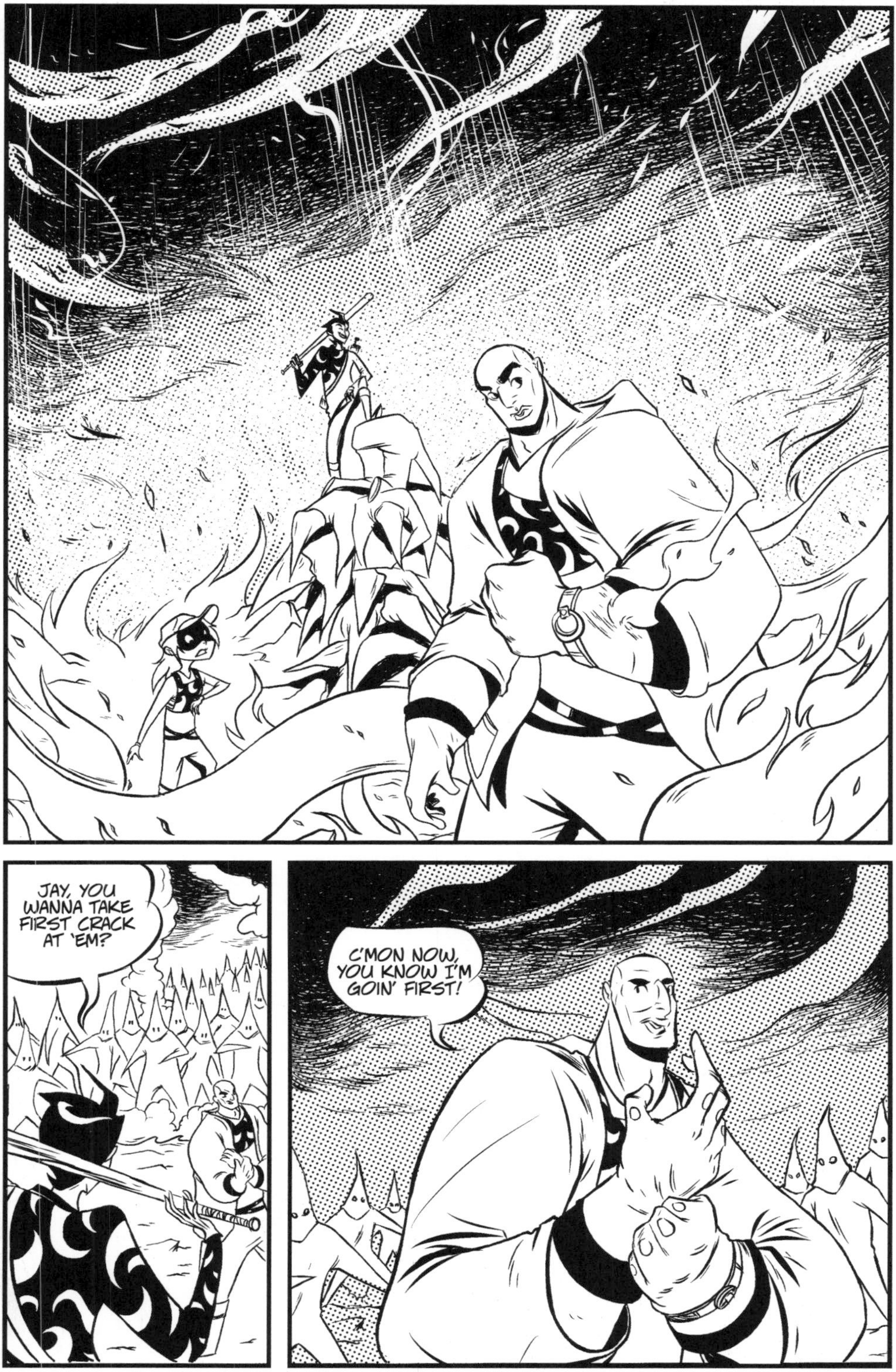
JAY, YOU WANNA TAKE FIRST CRACK AT 'EM?
C'MON NOW, YOU KNOW I'M GOIN' FIRST!

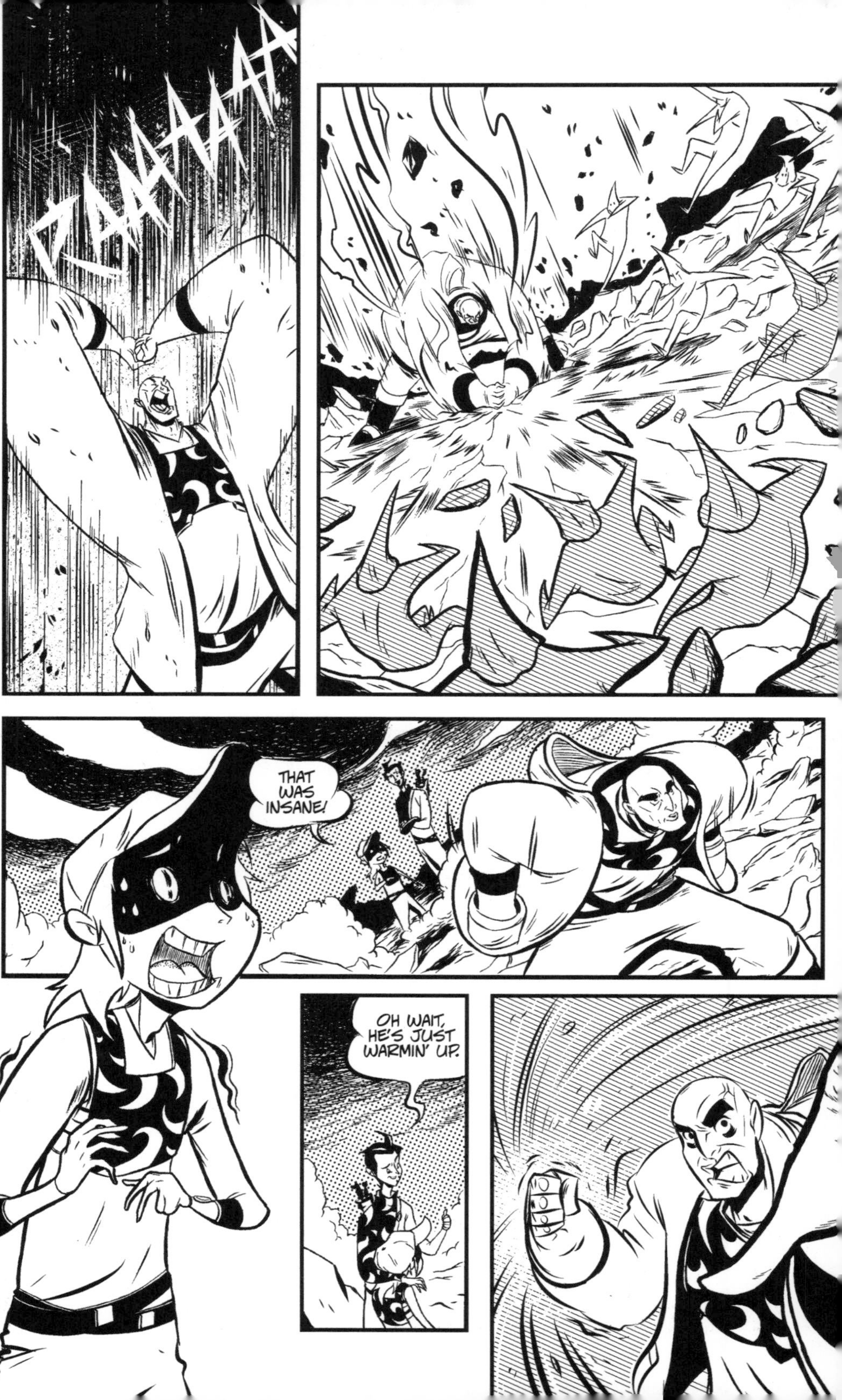
CRAAAAAA
THAT WAS INSANE!
OH WAIT, HE'S JUST WARMIN' UP.

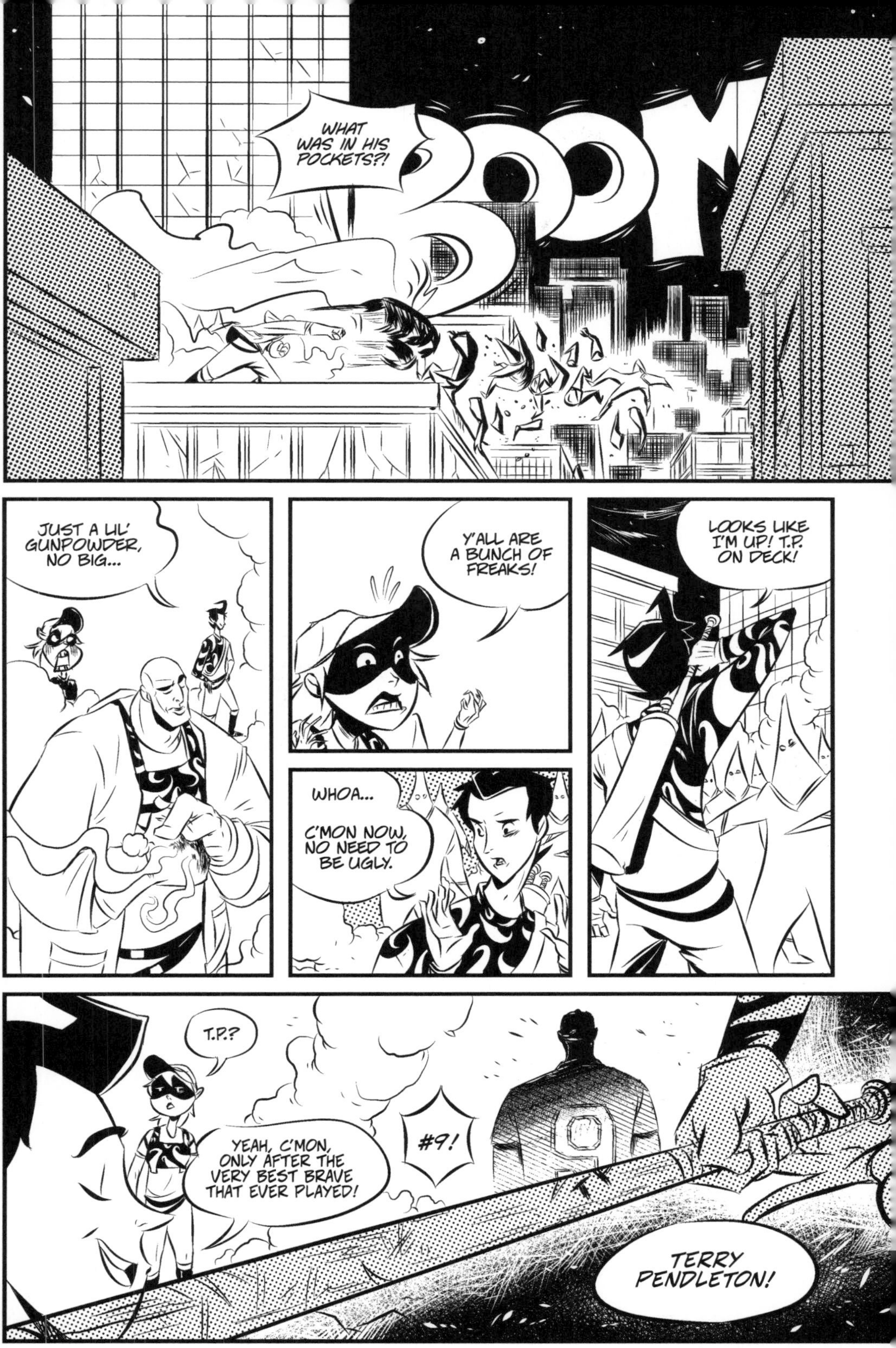
WHAT WAS IN HIS POCKETS?!
BOOM
JUST A LIL' GUNPOWDER, NO BIG...
Y'ALL ARE A BUNCH OF FREAKS!
WHOA...
C'MON NOW, NO NEED TO BE UGLY.
LOOKS LIKE I'M UP! T.P. ON DECK!
T.P.?
YEAH, C'MON, ONLY AFTER THE VERY BEST BRAVE THAT EVER PLAYED!
#9!
TERRY PENDLETON!

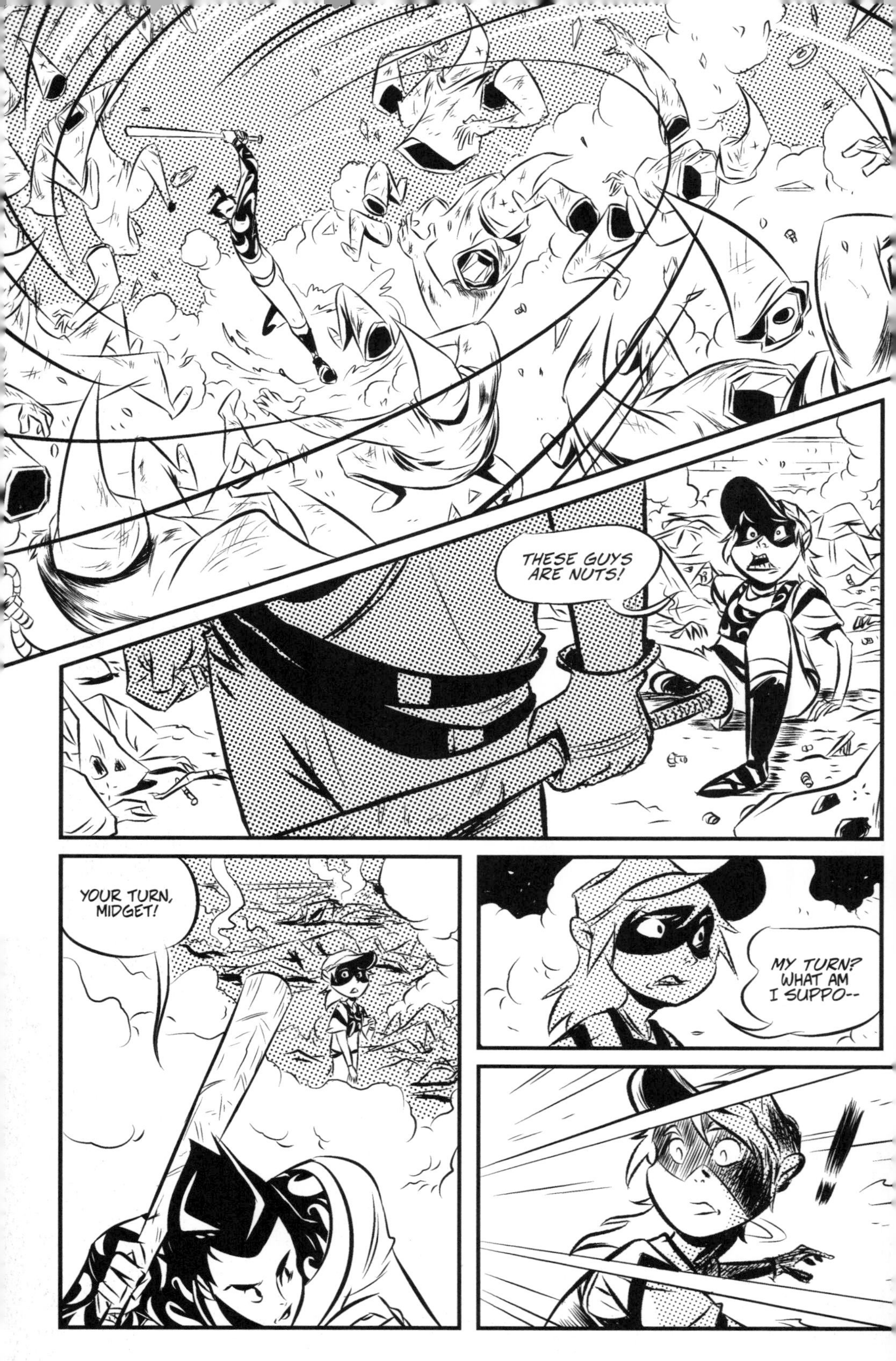
THESE GUYS ARE NUTS!
YOUR TURN, MIDGET!
MY TURN? WHAT AM I SUPPO--

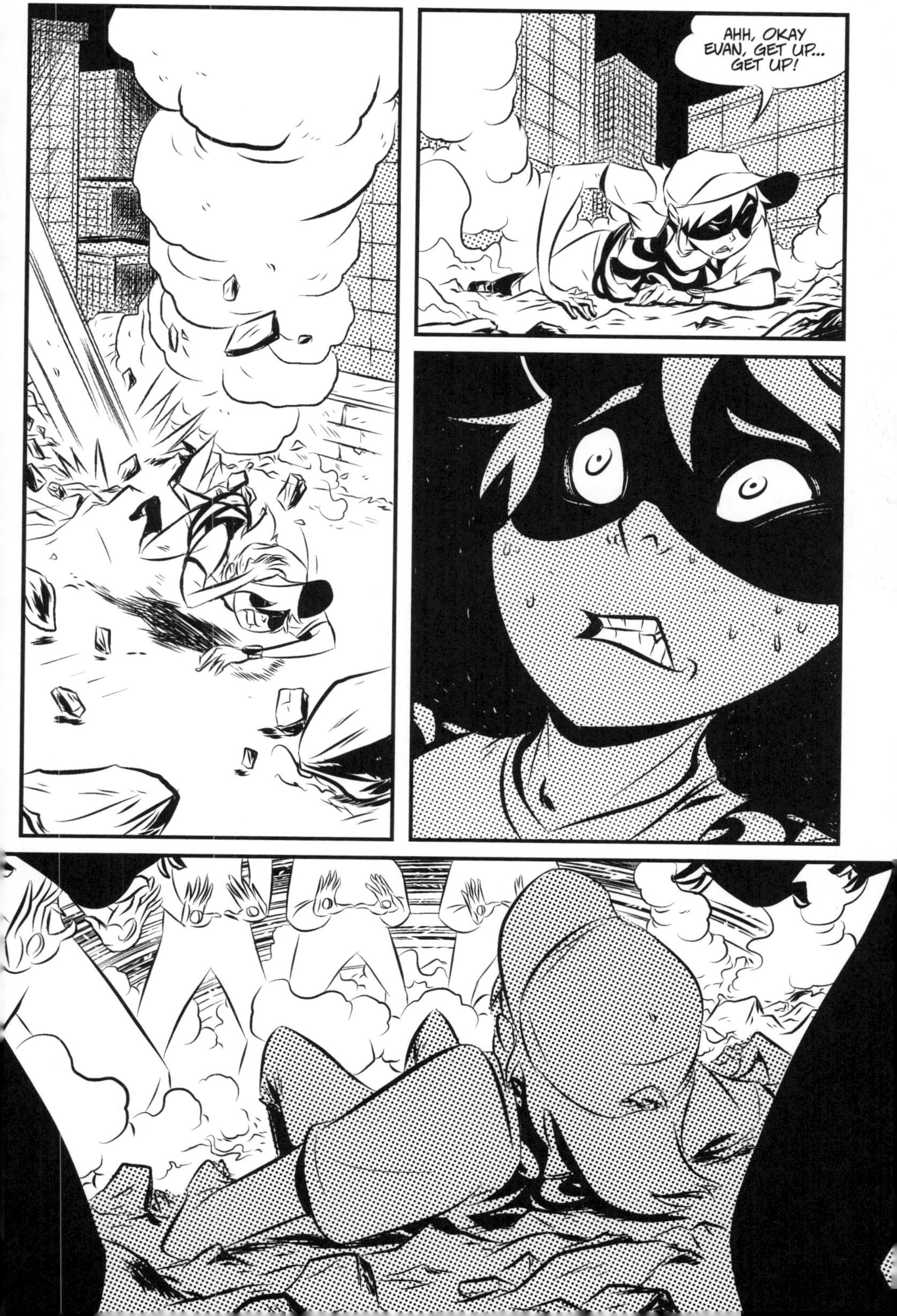
AHH, OKAY EVAN, GET UP... GET UP!

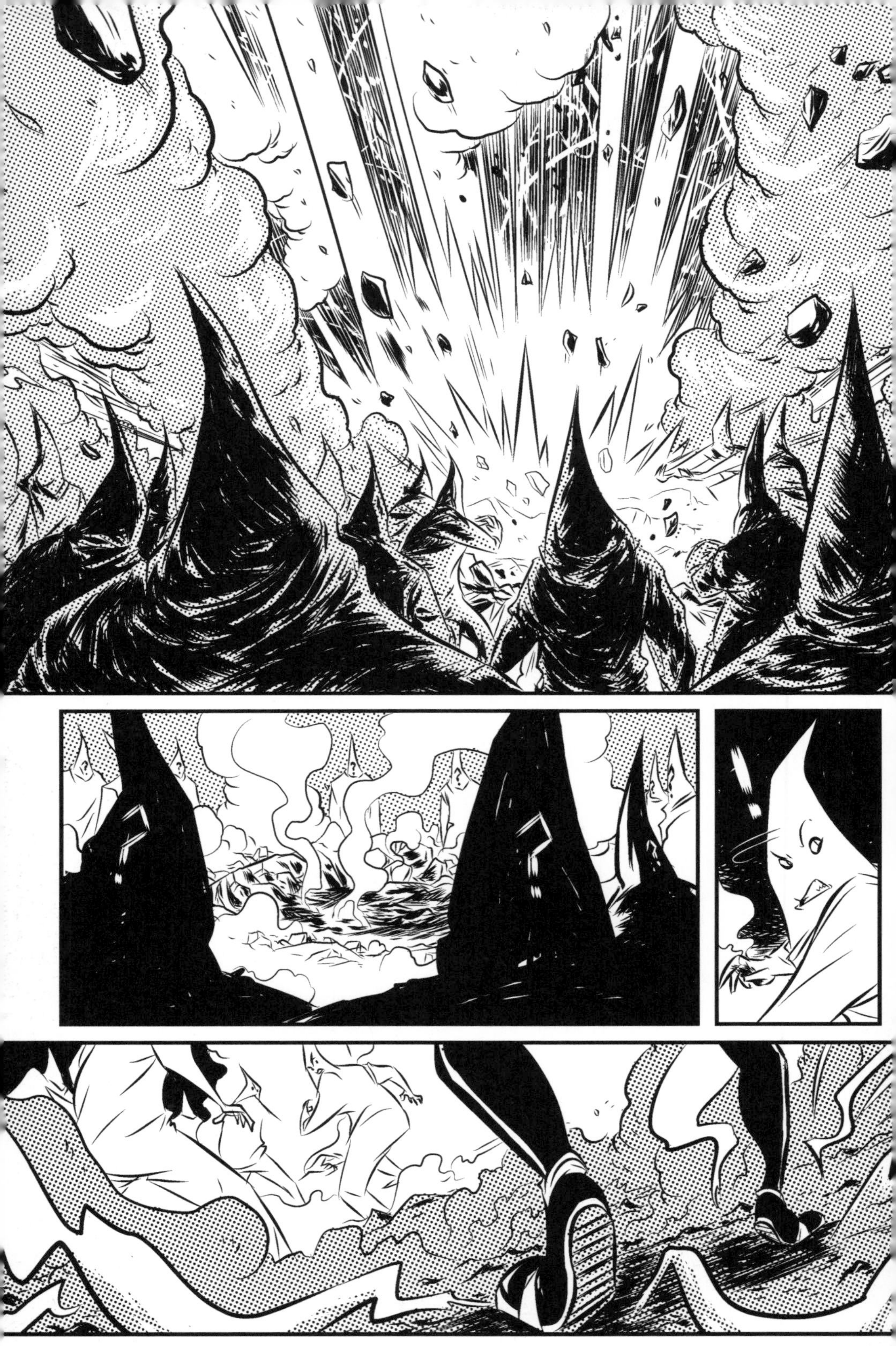

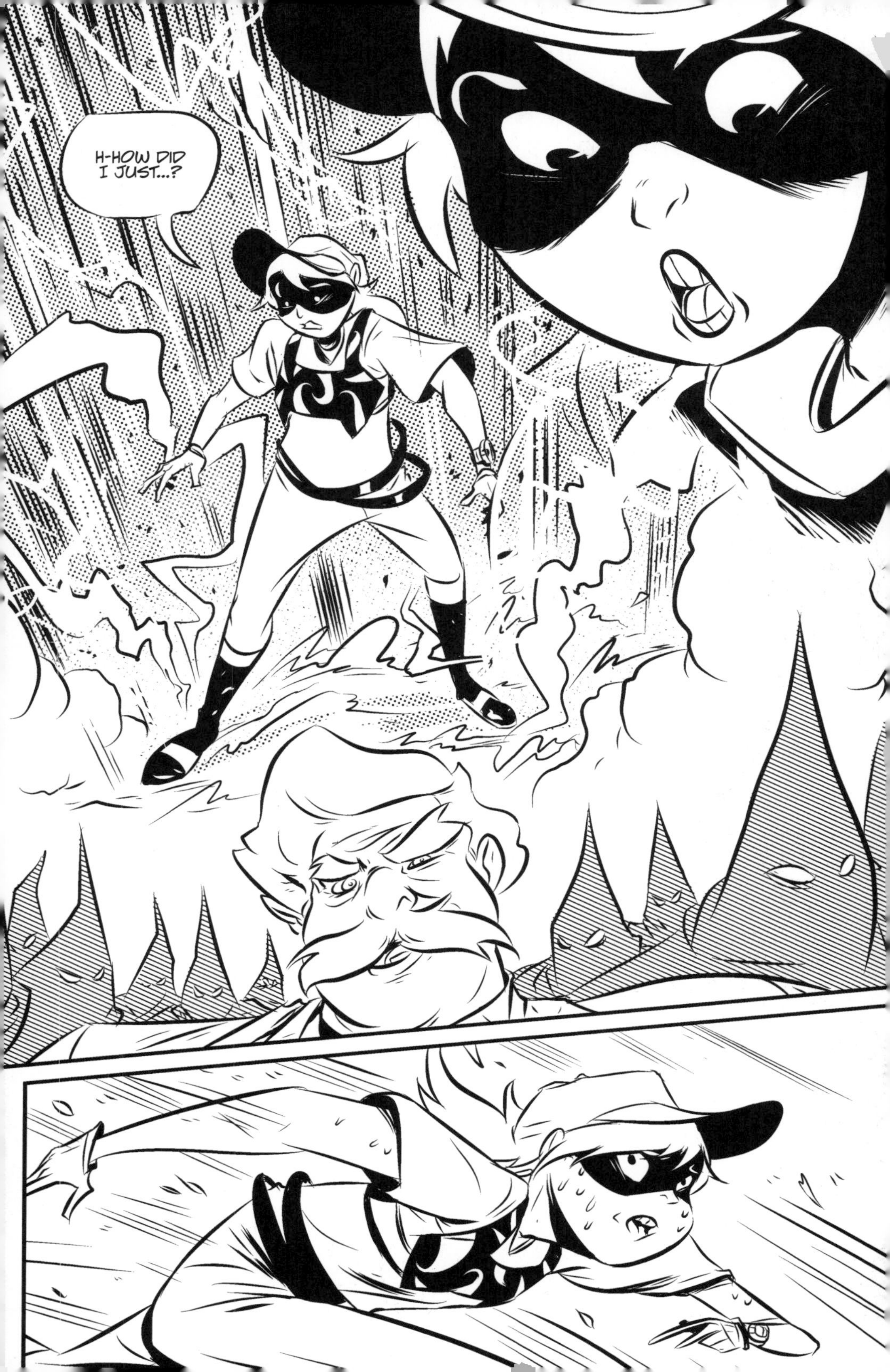
H-HOW DID I JUST...?

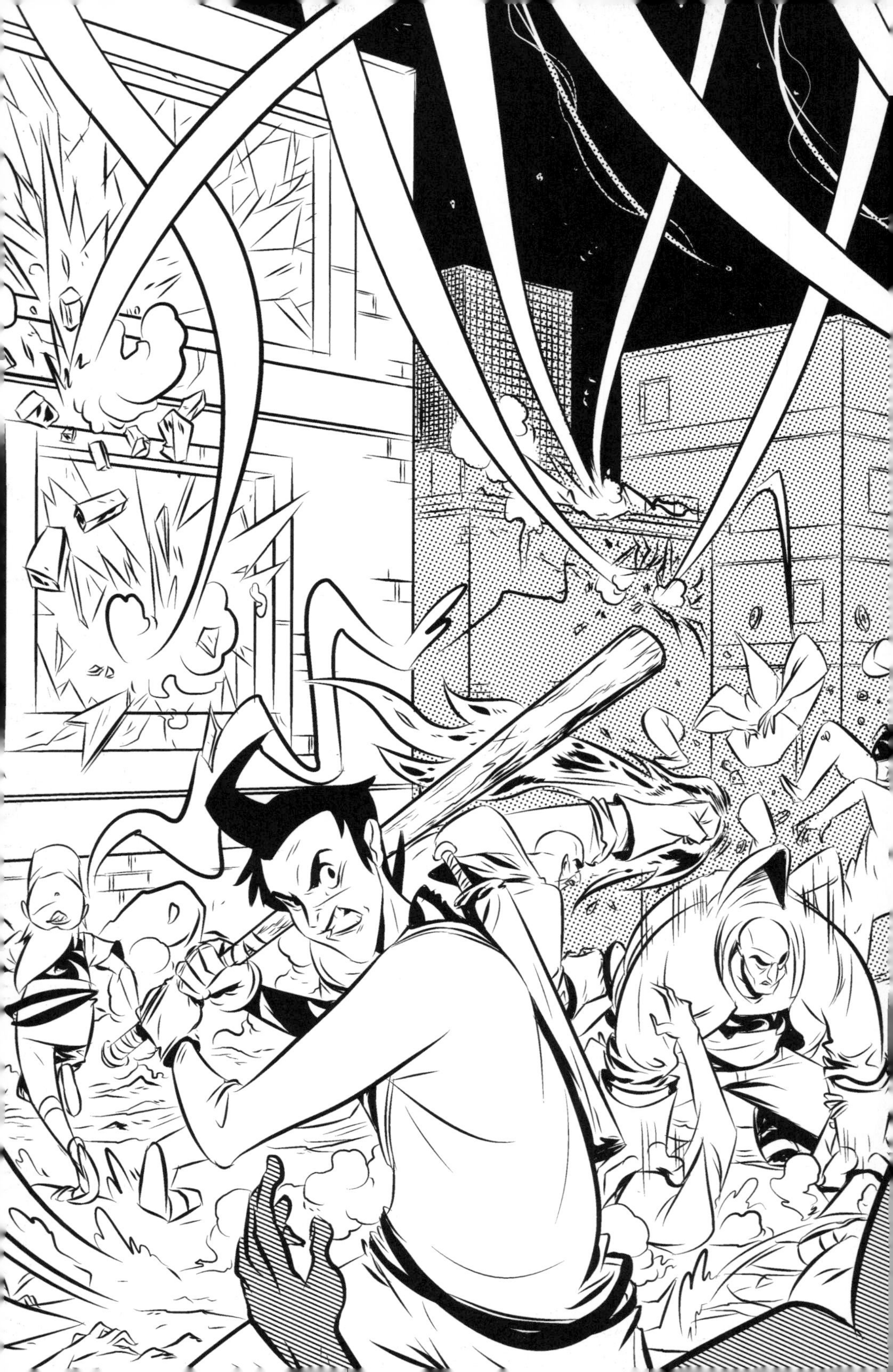

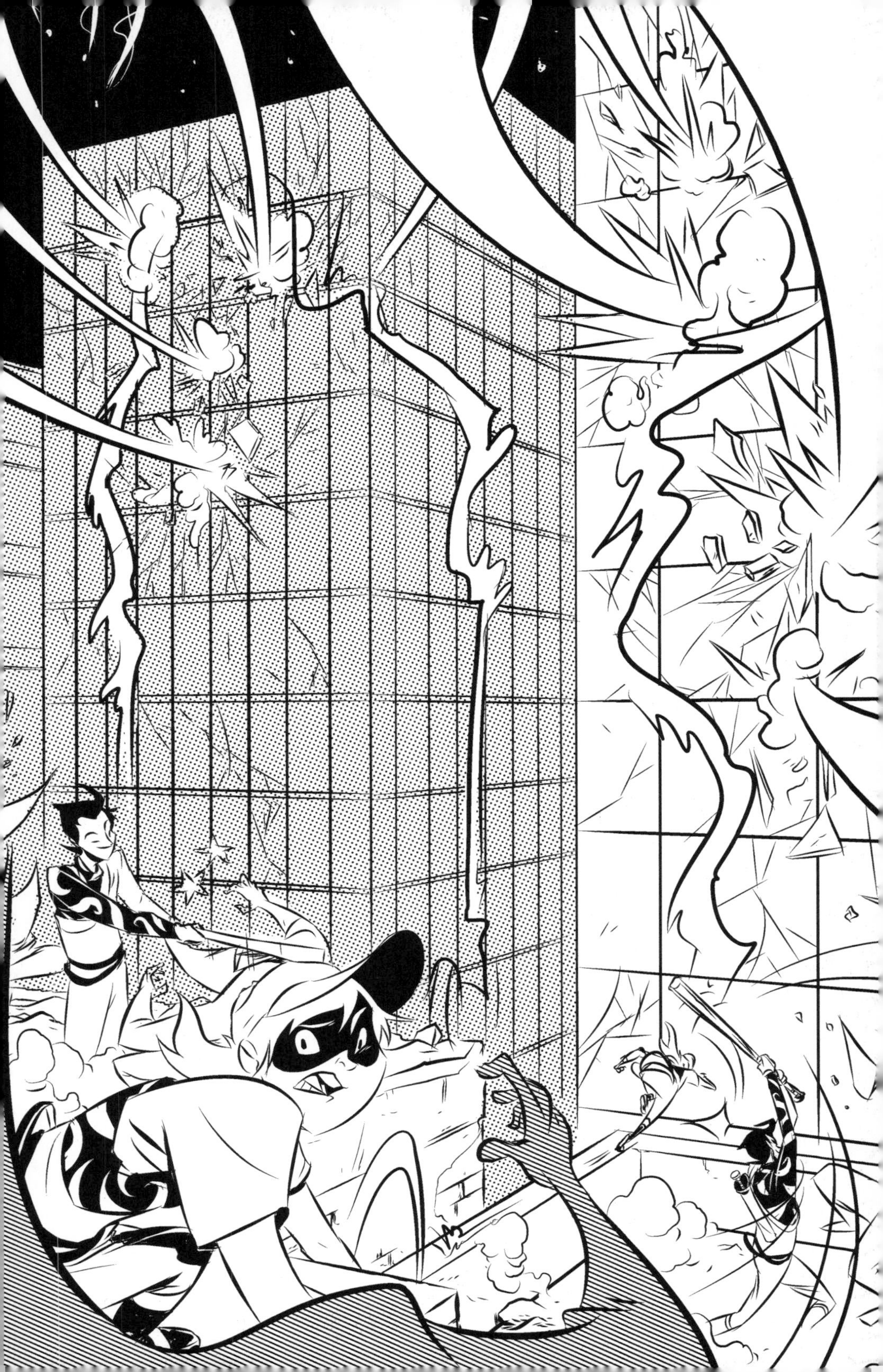

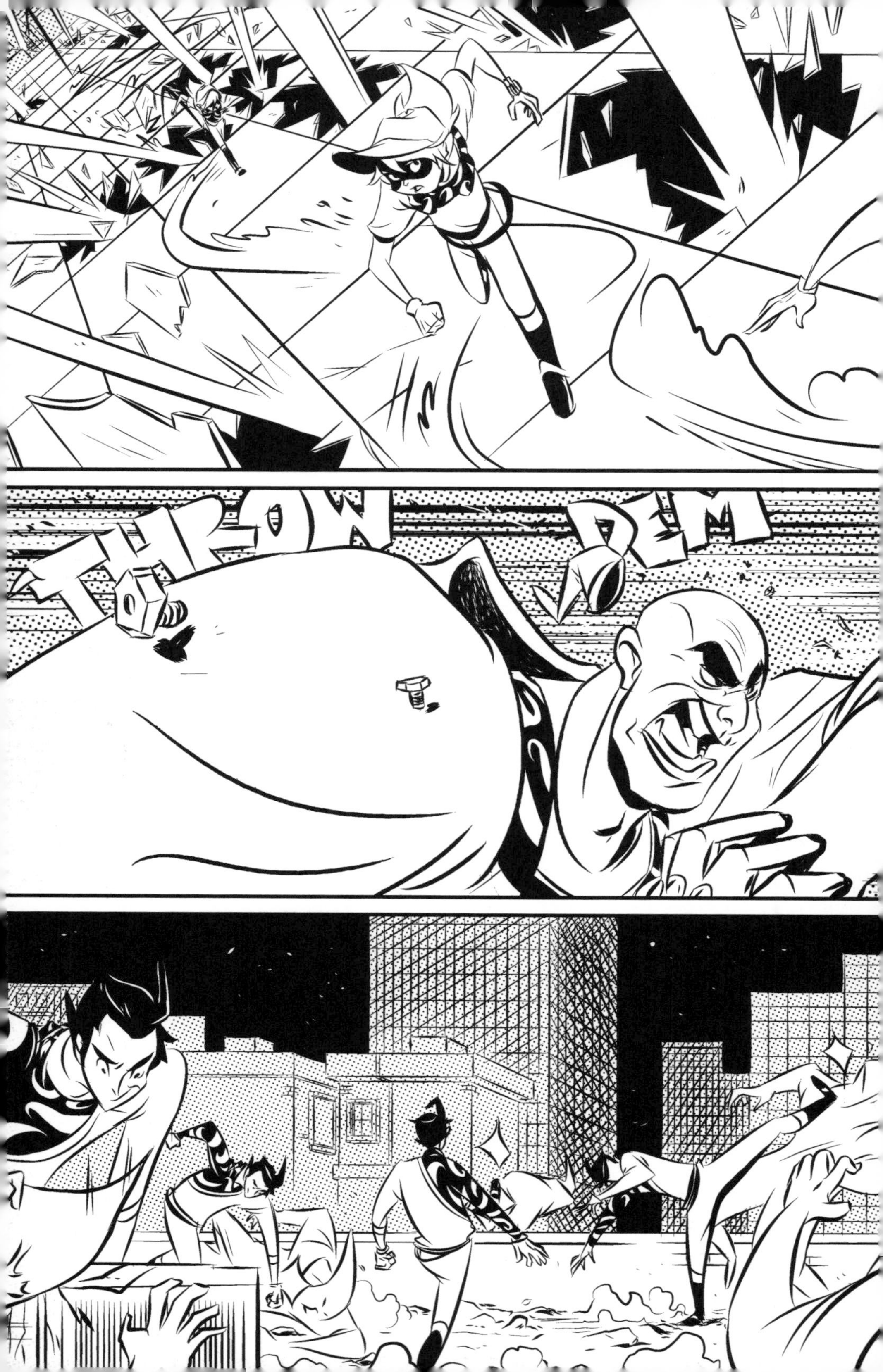
THROW DEM

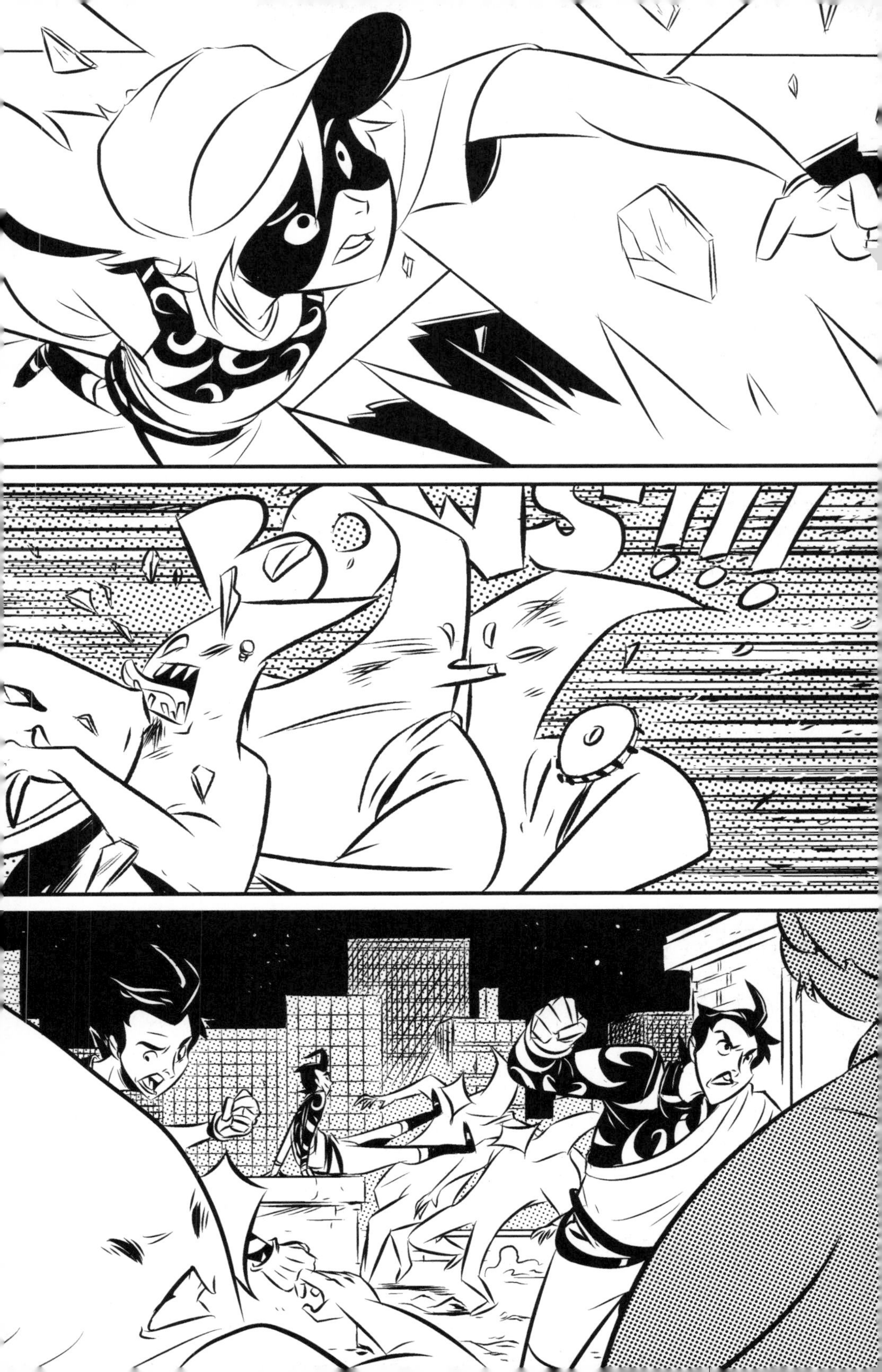

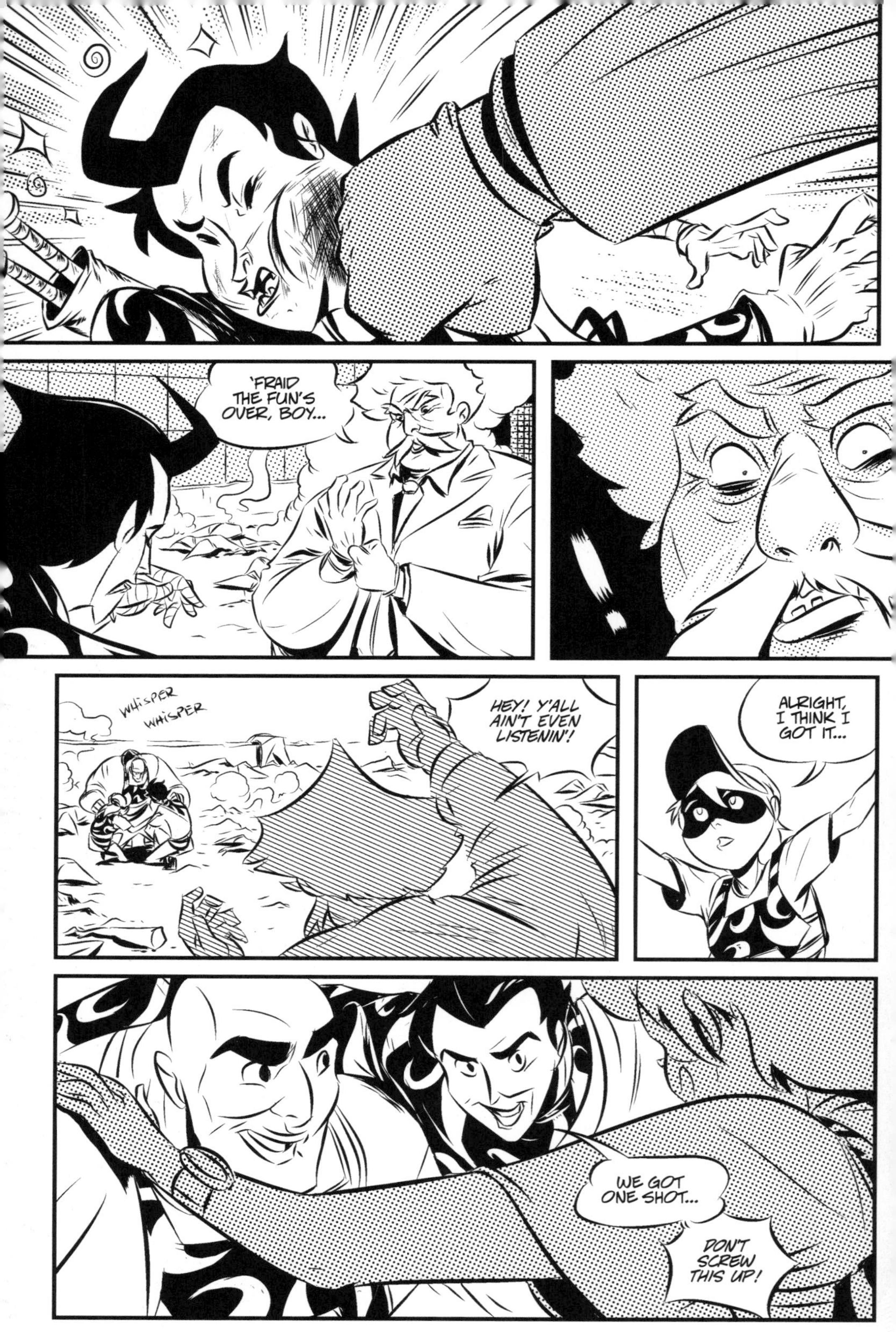
'FRAID THE FUN'S OVER, BOY...
WHISPER WHISPER
HEY! Y'ALL AIN'T EVEN LISTENIN'!
ALRIGHT, I THINK I GOT IT...
WE GOT ONE SHOT...
DON'T SCREW THIS UP!

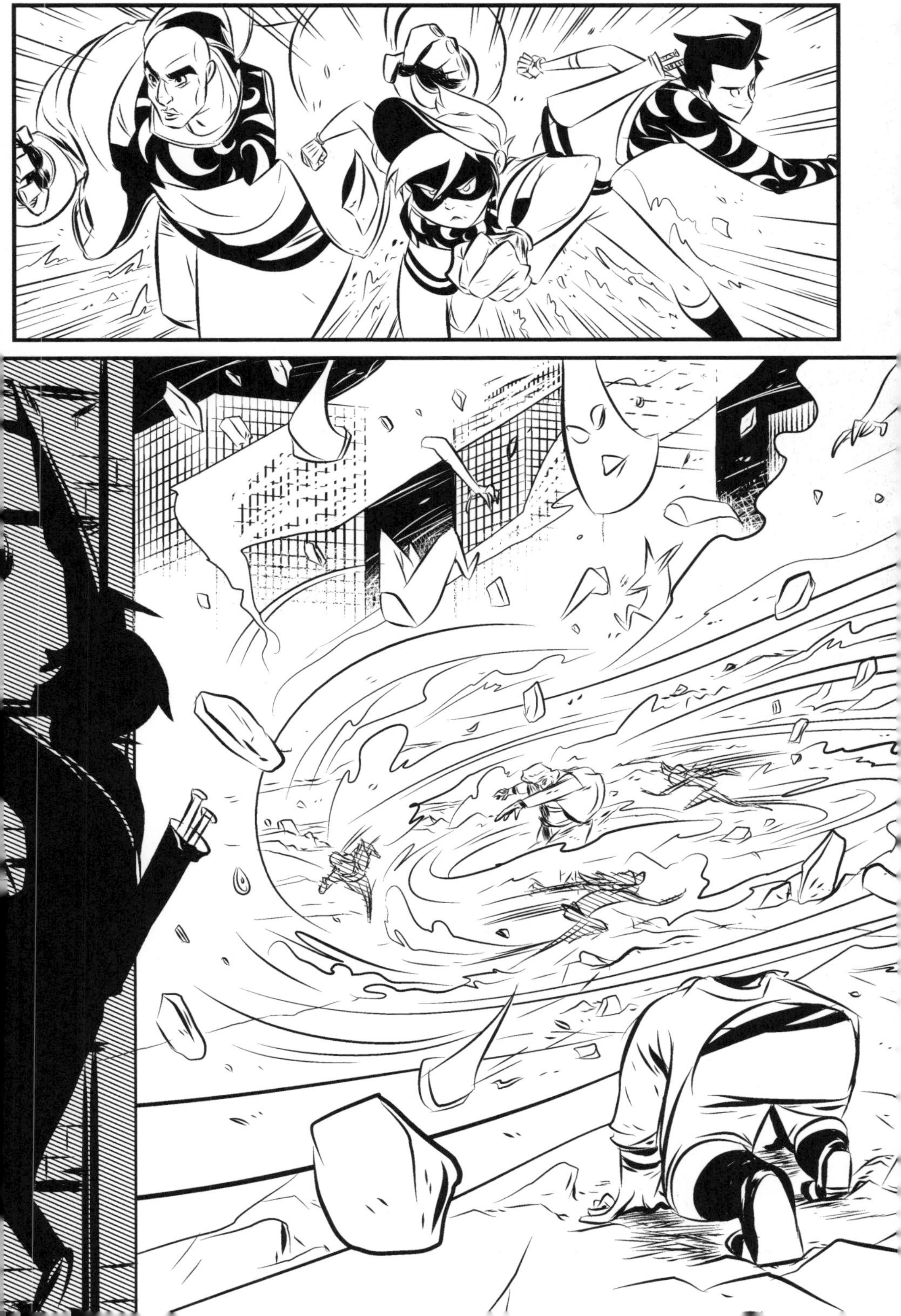

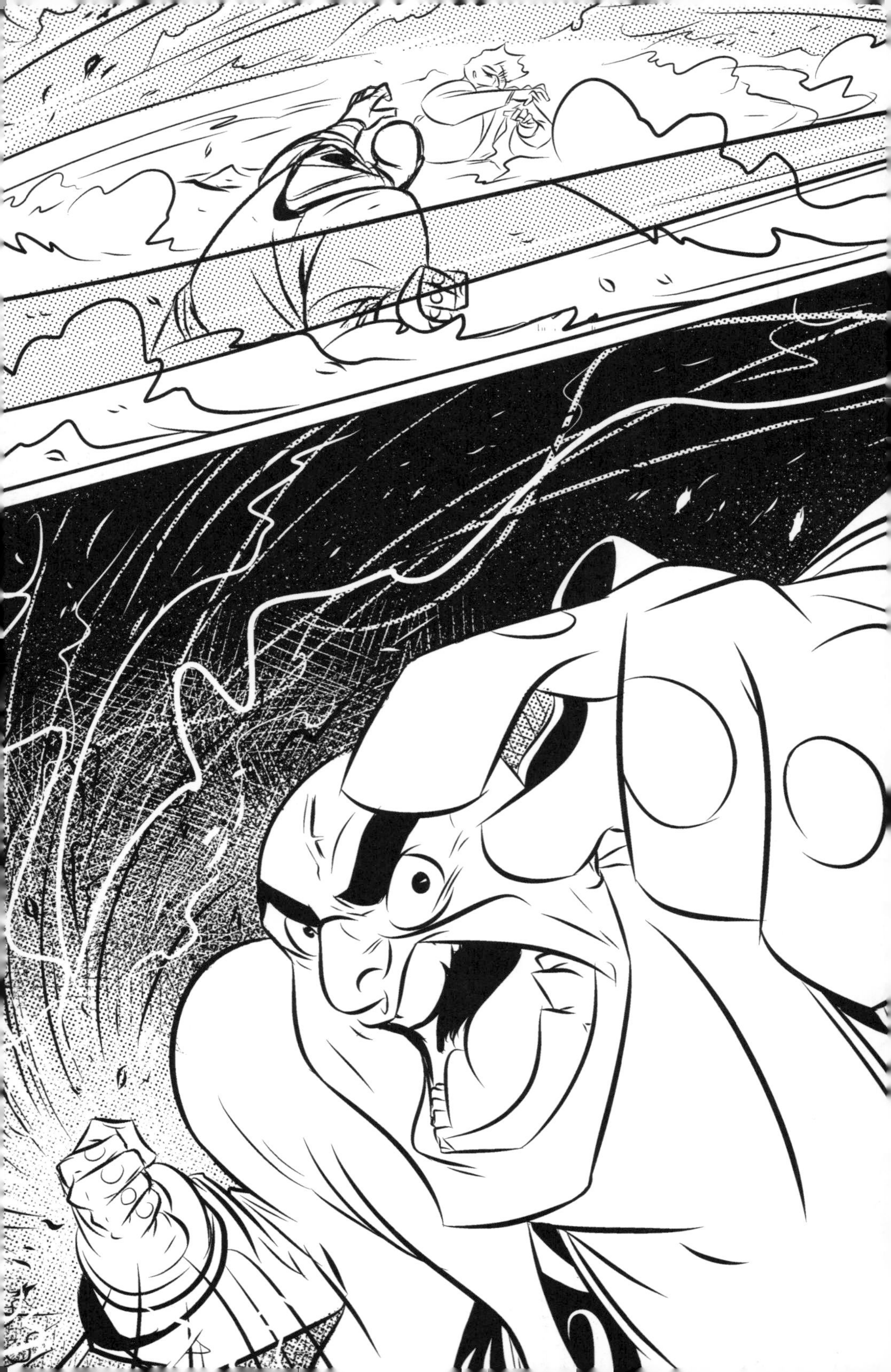

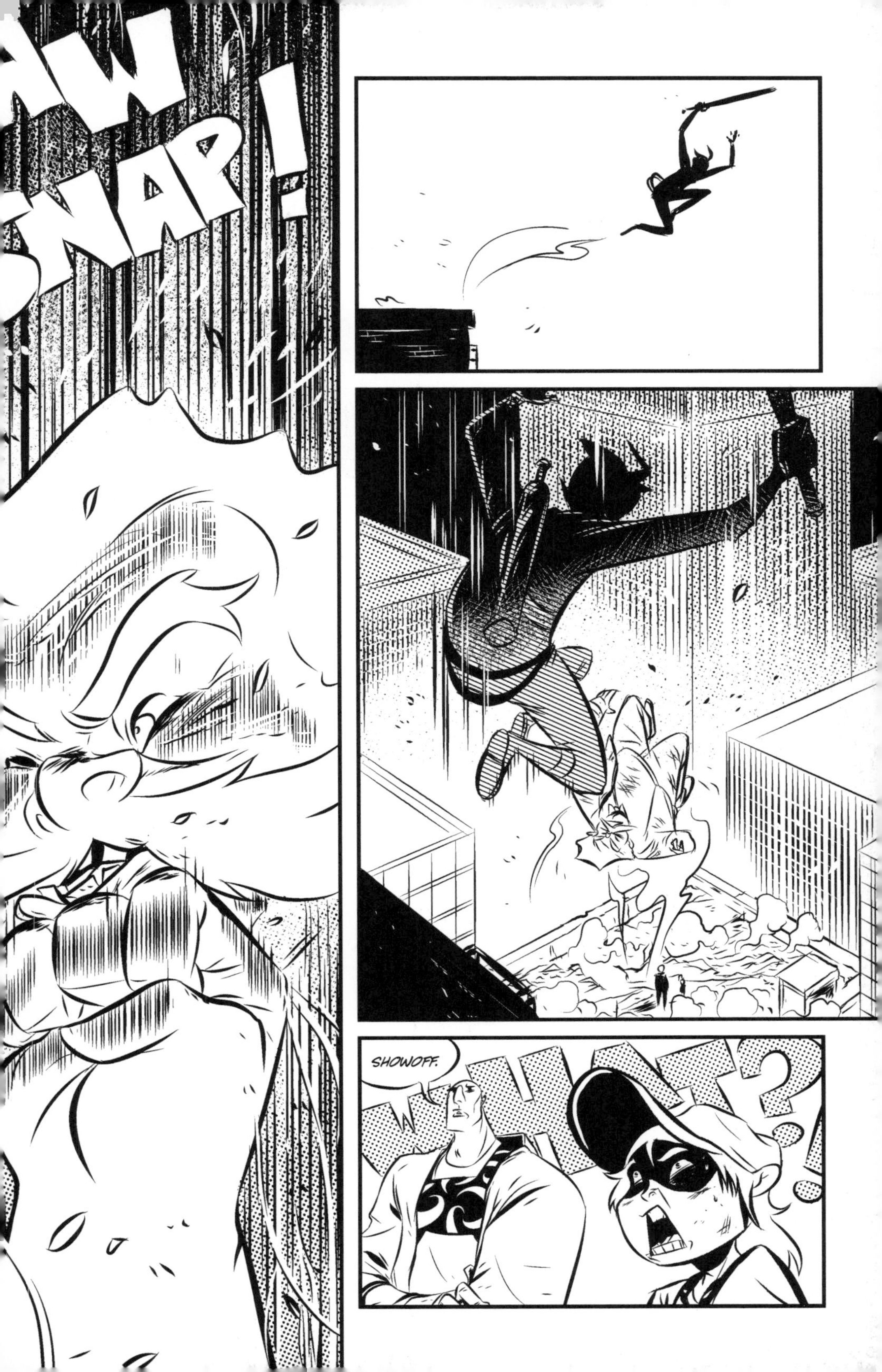

SNAP!
SHOWOFF.
WHAT?!

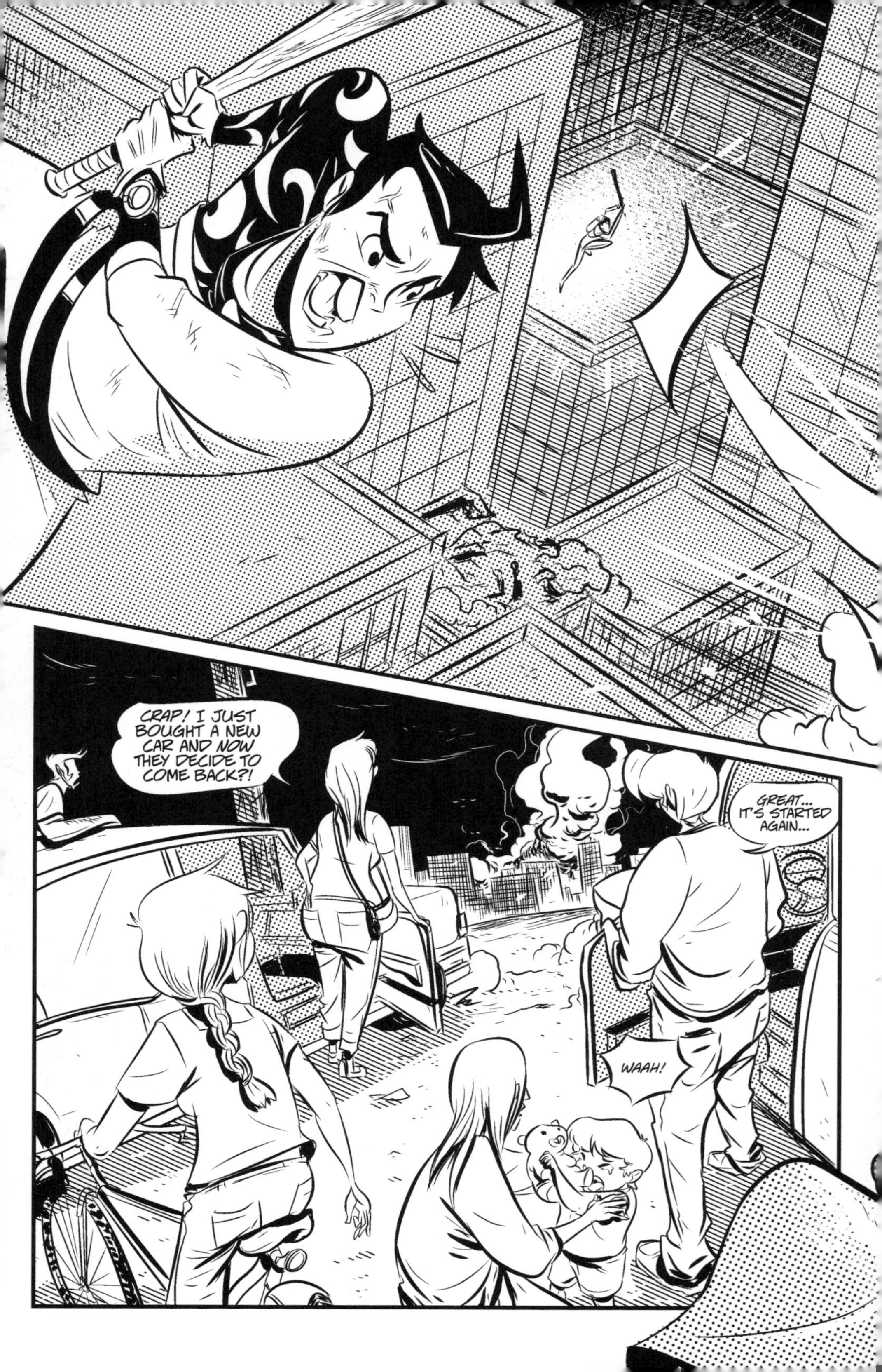
CRAP! I JUST BOUGHT A NEW CAR AND NOW THEY DECIDE TO COME BACK?!
GREAT... IT'S STARTED AGAIN...
WAAH!

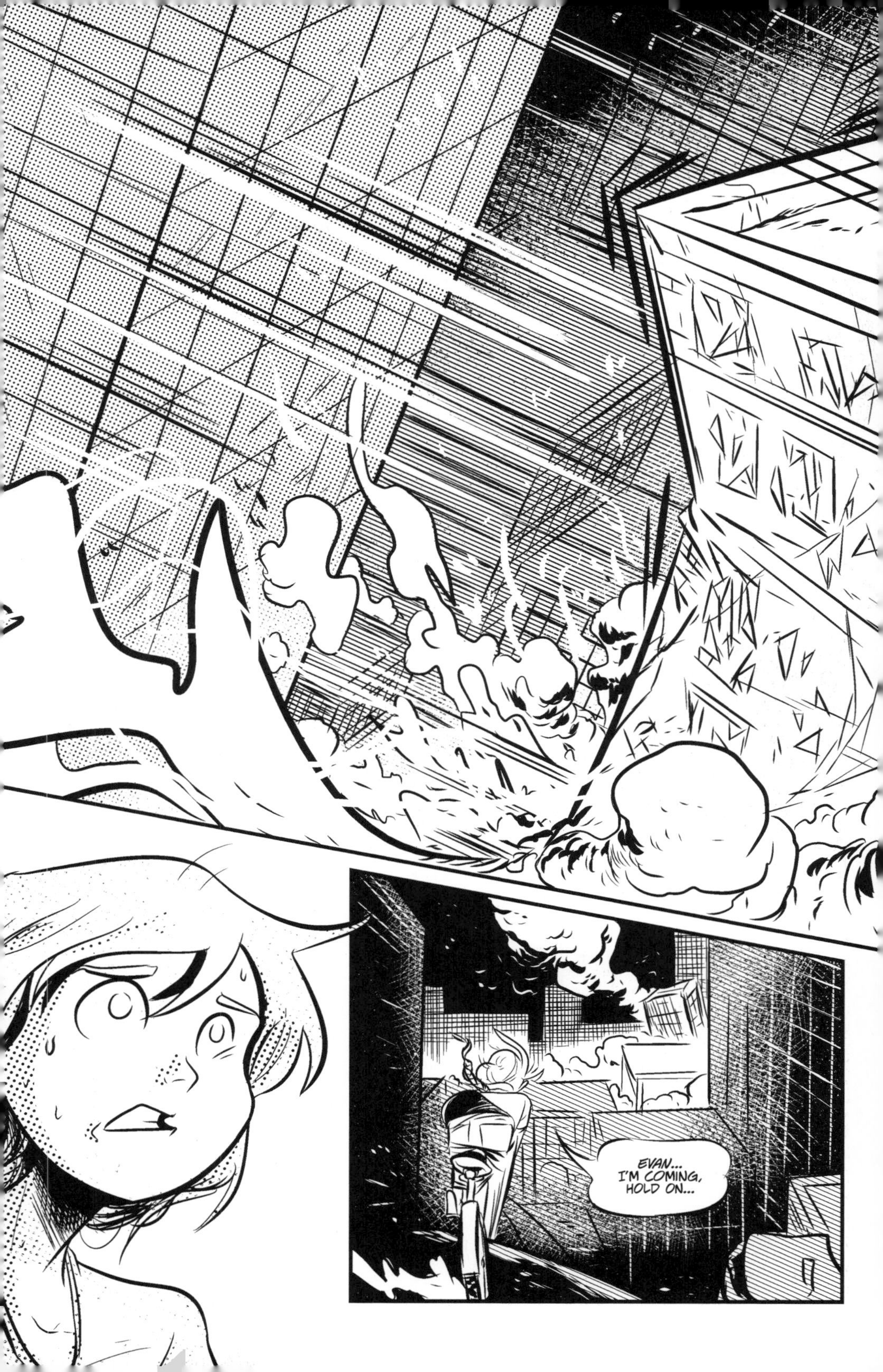
EVAN... I'M COMING, HOLD ON...

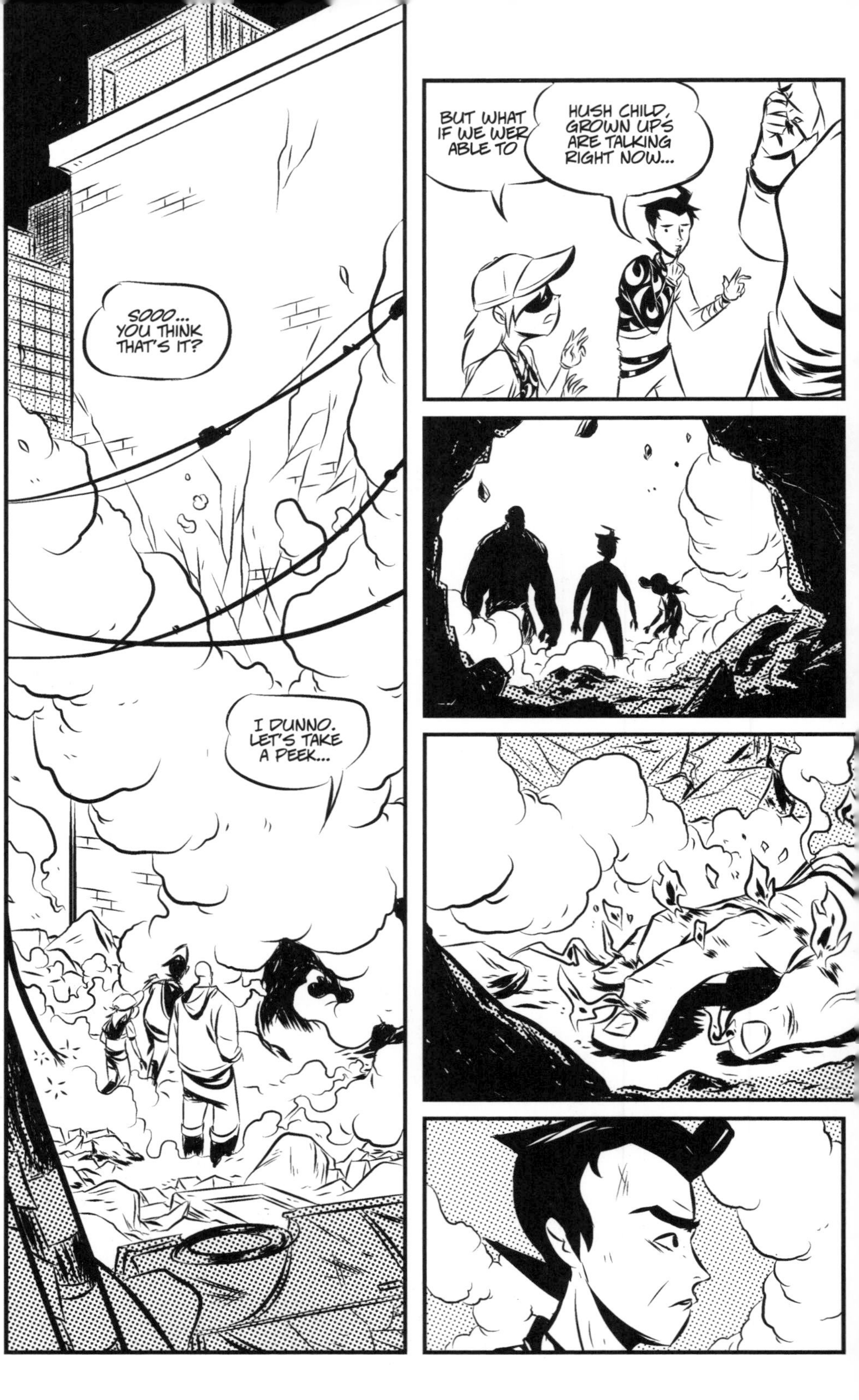
SOOO... YOU THINK THAT'S IT?
I DUNNO. LET'S TAKE A PEEK...
BUT WHAT IF WE WER ABLE TO
HUSH CHILD, GROWN UPS ARE TALKING RIGHT NOW...

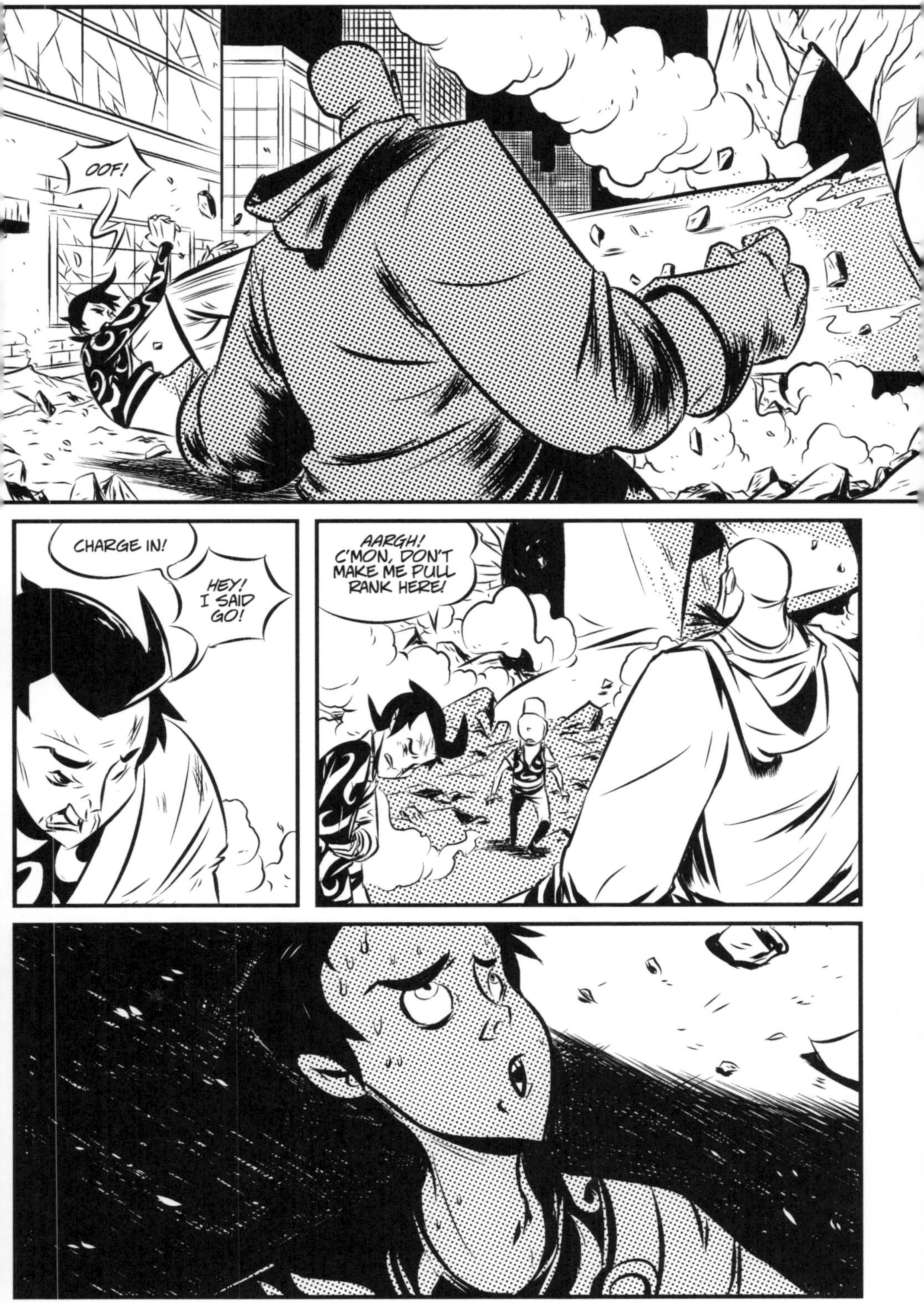
OOF!
CHARGE IN!
HEY! I SAID GO!
AARGH! C'MON, DON'T MAKE ME PULL RANK HERE!

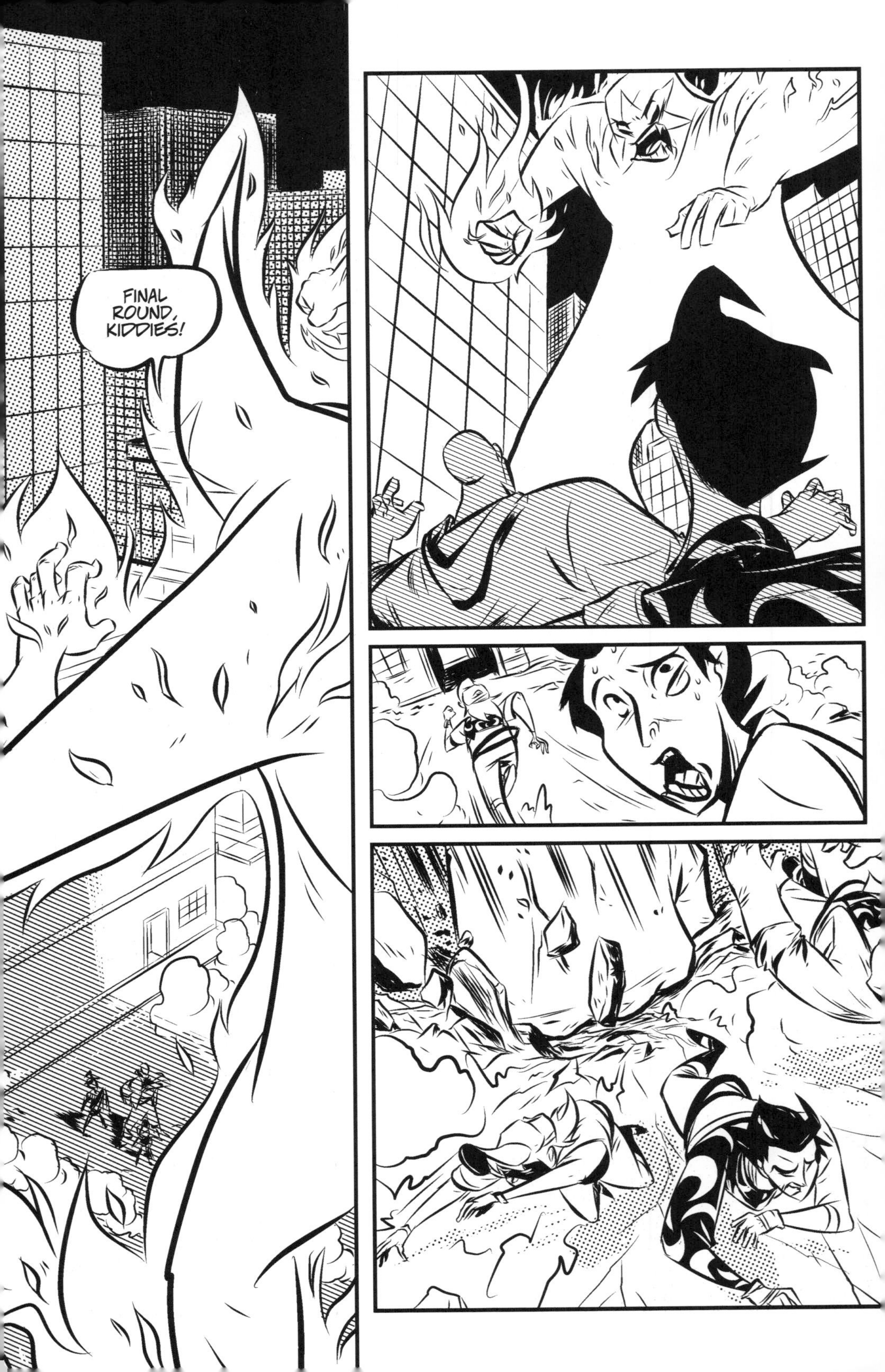
FINAL ROUND, KIDDIES!

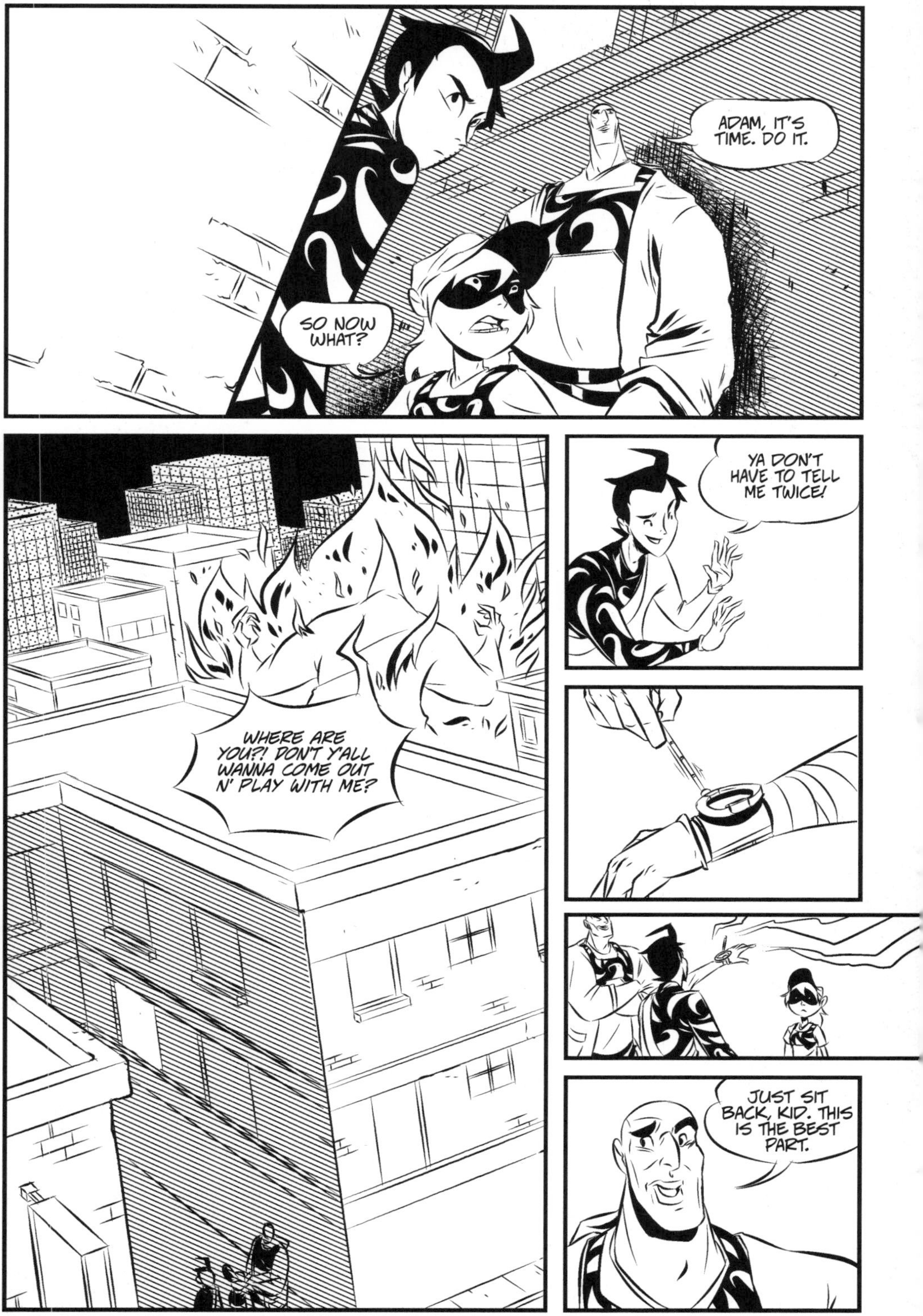
SO NOW WHAT?
ADAM, IT'S TIME. DO IT.
WHERE ARE YOU?! DON'T Y'ALL WANNA COME OUT N' PLAY WITH ME?
YA DON'T HAVE TO TELL ME TWICE!
JUST SIT BACK, KID. THIS IS THE BEST PART.

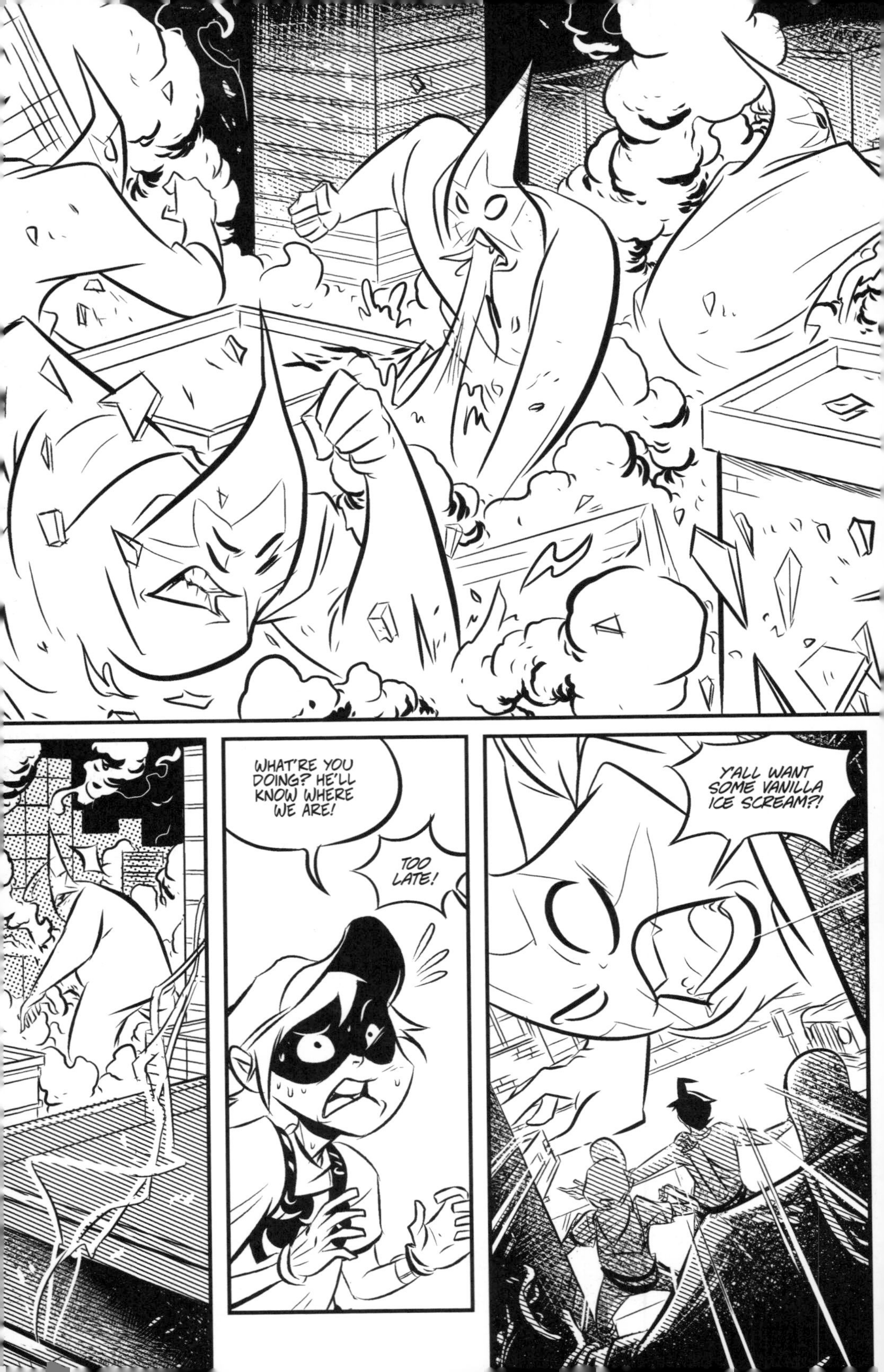
WHAT'RE YOU DOING? HE'LL KNOW WHERE WE ARE!
TOO LATE!
Y'ALL WANT SOME VANILLA ICE SCREAM?!

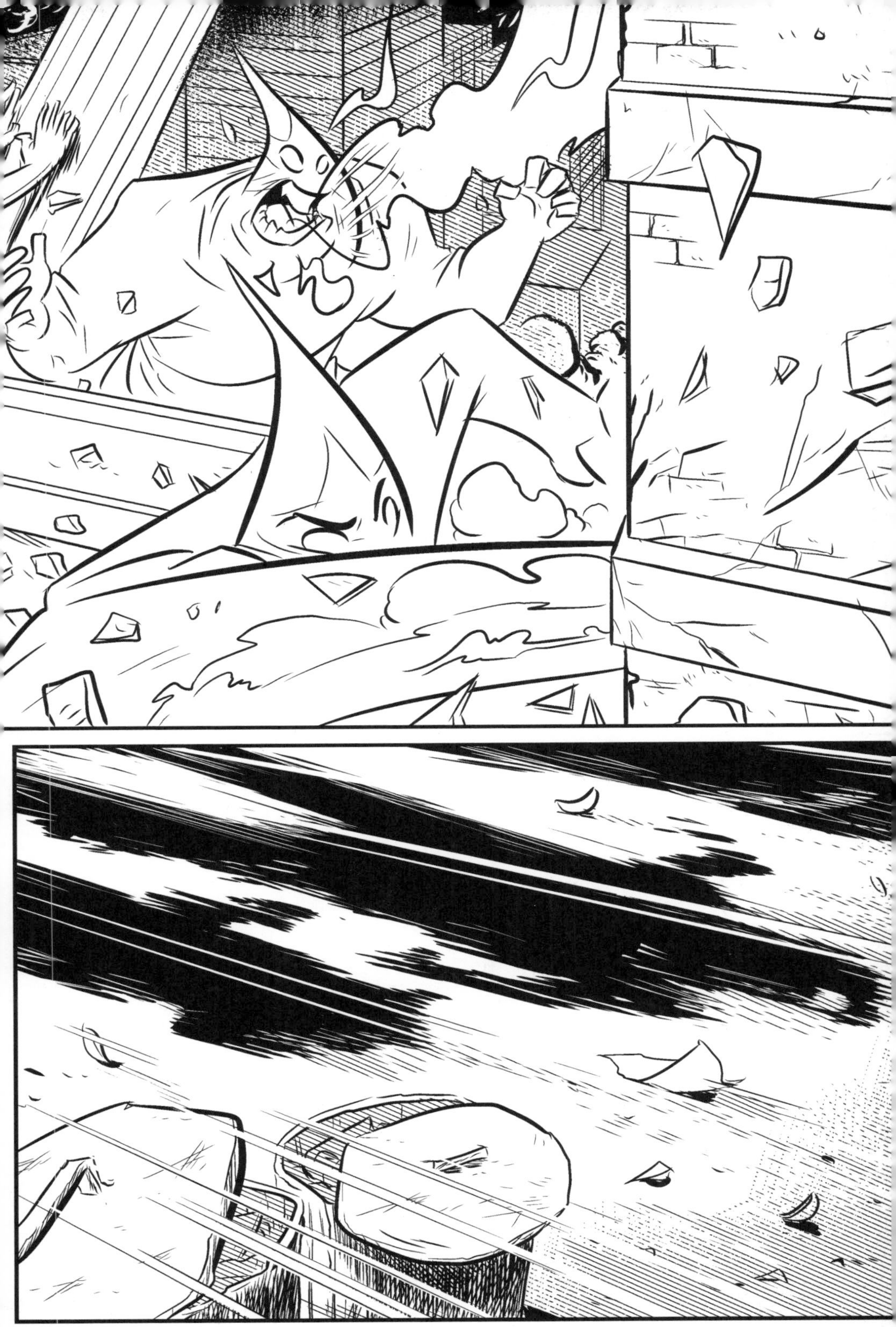

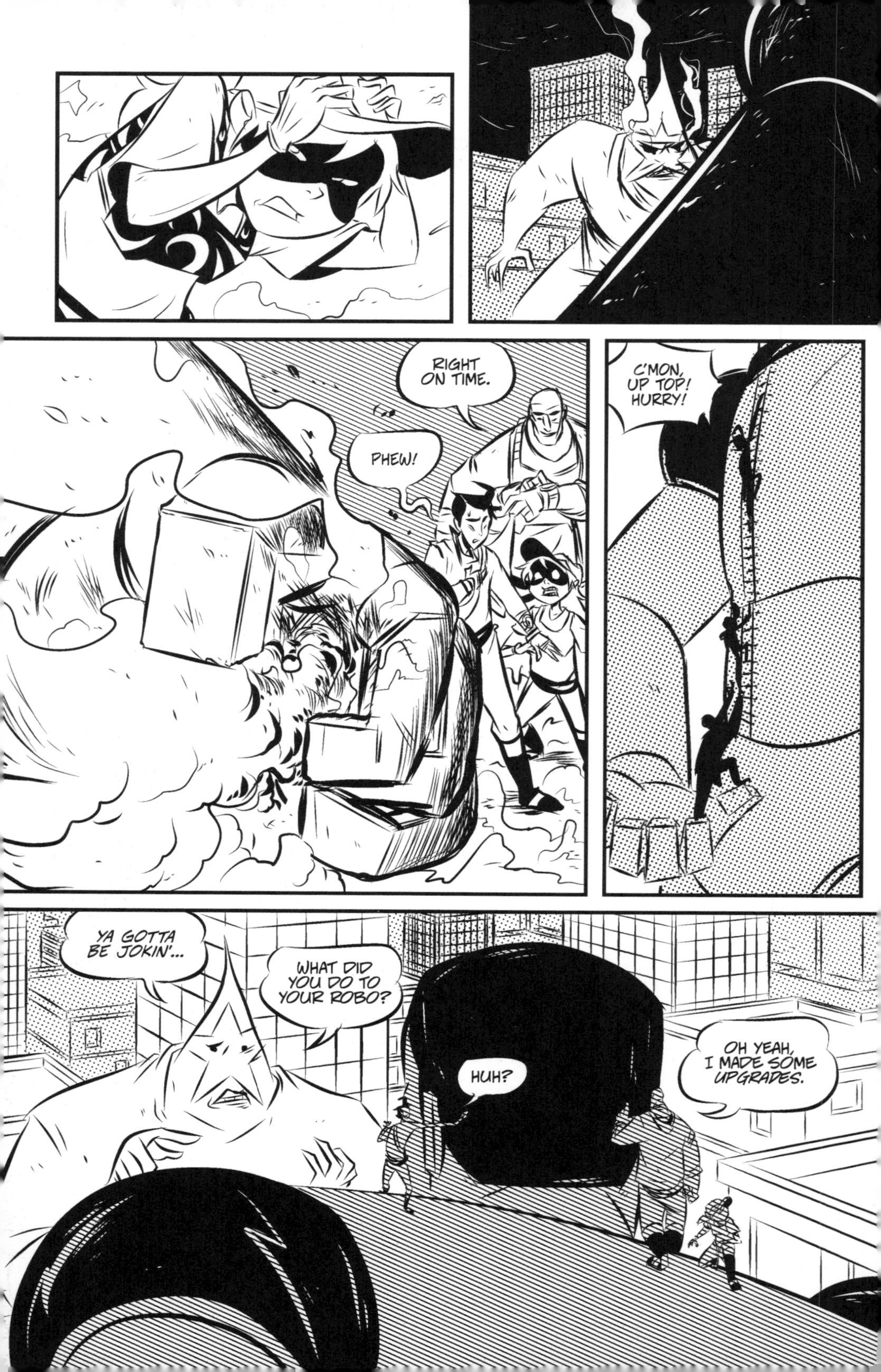
RIGHT ON TIME.
PHEW!
C'MON, UP TOP! HURRY!
YA GOTTA BE JOKIN'...
WHAT DID YOU DO TO YOUR ROBO?
HUH?
OH YEAH, I MADE SOME UPGRADES.

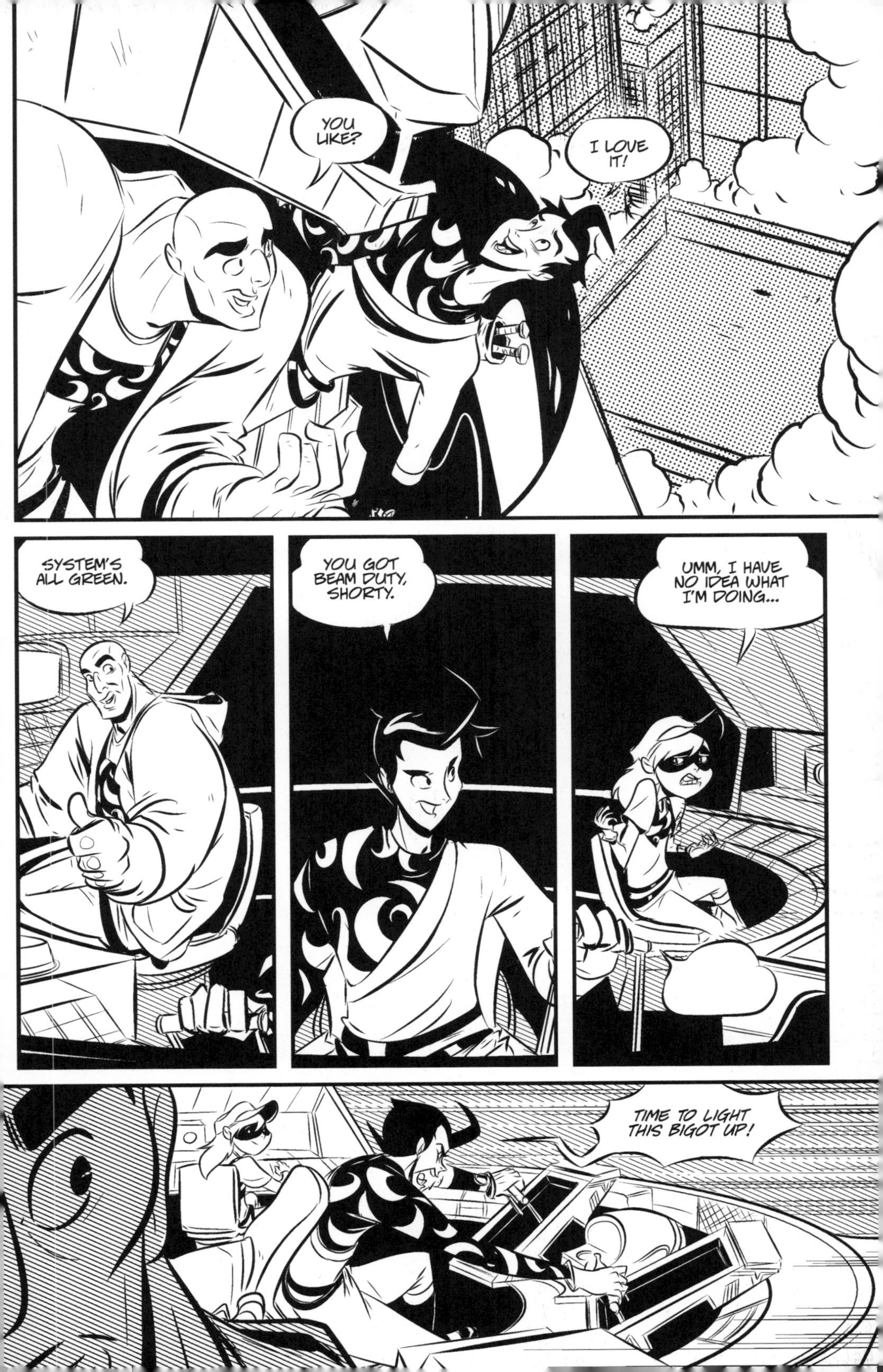
YOU LIKE?
I LOVE IT!
SYSTEM'S ALL GREEN.
YOU GOT BEAM DUTY, SHORTY.
UMM, I HAVE NO IDEA WHAT I'M DOING...
TIME TO LIGHT THIS BIGOT UP!

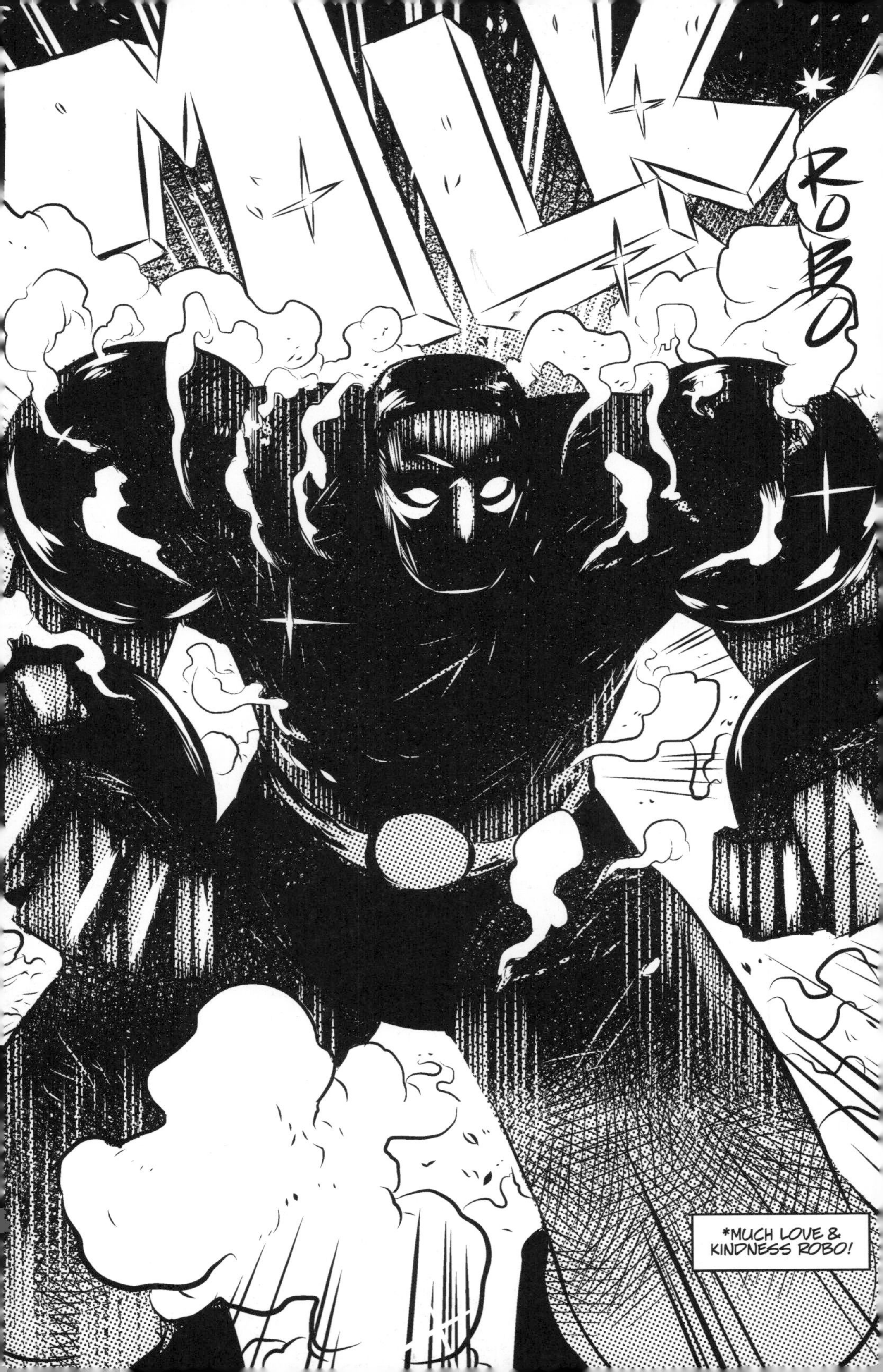
MILK
ROBO
*MUCH LOVE & KINDNESS ROBO!

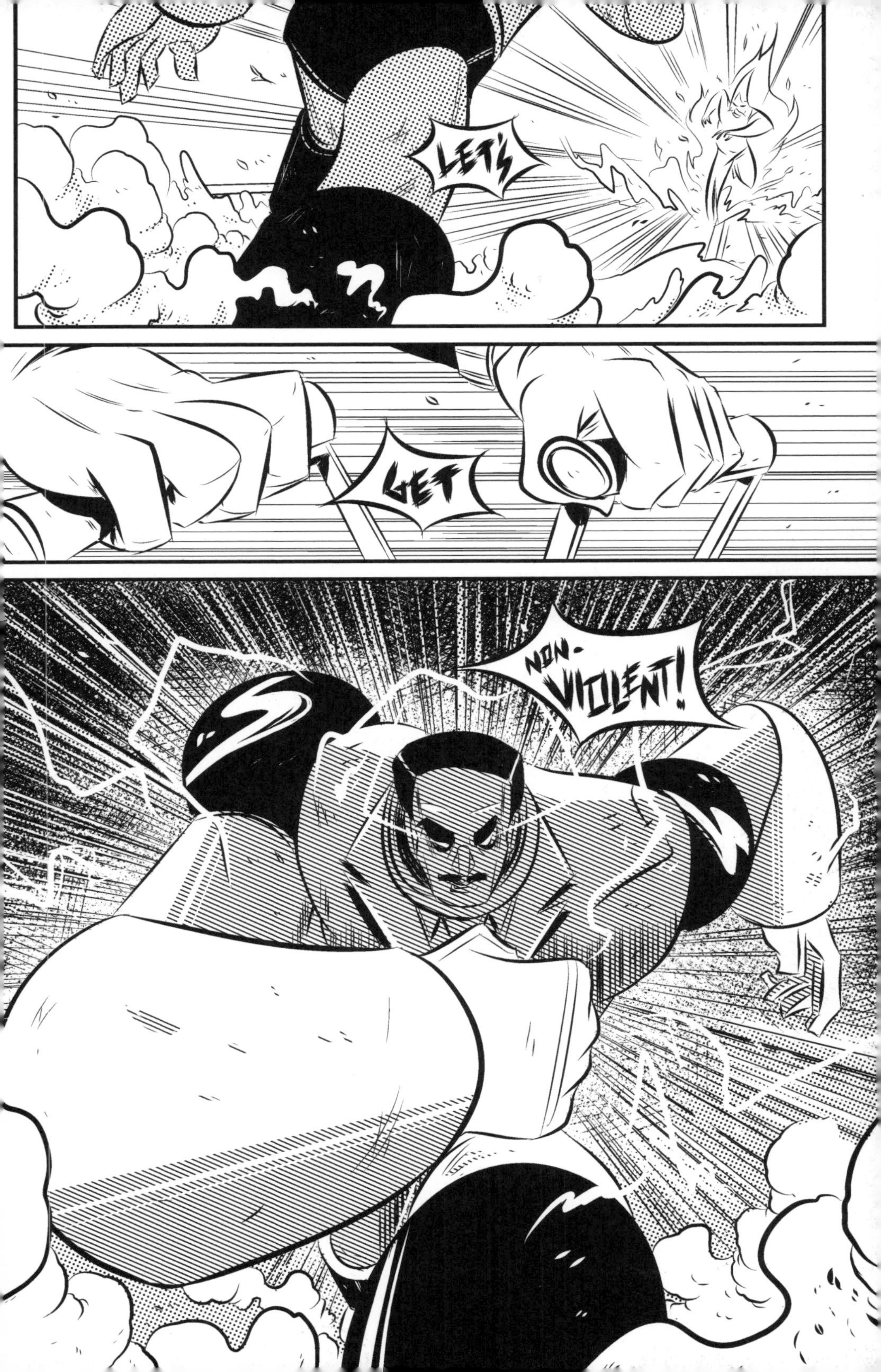
LET'S
GET
NON-VIOLENT!

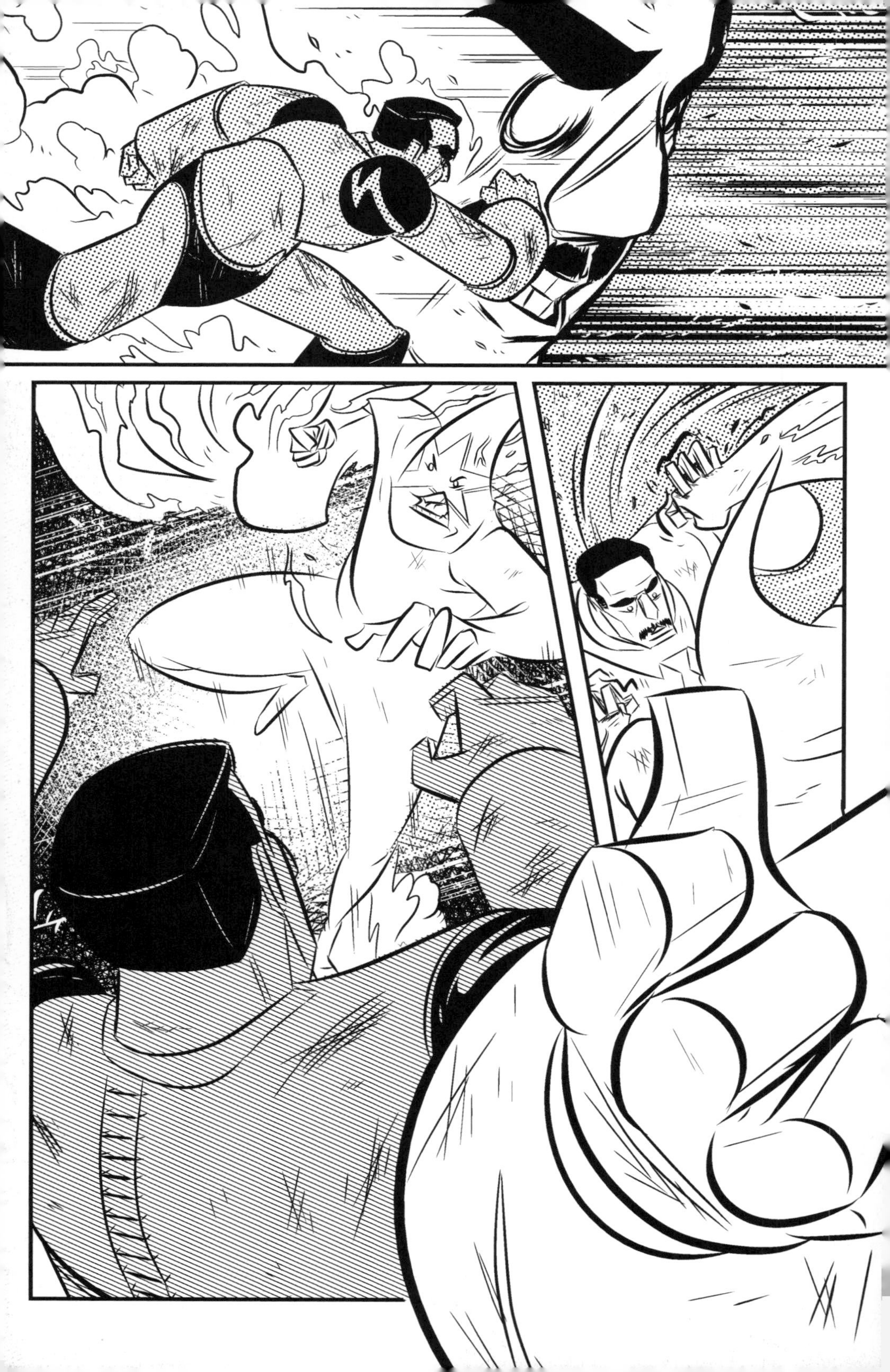

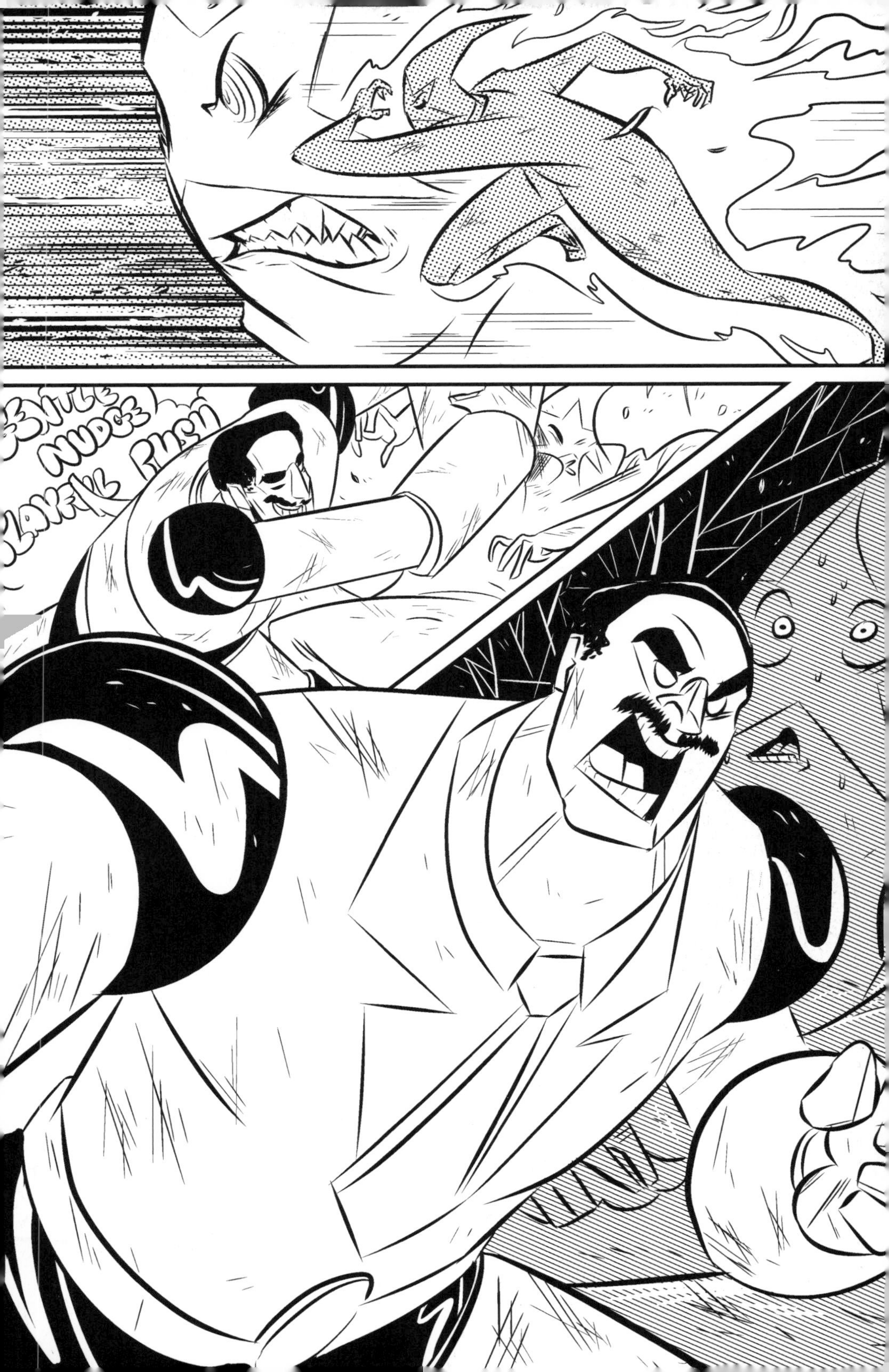
ENTLE NUDGE
LAYFUL PUSH

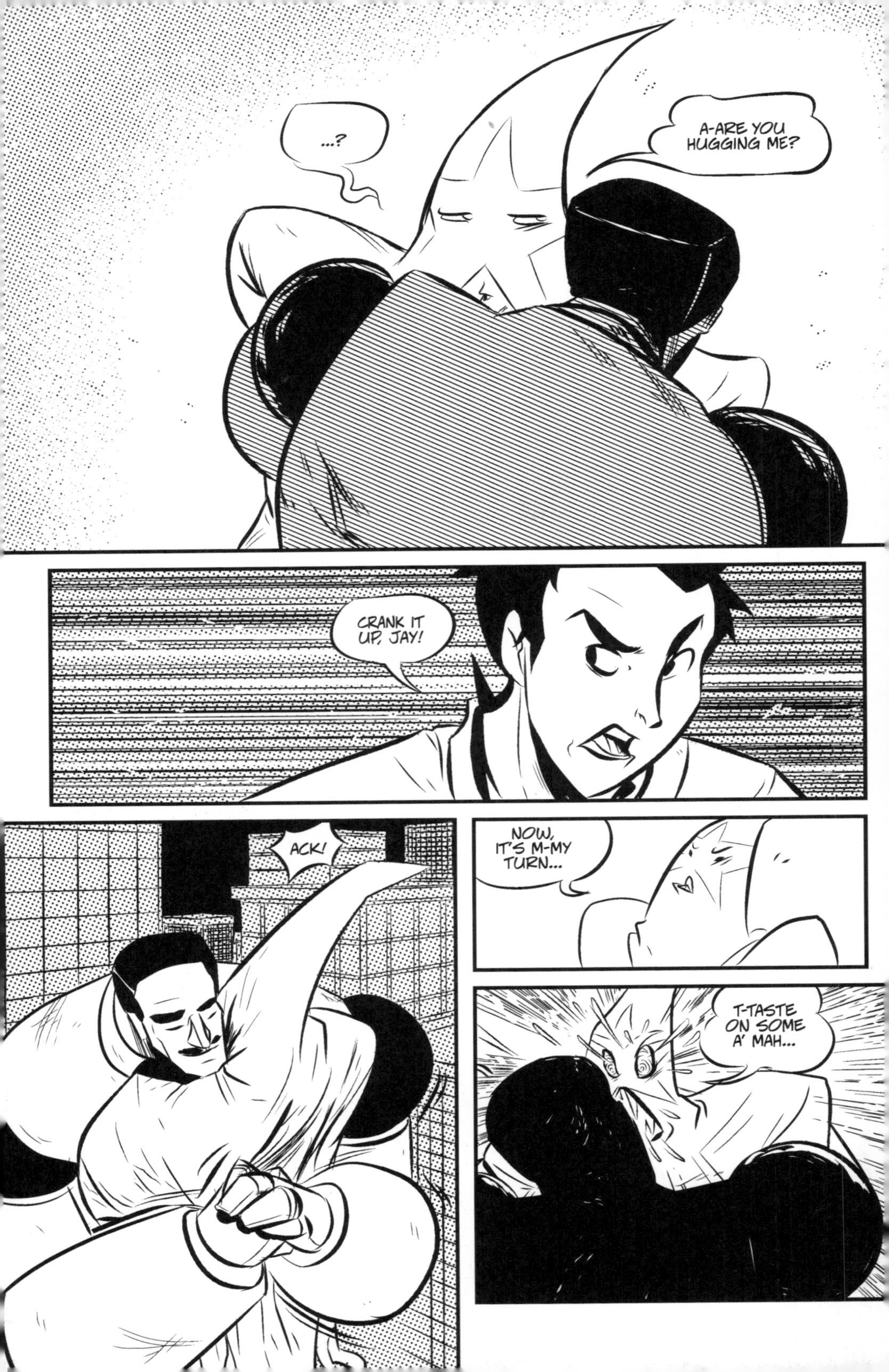

...?
A-ARE YOU HUGGING ME?
CRANK IT UP, JAY!
ACK!
NOW, IT'S M-MY TURN...
T-TASTE ON SOME A' MAH...

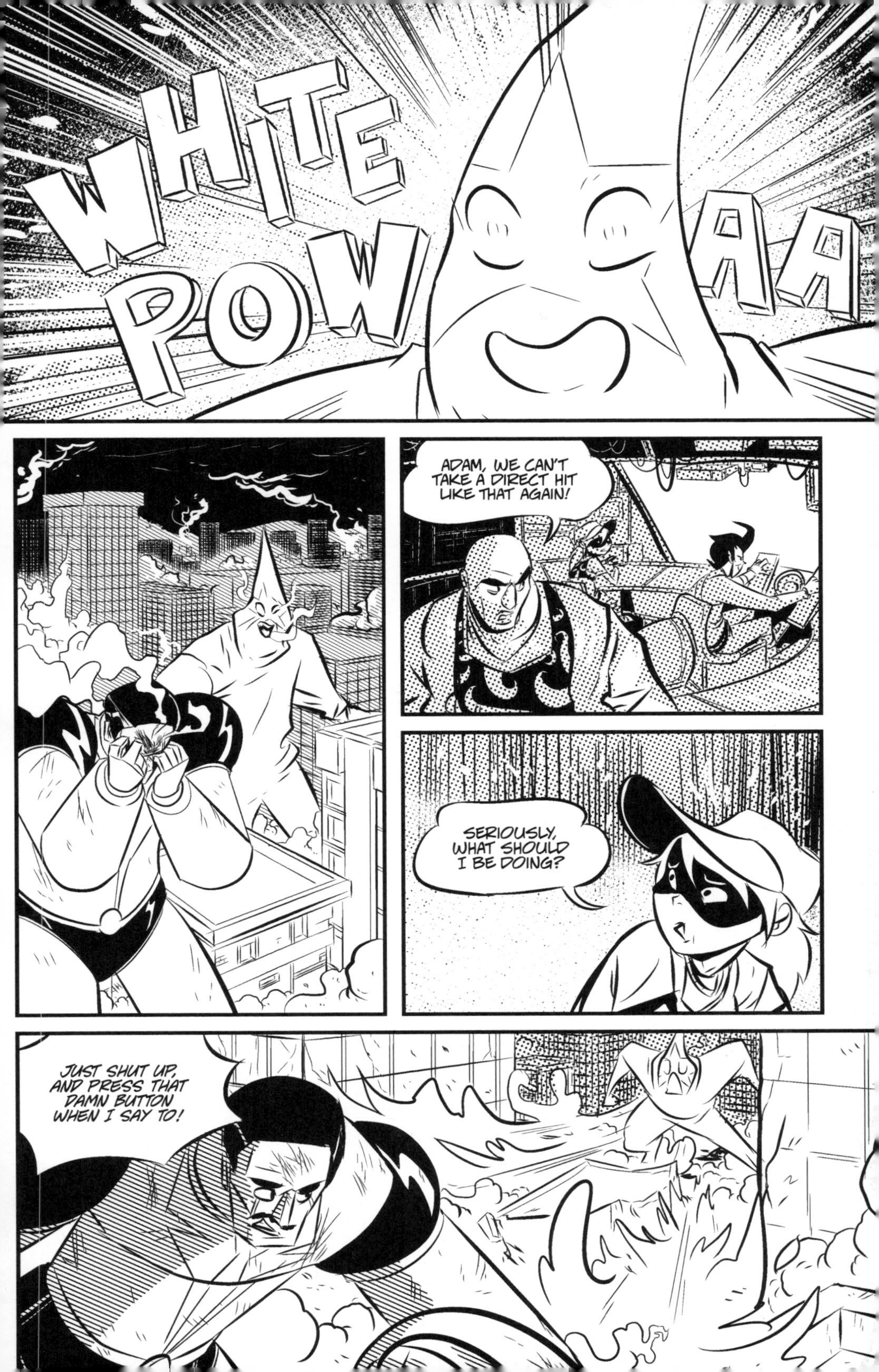
WHITE POWAA
ADAM, WE CAN'T TAKE A DIRECT HIT LIKE THAT AGAIN!
SERIOUSLY, WHAT SHOULD I BE DOING?
JUST SHUT UP, AND PRESS THAT DAMN BUTTON WHEN I SAY TO!

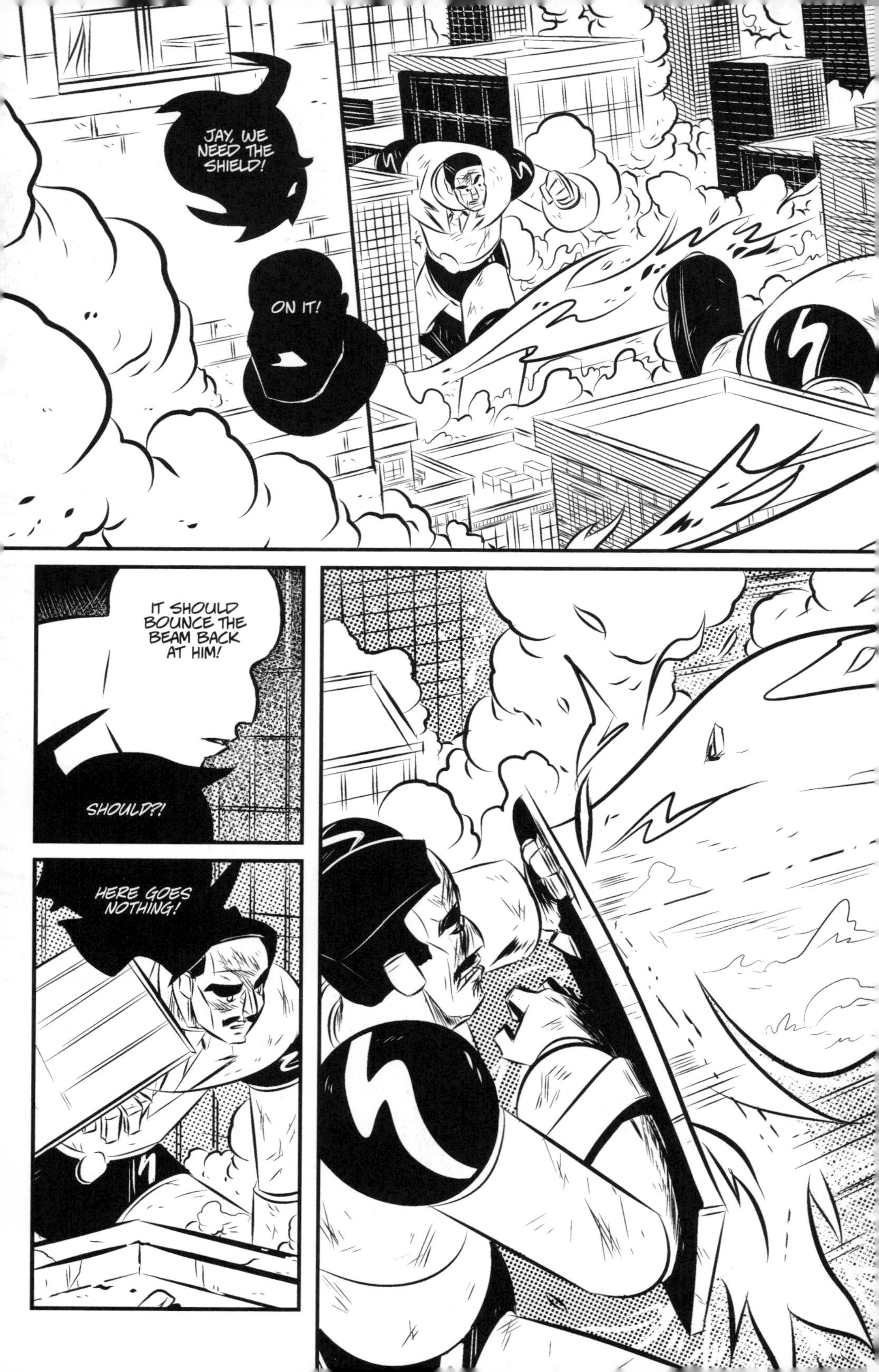
JAY, WE NEED THE SHIELD!
ON IT!
IT SHOULD BOUNCE THE BEAM BACK AT HIM!
SHOULD?!
HERE GOES NOTHING!

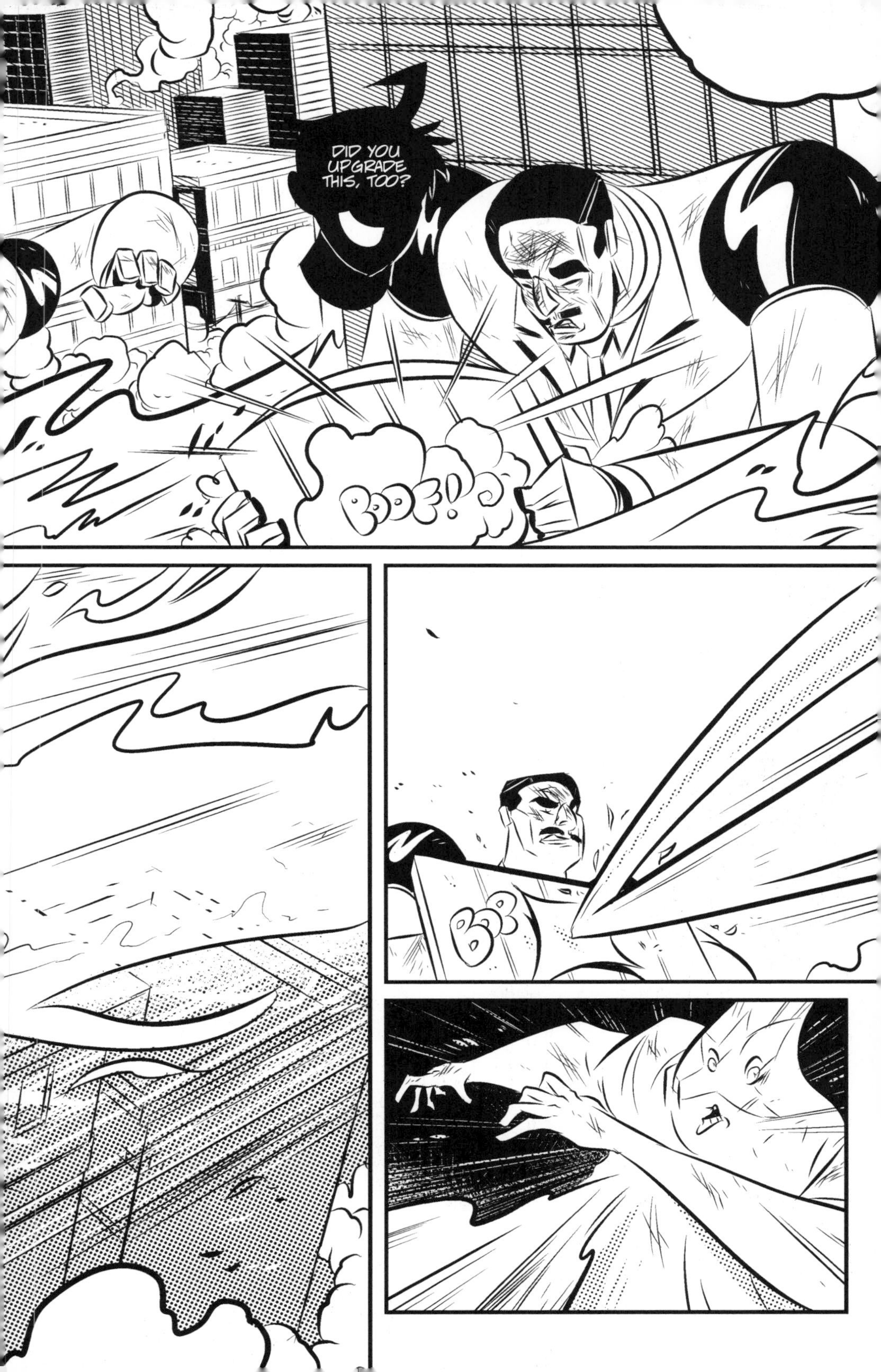
DID YOU UPGRADE THIS, TOO?
BOOF!
BOB

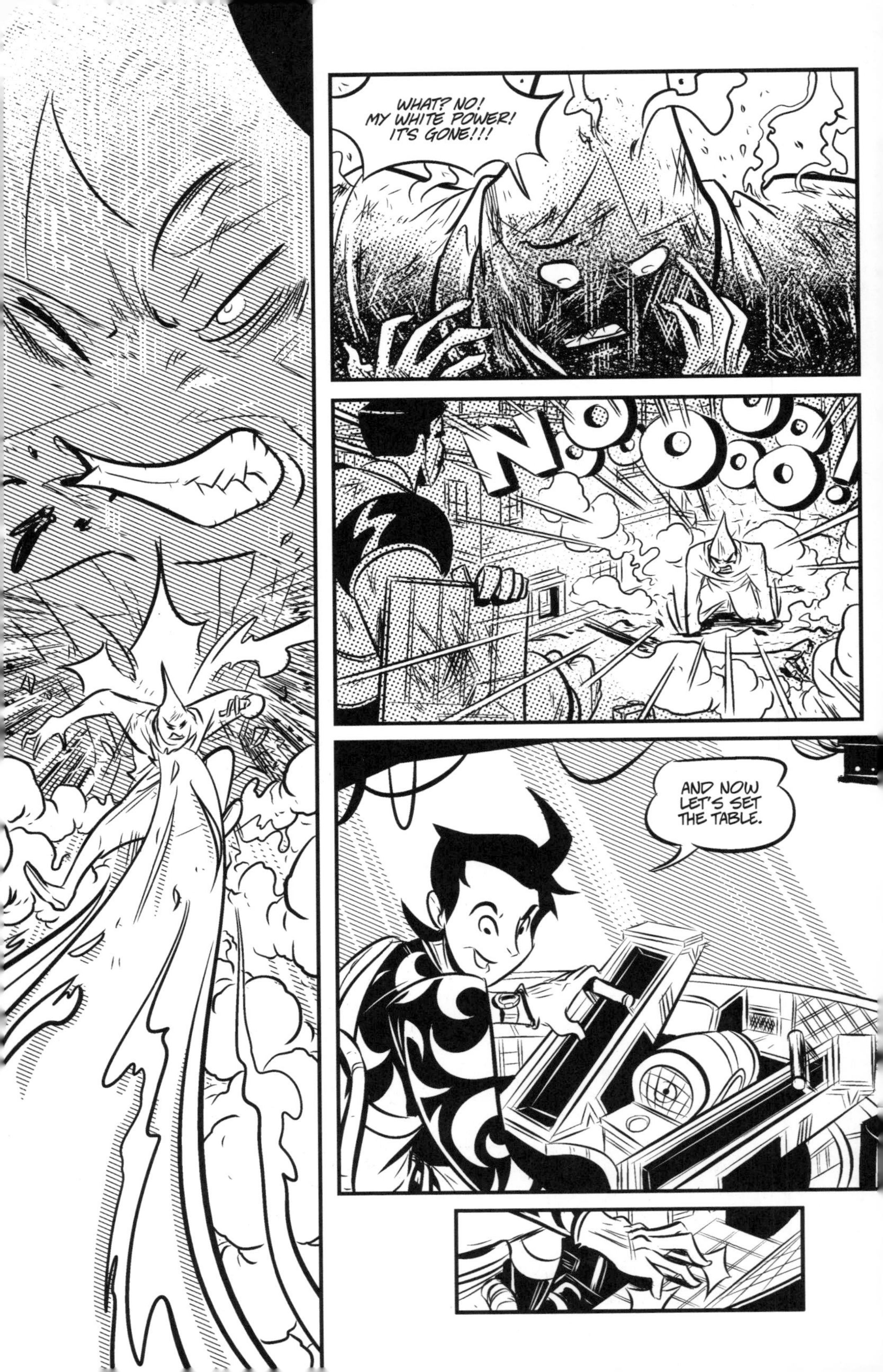
WHAT? NO!
MY WHITE POWER!
IT'S GONE!!!
NOOOOOOO!
AND NOW
LET'S SET
THE TABLE.

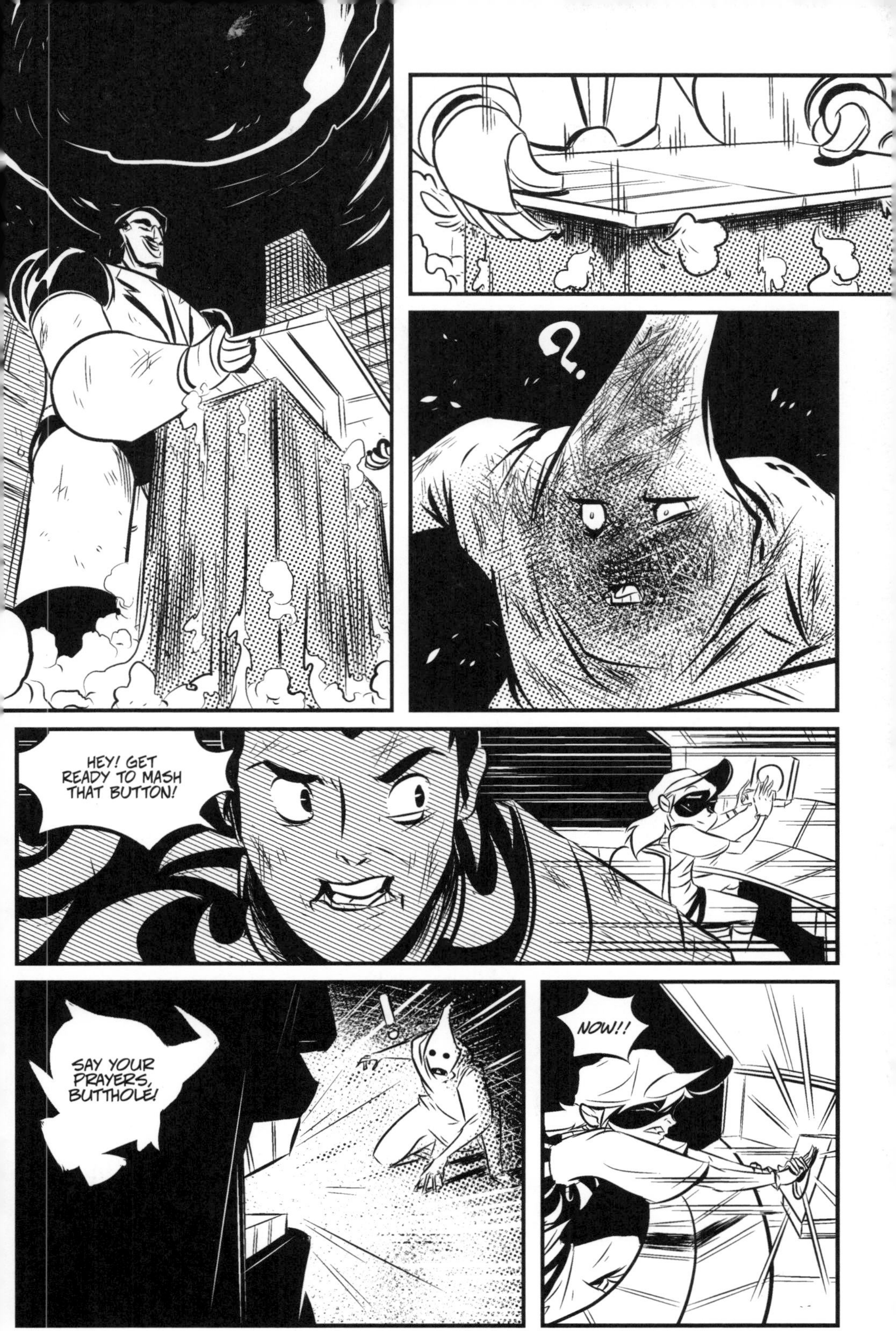
?
HEY! GET READY TO MASH THAT BUTTON!
!
SAY YOUR PRAYERS, BUTTHOLE!
NOW!!

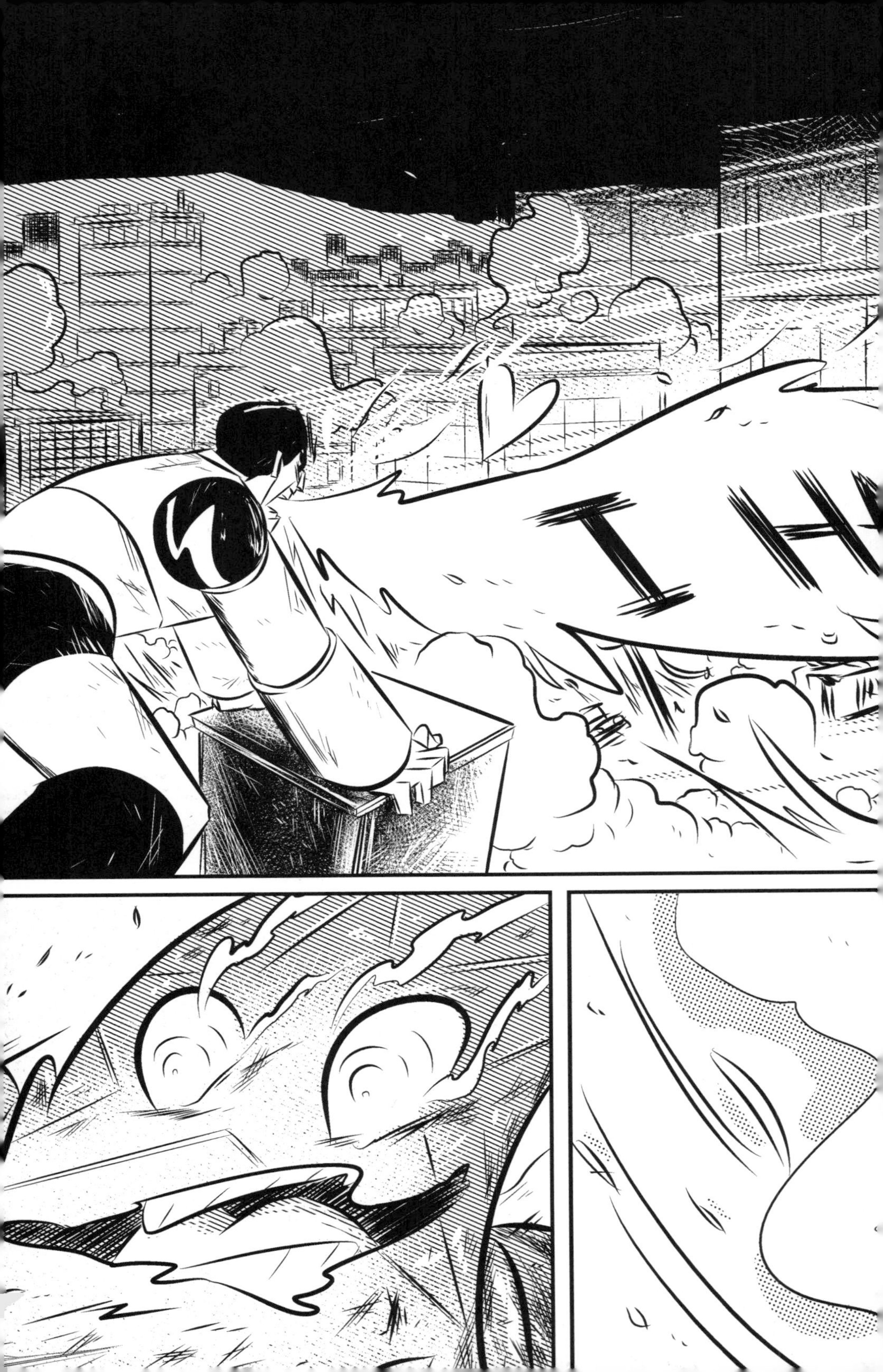
I H

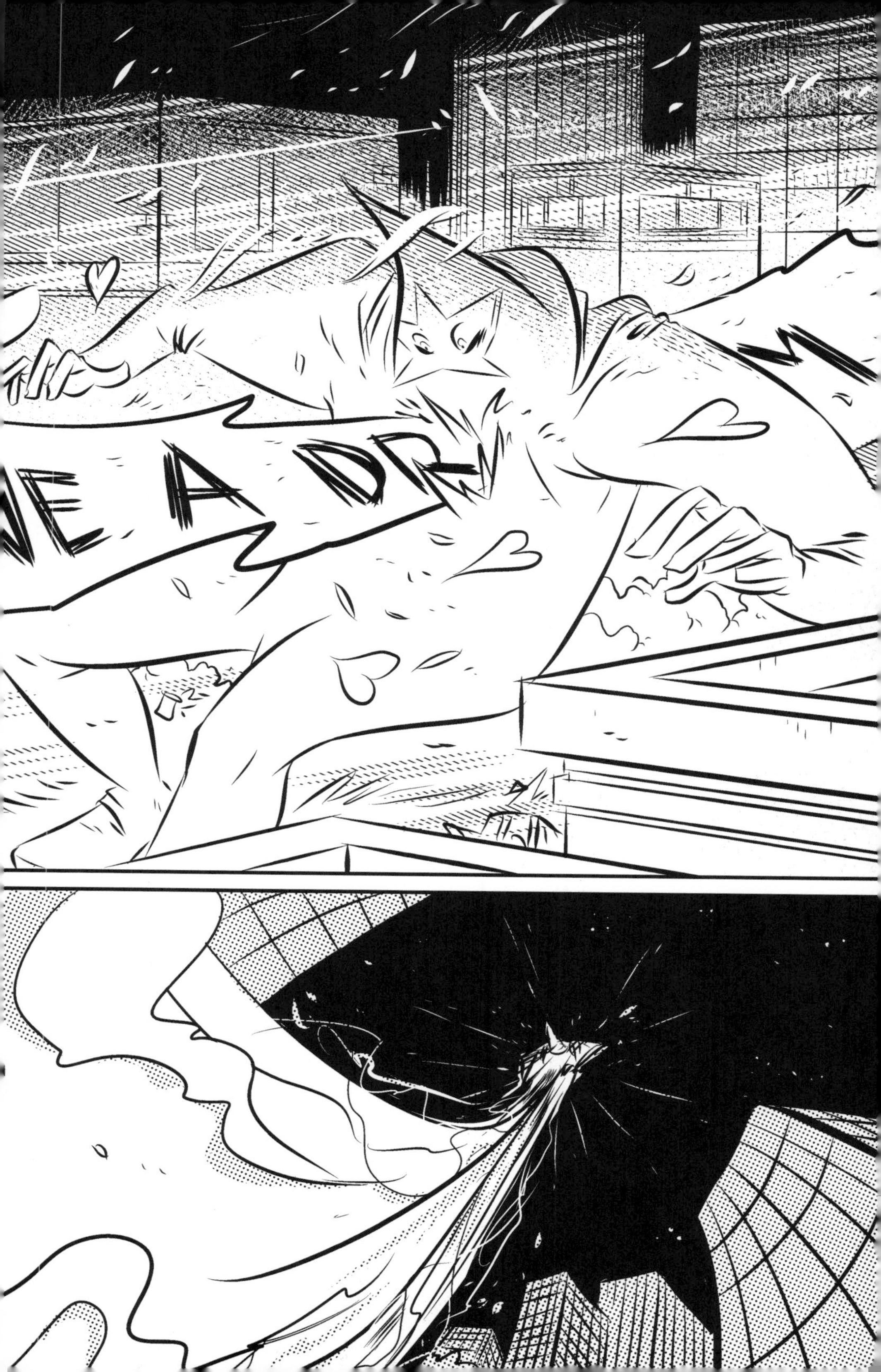
NE A DR
M

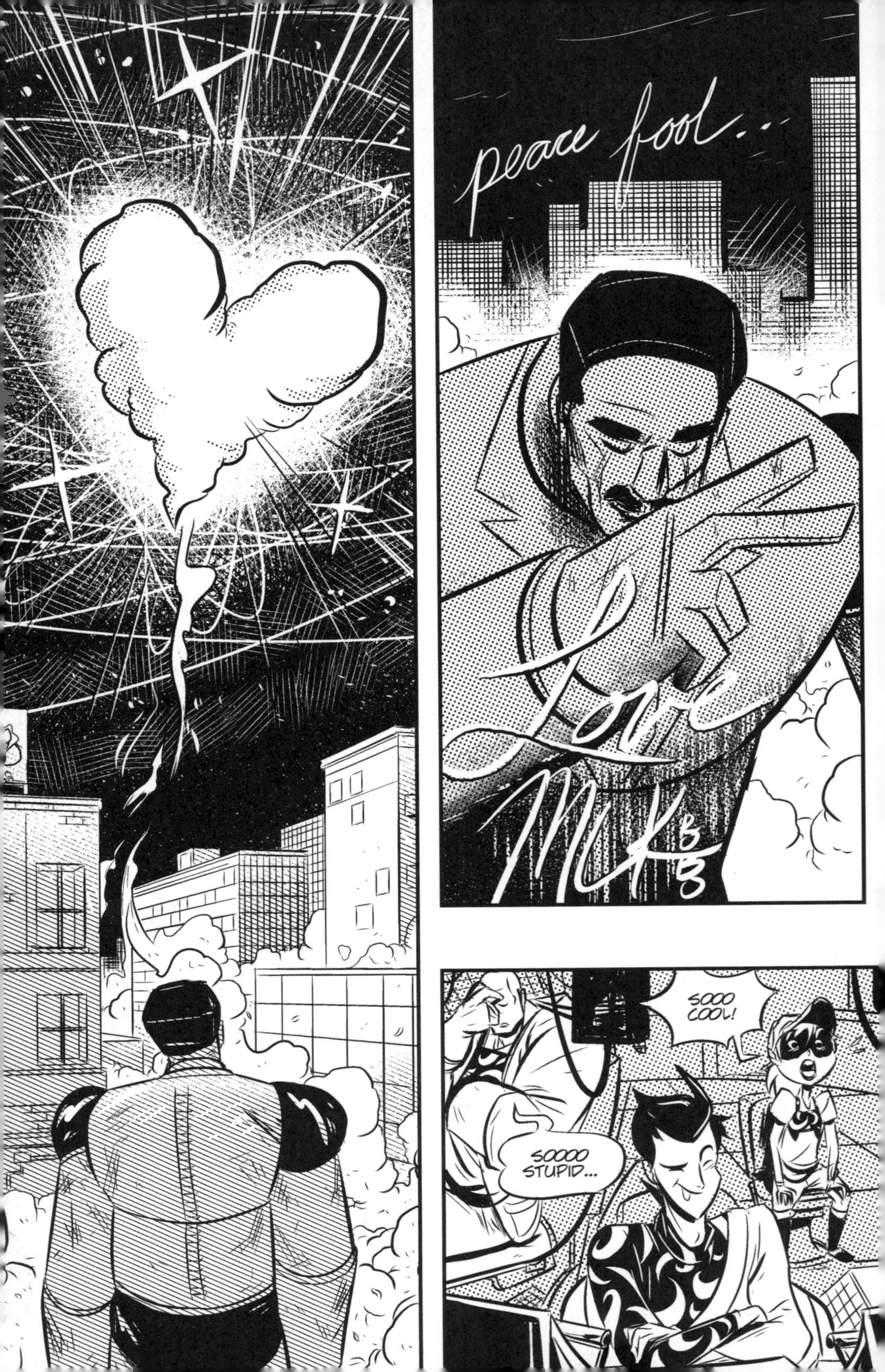
peace fool...
Love
Mk
SOOO COOL!
SOOOO STUPID...

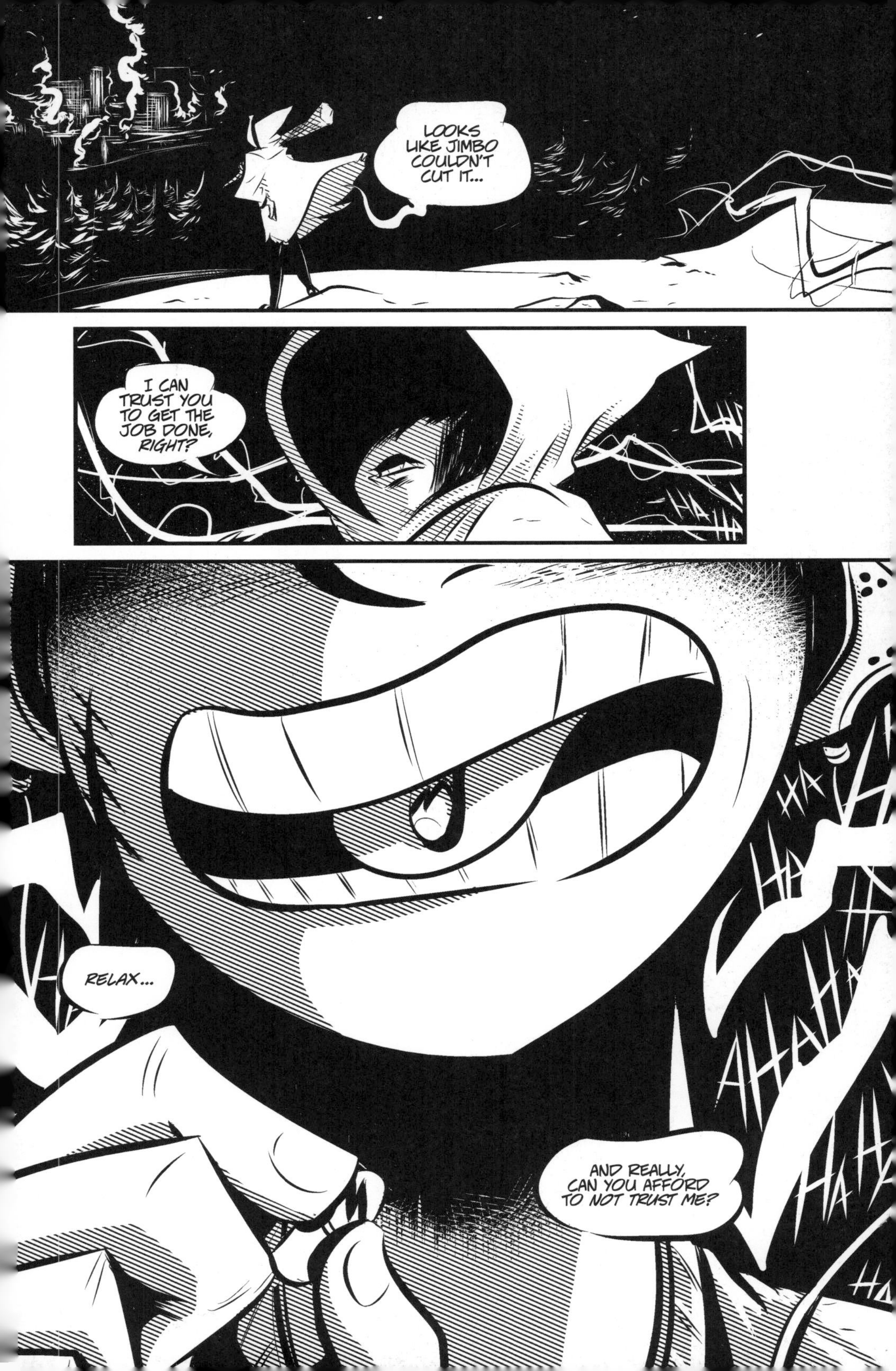
LOOKS LIKE JIMBO COULDN'T CUT IT...
I CAN TRUST YOU TO GET THE JOB DONE, RIGHT?
RELAX...
AND REALLY, CAN YOU AFFORD TO NOT TRUST ME?

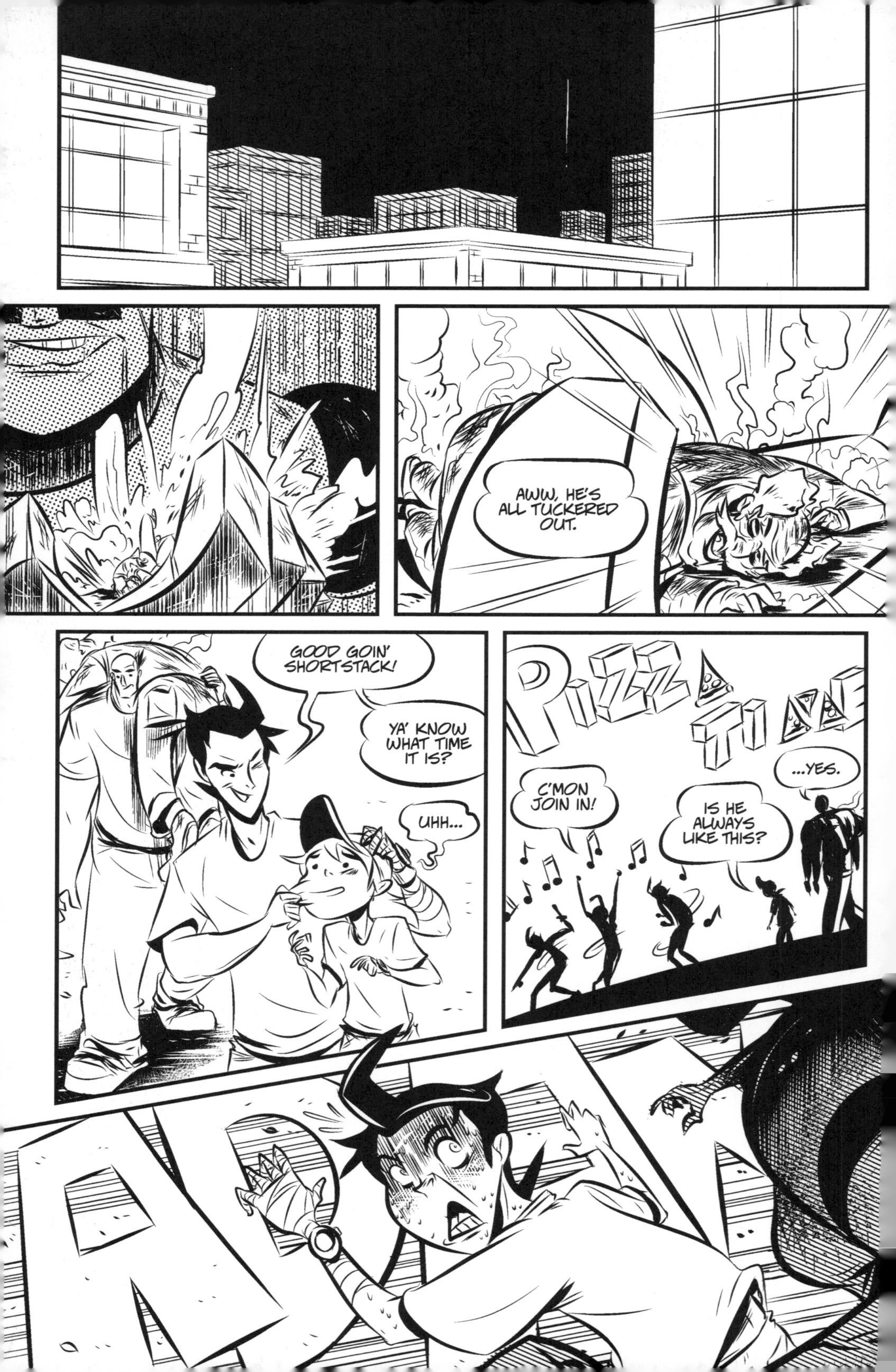

AWW, HE'S ALL TUCKERED OUT.
GOOD GOIN' SHORTSTACK!
YA' KNOW WHAT TIME IT IS?
UHH...
C'MON JOIN IN!
IS HE ALWAYS LIKE THIS?
...YES.

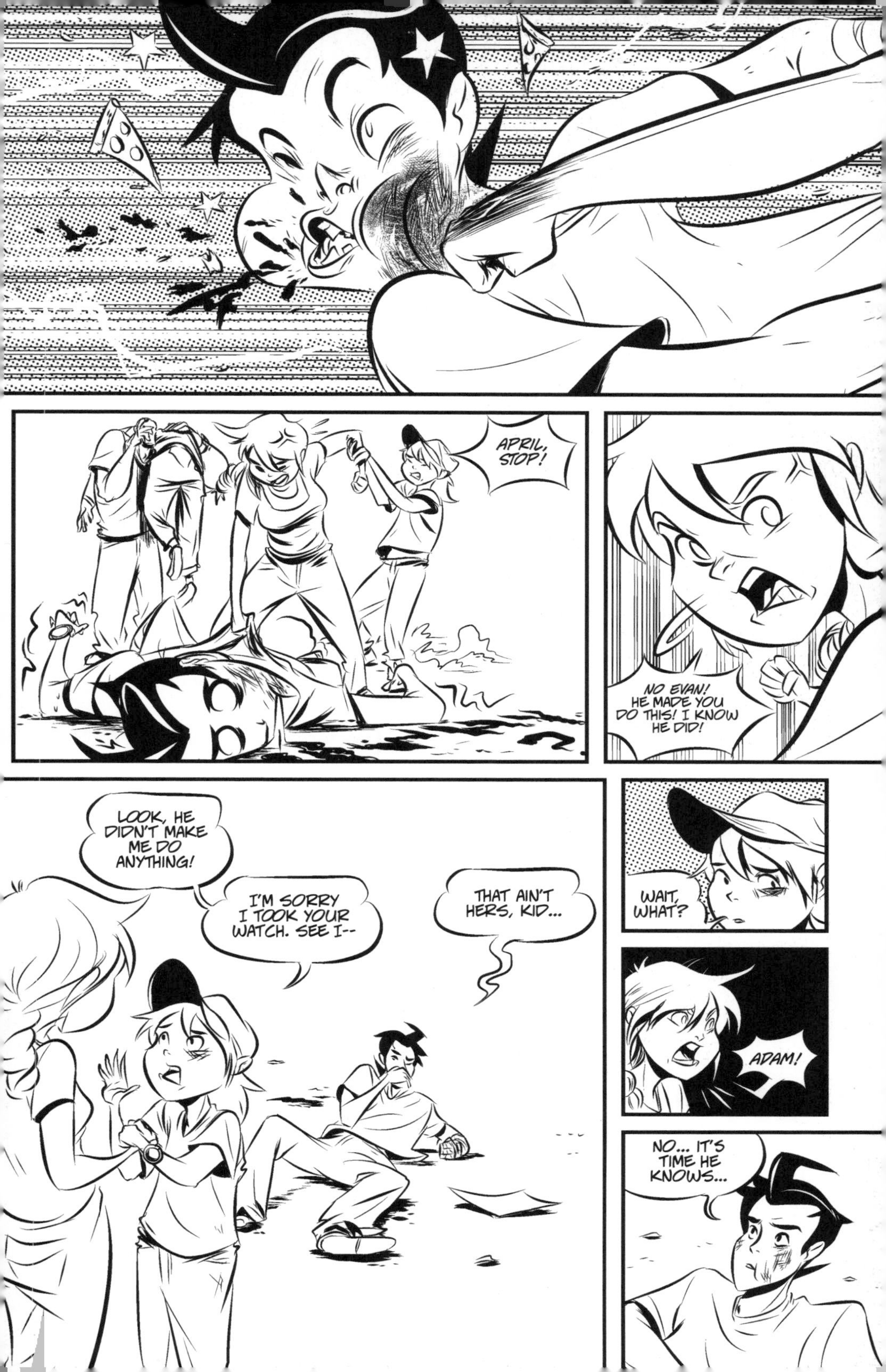
APRIL, STOP!
NO EVAN! HE MADE YOU DO THIS! I KNOW HE DID!
LOOK, HE DIDN'T MAKE ME DO ANYTHING!
I'M SORRY I TOOK YOUR WATCH. SEE I--
THAT AIN'T HERS, KID...
WAIT, WHAT?
ADAM!
NO... IT'S TIME HE KNOWS...

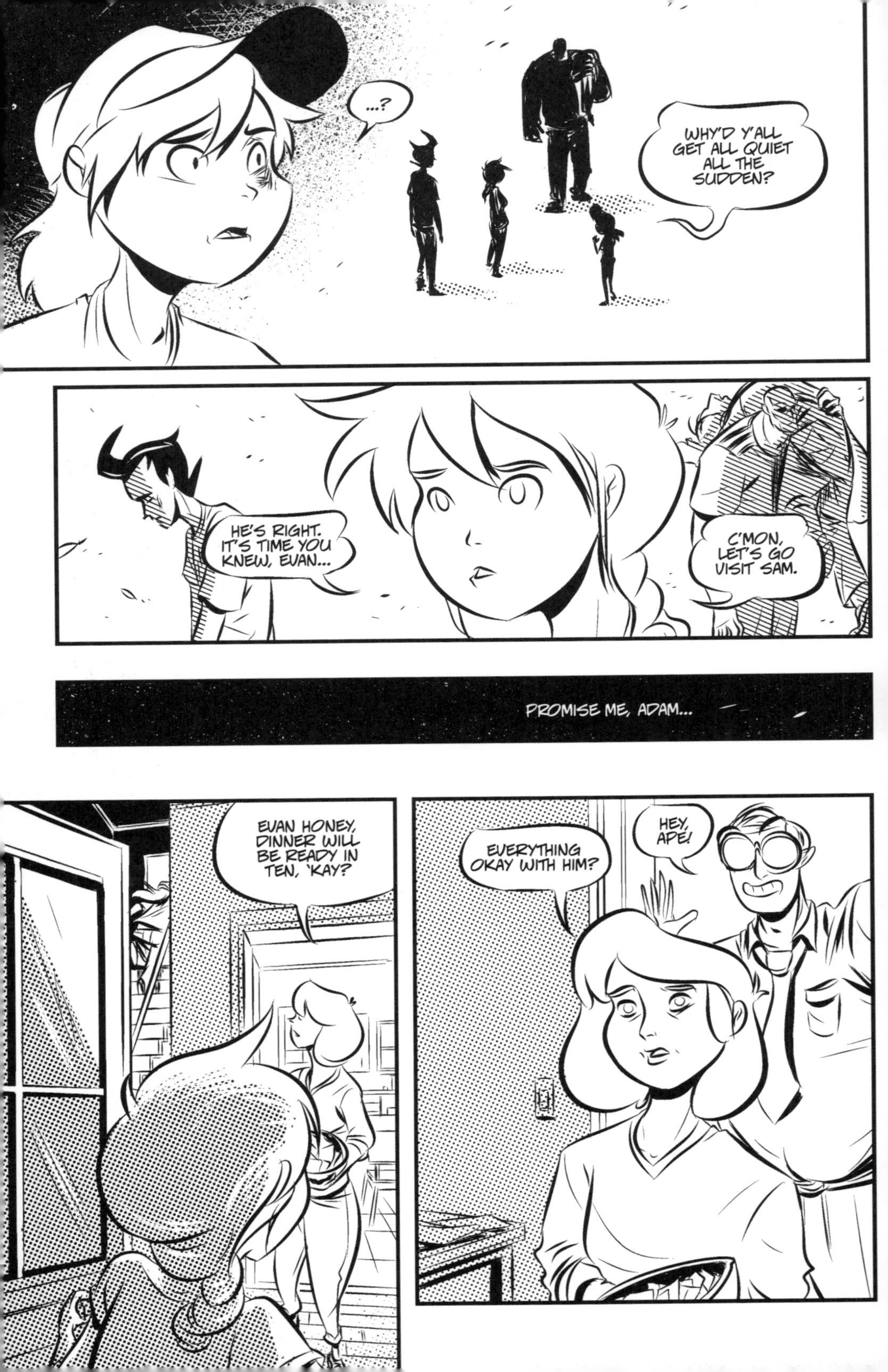
...?
WHY'D Y'ALL GET ALL QUIET ALL THE SUDDEN?
HE'S RIGHT. IT'S TIME YOU KNEW, EVAN...
C'MON, LET'S GO VISIT SAM.
PROMISE ME, ADAM...
EVAN HONEY, DINNER WILL BE READY IN TEN, 'KAY?
HEY, APE!
EVERYTHING OKAY WITH HIM?

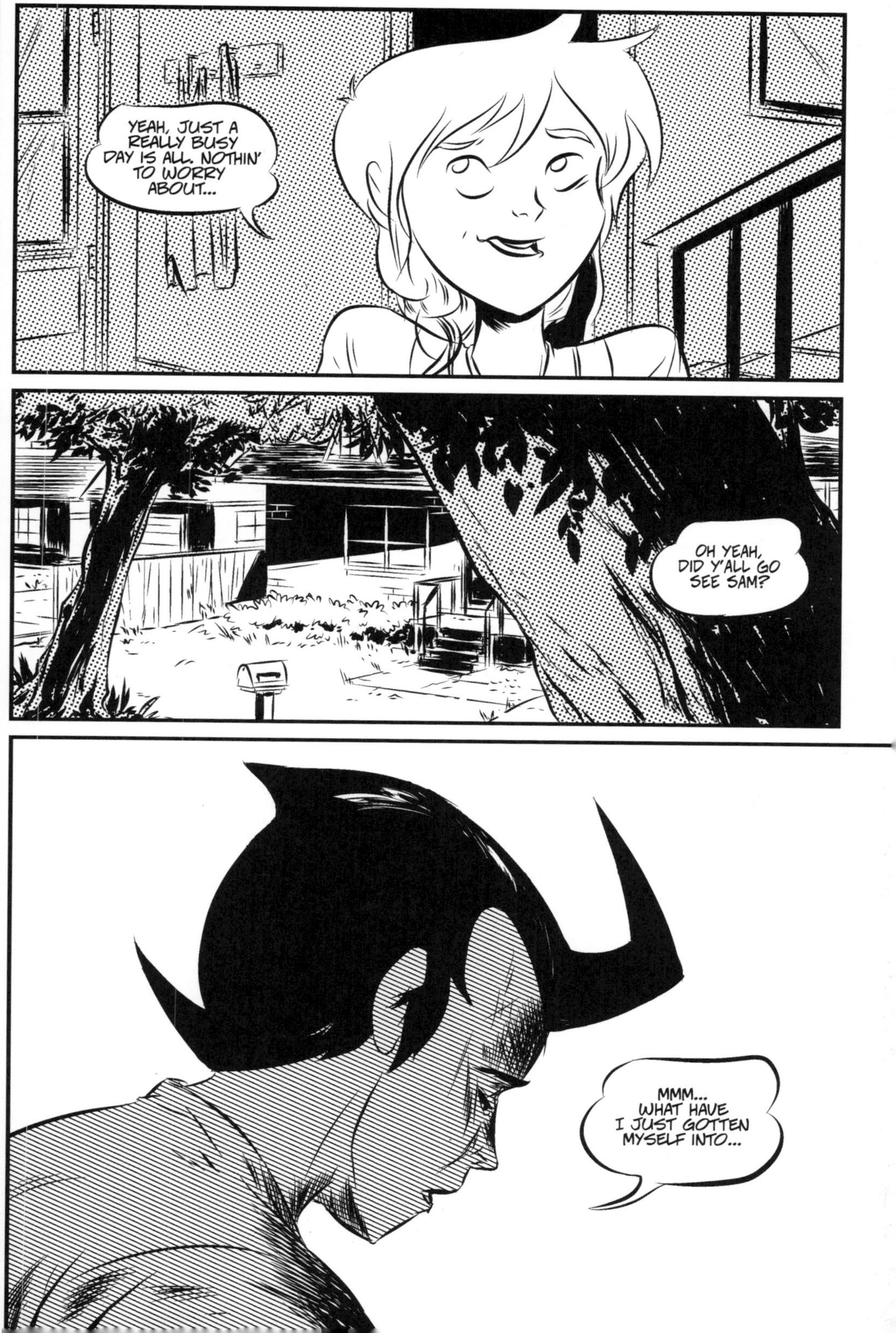
YEAH, JUST A REALLY BUSY DAY IS ALL. NOTHIN' TO WORRY ABOUT...
OH YEAH, DID Y'ALL GO SEE SAM?
MMM... WHAT HAVE I JUST GOTTEN MYSELF INTO...

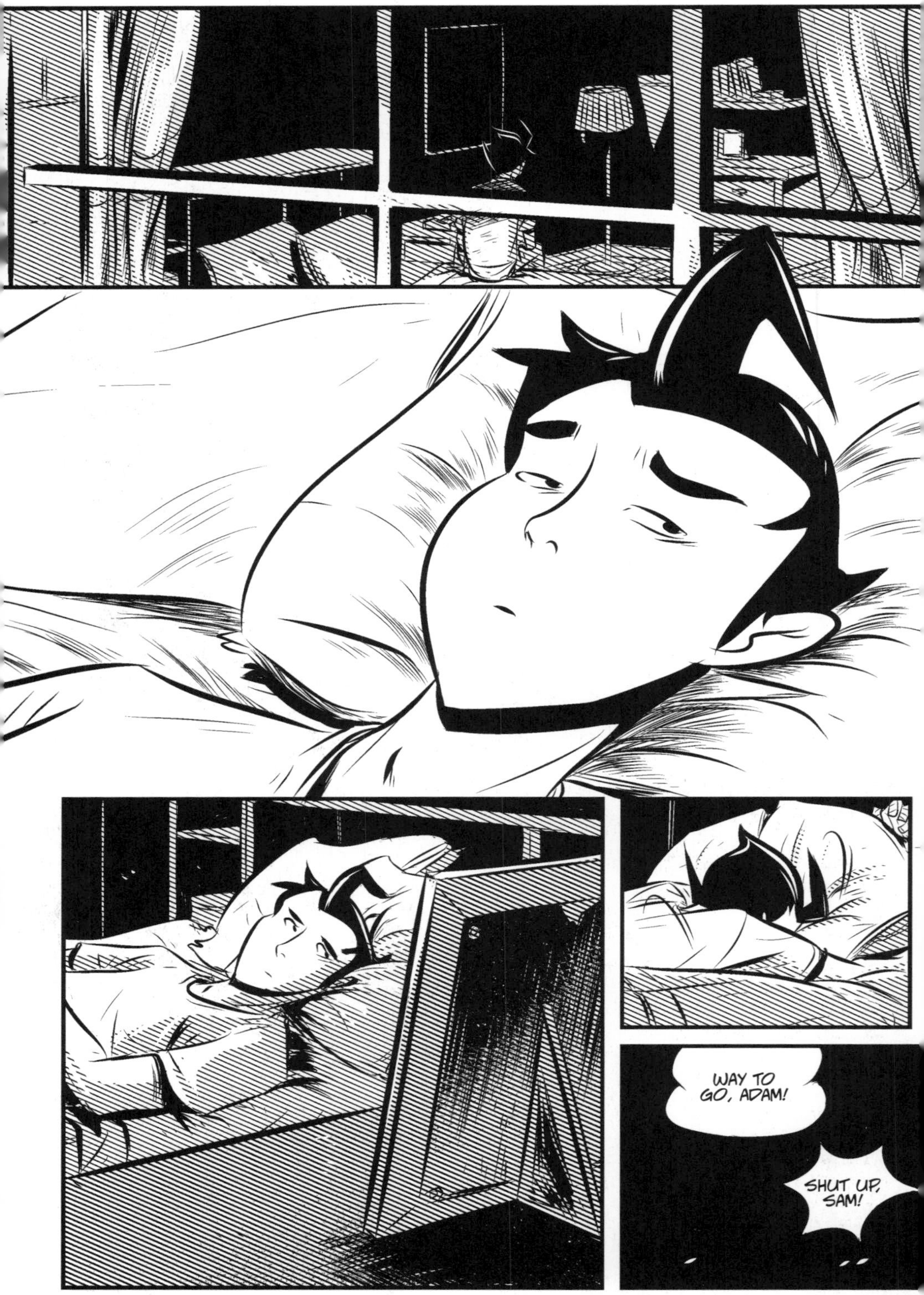
WAY TO GO, ADAM!
SHUT UP, SAM!

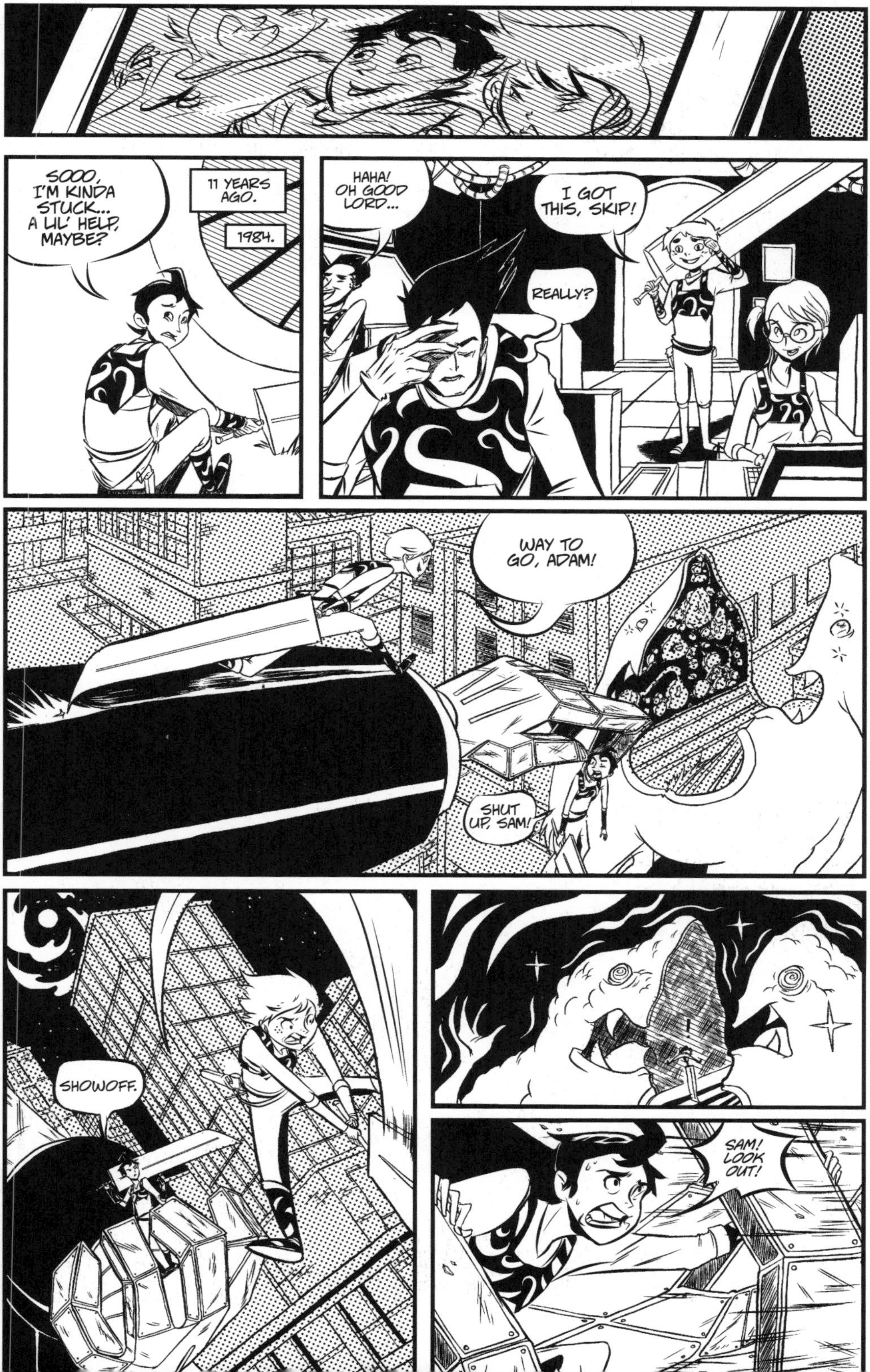
SOOO, I'M KINDA STUCK... A LIL' HELP, MAYBE?
11 YEARS AGO.
1984.
HAHA! OH GOOD LORD...
I GOT THIS, SKIP!
REALLY?
WAY TO GO, ADAM!
SHUT UP, SAM!
SHOWOFF.
SAM! LOOK OUT!

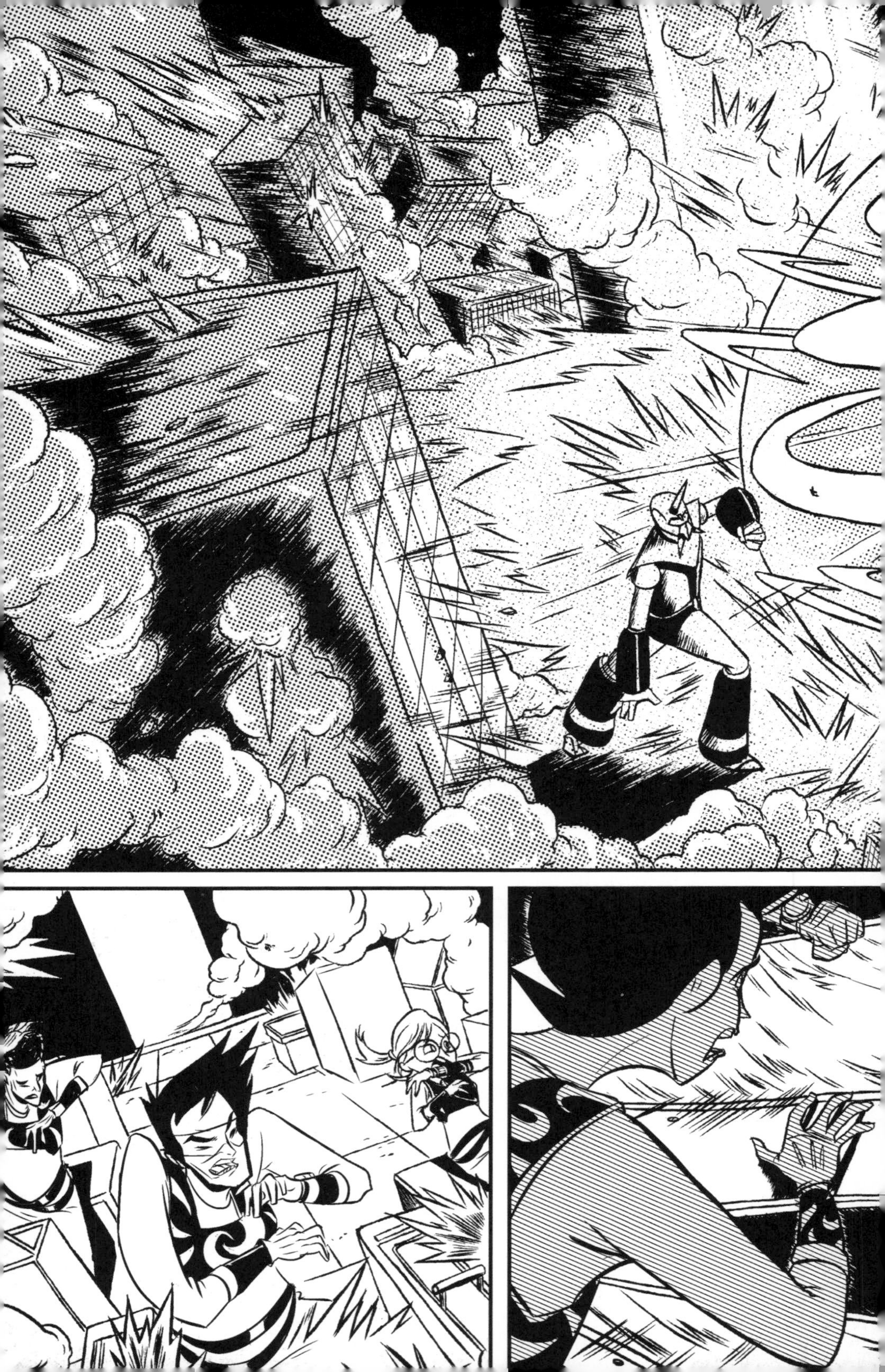

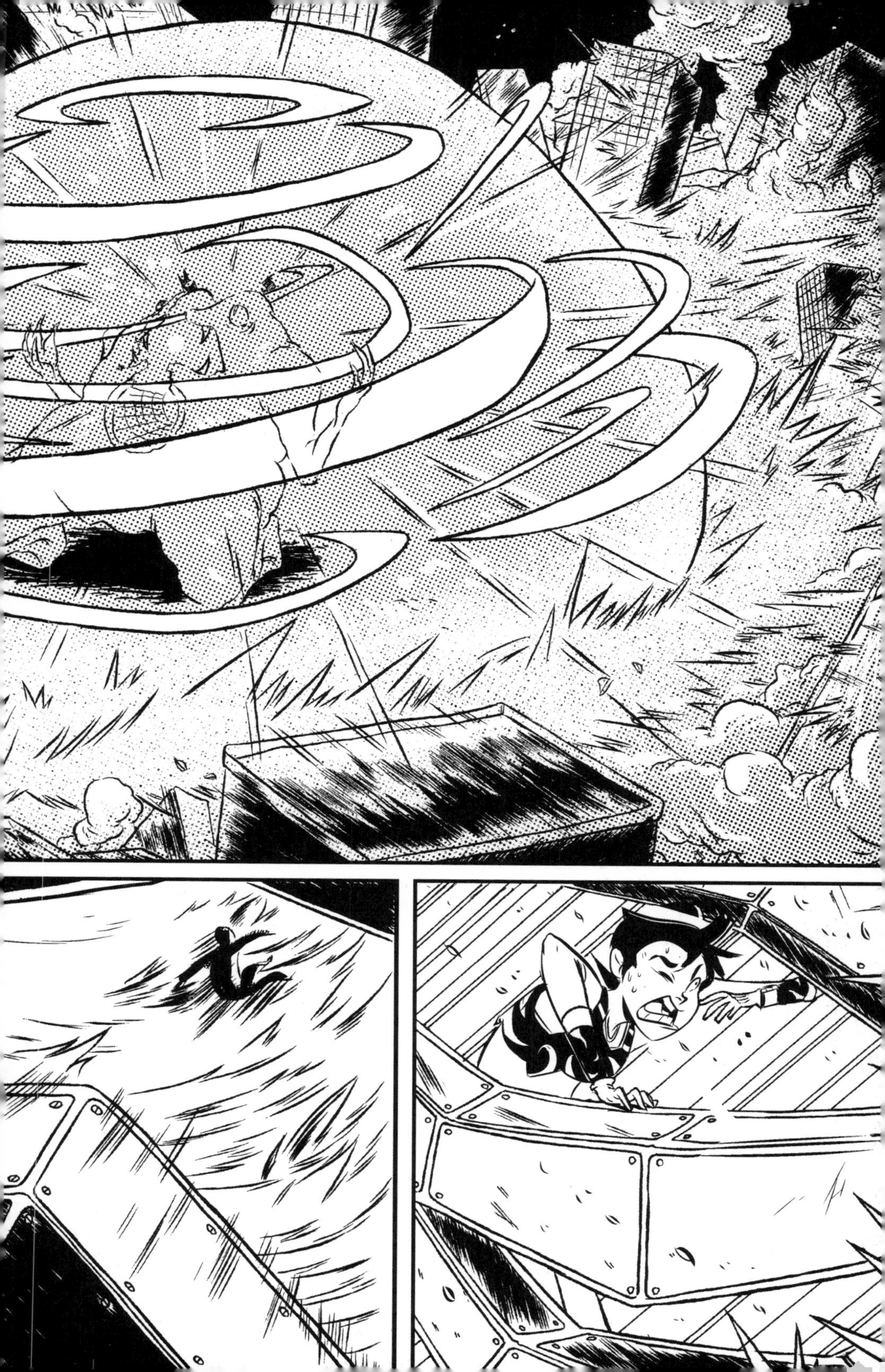

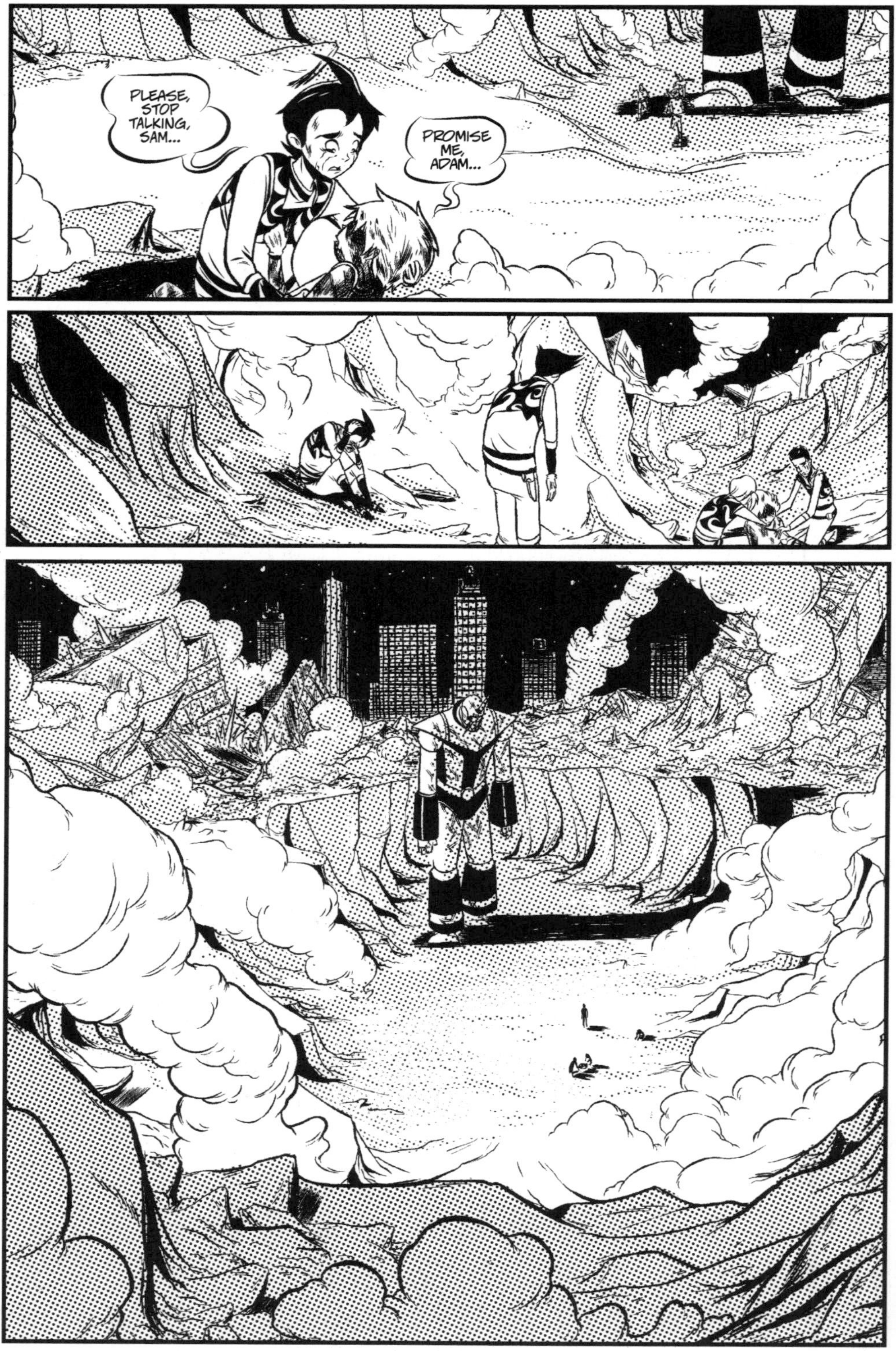
PLEASE, STOP TALKING, SAM...
PROMISE ME, ADAM...

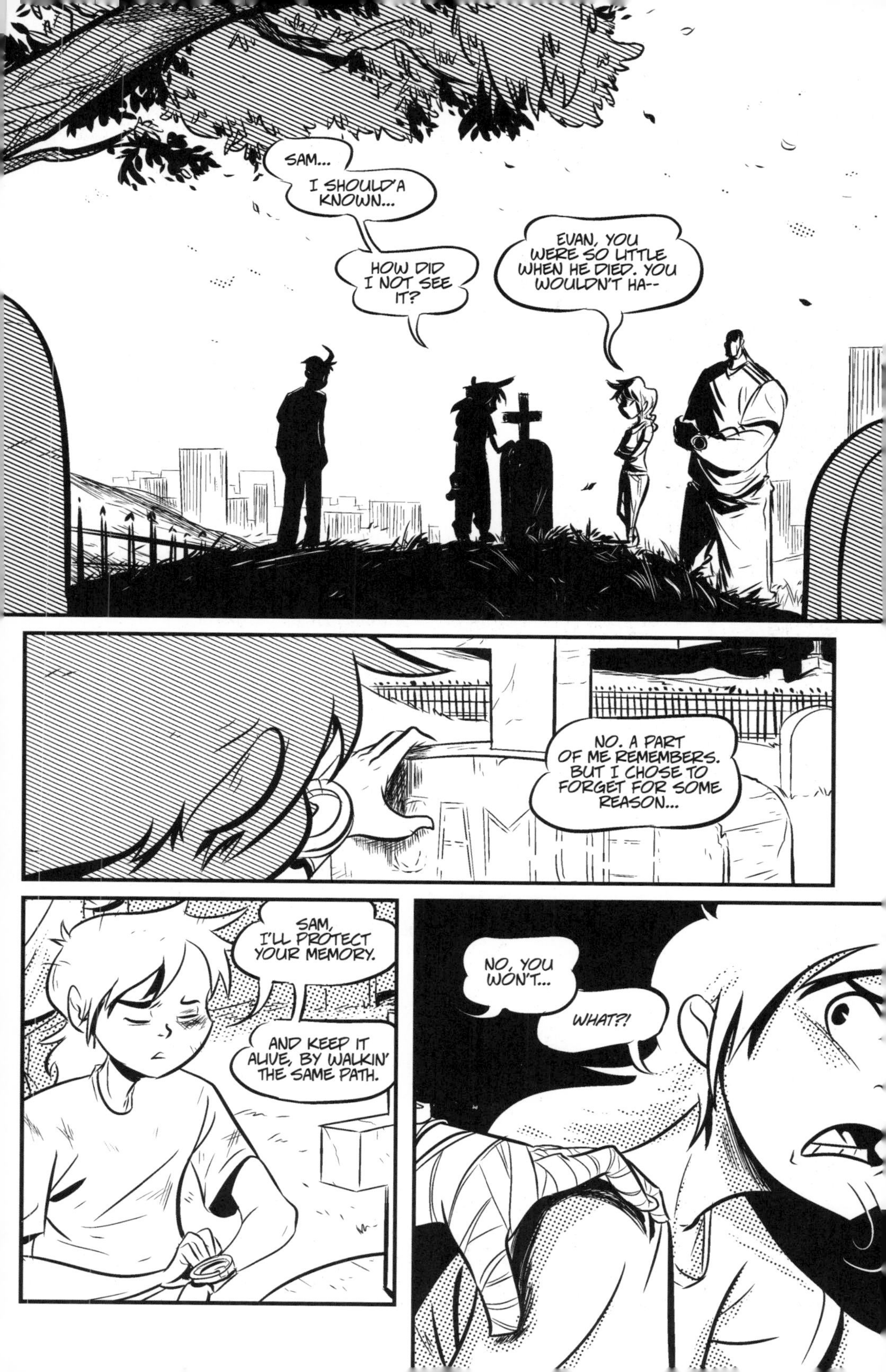
SAM...
I SHOULD'A KNOWN...
HOW DID I NOT SEE IT?
EVAN, YOU WERE SO LITTLE WHEN HE DIED. YOU WOULDN'T HA--
NO. A PART OF ME REMEMBERS. BUT I CHOSE TO FORGET FOR SOME REASON...
SAM, I'LL PROTECT YOUR MEMORY.
AND KEEP IT ALIVE, BY WALKIN' THE SAME PATH.
NO, YOU WON'T...
WHAT?!

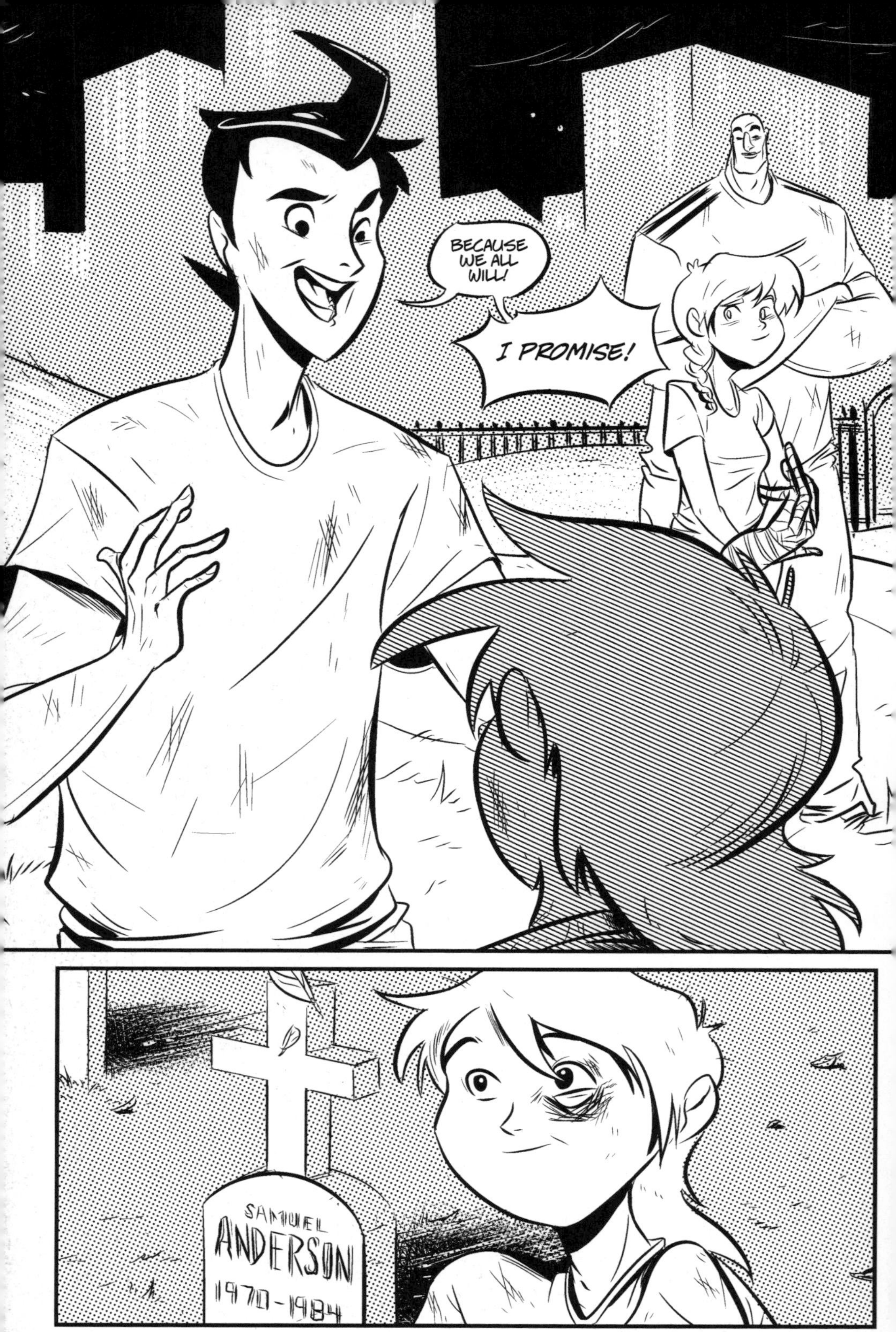
BECAUSE WE ALL WILL!
I PROMISE!
SAMUEL
ANDERSON
1970-1984

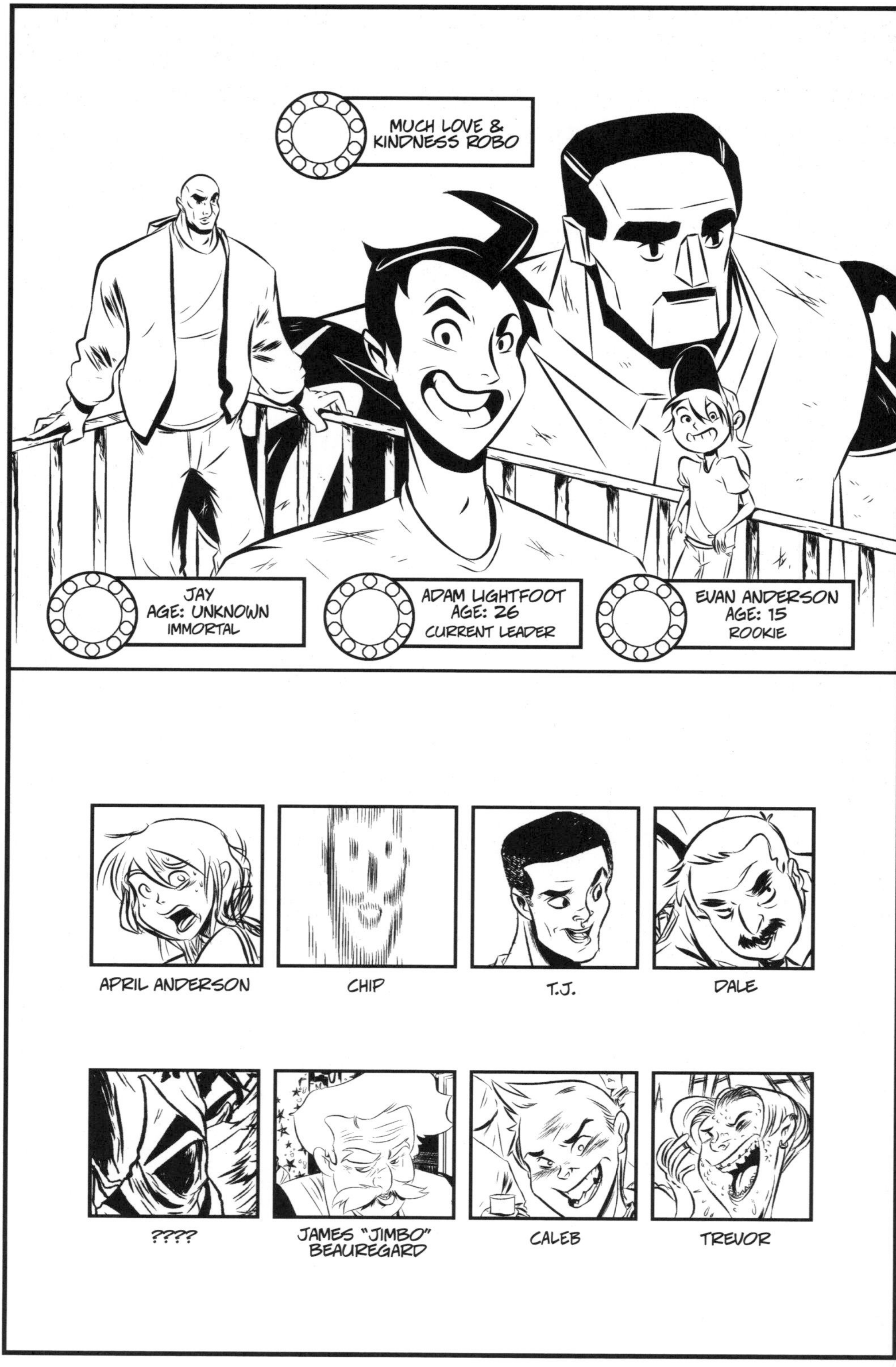
MUCH LOVE & KINDNESS ROBO
JAY AGE: UNKNOWN IMMORTAL
ADAM LIGHTFOOT AGE: 26 CURRENT LEADER
EVAN ANDERSON AGE: 15 ROOKIE
APRIL ANDERSON
CHIP
T.J.
DALE
????
JAMES "JIMBO" BEAUREGARD
CALEB
TREVOR

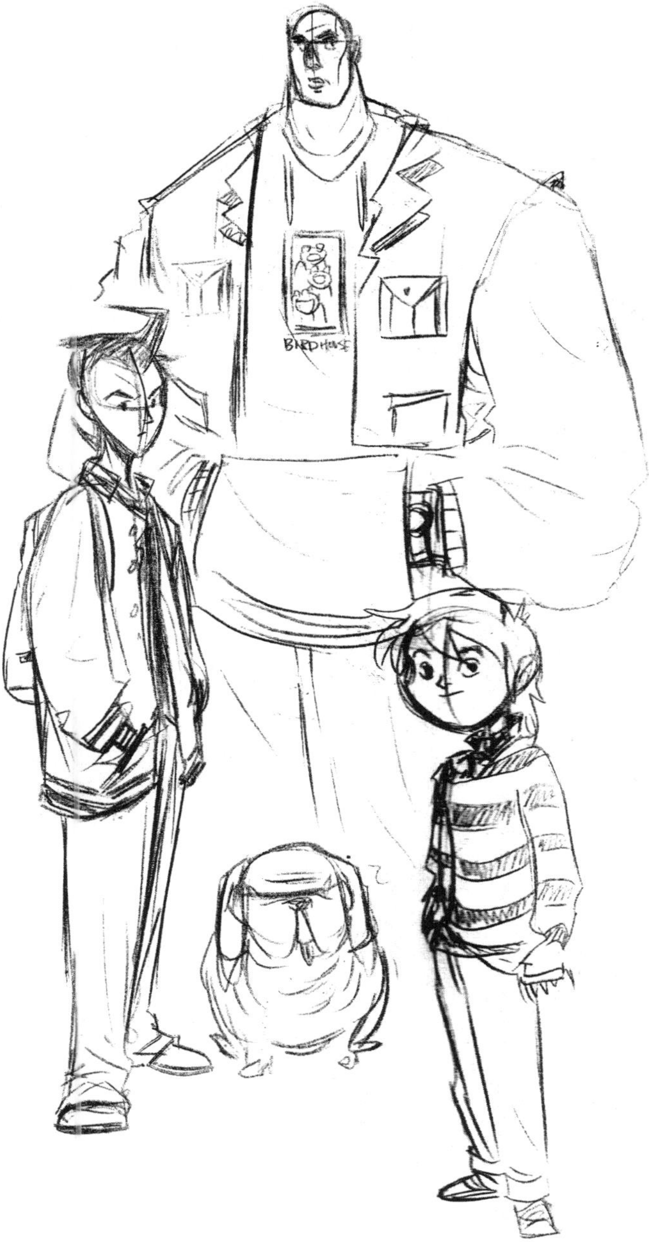
BIRDHOUSE

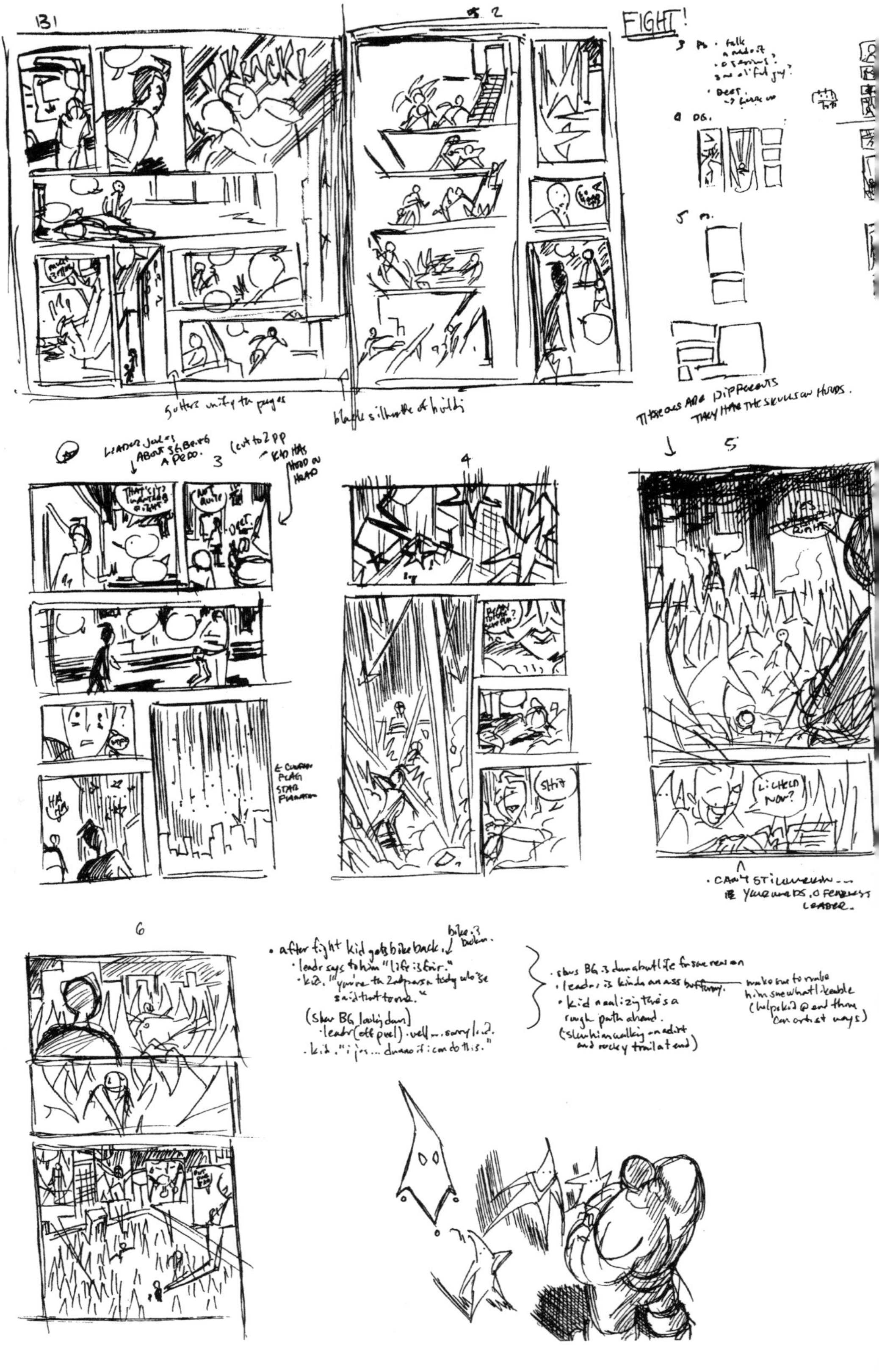

FIGHT!
gutters unify the pages
LEADER JOKES ABOUT SKABBING A PEDO.
(cut to 2 pp
KID HAS HOOD ON HEAD
THAT'S IT? I WANTED A FIGHT!
NOT QUITE
SHIT
CAN'T STILL WALK... YOUR WORDS, O FEARLESS LEADER.
· after fight kid gets bike back. ↓ bike is broken.
· leadr says to him "life is fair."
· kid. "you're the 2nd person today who's said that to me."
(Show BG looking down)
· leadr (off panel). well... sorry kid.
· kid. "i jus... dunno if i can do this."
· leadr is kinda an ass but funny.
· kid realizing this is a rough path ahead.
make sure to make him somewhat likeable

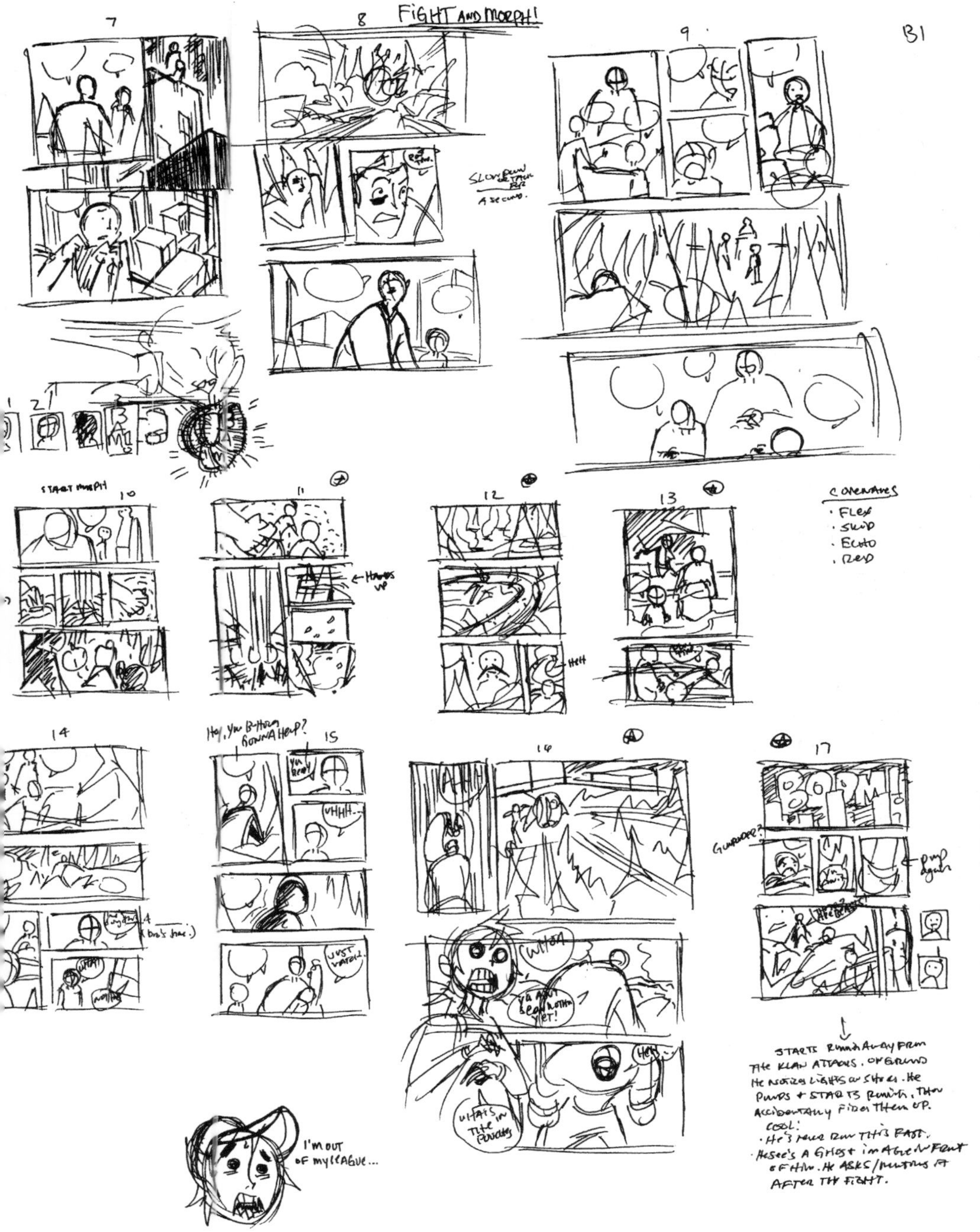
FIGHT AND MORPH!
B1
START MORPH
CODENAMES
· FLEX
· SKID
· ECHO
· RED
UHHH...
JUST WATCH.
BOOM!
WHOA
I'M OUT OF MY LEAGUE...
STARTS RUNNING AWAY FROM THE KLAN ATTACKS. ON GROUND
HE NOTICES LIGHTS ON SHOES. HE PUMPS + STARTS RUNNING. THEN ACCIDENTALLY FIRES THEM UP.
COOL!
· HE'S NEVER RUN THIS FAST.
· HE SEE'S A GHOST IMAGE IN FRONT OF HIM. HE ASKS/MENTIONS IT AFTER THE FIGHT.

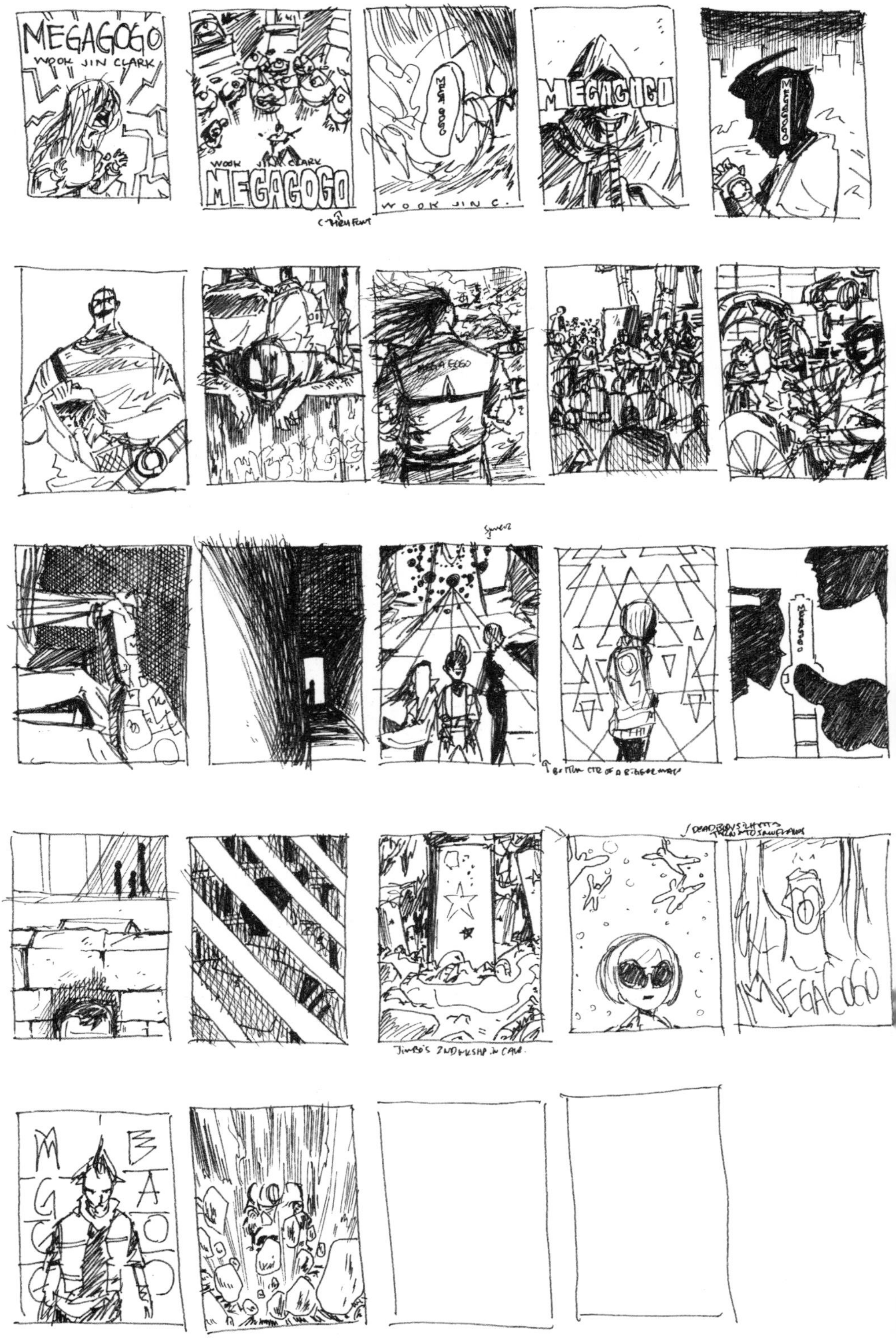
MEGAGOGO
WOOK JIN CLARK
WOOK JIN CLARK
MEGAGOGO
WOOK JIN C.
MEGAGOGO
MEGAGOGO

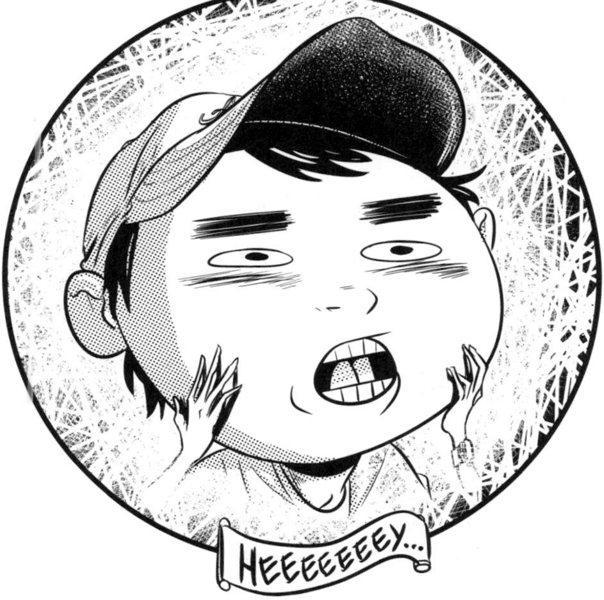
HEEEEEEEY...

Korean born, Southern raised.

Currently residing in Portland, Oregon as a member of Periscope Studio.

www.wookjinclark.com

MORE BOOKS FROM
ONI PRESS

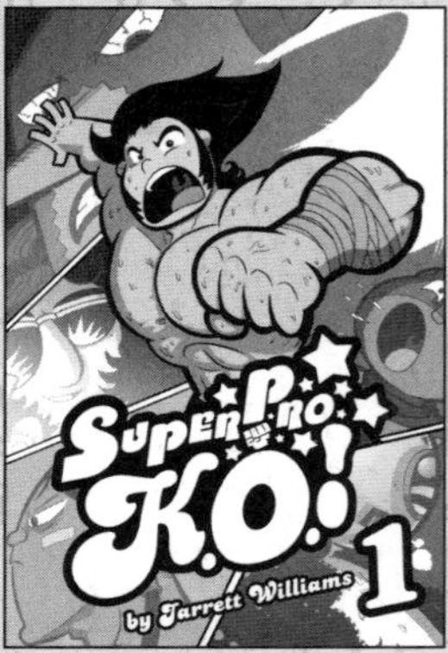
SuperPro K.O.!
by Jarrett Williams
1

SUPERPRO K.O., VOLUME 1
By Jarrett Williams
256 Pages · Softcover · B&W
ISBN 978-1-934964-41-5

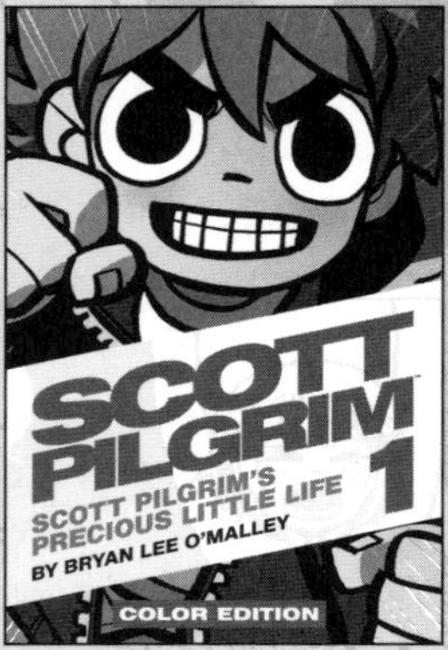
SCOTT PILGRIM
SCOTT PILGRIM'S PRECIOUS LITTLE LIFE 1
BY BRYAN LEE O'MALLEY
COLOR EDITION

SCOTT PILGRIM, VOLUME 1 PREVIOUS LITTLE LIFE
By Bryan Lee O'Malley
192 Pages · Hardcover · Color
ISBN 978-1-62010-000-4

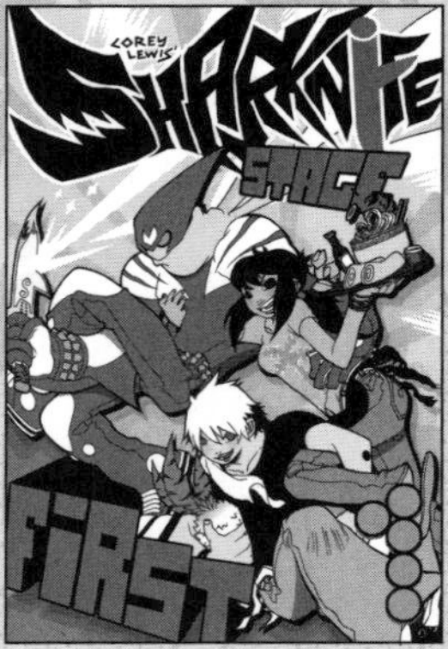
COREY LEWIS'
SHARKNIFE
STAGE
FIRST

SHARKNIFE, VOLUME 1: STAGE FIRST
By Corey Lewis
144 Pages · Softcover · B&W
ISBN 978-1-934964-64-4

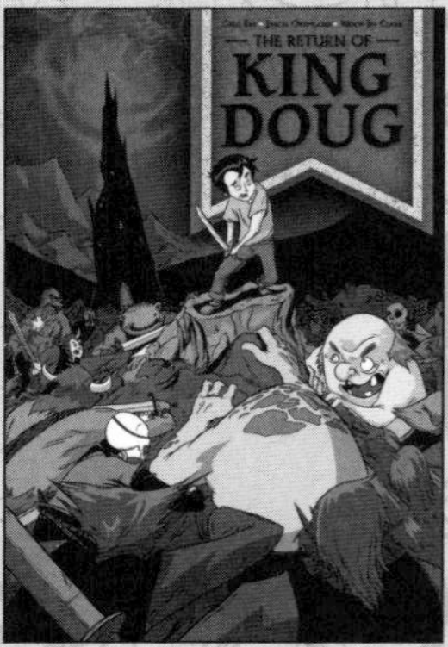
THE RETURN OF
KING DOUG

THE RETURN OF KING DOUG
By Greg Erb, Jason Oremland, and Wook-Jin Clark
184 Pages · Hardcover · B&W
ISBN 978-1-934964-15-6

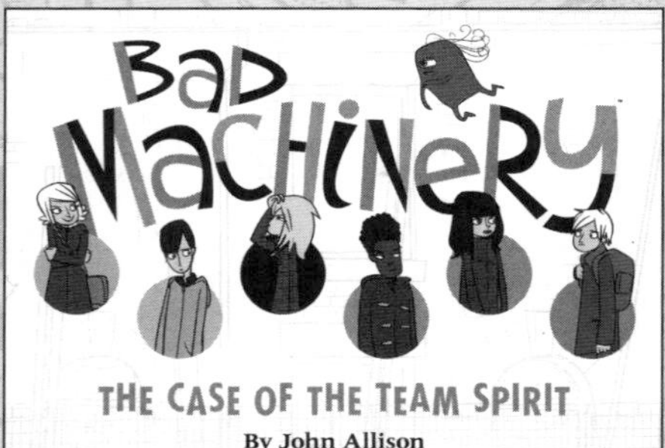
BAD MACHINERY
THE CASE OF THE TEAM SPIRIT
By John Allison

BAD MACHINERY, VOLUME 1
By John Allison
136 Pages · Softcover · Color
ISBN 978-1-62010-088-2

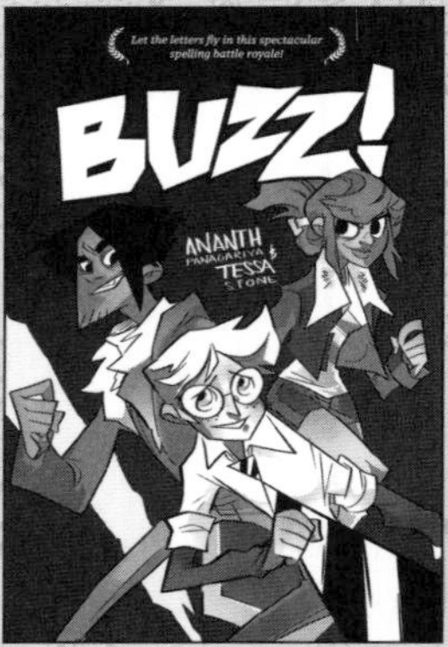
Let the letters fly in this spectacular spelling battle royale!
BUZZ!
ANANTH PANAGARIYA & TESSA STONE

BUZZ!
By Ananth Panagariya and Tessa Stone
176 Pages · Softcover · 2-Color
ISBN 978-1-62010-088-2

ONI PRESS
REVOLUTIONIZE COMICS
www.onipress.com

For more information on these and other fine Oni Press graphic novels, visit www.onipress.com.

To find a comic specialty store in your area, call 1-888-COMICBOOK or visit www.comicshops.us.

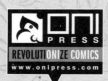